Fox's Nose

Fox's Nose

SALLY IRELAND

The publisher gratefully acknowledges the support of
the Canada Council, the Ontario Arts Council, and the
Department of Canadian Heritage.

Cover design by Bill Douglas@The Bang.
Printed and bound in Canada.

Cormorant Books Inc.
RR 1
Dunvegan, Ontario
Canada K0C 1J0

Canadian Cataloguing in Publication Data
Ireland, Sally, 1948-
Fox's nose : a novel
ISBN 1-896951-00-7
I. Title.
PS8567.R46F69 1997   C813'.54   C97-900496-9
PR9199.3.I683F69 1997

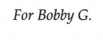

For Bobby G.

ACKNOWLEDGEMENTS

The author would like to thank the following people for reading various drafts of this book, and for making encouraging comments and suggestions: Robert Harlow, Jerry Newman, Cathy Ford, Monica Hogg, Pat Seebach.

Thanks also to Patrice Palmerino and Kevin Carter for the seeds that grew into Bette and Bradley.

ONE

It's the sound that takes me back, the muffled, distant, not quite recognizable summoning that might be only a ringing in the ears, or a hot water faucet that sings when the flow is constricted, or the chirp of crickets heard from behind closed windows. Whatever the cause, it captures the attention, alarms, excites, reminds me of Christmas Night in 1972, when I thought it was the call I'd been waiting for.

"Did you hear that?"

"What?"

"Can't you hear ringing?"

"Jees, Yule, it's just Mom on the piano." Aunt Xenia playing for the guests.

The sounds of the party were scarcely audible where we lay in the wintry attic under a naked bulb. My cousin's chin dug hard into my collarbone. There was now a roughness about everything he did that he had learned from his part-time job at the building supply in Chilliwack. He hadn't been like that the previous summer, in the days before he started working: stifling August days, one rainy afternoon in particular, when we'd sat snipping at each other's pubic hair with a pair of scissors as if we were trying to deny growing up. Strands of the hair were still scattered over the floor. Our hot flesh was beginning to warm the air trapped under the blanket, and I felt my body relax into comfort even though there was no more than an old moth-eaten coat and a pillow between me and

1

the fir planks. Christmas wasn't quite over, so the ringing I'd heard could have been the phone. It was already breakfast-time in England and I imagined Mama dialling between sips of her morning tea.

I put my arms around Nick's ribs to embrace the warmth. I could feel their separate ridges, began to count them: one, two, three.... Against my pubic hair Nick's penis felt serious and businesslike. I put my hand down around it, guided it, hardly needed to.

"Yule, oh, Yule."

He spoke to hear himself, to convince himself, I imagined, that this was what he wanted as well as what he needed. And he was inside almost before I knew it, the small pain only an echo of itself by the time I became conscious of it.

I groaned.

"What's the matter?"

"Hurts."

He started to pull away, as if he didn't want to ruin his own pleasure by hurting me.

"It's okay," I said, keeping him there.

My left foot was cold. I pulled it back under the blanket. The memory of the hurt was almost gone, and in its place a lovely swelling sensation. I closed my eyes against the naked lightbulb, felt Nick's breath on my earlobe. So this was what I'd been yearning after, very different from all the times I'd made myself come. Harder because it partly depended on someone else. I couldn't find the rhythm at first. Then I did. I was swelling and swelling and I knew I was going to burst and I wanted it and I thought soon, yes, any moment. Nick's bones were grinding against mine. He groaned, arched back, thrust, shivered and collapsed on top of me. The lovely swelling sensation dwindled.

"Did you like it?" he asked.

"A little."

He rolled away from me and I knew my answer had disappointed him.

2

A moment later he was breathing the slow even rhythm of oblivion. My crotch felt wet and sticky, and when I explored with my hand, I discovered blood. Downstairs Aunt Xenia was playing a folk dance; I could hear clapping and stomping. I drew my legs up and snuggled closer to the creature smell of my cousin's sweat. Nick. Nicholas. Named for my father. If I kept my head under the blanket and stayed close to Nick, I could almost believe I was warm.

As I lay there I considered that my mother might have tried to reach me, found all the lines busy and thought it would be better to wait a day. Or maybe on a moment's impulse she'd decided to fly out for a visit. She might be in the air at that very moment, over Reykjavik or the icy coast of Greenland. Because my parents had been separated for five years, and before that my mother had been so often absent, she was less a real presence for me than part of my cosmology. To her I attributed powers that my adolescing mind both believed in and denied. When I thought of her flying through the air towards me, it was as a goddess, fine-boned, her hair pulled back from her gaunt cheeks, streamlined and wingless, buoyed up by her will rather than the complex technology of flying machines. My expectations of her were contradictory: I wanted her to arrive like a goddess, but nurture me like an entirely human mother, then turn back into goddess again and banish the woman who had become my father's lover the previous fall. Her name was Bette DesRosiers.

"What do you mean, for her love is everything?"

Those were the first words I'd ever heard Bette say. I'd taken the Hastings bus downtown to meet my father at the hall on Thurlow Street, where he was rehearsing *Medea*, and when I arrived he and Bette were there alone. The rest of the cast had already gone.

"She's beginning to calculate *very coolly* how to get her revenge," she said.

"No, no. She is desperate," said my father, who was

3

directing the play. "At this point she cannot think. You are making her too cerebral."

He squeezed the first "e" in "desperate" as he spoke. When he was being challenged he sounded more Russian, but normally his speech was almost accentless.

"Too cerebral...?" Bette began. Then she saw me. She looked puzzled and, I thought, annoyed by the interruption.

"May I help you?" she asked.

"Yulochka," my father said, turning his chair around.

I went up to him and kissed him on the cheek. As much as a greeting, that kiss was a defence against Bette's polite, cold question.

My father introduced us.

"I didn't know you had a daughter." She glanced from me to him and back again. "You certainly look alike," she said, and then added, smiling, "I'm delighted to meet you." But what she was really saying was that she was delighted my father was not what she had supposed — an invalid in a wheelchair — but a man who could make, and obviously had made, love.

Medea was the first show my father had directed in over two years. He'd been ill with a chronic kidney ailment that for months had had him in and out of hospital and unable to work. Consequently he'd been forced to resign as artistic director of Fourth Wall Theatre, which he and his friend Bradley had founded eleven years earlier. After *Medea*, Bradley asked him back to Fourth Wall to direct *Blood Wedding* in the spring. It was Bette who persuaded him to accept Bradley's invitation.

Beside me Nick stirred, reached out, put his arms around me.

"Jees, it's cold. Do you love me?"

"Oh, yes." I did. I loved the way we had so suddenly and inevitably become lovers after all those years of sharing childhood secrets. This was the biggest secret

4

of all. And we'd have to keep it. Our parents would think us too young at fourteen and fifteen for anything more serious than an adolescent crush. And if the actual fucking had been awkward, the intimacy had not. We'd been two very good friends learning to touch in a way that was not so much new as a progression beyond childish hugs and prepubescent rough-and-tumble.

Nick started kissing me again. Already his cock was beginning to wake up.

"No, Nick, we can't, not again. What if I got pregnant? Anyway, I bet they're already wondering where we've got to."

"But it's too cold to just lie here."

So we got dressed, hugging each other as we fastened zippers and buttons.

"We'd better not go down together."

"Okay, you first."

"No, you," I said, even though my teeth were chattering.

Nick held me for a moment in his arms, which had grown muscled from hefting lumber; then he opened the door and, as he ran down the stairs, party chatter and the strains of "Moscow Nights" accompanied his footsteps.

The smell of Nick remained in the attic, and mine too, commingled with his, a precious union that turned me protective and fierce. By instinct I folded up the blanket and coat, checking them for blood, before I carried them back to the trunk where we'd found them. When I opened the trunk's lid it caught the edge of the curtain hanging above it. I'd never noticed before that it wasn't a real curtain but a piece of torn slip, lacy along the bottom, tacked to the frame of the small, drafty window. Neither had I seen, when we'd pulled the blanket out, that there was a paper bundle lying beneath it. The bundle was labelled in Russian, the ink sepia with age, and someone had undone it, then fastened it up again, putting clear tape over the old peeling and yellowed cellophane tape with which it had first been sealed. I lifted it up and sniffed it: a cold, damp smell like the attic, and something older, also wintry, but raw. Then I opened it, my fingers both eager and cautious; even the newer tape had turned brittle and begun to disintegrate. Inside was a cardboard folder, and inside that a small exercise book with a worn and dirty cover that had once been white. The pages were marked off in tiny squares, the front ones filled with neat Cyrillic writing which became increasingly unsteady towards the middle, then neat again at the end but crabbed, as if an old person had finished what a young person had begun. Between the last page and the cover there was a sheaf of better-quality paper. The pages were typewritten in English and stapled together, and on the first page I read the following:

Diary of Leningrad at War, 1941-45

Written by V. M. Kabalevskaya

Translated by X. A. Kabalevskaya Grant

V. M. Kabalevskaya was Babushka, my grandmother, while X. A. Kabalevskaya Grant was Aunt Xenia, who at that very moment was playing piano down in the living-room. I felt two things: the first, that I was trespassing, and the second, that the diary and the rawness emanating from the bundle were meant for me. With quick, secretive hands I slipped the exercise book and the translation into the folder and wrapped them up in the brown paper again. A gust of wind shook the window, making the lace-slip curtain shiver. My scalp began to tingle. I took this as both permission and omen. Instead of putting the bundle back in the trunk I took it with me when I went downstairs, and sneaked it through the hallway, past party guests, to the small office that became my room whenever I visited the farm. Under the cot where I slept, I excavated a small space between a pile of old ledgers and my suitcase, and hid the diary there.

On my way back to rejoin the party in the living-room, I passed the kitchen. It was a shambles of smudged glasses, greasy plates, sticky utensils, casserole dishes encrusted with unidentifiable remains. In the middle of it at the deal table sat Dedushka, my grandfather, a bottle of vodka nearby, a shot glass in his hand, singing out of tune in Russian. Though I had never learned the words, I recognized the song. It was about a young man whose girlfriend had died; all alone, he mourned for her on a lovely spring night.

Weeping drunk, Dedushka sang the descending minor phrases in his thin, querulous tenor.

"Verochka, Verochka," he cried out. That was his pet name for my grandmother whose first name had been Vera. Taking hold of my hand, he said, "It is not even Christmas. Why then this party? January seventh, that is the real Christmas. If Vera was alive we would celebrate then." He began singing again and tried with his insistent grip to get me to follow. I sang the melody as well as I could.

"Sing the words," he demanded.

"I don't know them."

"But they are so simple," he said, and began singing the song phrase by phrase, expecting me to follow, but I couldn't because Papa never spoke Russian at home and I only knew a few common words like *xleb*, "bread", and *glaza*, "eyes". He kept hold of my hand and every time I made a mistake he squeezed it, harder and harder, the more frustrated he became.

"You're hurting me," I cried out at last.

"Get out of here," he shouted. With a final squeeze that made me yelp he pushed me away. "You're useless. Go on. Get out."

I backed out of the kitchen and fled down the hall towards the living-room, where the music was no longer my aunt's traditional piano-playing but the hard, canned sound of electric guitar. On either side of the doorway stood a man and a woman talking across the space between them, guardians of an adult world. I slipped past them, their self-absorption so colossal they didn't even notice me. Inside it was hot and smoky. Half a dozen people were dancing in the middle of the room; around the periphery others stood or sat, talking, joking, laughing, except for my five-year-old cousin Kate, Nick's sister, who lay safely out of the way beside the fireplace, sleeping with her arms around Callack, the border collie. Along one side of the large room was a table, actually two large doors laid end to end over sawhorses and camouflaged with Aunt Xenia's ornately embroidered cloths. On top were plates and plates of *zakuski*: caviar and black bread; pickled tomatoes; *pirozhki* filled with meat, potatoes, cheese; gherkins; pickled mushrooms; and bottles of ice-cold vodka. I chose two *pirozhki* and slathered them with sour cream.

My father's brother, Alek, was standing at the end of the table with Bette. He was an anaesthesiologist, and when Papa had introduced her to him he'd said in a light but caustic voice, "He puts people to sleep, you know." Uncle Alek was the one person in the world I hated.

At that moment he was showing Bette how to drink Russian-style. He picked up one of the misty bottles — the word *Ekstra* was written in red Cyrillic letters across the label — and poured the liquor into two shot glasses. She lifted up one of the glasses and began to take a sip.

"No, not that way," Uncle Alek laughed. "You have to drink it all in one gulp."

"Straight up?" she said. "I'll be drunk in about two seconds."

"Nonsense. Watch me."

He pushed his dark hair off his forehead, glanced down at her as he lifted his shot glass to make sure she was watching him, then swallowed the vodka.

"Now, some *zakuski*."

He buttered a piece of black bread and spread some caviar over it. As he bit into it he nodded.

"Delicious," he said. "Now you try it."

I ate the cheese *pirozhok* as I watched her. She had a small reddish-brown mole at the back of her neck just above the round yoke of her dress, and out of its centre grew a red hair. As she knocked back the liquor — she had the look of someone who'd been drinking that way for years — the mole disappeared into a crease and then reappeared as her head straightened up again. This growth repelled me, and yet I guessed by Uncle Alek's fascination as he watched her that he found it sexy, as no doubt my father must have.

"Whoo," she exclaimed. "God, it burns. Oh my. Give me some caviar quick."

Across the room my father sat next to Nick's father, my Uncle Michael, who was holding a joint delicately between the thumb and forefinger of his rough farmer's hand. He passed it to my father, who sucked on it long and hard while he stared at Bette. She put the shot glass down on the table. Uncle Alek popped a morsel of bread and caviar into her mouth, and as he did so his finger touched her bottom lip.

"Hi," a voice behind me said.

I turned around and saw a girl about my age, though a little taller. She smiled, touching her light brown hair with her hand as she asked, "You're Nick's cousin, aren't you? Julie?"

"Yes," I answered.

"I've heard about you."

"You have?"

"Yes. From Nick. We go to the same school," she said in a false, bright voice.

The room was hot from the fire and the crush of bodies. I became aware of a faint smell, perhaps more in my imagination than on my skin, a souvenir from the attic: sex and sweat, more sophisticated than a French perfume. I hoped the girl could smell it too.

"Oh, I almost forgot," she said. "How silly of me. My name's Suzy."

At that moment Nick came in carrying two glasses,

one filled with fruit juice, the other with ginger ale.

"Oh, hi, Suzy," he said.

She smiled. "Nick, *comment ça va?*"

"Huh?"

Taking the glass of juice, I pulled him away into the centre of the cool saxophone sound that now filled the room.

"That was French. She was talking French to you."

"Yeah, I know. It was French."

I drank half the juice, which burned as it went down.

"What is this?" I demanded.

"Orange juice," he said, "with vodka."

Heat travelled down into my thighs and up through my chest into my arms. "Just who is she, anyway?" It was an animal question — territorial.

"Suzy Janssen? Why do you wanna know about her?"

"Because obviously she knows you well enough to speak French to you."

"Jees, Yule, she's a grade below me at school, is all." After a moment he said, "I didn't invite her, if that's what you're worried about. She just came with her mom and dad."

I was surprised at how relieved I felt.

Instead of hearing the saxophone, I felt it inside me. It was as if I'd swallowed the music with the vodka. My weight gently shifted from foot to foot in time with the lazy jazz beat. I noticed Bette sitting on the couch near the hearth, her red hair ablaze in the firelight. Uncle Alek, who was sitting beside her, said something to her and she laughed. I swallowed the last of the vodka and put the glass down on Aunt Xenia's piano. "Wanna dance?" I asked Nick.

He looked around, and when he saw there were others dancing he said, shyly I thought, "Okay, sure."

It was after midnight. Now I knew my mother wasn't going to phone: a disappointment, but not unexpected. Looking over Nick's shoulder I saw Uncle Michael lift Kate up in his arms. As he carried her, nuzzling against his neck, out of the hot and noisy living-room, I thought how much they looked like father and daughter, both with the same blondish hair and fair skin, though Uncle Michael's was ruddier and weathered from his life out of doors. Followed by Callack, he'd take her upstairs to her bedroom, where he and Aunt Xenia would tuck her in under the colourful quilt on her child-sized bed. *Lucky Kate*, I thought, but then reconsidered, and decided that after all it was better to have a lover.

As the music changed to ragtime I saw Bette get up from the couch. There was a tender look in her eyes, like the expression Aunt Xenia sometimes got when she was talking to Kate. She walked across the room to my father, bent down and kissed him. I watched their lips but couldn't make out what they were saying. My father looked sombre. Bette's feet started to move in time with the music, and she took hold of my father's hands as if she were inviting him to dance. He shrank away from her. She looked surprised and then hurt. I understood that she had not meant to mock him, but had wanted to share the music with him, to have him for her dancing partner even though he must remain in his chair.

The saxophone had stopped, but my feet kept moving through the silence between cuts as I watched Bette retreat from my father back towards the fireplace. Someone turned off the overhead light. The new music was more upbeat, still saxophone but warmer, and it felt as if it were radiating from the centre of me, like the vodka, up through my chest into my arms and down through my pelvis into my thighs. I thought that now was the moment we should have started to make love, instead of earlier up in the attic when it was too cold and our naked bodies were unsure of themselves. On the other side of the room Bette had begun dancing with Uncle Alek, and they too shaped the space between them, more expertly than we did, so that, eager to learn, I couldn't help dancing towards them, the space between Nick and me stretching and then

11

contracting when he followed. The firelight cast our shadows onto the walls, while the angles of the room distorted them. They mingled and separated, climbed towards the ceiling or shrank to the floor, as we danced back and forth over the carpet. I saw Papa watching Uncle Alek and Bette, and I could feel Nick watching me. The living-room was filled with horn and gyrating shadows. With our dance we were spinning the air taut.

Then I found myself alone, so I expanded my dance, whirling into the corners of the room, faster and faster as the tempo increased.

"Yule, Yule," an urgent voice said, and Nick tried to pull me out of the dance.

The music stopped. I went dizzy. Stumbled. Then everything around me turned black, as though all the shadows in the world had suddenly come together in a strange new place that had once been the firelit living-room at Lisii Nos.

In the blackness I heard a rushing sound and then voices. Familiar. Strained.

"Anything wrong?" Uncle Alek.

"Niki, my love, we were just dancing." Bette.

The living-room slowly emerged, whirling out of the dark. Bette and Uncle Alek stood close together, he looking down at my father, who confronted them from the disadvantage of his wheelchair.

"To hell with you both," Papa said, in a voice that was furiously quiet.

"Why so touchy?" Uncle Alek asked.

"Shut up."

"Niki, darling, it's not what you think."

"Shut the fuck up."

My father tried to punch Uncle Alek in the groin but he dodged him easily.

"I don't fight with paraplegics," Uncle Alek said, lofty, turning his back.

Then I heard an immense voice say, "Stop," and Aunt Xenia strode into the room in a scarlet gown, her outrage transforming her into a giant.

"I'm sick to death of this," she said, brandishing her disgust. "Christmas after Christmas. Taunts. Recriminations. Every year you ruin the holidays, both of you. This is my house. I won't have it. I want you to stop or get out. Right now."

Sweat began to trickle down from her hairline and there were dark wet patches on her dress under the arms. The bodice was stretched tight across her breasts as if the buttons were straining to contain her fury. Uncle Michael came up from behind and put his rough hand on her shoulder. She spun round, closed her eyes when she saw him and sighed heavily. For a moment she rested her forehead on his shoulder; then, patting his hand as if to reassure him, she turned back to Papa and Uncle Alek. Her voice was calm when she spoke.

"I meant what I said. Now it's up to you."

Shortly after that the party broke up, and Aunt Xenia — again pure hostess, smiling and genuinely gracious — wished the guests a merry Christmas and thanked them for coming. She stood side by side with Uncle Michael, who thumped all the men on the back and kissed all the women on the cheek as he ushered them out. When they'd all gone, my father went up to Aunt Xenia, took her hand, kissed it and said, "Forgive me." Although Uncle Alek remained aloof, he looked deflated.

"It's after two in the morning," Uncle Michael announced. "Why don't we all turn in?"

Nicholas whispered, "Good night," as he kissed me on the cheek, gallantly, more for the adults than for me.

The vodka sent me to sleep right away, but it was a troubled sleep from which I woke up only an hour or so later, dry-mouthed, too hot and uneasy. It was very dark outside; no moonlight reflected off the rapidly melting snow.

I pushed my quilt away from my shoulders, and the cool air soon made me more comfortable, though my unease drifted with me back into sleep; I dreamed fitfully until a noise interrupted, became a voice and woke me up.

"Xenia, Alek, somebody, please." It was Bette.

I got out of bed, and as I opened my door I heard footsteps on the stairs and Aunt Xenia saying, "What's wrong?" She appeared out of the gloom in the front hallway; Uncle Michael was right behind her.

"It's Niki," Bette said. "He's so sick."

Uncle Michael said, "I'll get Alek," and disappeared back up the stairs.

Aunt Xenia and Bette hurried into the bedroom, where, from the doorway, I could see my father lying in bed on his back, breathing shallowly and sweating.

"Niki, what is it?" Aunt Xenia asked.

My father groaned in response.

"Something in his gut, I think," Bette suggested hesitantly.

Yawning, Uncle Alek arrived in the lower hall.

"Jesus Christ, it's four o'clock in the morning," he complained as he strode towards me, the skirt of his short dressing-gown flapping open to reveal his well-shaped naked thigh. As he passed me and went into Papa and Bette's bedroom, he wrapped the belt more securely around his dressing-gown and straightened it, as if it were a business suit, and while he did this his whole person underwent a change, from a brother drowsy and annoyed at being wakened out of a sound sleep to a physician professionally composed and alert.

"Get my bag out of the car, will you, Mike?" he asked, in a neutral voice that was also persuasive.

As he began to examine my father, Aunt Xenia retreated to where I was standing in the doorway.

"Yulochka," she whispered, "you can't do anything here. Come away with me to the kitchen and I'll make you something hot to drink."

I almost went with her, but then my father groaned and, seeing Uncle Alek press down on his abdomen, I began to be afraid that he was hurting Papa on purpose.

14

Suddenly Bette left Papa's side and ran white-faced towards us.

"I'm going to be sick," she told Aunt Xenia, who put her arm around her shoulder and steered her into the bathroom.

From behind the closed door I could hear Bette retching, and I felt a small triumph because she obviously couldn't stand to see my father ill, while I was used to it and could stay near him, at the very least as a witness, and perhaps to help if he needed me.

Uncle Michael brought Uncle Alek his bag, and later a basin, his ruddy face as unperturbed as if he were helping his neighbour birth a lamb. I longed for Nick to be there with me, his arms around me for warmth and comfort, but I supposed the commotion hadn't even wakened him.

Uncle Alek was standing on the near side of the bed with his back to me, and my father was now hidden behind him. Opening his bag, he took out a thin piece of rubber tubing. I couldn't see what he was doing, but the corner of his robe swayed to and fro as he worked, and his sleeve creased neatly at the elbow whenever he bent his arm.

"Didn't you guess what was happening when you started running that temperature?" he asked.

My father didn't answer.

Uncle Alek walked around to the other side of the bed, and I could see my father lying half-naked amid the crumpled bedding. He tried to sit up, then fell back onto the mattress.

"Jesus," he said.

"Don't move, Niki. You'll feel better in about thirty seconds."

Suddenly my father turned his head and looked right at me. He didn't say anything, only stared as if he couldn't see me. I moved my hand. Still nothing. I thought, *Am I invisible?* Then I realized he was blind with pain.

Uncle Alek was making a threading motion with

his right hand. Watching him as he worked, I saw that all arrogance was gone from his face. Instead he looked serious and completely absorbed in what he was doing. And there was something else: a look of caring that I had never seen in him before.

I thought to myself, *Does he love Papa after all?*

Papa lay with his eyes closed, but there was a tautness in his face as if he was struggling for control. I heard him gasp; then a trickling sound. He groaned once or twice and grew quiet.

"Done," Uncle Alek said. He sounded pleased with himself. I heard the arrogance return to his voice before I saw it in his face. As he packed his instruments back in his bag he said to my father, "I suppose I don't have to tell you that you'd have done far better not to accept this new gig at Fourth Wall."

"Christ, Alek, don't start...," Papa began, but he didn't have the energy to finish.

Bette came out of the bathroom, still white-faced but looking determined. She gave Uncle Alek a tight-lipped smile as he passed her on his way out of the bedroom, a smell of urine rising from the enamel basin he was carrying. Bending over my father, she ran her fingers through his hair.

"Feeling better?" she asked in a whisper.

"Mn-hmn," he answered. The look on his face was that of a young child about to fall asleep.

Bette ran her hand along his arm, then turned and walked quietly over to the doorway, where I was still standing.

"Better go back to bed," she said, and closed the door.

TWO

The next morning, despite having slept only a few hours, I woke up just as the darkness was turning to dawn. I was entirely thirsty, as if every fluid in my body had turned viscous. My eyelids were stuck together, my tongue moved slowly through gluey saliva. I pulled myself out of bed and went into the bathroom, where I gulped down cold water to thin my blood. No one else was up, so I made some tea and ate a piece of black bread and jam before I picked up the scrap bucket and went outside. I pulled my collar up and my toque down over my ears to ward off the damp west-coast cold. My feet packed the snow solid as I headed down the slope towards the stable where the two donkeys were kept during nights that were too bitter for them to stay out of doors.

It was a bleak morning, the sky an indeterminate grey that might or might not imply another snowfall. The white rails of the donkeys' paddock were hardly distinguishable from the surrounding snow, while far off in the neighbour's fields the sheep, huddled together against the cold, looked like a large stain on a tablecloth. Down in the orchard the naked branches of the apple and cherry trees stood out sharply, and looked as if, with a gust of wind, they might scratch the surface of the low, monochrome sky. Dedushka's shed, which lay to the right about fifteen yards from the main path, looked secretive under its hood of snow. It was a forbidden place, where Dedushka kept his traps; none of us kids had ever been inside. Of course we'd tried to look through the window, but even standing right up against the glass we could make out no more than the dim but unequivocally functional line of a workbench; and so we imagined that in the darkest corners mysteries crouched, their faces turned away from the light.

Even before I opened the door to the stable I heard Chornik, the dark one, braying. When I walked up to him he started to nuzzle me. The other, White Isobel, sidled up to the pail to get at the scraps but Chornik kept pushing her away until she nipped and he bellowed. The sweet smell of the hay made me feel cosy though I could see my breath in the dim-lit air. When they had finished the scraps I found a curry comb and began to brush Chornik's flank. His hair was coarse beneath my hand as I ran my finger along the dark cross that ran over his shoulders and down his back. Once Aunt Xenia had told me a story about the donkey that carried Christ into Jerusalem on Palm Sunday. She said that before Christ rode on him he didn't have any markings at all, but afterwards a cross appeared on his back and, ever since, all his descendants have been marked with crosses. This made Chornik special and explained why I was fonder of him than of White Isobel. Perhaps the cross gave him extraordinary powers: he might be able to grant a wish or send a prayer directly to God. That was what I half believed; and so in the privacy of my own fantasy I fondled his silky ear and whispered into it, "Chornik, my lovely boy, make it so Papa gets well and Mama comes back home to live with us."

As I was walking back with the empty scrap bucket towards the square farmhouse, whose wide verandas I thought of as the outward expression of Aunt Xenia's generosity, it started to snow sharp small flakes that pricked my cheeks. At the side of the house the kitchen door opened and Nick came out, booted and mitted, with a lunch bucket in his hand and the flaps of his cap turned down over his ears. He saw me and, waving, walked down the path to meet me.

"Yule," he said, "how come you're up so early? Everyone else is still asleep."

Before I could answer, he kissed me on the mouth, then put his arms around me. His lunch bucket thudded against my hip, but my thick clothes protected me from bruising.

"Do you know if Papa's okay?" I asked.

"Uncle Niki?" He looked bewildered.

"So you didn't hear a thing, huh?"

"What are you talking about?"

That he'd been able to sleep soundly through that middle-of-the-night crisis, I thought, was a flaw in his character. He must have sensed it, because he began kissing me...on my cheeks, my forehead, my eyes, my nose; it was an act of contrition, which I accepted by walking with him hand in hand up the long driveway towards the road where he was going to thumb a ride to work.

About half-way up I heard Aunt Xenia calling my name. Her voice sounded urgent, and I thought, *Papa. Something's happened.*

"I gotta go," I told Nick.

"Kiss me first."

"He was really sick last night."

"You want me to come back with you?"

A rush of panic pulled me into isolation; I shook my head and ran away from him down the drive.

"Yule...," he called after me.

In the kitchen doorway Aunt Xenia stood, her arms folded against the cold.

"Hurry," she said.

"Papa?"

"A phone call, long distance. A man with a British accent."

But it wasn't a man, it was Mama. Her voice sounded close, as if she might be calling from the pay phone down the road at the nearest gas station.

"There you are at last, my darling," she said. "James

has been trying to get through to you for the past two hours, and I'm going out for tea in fifteen minutes; I was so afraid I'd miss you."

If she was going out for tea it must be about four o'clock in the afternoon, which meant she was still in London and not, as I had hoped, in some more westerly city, Toronto, for instance, en route to Lisii Nos. Vaguely I felt it was my fault James had had so much trouble getting through.

"Now, my dear," she said, "I know I'm terribly bad, just awful for not sending you a present, but I've been so busy lately, what with this new ballet and rehearsals, and God knows what else. Anyway, you must tell me what you want, and I'll send it post-haste."

I thought, *You.* I want you. But when I answered her I said, "Nothing. I don't care about a present," though I knew I could take advantage of her guilt and ask for something expensive.

"Come on now, darling, think," she said. "I want to get you something lovely."

"Presents are supposed to be a surprise, aren't they?" I felt insulted that she'd had James do the phoning instead of taking the trouble to get through the international exchange on her own.

"Oh dear, now you're angry with me."

"No," I said. Not just angry, I ached for her; but I couldn't tell her that because she'd laugh and say, "Oh, my darling, don't be so sentimental."

She tried to talk to me for a few minutes longer, but I hardly listened. To her direct questions I answered yes or no. Finally with a relieved sigh she said, "Well, my dear, James is standing right beside me with my coat. I really must ring off or I'll be late. I love you, my darling, darling. Goodbye."

"'Bye," I said into the half-moment of brittle silence before she hung up.

She wasn't in love with James. Half the time he functioned as her pet, the other half her protector. In return for her sharing her bed with him she expected him to be a loyal intercessor with the outside world. He guarded her dressing-room door so she wouldn't be disturbed, he vetted incoming calls so she wouldn't be taken by surprise, and he accompanied her to parties and opening-night receptions so she wouldn't feel lonely. And if she denied him equality, his usefulness made him indispensable, like a beloved servant who might one day transcend his servitude.

Whatever his status, at least he was with her in the flesh, actually saw all those physical details that made her real: how her left eyebrow arched higher than the right, how her collarbones stood out from the scooped-neck blouses she so often wore, the scrawl of veins on the back of her hand, the dancerly ruin of her feet. For me she was present only in my mind, and it was as if all the particularities of her body were like the aspects of God, imagined unreliably and at a distance.

"Your mama? She's well?" Aunt Xenia was sitting at the kitchen table in her bulky dressing-gown and old fuzzy slippers; even though much of the fuzz was worn away, they made her feet look larger than they really were.

"Oh, just fine," I said, my voice vehement. "She and James are going out for tea."

Aunt Xenia frowned. "Sit down, *golubchik*, have some bread, have some cheese. Tell me all about it."

She was offering me solace and understanding, but I could think only how dowdy she looked sitting there against the blank snow-laden light from the kitchen window. I put the scrap bucket back under the sink to stall for time so I could think up an excuse, then straightened and answered, "I haven't made my bed yet." She had often scolded me about this. No, not scolded. Not Aunt Xenia. She implored, sadly, as though my shortcomings caused her pain. And so I escaped before she had time to recover, but I heard her voice, *Wait, Yulochka, you can do that later*, her earthy contralto, following me down the hall, and I closed the door of the small office-bedroom behind me, reluctant to shut out what comfort she could give me, but helpless to feel anything but unreachable.

Wiping my eyes, I noticed my grandmother's diary, the corner of it sticking out from under the bed I'd made while tears trickled down my cheeks. I lifted it up and turned to the first page of the Russian version. The letters were carefully shaped, but there was a fluidity in the words as they spread across the page that was elegant. I ran my fingertips over the flowing Cyrillic.

Looking back from the vantage point of middle age I can say that this was the moment of choice, the nexus of small events — making love with Nick, finding the diary, witnessing my father's illness, receiving the phone call from my mother, who once again had let me down — these and so many others from my earlier childhood, most of them forgotten, that converged towards the simple act of running my fingers over the words my grandmother had written thirty years earlier. At that moment I accepted her legacy, which Aunt Xenia's typed translation made intelligible. Here was my family's history, the beginning of a new knowledge that during the next seven months informed and perhaps distorted all my thoughts and actions.

The first entry was dated June 22, 1941.

This morning we were heading out to the dacha near Lisii Nos: my Andrei, who is on leave, the children, Lev Antonich, a friend of Andrei's from the university, and I. There were no clouds in the sky. It was real summer weather and we found ourselves singing song after song: "Kalinka", "Far Away", "Along Peter's Street", "You Are So Beautiful". As we were driving along the road beside the reedy swampland, with the Gulf of Finland in the distance, Lev Antonich said, "Look at all those cars heading back to Leningrad." I had not noticed them because I was already thinking about how the sunlight shining through the curtains at the dacha would cast lacy shadows onto the old deal table under the window. I thought how foolish they were to be heading into the city on such a fine day. Soon we would be sitting on a blanket beneath the birch trees with our lunch spread out before us. I looked over at Andrusha. There were two deep lines in the flesh between his eyebrows. Those lines always mean he is worried. I put my hand on his knee. He cried out, "Stop the truck." Lev Antonich pulled over and, even before it had stopped rolling, Andrusha was climbing out onto the gravel.

"What is it, Andrusha? Are you ill?" I asked him, but he was already flagging down one of the cars driving in the opposite direction. I looked over at Lev Antonich. We did not speak. Even the children, who had been playing krestiki-noliki, *noughts and crosses, in the back seat, were silent.*

Andrusha talked to the driver for only a moment, then he turned around and walked slowly back towards us as the other vehicle started up again. He climbed onto the seat beside me.

"And so?" Lev Antonich asked.

Andrusha turned and looked at us.

"War," he said.

We were all silent. Then Nikolenka asked, "Does this mean we are not going to Lisii Nos?"

I stopped reading because the name Nikolenka reminded me that the children Babushka was talking about were my father and Aunt Xenia and Tatiana, their older sister, who had died during the war. There was a photograph of Tatiana on the dressing-table in Aunt Xenia and Uncle Michael's bedroom. I couldn't remember my father or Aunt Xenia ever talking about Lev Antonich, but I knew Andrusha was Dedushka because the two deep lines between his eyebrows had become set so that he had a permanent scowl.

Babushka had died when I was five years old, and there was little I remembered about her physically. I thought she had been quite a large woman, like Aunt Xenia, and I knew her face had been covered with unhealthy-looking wrinkles. Around her hung cigarette smoke. Her voice was smoky too, and she coughed a lot,

23

especially at night. I didn't remember liking her but, like her or not, she had now become my informant about events that still haunted my family thirty years later. It seemed fitting that the name of my aunt and uncle's farm, which was also Lisii Nos (Fox's Nose), harked back to the beginning of the war. Why the town and the farm were called Fox's Nose, Aunt Xenia never said.

I became aware of noises in the house — voices, running water, the opening and closing of doors — which meant the rest of the family was up. What if someone came into my room and found me with the diary? How could I explain? Though the war was a constant presence at the farm, no one ever talked about it, and forcing a break in that silence was not something I wanted to do. I decided to take the diary up to the cabin in the woods where Nick and I had played together during our childhood summers. It was a private place where I could read without fear of interruption, and in some comfort, because the cabin was furnished and had an old woodstove. So I packed the manuscript away in my knapsack and headed down the hall towards the kitchen, intending to check on my father before I left.

Everyone but Dedushka and Nick was there. Uncle Michael had the guts of a radio spread over the kitchen counter. He could repair almost anything, and neighbours often brought him appliances which he fixed for a small fee to supplement the family's meagre farming income. Papa was sitting at the table in pyjamas and a dressing-gown that made him look shrunken because they were too large, but he was sipping at a cup of tea and there was a half-eaten slice of bread and cheese on a plate in front of him.

"Don't look so worried," Bette said. "Your papa's all right."

"What makes you think I'm worried?"

My father looked up. "Don't speak to Bette like that," he said.

Uncle Alek's only comment was a smile with which

he looked down on the rest of us.

"I'm going out," I said, already headed for the porch to put on my coat and boots.

"In this weather?" Aunt Xenia's voice trailed after me.

Kate had followed me into the porch. "I'm coming with you," she announced.

"No you're not," Uncle Michael called out to her.

And suddenly Bette was there too.

"It's awfully cold outside. Here," she said, handing me a long and achingly soft scarf, the colours as vibrant as medieval illuminations.

"That's okay. I don't need it."

But she had already put it around my neck.

I was hardly through the back door when Dedushka appeared, his black leather jacket stark against the snow.

"*Krolishka*," he said, "little rabbit. Come with me."

Immediately he turned and strode off.

"Where to?" I asked after his black shoulders, which were receding into snowflakes so fine they looked like particles of detergent pouring out of the sky.

"You follow," he called back.

After my babushka's death nine years earlier he had begun to trap small animals — raccoons, marmots, weasels — in the woods around Lisii Nos. Some of these animals he sold for their pelts. From others, usually raccoons, he made stews which he ate alone and never shared. Instinctively I knew that this behaviour had something to do with the war, though no one had ever said as much. Once when Dedushka found one of his traps empty, he accused Nick of springing it and slapped him across the face, hard, four or five times. I hadn't witnessed it, but when Nick told me about it he lovingly fingered his cheek where the bruise had been, as if he was proud of it and had won it like a decoration for bravery. Dedushka had never raised a hand to me.

I'd been so busily following his black shoulders that

it was a complete surprise when I looked up and saw we'd reached his shed.

He undid the padlock, opened the door, and with a flourish of his hand said, "I invite you inside."

Never before had I or anyone else been allowed in that shed, and I stepped up into the doorway feeling not only awestruck but a little smug too, knowing how jealous Nick would be if he knew.

It felt almost like church, like being shown into the sacristy behind the icons, where the priests conducted the first part of the Russian Orthodox service, hidden from the congregation. Around my neck the scarf, sweet with Bette's perfume, reminded me of incense. There was a row of traps neatly lined up on the worktable, above which twelve calendar girls from 1947 smiled out at us from the wall. In the white, blank light from the falling snow their red lips astonished me. The girls were square-shouldered, long-legged, and wore scanty costumes that looked like décolleté evening gowns on top and bathing suits on the bottom, each decorated with flowers or berries or grain or red leaves, depending on the month represented. Immediately I fell in love with Miss December, who wore a costume trimmed with ermine. I wanted to reach out and touch the soft pelt, then let my fingers stray over onto her smooth skin and down into the space between her round breasts. One day, I thought, *I'll* have breasts like that.

Dedushka said, "There," and pointed to a wooden bench that stood against the wall. I shrugged off my knapsack and sat down.

He turned to the worktable and lifted up a trap from the meticulous row where each one was placed, smallest to largest.

"I used to trap foxes, you know. Near the Polish border."

I thought how, whenever I came to Lisii Nos, the war felt much nearer than it did at home in Vancouver.

"Real traps, not snares," he continued. "For foxes I used only traps." He put the one he was holding back in its place, then his hand hovered with intent over the rest of them before he selected the most fearsome.

"You want to see how does it work?" He didn't wait for an answer.

Slowly he pulled the jaws of the trap open. It had sharp triangular teeth, and looked like the jaws of a shark I had seen at the aquarium. He took a small can, oiled the hinges, and from the back of the worktable picked up a piece of wooden dowelling. For a moment during which I heard snow whispering against the window, he held the dowelling above the trap; then with a quick downward jab, while the calendar girls looked on, he sprang it. The jaws snapped. They crushed and splintered the wood with a dull sound that made my teeth ache. I felt ligaments tearing, bones breaking. Without looking up at me Dedushka said in a quiet voice, "That is how I used to trap pretty little foxes."

He reached into the pocket of his leather jacket, brought out a ten-dollar bill, and handed it to me, then tapped his cheek to show me where he wanted to be thanked with a kiss. When I touched my lips to his skin, I felt as if I had just sealed a pledge, but for what I had no idea.

Ten minutes later I turned off the road that ran along the fenceline above Lisii Nos onto the path to the cabin. It had stopped snowing and the sun had come out. There was a hush in the woods: no twigs snapping, no birdsong, no scrabbling in the undergrowth; only the occasional plop as snow fell from the burdened branches to the ground. The snow was deeper than on the driveway or along the road. It reached almost to the top of my boots, and on either side of the trail it rose in humps that looked like the rounded backs of crouching animals, the raccoons and foxes and marmots that Dedushka trapped.

I felt in the pocket of my coat for the ten-dollar bill. It was a lot of money, and Dedushka had given it to me after Christmas instead of before, when I'd have felt bound by the generosity Aunt Xenia exemplified to spend it on presents.

What I really wanted to do was keep it for myself. Mama paid my tuition for private school and, because all the projects and excursions were for rich kids, towards the end of every term I ran out of the allowance money she sent. It was no use asking Papa because he never had any, and Aunt Xenia and Uncle Michael hardly had enough to keep the farm going, so I had to phone England to get Mama to wire me some. I hated doing that, not because she didn't want to send it, but because I rarely got to talk with her directly. I had to beg through an intermediary, either her answering service or sometimes, which was worse, James. In my discomfort I was usually rude with him and in revenge he often forgot to give her the message. Then I'd have to phone all over again, and hope I got her answering service instead of him.

The trail suddenly went dark. My chest tightened even though I knew it was only that the sun had gone behind a cloud. The deep snow had begun to tire my legs and, as I trudged through it, I heard a spattering sound that made me think one of the snow beasts was coughing. I arrived at a fork; the right-hand path eventually led up to an outcrop from which there was a view of the fields and buildings that made up Lisii Nos. Because I was cold, I took the darker, shorter, left-hand path to the cabin, where I knew I'd find shelter and could build a fire in the old woodstove. But when I got there it looked desolate and unwelcoming, with its windows shuttered against the season. So different from my memory of door and window standing open to the summer heat and green light filtering down through the cedars and Douglas fir.

At first I couldn't open the door; my gloved hands kept slipping on the knob. I took the gloves off. The coldness of the metal made my fingers ache as I tried to free the rusted latch. Finally it gave way with a screech that sent a sharp pain through my skull.

The door opened into darkness, which frightened

me until I remembered that the shutters were closed. As I groped my way towards the windows, I smelled a pungent, rotting odour. When I pushed back the shutters the winter light had brightened again. I dropped my knapsack off my shoulder onto the bed, which stood beneath the window. The naked mattress smelled of mildew and was damp to the touch. I thought, *If I build a fire, it will drive the mildew and the rotting smell away.* There were still eight or ten matches in the screwtop jar on the hearth, and there was a ragged but adequate pile of wood. I scrunched up some paper and laid a few sticks of kindling into a tent over it. Within a few minutes the cabin was warm with a heat that dissipated the smell of mildew but only intensified the rotting odour. I had to find out what it was and where it came from. I walked all around the inside of the cabin — along the walls, beside the bed, near the stove — until I stopped in front of a cupboard where the smell was very strong. When I crouched, it became still stronger. I ran my fingers over the seams of the floorboards and in an instant I knew: the stink came from beneath the cabin.

I took a knife out of the cupboard and started slicing at the seams between the floorboards, but I managed only to scrape out clumps of dirt. When I tried to use the knife as a lever the blade broke off near the handle. I felt tears starting and I almost gave up, but then, as I looked around me, I caught sight of the handle for the stove lids hanging on a nail beside the stovepipe. I took it down and began working at the floorboards again. One by one the nails gave way, shrieking. As I pulled the boards up, the smell made me gag. I put my hand over my nose and mouth and peered down into the darkness. Something moved. *It's alive*, I thought. Then I saw that the movement didn't come from one living thing, but from many: maggots crawling over the carcass of a small animal. In the dimness beneath the floorboards the creature's white teeth reflected what little light there was. I looked closer at the eyeless face that was turning into a skull, at the haunches that were shrinking to bone. The hind legs were long and thin: the legs of a runner, a rabbit. One of the forelegs was only a stump. I thought of the snapping sound of the trap Dedushka had sprung. The poor creature must have been caught in one and gnawed its foot off to escape. I pushed the floorboards down again. If I looked at that pullulating mass a second longer I knew I was going to throw up. But I had to find a way to get rid of the little corpse, or be driven out by its stink.

The place where I'd pried up the boards was near the cabin's outside wall, and it occurred to me that it might be much easier to get at the rabbit from the outside rather than try to lift it up through the floor.

With an axe that was kept beside the stove for chopping firewood, I went outside and carved a hole in the hard ground. I returned to the cabin for the ashbucket; then, tying Bette's scarf over my nose and mouth, I crawled under the cabin floor, shovelled the creature's remains into the bucket, dumped them in the hole without a ceremony of any kind and filled it up again with dirt.

I left the windows open when I returned to the house for lunch, and came back afterwards to discover the cabin freezing but the smell almost gone. It was still early afternoon when I got the fire going again and the cabin warmed up. At last I lay down on the bed under a blanket I'd brought from the house. I picked up Babushka's little exercise book and opened it at random. The entry was dated September 9, 1941. Looking up the same date in Aunt Xenia's translation, I began to read.

I was visiting Danya last night when the air raid began. We were working on the letter scene for Yevgeni Onegin. *One of the phrases contains a high B-flat and, although I have heard her sing a D in alt, in a lovely pure whisper of a tone (she usually has so much control), she kept running out of breath and could not support the note.*

Right after a particularly unsuccessful run at the phrase, when she had sung it a quarter-tone sharp, the air-raid alarm suddenly shrilled. We stared at each other. She looked panic-stricken for a moment, then a smile passed over her lips, but she said with convincing sincerity, "If I am expelled from the opera because I cannot sing high B-flat perhaps I can serve the motherland as an air-raid siren."

We did not go down to the air-raid shelter, though Danya suggested it, because, as the bombs began to fall, fire after fire broke out in the southwest quarter of the city and the sight bewitched us. Danya's windows look out over the Vitebsk Station and beyond to the Kirov Metallurgical works. As we watched, oily black smoke spread across the sky. Flames slithered up through the smoke and turned it red. More and more bombs fell. More and more fires broke out. They were so intense they almost blinded us.

As soon as the all-clear sounded I ran down into the streets. I wanted to get home as quickly as possible because I had left Tanyusha to look after Xyusha and Nikolenka, and I knew she would be frightened. Danya came with me to see the damage from street level. It looked as if all of Leningrad had come out into the streets. Crowds of people were walking south. None of the streetcars could get through so I said goodbye to Danya and walked home.

I arrived at about nine-thirty to find the children safe but wide awake with excitement and fear.

"Yura's apartment was bombed," Nikolenka told me. "His mama is under the rubble. They are trying to dig her out."

I had only just got the children into bed when the sirens shrieked again. We have no shelter nearby so we stayed where we were. By this time the smoke had spread right over the city. Searchlights crossed the sky back and forth, again and again. Our anti-aircraft guns rattled away but the bombs kept falling. Occasionally I thought I saw rockets shooting up into the clouds.

By the time the all-clear sounded the children were asleep. I ran downstairs and found the streets filled with a peculiar, hectic light, as the clouds of smoke reflected the flames from the fires.

A woman I recognized from the next apartment building, though I do not know her name, ran up to me.

"Have you heard, Vera Mikhailovna?" she said. "The Badayev warehouses have burned to the ground."

The warehouses were located near the Vitebsk station, which meant the food supply for the entire city had gone up in smoke.

"Yes," I told her, "I saw them burning."

"And did you see those rockets?"

I nodded.

"German agents," she said, "guiding in the bombers. Ah, the filthy creatures. And do you know, I saw someone signalling from the rooftop of that building on the corner."

"Signalling?"

"With a torch. There are traitors among us, and some of them speak Russian and pretend to serve the motherland. We must be vigilant."

This morning I saw Danya at the conservatory. She said that where she lives the air is filled with the stench of burnt meat and sugar. As she told me she started to cry.

"My God, my God," she said, "we are all going to starve to death."

Every fifteen minutes or so I put more wood in the stove. When all the wood had gone I still huddled on the mattress beneath the blanket and continued reading. It was dusk when I finished. The words and the pages upon which they were typed were fading to the same uniform grey. When I got up, my shoulders were sore from hunching over the diary. Through the windowpane I saw a few flakes drifting down from the twilight sky, and when I left the cabin I found a new covering of snow on the stoop two inches thick. It had been snowing most of the afternoon.

THREE

A large window in the living-room at Lisii Nos looked out onto the veranda and beyond it to the garden, where a balsam grew. The window was divided into three panes, and one of these panes, which dated from the 1920s, had a flaw in it. All through my childhood that glass had been a source of wonder: to look through a flawed lens and see the world transformed. It magnified the balsam so that over the years I became aware of the gradual metamorphosis of its bark from smooth and mottled to furrowed and ridged. But what fascinated me most were the edges of the flaw, the boundaries between extraordinary and normal seeing: on one side, a jagged break so that the bark resembled tectonic plates, the ridges seen through the flaw sliding over those beyond it; on the other side, a queasy rippling like the lapping of waves on a shore that made me deliciously light-headed.

My grandmother's diary transformed my vision as surely as that remarkable pane of glass, and I couldn't help seeing my family through the lens of wartime, the present reshaped by their past. At dinner that night I could not look at Dedushka without seeing a young soldier, or at Papa and Aunt Xenia without remembering that in the winter of 1941–42 they had been children, younger than me, who very nearly starved and froze to death. Uncle Alek had left Lisii Nos that afternoon while I was still up at the cabin, and his absence felt entirely appropriate, because he hadn't been born until after the siege. Nick, who was sitting beside me, kept touching my thigh under the table, not passionately, but as if he were trying to pull me back to the present.

There was a mood of celebration in the dining-room, and I wanted to be part of it instead of observing it from behind my flawed-glass barrier. Papa had some colour in his face. There were no signs of strain around his eyes, and by the way he looked at Bette I knew they were sharing some private happiness. I was jealous, but only a little. It was a relief that Bette had taken on some of the responsibility for keeping him safe.

The table was laden with food, most of it left over from the party, including a tin of caviar that Aunt Xenia had just opened. There was also tomato salad, soup, potatoes, blini, smoked salmon and chicken. Aunt Xenia said, "Since we won't all be together at the New Year, I thought we should have a little feast tonight, before all this food goes bad." Dedushka lifted up a glassful of vodka and said, "*S novim godom*, Happy New Year." Like everyone else around the table — even Bette, who laughed as she mispronounced the unfamiliar Russian words — I answered, "*S novim godom*." But the New Year's celebration that claimed my attention had taken place in Leningrad on December 31, 1941.

Last night the Germans shelled the city and our ships on the Neva fired back at them. Even so, we celebrated the New Year. Yesterday morning Xyusha went out with Tanyusha and came back about an hour later with a fir branch. They would not tell if they had found it, stolen it or traded something for it; and I really did not care, because they were so pleased with themselves, laughing and whispering. They were quite transformed, and for an hour or two I felt curiously euphoric, convinced that the Siege would soon be over.

In the evening Danya came to visit us. She had scarcely got in the door when the lights came on. It is weeks since we had electricity. Nikolenka, in spite of his swollen feet, did a funny, stumbling dance around the table while Tanya and Xyusha clapped in accompaniment. Danya had brought a little bottle of something she called wine. It was thick and sweet. She said she had made it from dried mossberries.

"And there is real alcohol in it," she added, sounding very proud.

I had traded my recital gown for some dog meat, and we had all saved our bread ration so that we might have a little feast. The five of us sat around the table, with the fir branch standing in a jar in the centre. We ate very slowly to make our feast last as long as possible. The noise of shelling boomed in the distance, and several times shells exploded nearby, making the dishes tremble and the electric lights flicker. During those moments we sat silent, staring up at the lights, but the bulbs kept glowing, so we started back in on our feast. Over the radio we heard a broadcast of the Spassky chimes playing the Internationale. It made me long for Moscow, or rather, for Andrusha.

I kept thinking of the little square where he and I first met. We sat for a long time in the summer twilight talking about Eisenstein's films. Then, without knowing I was a musician, he invited me to a chamber concert the following evening. It turned out that I was playing in that very same concert.

I must have had a strange expression on my face because Danya asked me, "What is it?"

"Nostalgia," I answered.

"Oh, yes," Danya said.

We both began to cry.

The lights went out and we lit the candle I had saved for our New Year's celebration. The children finished their feast and moved to the other side of the burzhuika, our makeshift stove, where Nikolenka got his sisters to play White and Red Russians. He likes to play that game when we are being shelled. At first I thought it was because of the sound effects, but now, when I see how absorbed he becomes, I think it is because he can pretend the shelling is part of the game and it makes him feel safer.

Danya and I finished the little bottle of wine. My head was very clear, and my mind moved lightly from thought to thought. I watched Danya's face in the candlelight. Her cheek-

bones have become very prominent and, because she is so thin, her eyes are very large.

I got up and went over to her and put my arms around her.

"My God," I said, "you are so beautiful."

I kissed her and suddenly felt how fragile the moment was; how fragile we all were, in this cold apartment, bundled in our coats, with scarcely a morsel to eat, celebrating the New Year by candlelight because there was no longer any electricity.

I looked past Danya at the children. Suddenly I was sure we would not all survive; by the same time next year at least one of us would be dead. I looked at Danya, Xyusha, Nikolenka, Tanyusha, each of them in turn, as I tried to imagine who of us would live and who would die. I grew afraid. I thought that by imagining it I might make it true, and I worried that I might already have marked one of us for death. I found myself avoiding the eyes of these four people: my best friend and my children, who, together with Andrusha, are so close to me. For the first time since the war began, or rather, for the first time in my life, I have admitted that death is only a touch away: I feel implicated. And ashamed.

At my knee Callack sat decorously, but her eyes begged for the morsel of smoked salmon I had on my fork. Even she couldn't escape my new vision: I found myself blurting, "Did you really eat dog meat during the war?"

"Who told you that?" Dedushka demanded.

My father, who had been holding Bette's hand, let go and stared at me with a wounded look, as though I'd said the words deliberately to hurt him.

"I read it somewhere," I said. I was trying to sound offhanded, but I knew I'd broken a family taboo. My cheeks went hot, and I didn't dare look up from the potato I was cutting.

"Yes. It's true. We did eat dog meat," Aunt Xenia said, coaxing me with a gentle voice to look at her. When I did, I saw that she knew I had been reading the diary. She must have seen it on the floor under my bed. And what else did she know? That Nicholas and I had been up in the attic alone? But she went on talking about the war in a purposefully quiet voice to soothe my father's alarm.

"Dog meat was not the worst of it," she said. "We ate sawdust, glue, boiled leather...and do you know what was a treat? A bowl of hot water with a single cabbage leaf in it...we called that soup."

"Yuck," Kate said.

"Gross," Nicholas added.

Aunt Xenia was now laughing, trying to make light of it.

"I remember one day Mama, your babushka," she said, looking straight at me, "came home with a dead cat. She'd found it down by the Fontanka Canal. It was weak and starving, so she hit it over the head with a board and killed it. Well, she skinned it, cooked it. My God, there was hardly any meat on it, but I swear it's just about the best meal I've ever eaten. Delicious. Better than this caviar," she added, holding up the hunk of black bread she had just spread with butter and a spoonful of the fish roe.

"I never heard this story before in my life," Papa said, his voice sharp with anger.

"But don't you remember how stringy the meat was?" Aunt Xenia asked, her tone aggressive now, because she wanted him for a witness. "And you must remember how she played for us afterwards. She hadn't touched her piano for months and her hands were so stiff and swollen. She had stopped giving lessons at the conservatory because it was too far to walk and most of her students were dead anyway."

My father didn't answer. He had closed himself off.

"Poor darling," Bette said. Her tone was noncommittal. I wasn't sure who she meant. It might have been Papa, or Babushka, or even the dead cat.

Dedushka's eyes filled with tears as he drank another glass of vodka.

"Don't you think you've had enough, Andrei?"

Uncle Michael asked, but Dedushka ignored him, whispering to himself, "Verochka." Then, suddenly, he sat back in his chair and slapped the table with his hand.

"You need never be without food if you have a trap," he said, his melancholy completely evaporated. "I used to supply food to our whole group of partisans — twenty men. I trapped foxes, and wolves, yes, and bears. Month after month. And why did I have such success?" he asked, beginning to sound like a teacher. "For two reasons: first, I thought like an animal; second, I made certain there was never any smell of human...."

"It's all very well if you live in a forest," my father interrupted, "but in a city under siege there aren't any animals, and you'd be damn useless there."

"Niki, that's not fair," Aunt Xenia said. "It's not Papa's fault that he wasn't in Leningrad."

"No," Dedushka said, "but it is correct. I would be useless." Then he swallowed yet another glass of vodka. "*Pravilno*," he whispered, nodding. "It is correct."

The next afternoon, on Nick's day off, he and I climbed up through the woods and, at the fork, took the trail that led to the outcrop. Far below, the donkeys stood in the meadow. It was their first day out after the low temperatures. Most of the snow had melted or dropped from the trees, and what remained on the ground was marked by footprints and tire tracks. At the edge of the farthest meadow the bare branches of the trees were tinged with pale orange, reddish brown, olive and many other shades of green, all of them subtle, damp colours. Up the slope evergreens mingled with leafless maples and alders.

It had begun to drizzle. I put my hand on Nick's arm and turned him towards me. His damp, light brown hair and khaki jacket had the same pale subtlety as the surrounding woods: the diffident lichen greens; the granite greys of the outcrop. I looked past him into the mist-fine rain. The colours were even more sombre where the evergreen boughs filtered the winter light, except for a patch of bright red from a cedar root that lay exposed in the wet.

He pushed back my hair and touched his cold lips to my neck. I shivered. "Let's go to the cabin," he said in a whisper, and once more touched his lips to my neck, so that I could no longer tell if the shivering came from the coolness of his lips or the warmth of his whispering breath.

When we got to the cabin we lit the fire, pulled the mattress in front of it and lay down together. Our bodies remembered each other, and after only a few awkward kisses we touched easily. He was eager to bear down on me and put his penis inside. I wanted him there, but I remembered the lovely swelling sensation I'd felt up in the attic and how it had dwindled when it should have burst.

"Nick," I said, "roll over on your back."

"Aw, Yule."

"Please."

I crouched over him and guided his penis. It rubbed against me uncomfortably for a moment; then, quite suddenly, it became easy, and the lovely swelling itch began to grow.

"Is this okay for you?" I asked.

"Yeah, it's okay," he said. But he began to struggle under me.

"Please, Nick, a little longer, and then we'll roll over."

The swelling grew and grew as we worked back and forth against each other. Our skin was sweaty in the glow from the stove and our chests made sucking sounds as we stuck to each other and then came apart.

"Our bodies are kissing," he said.

My mouth found his. We swallowed each other's saliva while our tongues explored. He thrust against me harder and harder.

"Now, Yule," he shouted. "NOW."

We rolled over. He shuddered. The swelling inside me burst, turned into a current of sharp pleasure, travelled up my spine to the crown of my head and set my scalp on fire with tiny cold flames.

"Lovely. Is it lovely for you?"

"Yes."

We held onto each other until his penis shrank, and then we drew away slowly until only my hand touched his belly. The heat from the stove wafted the smell of our sex over us.

As I got up to put more wood on the fire I caught sight of Babushka's diary lying on the table. I looked back down at Nick. His hair was damp with sweat as earlier it had been damp with drizzle. I felt a tenderness for him so radiant it was like the heat that emanated from the stove's belly. I thought, *Why shouldn't I share what I've learned with Nick?* It would be easier than trying to talk about it to the adults, even Aunt Xenia, because they'd been through the war, suffering it directly. I had not frozen or starved, but what I'd learned made me more intimate with death, and therefore less of a child.

I lay down beside Nick again and pushed my face under his arm, sniffing at the vitality of his sweat.

"Has Aunt Xyusha ever spoken to you about the war?" I asked.

"You mean like eating dog meat and glue and stuff?"

"Yes, that, but other things too. What it was like to live under siege day after day."

"Nah. Anyway it's pretty boring compared to what Dad did in the war. He was only seventeen, but he lied and got into the air force, and flew a Spitfire in the Battle of Britain. "Ah-ah-ah-ah-ah-ah-ah-ah-ah," he said, gripping an imaginary joystick with his hand and pressing down on the firing button like an eight-year-old playing pilot. "Even when Dedushka talks on and on about his traps it's a lot more interesting than that freezing and starving stuff."

He pulled me closer to him and kissed me, his tongue exploring my mouth like a soldier in occupied territory.

40

"I love you," he said. And then, "Holy shit."

"What?"

He pulled away from me and sat up.

"Someone's been watching us."

"What do you mean?"

"Through the window."

"Who?"

"Dedushka."

"Are you sure?"

"It might have been Dedushka."

"Are you making this up, or what?"

"Yule, I saw someone. Holy shit, are we ever gonna get it now."

But we didn't *get it*, either when we arrived back at the house that afternoon, or at dinner. Afterwards, excited by each other's bodies and the belief that somehow we'd escaped adult censure and punishment, we chased each other around the house. It was a contest of sorts, surreptitious and silent, like kids trying to act up in a classroom without getting caught by the teacher. We poked and elbowed each other, but only mimed our mock agony, opening our mouths wide in voiceless screams. By the time we reached the upstairs hallway we could no longer contain our pent-up energy. I pulled him down on the carpet, where we wrestled and tickled each other into squealing laughter, pretending for the sake of the adults and for our own protection that we were only playing a children's game. But it attracted Dedushka's attention.

When he appeared on the stairway, I thought he was going to scold us and tell us we were disrupting his quiet evening. We stood up and brushed ourselves off. As Nick tucked his shirt back into his jeans, he hung his head like a caricature of a naughty child. I looked at Dedushka to see if he was fooled, and instead witnessed a strange metamorphosis. His eyes narrowed, his upper lip curled, his mouth opened and he roared. In a fraction of a second he turned into a wild creature: neither bear, nor wolf, nor wildcat; rather, a crazed human cousin to all three.

I glanced back at Nick. An expression of bewildered fear had come over his face, and he stared at me as if to say, *Is Dedushka for real?*

Suddenly Dedushka charged at us. Nick sidestepped him and ran down the stairs. I would have run down too, except that Dedushka got there before I could and blocked the way.

I was trapped. All the doors led to bedrooms or the bathroom. Dedushka stalked me slowly, growling and hissing to keep up the appearances of a game. I stood frozen, afraid to look into his face, watching only his feet as they slowly approached me. Kate's room was just behind me. I thought, *If I can get in and shut the door....*

I bolted into Kate's room and slammed the door as hard as I could. There was a yowl of pain. I leaned with all my weight against the door, but I wasn't strong enough. Dedushka forced it open, and just as I was about to dash behind Kate's bed he grabbed me around the waist.

He whispered into my ear, *Krolishka*, and spoke other words I didn't understand. Then he began to tickle me. Nothing like the tickling that had gone on only a few minutes earlier between me and Nick. There was no joy in it. Dedushka's fingers were like insects crawling over my ribs. I tried to pull free and, for a moment, the insects stopped. Then, just as I was about to escape, I felt myself being dragged roughly back. The insects started crawling again and I was choking with desperate laughter.

A moment later I heard fierce high-pitched barking that deepened to a growl. Dedushka let go of me and shouted, "*K chortu.*" I turned around and saw Callack, her jaws clamped on Dedushka's pant-leg, baring her teeth and snarling as she tried to pull him away from me. Dedushka slapped her hard, five or six times. Finally, with a yelp, she let go and, barking loudly, backed away from him. Nick was standing in the doorway.

"What's going on?" he demanded, as Uncle Michael might have if he'd been the one to catch Nick and me making love in the cabin. He patted Callack's head until she stopped her mad barking and only growled, slowly giving up her rage.

"What business is it of yours?" Dedushka replied, but he sidled towards the door, keeping his distance from Callack. Nick blocked his way for a moment before he let him pass.

"*Durak,*" Dedushka called out as he went down the stairs. "Fool."

January 27, 1942

Towards dusk today I took two pails down to the Neva on Nikolenka's sled to get water. The lines are shorter then, although I do not like the trip back home in the dark. I left the sled at the top of the bank and carried the pails to the river down steps that are treacherous from all the water that has been spilled on them as people haul their pails back up the bank. On the way down I slipped and banged my knee. The shock made me so dizzy that I had to sit down and rest; but I soon got up again because, as I sat there, I counted five new corpses around the water-hole, and I did not want to be the sixth. I have begun to keep a tally of the corpses I pass along Nevsky Prospekt and along all the streets I routinely travel. I notice when a new corpse arrives and when the old ones are taken away. Whenever I smell turpentine I know it is a truck bound for the cemetery and I think, Good, they are cleaning up the streets. *It is important for me to know that we still have some control over death.*

As I filled my pails I worried that someone might steal Nikolenka's sled from the top of the bank, so I returned quickly to the steps. I left one pail at the bottom in order to have a free hand to steady myself, and as I half climbed, half scrambled up the steps I was in a panic that both the sled and the pail I had left behind would be stolen. But of course they were not.

When at last I had carried both pails up to the sled, I was thirsty, so I bent over one of them and lapped up water as a dog might, or a cat. Now that we have killed all our pets we are becoming more like them. By eating their flesh we have inherited their behaviour.

43

The water tasted sweetish and faintly mouldy. I have grown used to that too. It is the taste of decomposing corpses. But it does not matter. I am thirsty and so I drink. Even if I boiled the water the taste would still be there. Those of us who survive the winter will probably die in the spring from cholera. Meanwhile the low temperatures keep away disease, and so, for the time being, we only freeze to death.

Before I left the river I turned back and gazed at it for a moment to delay the forty-minute walk back to our apartment. The ice had turned lilac-coloured in the dusky light. It was amoral, this lilac light, neither malign nor beneficent. It touched ice, corpses and the stumbling, gaunt-faced water-bearers with the same intensity. Suddenly I was close to tears and I was surprised to notice that the tears had nothing to do with joy or with sorrow, it had to do with relief, because the lilac light did not choose between life and death, but illuminated both.

I began pulling the sled towards Nevsky Prospekt. I was in a tender mood, and I felt that the frozen buildings regarded me tenderly. Even the sled's rope felt tender against my palm, when usually it demanded effort. I pulled, I made an effort, but I knew I might also choose not to. I might choose to lean against a lamppost, close my eyes and sink slowly to the ice as so many others have done.

Out of habit I began to count the lampposts as I passed. Out of habit I took note of the corpses: male, female, unknown. There was no more colour in the dusk. Suddenly I felt a hand on my shoulder. A voice said, "Vera Mikhailovna." I turned around to see a healthy face, round-cheeked, full-lipped and smiling.

"Lev Antonich," I answered. I was shocked by his looks. He must have noticed, because he glanced away and then, turning back to me, smiling slightly, he said, "I have only just returned to Leningrad. Over the ice road."

"Lake Ladoga?"

"Yes. Please, Vera Mikhailovna, let me pull your sled for you."

I surrendered the rope to him. He began to talk about the time we had last been together, on the road to Lisii Nos, the day the Germans invaded. He sang, "Far away...far away...," *because we had sung it then.*

"Sing with me, Vera Mikhailovna," he said. I tried, but the frozen air was too much for my lungs, my voice was too weak and the words wouldn't come. His voice was rich and full even though he sang with his scarf over his mouth to protect his lungs. My tender mood began to deepen.

He asked me about Andrusha, and I explained that he was fighting somewhere in Belorussia. He nodded. I was about to ask him what he had been doing when he turned to me, took hold of both my shoulders and said to me in a low-pitched, intense voice, "Vera Mikhailovna, I know a man who has meat patties, real horse meat. If you come with me, I can get you four or five for fifty rubles. Only you must come with me now."

During the first moments I listened to his words with indifference; the tender mood slipped away from me and I thought of Tanyusha, Xyusha and Nikolenka for the first time in many minutes. If I got four meat patties we could each eat a whole one. If I got five, we would divide the extra one among us, or I could make a stew with it. My mouth began to water. How long had it been, I wondered, since we had eaten meat? And Lev Antonich had said it was real horse meat — no cat meat, dog meat, rat meat, cellulose or sawdust. And fifty rubles was cheap. On the black market meat patties sometimes sell for 150 or 200 rubles.

"Lev Antonich," I said, "I do not have fifty rubles, not with me. But if tomorrow...."

"Tomorrow?" he said. "No, Vera Mikhailovna." He squeezed my shoulders and added fiercely, "I will lend you the fifty rubles. Yes? Only you must come with me now."

I felt tired, and no longer sure of myself or Lev Antonich. I sighed. He took it as a sign that I agreed. He turned off Nevsky Prospekt and began leading me down a small back street where I had not walked since before the war.

He stopped for a moment, took out a cigarette, lit it and passed it to me. I drew the smoke down into my lungs, where it burned and delighted me both. I passed the cigarette back to Lev Antonich, who puffed on it quickly and then, exhaling, turned to me and said, "Vera Mikhailovna, we must hurry."

Even though he was pulling the sled, I could hardly keep up with him. It was almost dark and the burning end of the cigarette, swirling and jumping from the movement of his hand as he walked, became my beacon. We passed a building that the German shells had turned to rubble. When I was a child, a friend of mine lived there. I wondered if she was still in Leningrad, alive or dead, or perhaps in some safe place beyond the Urals. She had always said she would become a mining engineer.

"Vera Mikhailovna, please," Lev Antonich said sternly.

Without realizing it, I had stopped in front of the shelled building. I hurried to catch up with him. As he stood waiting for me I saw the glowing cigarette drop from his hand to the ice. When I reached the spot where it had fallen it was still burning and I found myself hesitating, wanting to stay there until the glow went out.

"We must hurry, Vera Mikhailovna," he said again. I did not like the insistence in his voice. There was no daylight left and the darkness made me uneasy because for weeks, in the lines for bread rations and for water, there had been rumours about crimes committed at night: people murdered for their ration cards, or their fur coats or their felt boots; men and women lured by the promise of bread or meat to their deaths.

"Lev Antonich," I said, "you have not told me what you have been doing since the beginning of the war."

"I have already explained that I have only just come back to Leningrad," he said in an irritated voice. "I was with the army near Slutsk."

But if he had been near Slutsk, why did he come back over Lake Ladoga? Anyway, I had seen the soldiers from the front and they were almost as gaunt as we Leningraders.

He led me into another street. I could see the dome of St. Isaac's and knew that we were heading towards the Haymarket, where jewels are exchanged for a small jar of soil and carbonized sugar salvaged from the ruins of the Badayev warehouses, and where, it is said, some traders deal in human flesh.

"Lev Antonich," I said, "I have changed my mind. My children are waiting for me at home. They will be frightened all alone in the dark. I must return to them."

His hand clutched my shoulder. "Are you mad?" he said. "Horse meat for fifty rubles. You will never have another chance like this." His face was very close to mine, so that when he spoke his breath warmed my cheeks, but I was now convinced I could not trust his healthy face.

"Thank you, Lev Antonich," I said. "I am going home."

I pulled away from him and began to run. He started after me, but the sled was in the way and he tripped over it and fell down hard. He must have been stunned, because there were several moments when I heard only the sound of my own running feet, before he called after me, "Go to the Devil." But I knew Lev Antonich was himself the Devil, and I kept on running.

When I got home, Tanyusha made me tea from some pine needles for which I had traded four of my silver-wire glass holders. Now I have lost the sled and two pails. Fortunately our neighbour gave us a tin of water, but I do not know what I shall do tomorrow.

It is said that people who experience physical and psychological trauma may, months or even years afterwards, put their lives at risk again and again, in the hope that this time, instead of the danger vanquishing them, they will vanquish the danger. This is what happened to my father, who — years after the Siege of Leningrad, in a new country, in his mid-twenties, at an age when many young men have given up the most reckless acts of their youth — began to race down highways and lure police cruisers into high-speed chases. When his licence was suspended, he took to the air. Though he did not know how to fly himself, he befriended an inexperienced pilot. On their third flight the aircraft stalled and then plummeted to the earth. The pilot was killed; my father broke his back. My aunt once hinted that it was my father and not the pilot who was at the controls.

The morning after Dedushka trapped me in Kate's bedroom, I too began to take risks. Partly I didn't want to be intimidated by Dedushka, partly I was curious. And there was another reason. It had to do with a personal history that went back beyond my own short life to the unassimilable wartime traumas my father's family had survived. Through the diary I sensed those traumas rising up to me out of the past, and, because I was only fourteen, I confronted them out of ignorance, in ways that didn't seem foolhardy at the time but in the long run proved dangerous, mainly to myself.

When I saw Dedushka come out of his shed into the daylight with a bag slung over his shoulder, my first instinct was to veer off onto the path down to the stable and avoid him altogether. I sensed the need to be as wary of him as Babushka had been of Lev Antonich; on the other hand I felt an even greater need to challenge him and watch him through the transforming lens the diary had given me.

So I began to follow him. As he trudged up the driveway towards the road and the woods beyond, I kept close to the trees so that I could hide if I needed to. The snow had melted from the drive, and when we got to the woods it lay over the ground in eroding islands. I stepped carefully between them so I wouldn't make any footprints as I walked. When Dedushka looked back to where I was hiding behind a young fir tree, though I'm sure he didn't see me, I realized he knew someone was stalking him, and I began to revel in the sense of power a hunter wields over the hunted.

That day it felt as if the woods were on my side, dripping melted snow, covering the sounds of my movements with the noise of running water. Birds rustled through the undergrowth and searched for seeds on the newly exposed ground, fluttering and snapping twigs as they went.

Dedushka turned around more and more often. I grew agile with stealth. I felt I walked a line of perfect balance, ready to dart to the left of the trail or to the right, hang back or pursue, do whatever I must to keep out of Dedushka's sight but at the same time keep him uneasy.

Each time he turned around I saw the fear grow on his face, and I guessed he was remembering his days in the forest, behind enemy lines, when he'd stalked the Germans and was sometimes stalked by them.

At last he stopped, took his bag off his shoulder and crouched down. His arms became busy. From the back he looked like a wild creature scrabbling in the soil, foraging on this day of rapid thaw like the other woodland creatures. Soon he lifted up a raccoon carcass and put it in his bag. As his breath fogged the air around him, he took a jar out and opened it. A few moments later I smelled something rotting that made me retreat a few steps to a cedar tree whose fragrance I breathed to protect myself from the taint. Through the needles I watched Dedushka's arms making scrabbling movements again. He got up, glanced back down the trail past the spot where I was hidden and continued on to the next trap.

I followed him as he harvested his prey from three more traps and set them again. By the time he was working on the third trap, I had got close enough to see that his hands were shaking. Every minute or so he glanced back over his shoulder. He stuffed a weasel into his bag and took out the jar of tainted meat, but as he opened it there was a cracking sound in the woods about twenty feet away. Dedushka dropped the jar, stood up and lurched off into the trees in the opposite direction as a branch split away from the trunk of an alder and crashed down through the undergrowth to the ground.

I've got him, I thought, but my stomach fluttered. Though I'd paid him back, I felt disappointed that a fourteen-year-old could cow a man so easily. I thought he and all the grownups, Papa and my mother included, should be much braver than I was. If they weren't, how could I depend on them?

I crept over to the trap. It was smaller than the one with the shark-like teeth that he'd shown me in his shed. As I examined it I held my breath, because the jar of tainted meat had spilled over the ground. There was dried blood along the jaws. Immediately I thought of the rabbit's carcass under the cabin floor and I began to gag. Other animals would inevitably suffer the same agony. I wanted to make it stop. A chain ran from the jaws to a metal stake that had been driven into the soil to hold the trap firm. I tugged at the stake, but it wouldn't come out. I tried again and, as I pulled, it occurred to me that if I stole the trap, not only would I save animal lives, but I could also use it against Dedushka for my own protection.

Finally, when I'd worked the stake free, I lifted the trap in one hand and the chain in the other. I made my way back down through the woods, eyes searching the ground to avoid snow islands and hollows or roots that I might trip over. My ears were alert for any snapping or rustling that might signal Dedushka's return. I got back to the road, found the trail to the cabin and walked up to it through the familiar trees, beneath which the snow creatures had almost entirely melted away.

About fifteen feet from the cabin door, where the trail ended in a clearing, I scraped a hollow in the soil, set the trap down into it and, with a stone, drove the metal stake into the dirt. Then I brushed some of the loose soil over the chain with a branch and spread the rest evenly over the ground. When I'd reset the trap, I covered it with twigs, moss and leaves. Then I tested the camouflage from a few feet away. The trap was well hidden and I knew that without bait it was unlikely to attract any of the woodland raccoons or foxes or weasels. As I stood up and began walking towards the cabin I thought, *See what will happen if he ever tries to spy on Nicholas and me again; just let him try.* But remembering the smell of the tainted, rotting meat, I heard a smaller, more timid part of myself say, *Now I am the bait.*

February 5, 1942
 Ever since the day I lost Nikolenka's sled, I have been borrowing my neighbour's. At first Nadezhda Nikolayevna was very kind. She offered me the sled before I had to ask. But the

last few days she has lent it only grudgingly. I have had to bribe her with food: that jelly I made from the wallpaper paste; bread from the Haymarket. But I cannot afford to give her these things when my own children are starving. Also I know that the more I use the sled, the more she will expect in return. This morning I decided that I must find a sled of my own.

The city is dying. There are corpses everywhere, and few of us have the strength to bury them. There are no human smells left in the city: no cooking odours, not even the smells of indus-try, only the raw smell of snow. The streets are silent except for the squeak of sled runners. How I long for the noise of streetcars rushing along their tracks outside our window. At the corner one of them stands frozen, its door stuck open ever since the electricity was cut off. For over a month it has been carrying two passengers, a man and a woman, who must have stopped to rest but never got up again. This morning as I went past I saw that a third passenger had joined them.

I had gone out to stand in line for our bread rations. Now that some supplies are coming in over the Lake Ladoga ice road there are rumours that the rations are going up again to five hundred grams for workers and four hundred grams for us. But I am afraid it is too late. The other day Danya told me she heard that over a hundred thousand of us died in January. She told me in a whisper, because she cannot speak any louder. Her lips were a hideous blue, and cracked. I do not think she will survive.

On my way back with the bread I walked along the Fontanka Canal. Ahead of me a woman was pulling a sled. A corpse wrapped up in an old red and blue oriental carpet was lashed onto it. The top of the head was exposed, and the hair was short and light brown, the colour of Andrusha's. I listened to the squeaking of the runners enviously.

As we approached the Summer Garden the woman slipped on the ice and fell. I waited for her to get up, and the longer I waited, the more excited I became. I felt giddy, but my mind was clear. The wrought-iron fence of the Garden stood out sharply against the snow. The woman did not get up. I went over to her and knelt beside her. Her mouth opened and closed like the beak of a young bird who waits for its parents to bring it

51

food. When it was closed she began chewing, but she did not swallow, and when her mouth opened again I saw that there was no food inside. I put my arms around her and rocked her. For some reason the song about the birch tree in the meadow came into my head. I sang it to her quietly. "Ai, Ai," she whimpered. Her mouth stopped working and I knew she was dead.

I pulled her over to the wrought-iron fence and laid her beside it. There were other corpses along the fence, some sitting, others lying. I felt I could not leave the man's corpse in the same place. None of the other corpses was wrapped. People had simply stopped there, or had fallen like the woman and died.

I knew she had been taking her husband's body somewhere and I felt obligated, because I intended to keep her sled, to find a more appropriate spot to dump it. I continued along the Fontanka, and as I neared the Neva I found a pile of four or five corpses, all of them wrapped, on a street corner. I unlashed the body from the sled and dragged it over to the pile, but I kept the rope. It may prove useful, though I dare not think for what.

When I got home, Nikolenka, who can hardly walk from the chair to the stove, examined his new sled and told me, "I am glad you lost the old one. This is much better." What frightens me now, and what I fear will haunt me in the future, is the excitement I felt when I saw that the poor woman was going to die. I know I would not have gone over to comfort her if I had not wanted her sled. I do not think I will ever be allowed to forget how her mouth opened and closed and chewed and opened again.

FOUR

Aunt Xenia stood in the driveway wearing nothing over her dress. Her arms were folded across her chest and she rubbed them with her hands to keep warm.

"I'm so happy for you," she said to Bette, who had just put her suitcase into the trunk of Papa's car. With her scarf wound around her neck and her coat buttoned to the top, Bette appeared to be standing on the other side of a climate line that separated a frigid zone from a temperate one. The two women reached across and hugged each other.

I felt warm breath on my ear and, knowing who it was, stretched out my hand without looking and touched the rough wool of Nick's jacket. He pulled me over behind a tree to a half-private place and kissed me on the cheek, then, drawing me further into privacy, on the lips.

"Don't, they'll see," I whispered.

"So what?" he said.

And I realized that, instead of trying to conceal our relationship, he was exhibiting it, and that the coy pretence of stealing a kiss was meant to provoke some remark from our parents that would strengthen his claim on me. But the only reaction he got was from Kate, who pushed her way between us saying, "Me too, me too," to make her own claim: that we turn our kisses back into a childhood game she could share.

My father began to transfer from his wheelchair into the car, with a movement that was both agile because of his strong arms, and furtive — as though, if he did it fast enough, no one would notice. But of course everyone did, and Kate was the most straightforward about it, staring while Papa lifted his atrophied legs one at a time into the front seat.

As soon as Uncle Michael took away Papa's chair to put it in the trunk, Dedushka pushed in beside Papa, before he could close the door, and slipped him an envelope — like Nick, exhibiting his gesture by pretending to hide it, and choosing a moment when Papa was most vulnerable. The envelope, I knew, contained money, which Papa accepted because he needed it. Dedushka gave him some of his pension money at least once a year, often twice, to try to bribe him to give up theatre and become an invalid. As an invalid, he believed, Papa would be safe, while directing, he claimed, only exhausted him and put his health in greater jeopardy. Partly he was right: directing did exhaust him, but it gave him a purpose too, and the year Papa had taken off after his resignation had convinced everyone except Dedushka that he was better off working.

When I was getting into the car Dedushka came up to me and, whispering, *Xoroshenka*, pretty, stroked my hair, then gave it a tug that wasn't quite playful, before he released me into the back seat. As we drove off a few drops of rain fell on the window, and I looked back through the spattered glass to see Nick pegging stones at a stump halfway up the drive, while Callack chased after them, barking in joyful high-pitched yips. In the distance — faintly, because all the windows were rolled up — I heard the donkeys braying.

Along Highway 1 into Vancouver almost all the snow had melted, except for the odd pile speckled with gravel and dirt where the plough had heaped the snow into ridges. As the rain came and went, the intermittent squeak of the wipers on the windshield reminded me of Babushka and the noise of sled runners on snow. Her diary was in my suitcase, packed carefully between two sweaters like a precious and fragile artefact. Bette was singing "Can't Buy Me Love" in her strong stage-trained voice. When she got to the refrain, my father sang it with her.

I wondered where he could have learned the song, then realized that, of course, Bette must have taught it to him. I pictured them at home lying in bed together, in my father's room with its heavy curtains that closed out all light, singing quietly, their heads touching, so they wouldn't wake me where I slept upstairs in my slant-roofed room with moonlight falling across my bed.

The small pang of jealousy I felt didn't prevent me from being excited about my father's renewed vitality, which meant he was making the transition, as he so often had, from invalid to artist. I was also frightened, knowing how much directing a full-length play would deplete his slight energy. The play was Lorca's *Blood Wedding*. When Bradley had proposed it to him the previous summer, Papa had been less than enthusiastic. The production of *Medea* he'd directed in the spring had received mixed reviews, and then an attack of nephritis had put him in hospital for most of May, so he was unsure of both his creative powers and his health. But Bradley was persistent. He phoned Papa every few days, and their first perfunctory conversations slowly evolved into long brainstorming sessions that energized my father and eventually convinced him to return to Fourth Wall.

It had been a busy fall. He and Bradley solicited donations and applied for grants. Meantime Papa got down to the work of directing: researching the script, making innumerable notes in his director's book, meeting with the technical director, the lighting designer and the costumer, Pip Salisbury, with whom he'd been working almost as long as with Bradley. He also began to spend more and more time with Bette, who in October suddenly became his lover after almost a year of being no more than what I thought of as an occasional friend.

The closer we got to Vancouver, the heavier the traffic became. I tried to imagine myself back in the quiet of

Lisii Nos, where each sound was discrete: the thwack of an axe splitting wood, the plop of snow falling from tree branches to the ground, the Slavic melodies Aunt Xenia played on the piano, the suck, like a wet kiss, of our sweating skin the day Nick and I made love in the cabin. But the low-grade hum of tires on pavement made me think about my school, which stood on Cambie Street, shielded from the traffic noise by only a high fence and a row of tall chestnut trees. It was a girls' school, and I lived on its fringes, liked, but not fully accepted though I wore the same uniform as everyone else. The fact that my parents were divorced, that I lived with my father, a stage director, a paraplegic in poor health who earned far less money than my mother, made me somewhat exotic to the other girls, but it also discouraged most of them from becoming close friends. And until Ursula arrived I had been known as a loner.

Ursula von der Linde made an entrance into our school. Instead of arriving on the first day of the school year like all the other new girls, she arrived in mid-November, from Germany, where her parents had been giving a series of concerts while her father was on sabbatical from the University of British Columbia. She was tall, blonde and daring. The first words she said to me were my full name: "Julia Nikolaevna Kabalevsky. Julia Daughter-of-Nicholas Kabalevsky."

We were standing in line, waiting to go up to our classroom after lunch. The second bell had already gone, which meant we weren't allowed to talk. We'd arrived at the end of the line at exactly the same moment, and I had stepped back to make room for her, but she made a gesture with her hand, both gallant and imperious, meaning that she wanted me to go first.

"Julia Daughter-of-Nicholas," she whispered, "are you related to Dmitri?"

"Silence," commanded the head prefect.

Dmitri. I sensed that her question was a two-part test: Did I know who Dmitri was? And would I dare risk a detention to answer her? The first part was easy. Since her parents were musicians I knew she must mean the composer Dmitri Kabalevsky. But the second part? Usually I didn't break rules, but I didn't want her to think I was a coward either.

"No," I said. But because I was facing forward and she was behind me, she apparently didn't hear me.

"Are you related to Dmitri?" she asked again.

I heard the footsteps of a prefect coming towards me, and in a panic said, "No," quite loudly, so that the girl in front of me turned around, a look of confusion on her face. The prefect pounced on her bewilderment.

"Jane," she asked, "were you talking?"

Jane hesitated and the prefect said, "I'm giving you a detention. Report to Room 7 on Friday afternoon. Three-thirty sharp."

As the prefect turned away Jane said too late, and in a voice that was too quiet, "But it wasn't me."

A few days later, after Ursula and I had become best friends, I told her how guilty I felt about Jane getting the detention that was meant for us. I even suggested we go to the prefect and confess.

"Julia Daughter-of-Nicholas," Ursula said, "don't be a ninny. Jane knew it was us, and she should have told the prefect that. It was her own silly fault."

The traffic on Broadway was heavy and almost a third of the trip was taken up driving west from the highway to Kitsilano. Bette had moved across the front seat, closer to my father. Several times she kissed the soft flesh of his neck showing above his jacket collar, but he could respond only with a slight tip of his head, because he was busy with the hand controls. As I watched them I tried to conjure up my old resentment against Bette, but over Christmas she'd become less of a threat, either because the rest of the family accepted her so well, or because I now had Nick and felt more her equal. In the warmth from the car heater I began to doze, content as I had not been for a long time, feeling it wouldn't be so bad even if Bette came to live with us.

Like a dog rousing itself at the end of a journey, I woke up only when we left the mind-dulling noise of Broadway, jogged onto Tenth Avenue and turned up our street, where pods from the catalpa trees still lay rotting on the grass boulevards. As we pulled up to the curb, Bette said to Papa in a low voice that was only a little less dramatic than a stage whisper, "Don't you think we should tell her?"

"What?" I asked, trying to ignore the keen blade of alarm that pressed against my throat.

My father turned the engine off, put his arm on the seatback to keep his balance and pulled himself round so he could see me.

"Bette is pregnant," he said and looked away.

I reached for the door handle.

"Be happy for us, my sunshine," he pleaded as I got out.

Without another word we unpacked the car, Papa got into his chair and we went inside the house.

"Of course, Bette will be coming to live with us."

"Of course," I said.

We'd thrown our bags on the chest in the hallway and, though I'd immediately started up the stairs to my room, Papa persuaded me back down to have a glass of tea with them in the kitchen. I sat silently, and to Bette and Papa I must have appeared sullen, but it was fear as much as anger that made me mute. I kept thinking to myself how foolish I had been that night at Lisii Nos, when Papa was so sick and Bette ran white-faced into the bathroom. I should have understood then that she was pregnant. I thought of Babushka's diary entry about the burning of the Badayev warehouses, in which her neighbour warned her to be vigilant because there were traitors in Leningrad. I had not been vigilant, I'd been too absorbed in my own adventures to see what must have been obvious to everyone else. Compared to Bette's pregnancy, making love to Nick seemed small and inconsequential, a mere distraction.

Although I'd already begun to give up the idea of having my father exclusively to myself, I thought I could never give up being his only child. Somehow I believed, as I think Papa did, that I was a miracle: a child conceived against the odds. The doctors had told him that although his paralysis had not left him impotent, it had made him sterile. My mother hadn't wanted a child, and this, I imagined, was one of the reasons she'd agreed to marry him. But my father did want me, and I had survived against even greater odds than my father's supposed sterility because sometimes miracles were allowed to happen. This was the basis of whatever faith I had in the world. But if Papa could have a second child, then it meant I wasn't a miracle after all. I was merely an accident.

"My sunshine," Papa said, "tell us what you think. You must say something."

I knew my eyes had gone dead with a misery that had as much petulance in it as pain, childish even to my fourteen-year-old sensibilities. Nevertheless I wanted them both to notice, so I looked up at Bette, then shifted my gaze slowly to Papa, and said in a withholding, stingy voice, "Congratulations."

The phone rang, and while Papa answered it Bette said to me, "How about showing me the upstairs? Your dad thought I might have the front room," she added carefully.

"You mean my mother's room," I said. "This is my mother's house, you know. She bought it, she paid for it."

Without answering me Bette started climbing the stairs. In the years since my mother had left, the whole of the upstairs had become my territory, and I didn't want to share it, especially with Bette. I'd never quite given up the hope that one day my mother would return, and if Bette took over her room it meant for certain she never would. Bette was an invader and, like the Germans who had laid siege to Leningrad, she needed to be defeated and driven out. She and the baby, my enemies. Most

59

especially the baby.

Bette opened the door to my mother's room and stood for a moment on the threshold. "It's lovely," she said.

What made Mama's room so different I never understood. All the other rooms were as undistinguished as the house itself, but hers, not quite as large as the living-room though considerably larger than the other two bedrooms, was elegant. It was painted the palest, coolest green. There was a small single bed and a chest of drawers made of rosewood on one side, while a row of tall mirrors and a barre ran all down the other. When she lived with us, my mother had spent most of her time in that room, and just to be near her I sat for hours on the little bed, watching her practise at the barre until I knew all the exercises by heart: pliés, extensions, stretches, kicks. Later I'd go into her room by myself so I could do the same exercises and pretend I was a dancer. But I never asked to take classes, because my mother had always made it clear that I didn't have the right sort of body for ballet.

As Bette explored the room I stood at the window looking out at a rowan tree, now bare of leaves, with only a few shrivelled berries still attached to the branches. In the spring the tree was a garden of delicate white flowers. At night, if the lamps were on and the curtains not yet drawn, the rays reached out into the darkness, lit up that miniature treetop garden and brought it inside, so that the pale flowers became part of the decor of Mama's room. Often I went into her room on spring evenings and switched on the lamps just to see the effect. If Bette stayed, that pleasure would be hers alone.

I turned around and found her near the barre, examining herself in the tall mirrors. She was standing sideways. Her fingertips lightly touched her abdomen, which protruded a little. She pressed her stomach with her fingertips and tightened her muscles so that the slight bulge disappeared. Then she stroked her belly with the palm of her hand, looked up, noticed me watching her and smiled only a little self-consciously.

"I'm going to enjoy living here," she said.

The next day it snowed again, and that evening I went for a walk with Ursula. She lived only six streets away, but her house was large and old enough to be venerable. Her parents had renovated it with their practical musicians' hands. They'd put in a sundeck, new kitchen cabinets and appliances, an extra bathroom with a sunken tub, a Heatilator fireplace and a music room that was panelled with special acoustic tile. The only renovations that had ever been done to our house were a ramp to the front door and a widening of the downstairs bathroom to accommodate Papa's wheelchair.

As I crunched my way through the newly fallen snow I began to look forward to the coffee Mrs. von der Linde always offered me, and wondered if tonight she would feed me streusel or kuchen. But when I turned onto the street where the von der Lindes' house stood, Ursula was on the steps, leaning against one of the columns that held up the porch roof. As soon as she saw me, she ran down to the sidewalk, looking taller than usual until I discovered that she was wearing a new pair of boots with platform soles, then very stylish. As we hurried towards each other it occurred to me that during the war her parents and my father's family would have been enemies. And I marvelled that a generation later she and I could be best friends.

"Willi got expelled for the *third* time," she said. "Mutti got a phone call on the last day of term, from the head of his new school, and he said he couldn't do anything with Willi so he was sending him home for good. This time he got caught smoking *and* drinking." Ursula laughed — a nervous sound, high like a piccolo, and different from her usual laugh, which was deeper and full of mockery.

"Papa's been in a state ever since," she continued. "And Mutti creeps around the house: '*Ja, Wilhelm. Nein,*

Wilhelm. Can I lick your boots for you, my dear one, my treasure.' It's disgusting." Ursula dismissed her mother with a wave of her hand. *"And* he's started smoking dope. Stinks the whole house up, but they don't say a word. I told him he could do what he liked, as long as he didn't stink up *my* room."

I had met Willi only once, just after he got expelled the second time. It was at the bus depot, when Ursula and I had spent a weekend at Lisii Nos and her mother came to pick us up. With her was a tall boy, strong-boned, thin-lipped, as dark as Ursula was blonde.

"That's my half-brother, Willi," Ursula whispered to me before we were close enough for Mrs. von der Linde to introduce us.

He took a cigarette out of his pocket.

"Ach, Wilhelm, nein," Mrs. von der Linde said, but he placed the cigarette between his lips and lit it with a silver lighter.

"Where did you get that?" his mother asked. He didn't answer her.

Ursula went up to Willi and kissed him on his cheek. He dangled his arm over her shoulder. Mrs. von der Linde curled her lips in a smile that looked forced.

By the time we got to the car, Ursula and Willi were already sitting together in the back seat. I pushed my bag into the front and got in beside Mrs. von der Linde. She started the car, but when she tried to pull out of the parking place the car bucked and the engine died. Willi mumbled something. Ursula gave a loud sigh and said, "Oh, Mutti."

I remember on the trip home I felt a discomfort in the back of my neck that was neither quite pain nor a burning sensation. I suddenly felt sure it was because Willi was staring at me from the back seat. I wanted to turn around to see, but didn't dare, so I kept looking straight through the windshield until the discomfort in my neck turned to sickness. Years later it occurs to me that this is what Dedushka must have felt in the woods, when I was pursuing him and he kept turning around to see if any-one was there. It's just possible it was that first meeting with Willi that taught me the only lesson I've ever learned about the tactics of fear.

I heard Willi's lighter flick again and then snap shut. Smoke tickled at my nostrils while Mrs. von der Linde coughed.

When they dropped me off at home I pulled my bag out of the car as quickly as I could and said, "Thank you, Mrs. von der Linde. 'Bye, Ursula." I glanced at Willi. His cigarette was dangling from the corner of his mouth and he was squinting at me. "'Bye," I said, and slammed the door.

The temperature was below freezing but the air was still, so Ursula and I walked cosily muffled in scarves and gloves and the lined boots we wore so rarely during a Vancouver winter. Few people had been out walking, and we were the first to make footprints along the sidewalks. The snow complained with pleasant squeaks and crunch-ing noises as we stomped through it.

"I got my very first period," Ursula declared, "and a scholarship to go to music school in Vienna for the whole of August." She spoke with pride, as if menstruating for the first time were as much an accomplishment as getting the scholarship.

"And I suppose you think that makes you a wo-man," I said. It was what she'd said to me when, a few months earlier, I'd told her about having my first period. I tried for the same tone of mockery she had used, but she simply answered with utter seriousness, "Of course."

We walked for another block before she asked "So what happened out there in the country? Did you have a good time?"

"I read my grandmother's diary about the Siege of Leningrad," I answered.

"How horrible," Ursula said.

"I set a trap to catch my grandfather."

63

"Weird," Ursula said.

"I made love to my cousin Nick."

There was a moment of silence. Ursula's pace slowed.

"What?" she asked. "Really made love?"

"We *fucked*," I explained.

Ursula looked down at the snow. She didn't know what to say and it made me feel powerful suddenly, so I went on.

"We fucked twice. Once in the attic and once in the cabin. We'd have done it more if Nick didn't have to work."

She walked a few steps, then said offhandedly, "So what was it like?"

"Fucking wonderful," I answered.

Ursula was silent again. At last she turned to face me.

"I don't believe you," she said.

"It's true," I replied very quietly. "Except the first time it hurt and it was over too quickly, but the second time it was okay."

She considered this for a moment and then said, "You can't marry your own cousin, you know, because you'll have moron children."

"I never said I wanted to marry him," I answered, but her words deflated me a little.

We walked a few more blocks, then turned down my street. I looked over at the house. Except for the porch light the downstairs was in darkness, but upstairs there was a light on in Mama's room.

"Bette is coming to live with us," I told Ursula. "And she's going to have a baby."

"Is it your father's?" Ursula asked. "Willi told me that cripples can't have children." Then she asked, with just enough mirth in her voice that I couldn't take offence, "And where the hell did you come from?" In fact I felt flattered, knowing that she and Willi had found me interesting enough to discuss.

"Bette's an invader," I said. "She's the enemy and I want her out of my mother's room."

"Your mother's not coming back, you know."

"I know," I said, though even as I spoke I was still hoping. "But I want to get rid of Bette," I repeated, "and that *thing* growing in her belly." Both Ursula and I understood that I was enlisting her help: the daughter of my old enemy to drive out the new enemy.

"Actually, I think Bette's quite nice," Ursula said. "But I sure understand why you don't want a baby around. God, they're so smelly and noisy. But you've come to the right person. I know how to get rid of babies."

I looked at her, expecting irony, but saw she was serious. "How?" I asked.

"The next time you get your period, tell me," she said.

"What do you mean?"

"There's nothing we can do till you get your period."

March 27, 1942

My neighbour, Yelizaveta Andreyevna, who was pregnant, knocked on my door the day before yesterday.

"It is time," she said.

I had promised I would take her to Erisman Hospital on Aptekarsky Island when she went into labour.

Looking at her I found it hard to believe she was pregnant, let alone in labour. Except for her abdomen she was so thin: no breasts; no muscles in her arms or legs. It was easier for me to think of her dying of some wasting disease than giving birth.

She bundled herself up in a coat and shawl. I put her on our sled and gave her an extra shawl of mine to wrap around her legs.

There had been a thaw the previous night. In a few places the pavement lay exposed and the sled's runners bounced over the uneven surface of the ice. Several times Yelizaveta Andreyevna called out, "Stop. It hurts so much." But I wanted to get her to the hospital as soon as possible. Her other children had arrived quickly.

At the corner of Griboyedov Canal and Nevsky I noticed a hand emerging from the ice. As I went past, I saw that a corpse lay under the snow, and that the thaw had begun to expose it. It must have been covered by a heavy snowfall early in the winter, because I had walked past that corner almost every day for months and had thought I was walking only over the ground. I wondered how many other corpses lay buried by winter, awaiting discovery. I am afraid that this spring will bring no hope at all.

Yelizaveta Andreyevna grew quiet as we crossed over the Palace Bridge. By the time we reached the hospital her jaw was set and her eyes appeared to be focused inward, on her pain or her child, I could not tell which. It took all my strength to lift her from the sled. When I brought her into the hospital the hallways were lined with benches on which fifty or more people sat: some huddled around a tin stove; some bandaged; others wounded and still waiting for treatment; but most so weak from hunger that I knew they had been brought there to die. At last I found a woman bathing an old man's frostbitten ear with water.

"Yes, citizen, what is it you want?" she asked without looking up as I approached her.

The old man groaned. She bent down over him, looked into his face and said, "Sh, sh," in a voice that commanded and comforted at the same time.

I told her about Yelizaveta Andreyevna.

She sighed, put down the water and came with me back through the hallway.

"Doctor, doctor," voices called out to her as she passed, but she did not answer.

She examined Yelizaveta Andreyevna, then said to me, "Come this way. Your friend is lucky. We have a free bed."

I knew she meant that someone had just died.

Together we held up Yelizaveta Andreyevna as we walked her past the other patients to a tiny room with two cots in it.

"My name is Dr. Kushovskaya," she told me as we

settled Yelizaveta Andreyevna. She then went over to the other bed, examined the woman who was lying there and pulled the sheet up over her face. I placed myself in front of Yelizaveta Andreyevna so that she could not see what the doctor had just done.

Somehow news spread through the hospital that a child was about to be born, because more and more people came and milled around the doorway, whispering to each other in order not to disturb the mother. The presence of these people comforted me and Yelizaveta Andreyevna too, I think, because once or twice she said to me, "What is that sound? Is it music?" And I answered, "Yes."

The contractions came rapidly. Yelizaveta held onto me whenever she was in pain. Then suddenly, easily, a boy child slid out. His cry was not lusty, but at least he was breathing.

Dr. Kushovskaya said to me, "She has no milk. There is no milk in the hospital to give to the child. We will give him sugar and water for now. But you must find some milk."

As I went out of the room I found myself surrounded by four or five people. One of them, a woman who looked old but was probably only thirty-five, moved close to me and said, "The child is alive, then? We heard a cry."

"Yes," I answered.

The others began asking questions: Was it a boy or a girl? Was it whole? Did it look healthy? Did it weigh enough? Their interest cheered me and I answered the questions, though at the same time I wanted to be free of them so I could think of a plan to find the little boy some milk. When they did not disperse, I told them about my problem.

"Ah, that is bad."

"No milk? Then the little creature will die."

There was a long silence. Then one tired-looking man said in a quiet voice, "I know a driver. Perhaps I can get him to take me into the country. If we can pay him, if we can collect some things valuable enough to trade for milk...."

There was another silence. At last a woman with a shawl wrapped around her head said, "I can get some vitamin C."

"I have a little bottle of cognac: real cognac from

Moldavia," said another.

"Coffee."

"Bread, about 750 grams for your journey."

"This is silver," one of the men said as he took a cigarette case from his pocket.

They all looked at me.

"The only thing of value that I have with me is my wedding ring."

They waited silently. I looked down at my ring. It was loose on my finger because I am so thin. I had been afraid of losing it and yet I had kept wearing it for fear that, by taking it off, I might bring harm to Andrusha. At last I pulled it off. I held it out to the man who knew the driver, and as he took it I said to him, "Safe journey."

Yelizaveta Andreyevna was too weak to care for the child, so Dr. Kushovskaya had a solution of sugar and water brought to me. Alternately I fed it to Yelizaveta Andreyevna with a spoon, and to the boy child with my finger. He sucked hard at the small nourishment, and even when I withdrew my finger his mouth kept making sucking movements. Often I had to take the solution back through the hallway of wounded, dying and dead, to heat it up again on the tin stove. I always took the baby with me, and a few of the patients stretched out their arms to him or clucked their tongues or said, "Poor little thing," as I passed by, but most could not rouse themselves from their own suffering. Even by the light of the stove the child's face looked grey. It was hard for me to keep from drinking the sugar-water myself because I was so hungry; but later, back in Yelizaveta Andreyevna's room, the woman with the shawl around her head, who had donated the vitamin C, came to me with a cup of weak liquid she called tea and a morsel of bread.

"Do you work here?" I asked.

"Yes," she answered, "I am Dr. Roschenko."

She saw my surprise.

"You thought I was an old babushka who sweeps the floors? But I tell you, we have so little medicine and so little food that often I can do nothing better than bring a patient or someone like you a cup of tea."

I held up the child to her and asked, "Will he live?"

She smiled at me. "I am not a seer," she said. "Before the war I would have looked at that child, or his mother, or you, or me, and said, 'Of course they will die. They should already be dead.' But as you see, we are, all of us, alive."

She smiled at me again and shuffled off.

A little after dawn the child died. Dr. Kushovskaya gave me a torn piece of sheet, and I wrapped the corpse up in it and put it on top of a pile of thirty or forty other corpses which lay in a small yard off the side door of the hospital. I went back to sit with Yelizaveta Andreyevna. She did not cry for the child. None of us did. She kept falling into a doze, and when she woke up she always asked me the same question: "Was it a boy or a girl?" Each time I answered her she nodded and closed her eyes again.

I wanted to leave the hospital. I was no longer useful and I was worried about the children, but I could not leave without hearing what had happened to my wedding ring. Throughout the morning I kept thinking about the man whose name I did not even know, who had left with our precious things. Perhaps he was a thief or a black marketeer. Perhaps the driver was not trustworthy. Perhaps he would be murdered for the valuable goods he carried. Perhaps no one would trade with him.

But in the middle of the afternoon he returned, not only with milk but with a sack of potatoes too. There were white frost-bite marks on his cheeks. "I had to travel in the back of an open truck last night," he explained. When he asked how the baby was, none of us wanted to answer. But at last Dr. Roschenko said, "He is dead." The man leaned against the wall and started to retch. We sat him down. Someone brought him tea. When he had drunk it, he looked up and said, "That means we can divide the milk and potatoes among us." He smiled with embarrassment. We all smiled at our sudden good fortune.

We divided the food carefully. The largest share went to the man who had haggled for it. I found out that his first name and patronymic were Fyodor Ilyich, though I did not learn his family name. Yelizaveta Andreyevna and Dr. Kushovskaya both got small shares, though neither had contributed, and the rest of us got medium-sized shares. Mine was a litre of milk for the children, and three potatoes.

69

FIVE

The first weeks of the winter term were the best I'd ever spent at St. Mary's. In spite of the drab navy and maroon of our school uniform, it was as if I were wearing vibrant colours. Never had I felt so rich. Ursula and I were inseparable. Nick was a memory I brought to school with me every day, not to parade in front of my classmates, but to call upon privately during moments of boredom or drudgery. No one except Ursula knew about us, but everyone sensed how much more self-assured I was and, as a result, the change in my status was almost palpable. I had utter faith, too, that with Ursula guiding me I'd be able to get rid of Bette. Not that Ursula had so much as revealed a plan. All I had was her cryptic request to call her the next time I started to bleed. But I was as convinced of her ability to defeat Bette as of her pianistic talent. And though some part of me knew I was deluding myself (I was away from home all day long, so I could conveniently forget that Bette now occupied my mother's room), there were moments when I still believed that, with Bette gone, my mother one day might be persuaded to come back to Papa and me.

And then there was the Siege diary, which became that winter's secret obsession. Its pages contained not just the story of the Russian side of my family, both living and dead, but my own story too, which continued beneath the surface of my North American life, unacknowledged most of the time, but influential. I became aware not so much of a lack of safety as of the superficiality of my daily existence. Beneath the relative prosperity and ease of my childhood ran the deeper history of starvation, cold, homelessness, danger and the presence of enemies. I had sensed this all my life, and my grandmother's diary was full-blown evidence that my instincts were right.

And then came an opportunity to reveal what I'd learned from the diary to the rest of my small world. At school our winter drama project was to rehearse a one-act play and have it ready to perform for the Middle School just before the Easter break. Immediately I knew I wanted to do a play about the Siege of Leningrad, but when I put it to Ursula she said, "God, how tiresome. I've already heard way too much about war from Mutti and Papa: sausages made out of sawdust, bombs falling — I don't know how many times Mutti's told me about how her best friend got her legs blown off on Kurfürstendamm and then died in her arms. She always starts crying at exactly the same place — when her friend looks up at her and says, 'Ach, Trudi, now is the twilight of the gods.' What a production. And she says she's only telling me because she wants me to understand how much better off I am than she was at my age."

It wasn't until a week later, in the von der Lindes' downstairs rec room — when we'd already decided to work on a murder mystery — that I found another opportunity to send my Leningrad passion sidewinding towards her.

"I think our play should be about the murder of a famous pianist," Ursula was saying. "We'll have to figure out who did it and then plot the story backwards to the beginning. That's how professional mystery writers work."

"You could be a famous Russian pianist living in Leningrad," I ventured, not daring to add *during the Siege.*

"But I don't look like a Slav," she said, and I thought I heard contempt in her voice. She laughed, as if to say I wasn't to take her seriously, and the expression on her face softened. I wondered if she was warming to my idea after all, but then I saw that she was looking past me, so I turned around. Willi was standing in the doorway with a cigarette hanging from the corner of his mouth.

He was an intrusion I didn't want. From the very first moment I'd met him I had felt marked by his bold and avid stare. It worried me, too, that Ursula, who made fun of him when we were alone, in his presence tried to flatter him by imitating his tough demeanour.

Approaching him with an odd swagger that was obviously meant to emulate his loose-hipped walk, she took the cigarette from his mouth and puffed on it herself before she gave it back to him. It was a ploy to get his attention, which was mainly focused on me.

"Hello, Willi," I said. His thin lips parted over his teeth in a smile, and he held out his cigarette towards me. I shook my head, knowing that I would probably choke on the smoke and embarrass myself. I recalled how, during the Christmas party at Lisii Nos, I had watched Uncle Michael and my father sucking on a joint, and I found myself blurting, "I only smoke dope."

Ursula glared. Willi looked interested.

"Yeah, you got a joint on you right now?"

I shook my head.

Ursula said, "Oh, Willi, can't you see? She doesn't really smoke dope. She's just trying to impress you."

But I insisted that I did, and Willi believed me.

This was an initiation of sorts. I became aware of power and the possibility of wielding it. I couldn't resist. Oh, I felt so sharp. I sensed unerringly how much influence Willi had over Ursula, and how interested Willi was in me. And my instincts drove me to exploit this, for the benefit of my obsession.

"Help us decide about our play," I said to him, even though I knew that, as far as Ursula was concerned, the decision was already made.

I described her idea for the murder mystery; then, in greater detail and with much more conviction, my idea for a three-scene play based on the Siege of Leningrad. In spite of that stare and his frightening history of expulsions from boarding-schools, I didn't falter once, and as soon as I was finished he said, "Great idea." Then, with a laugh that sounded forced, he said to Ursula, "Wait till old Papa and Mutti find out you're doing a Russian play about the war. That'll choke them up a little, won't it?"

Ursula looked bewildered, then angry, but she forced a laugh too.

"I'm going to play a famous Russian pianist," she said.

On the following Friday, just one day after Bette left to take a three-week acting job in Victoria, I got my period. I phoned Ursula, who declared that it was perfect timing, and that evening the two of us climbed to the upstairs bathroom and got down to the business of implementing her mysterious plan.

She rinsed out a small glass that stood beside the sink, then told me to take off my panties and fill the glass with as much blood as I could. I followed her instructions the way I'd been taught to follow church ritual: light the candle, kiss the icon, cross myself. No questions. With her coaching me, I stuck my finger up into my vagina and pulled down the sacred blood into the glass, or *chalice*, as Ursula called it.

"I'm just finishing my period," Ursula declared, and added her own blood, which looked old and brown. "This way it'll be much more potent," she said. "I'm still a virgin, so even though there's less of my blood, it counts for twice as much."

After we'd washed our hands, she took a bright red lipstick out of her pocket and painted first my lips and then her own. The contrast between our fully adult mouths and our navy-blue school tunics startled me into reverential awe: this was real magic, and Ursula the magician.

"Come on," she said, lifting up the glass that contained our blood. "We've got work to do."

Mama's room was no longer spare and palest green. Bette had filled it with bright colours. There was a small vase of dried flowers — rust-coloured and yellow; a blue bedspread; a blue and white Chinese rug covering Mama's floor, so that there was no possibility of dancing; yellow curtains; pictures hanging on the wall of mirrors; multicoloured scarves and belts and an umbrella hanging over the barre. The richness, the untidiness of it, was so much easier to fall in love with than my mother's life-denying asceticism. But I was already committed.

"What we have to do," Ursula said, "is smear the blood around the room, carefully, in hidden places, so she won't notice it."

"Oh yes," I said, reinventing my malice towards Bette so successfully that I found myself yearning to spatter the blood all over her bedspread, or bleed a whole river so that I could flood the room and leave everything stained.

Ursula stuck her finger into the glass and smeared a little blood on the corner of Bette's pillow. "It'll be close to her face when she's asleep," she said. "That's important because the blood curse works best when a person's asleep."

"If it's a curse, shouldn't we say *abracadabra* or *hocus-pocus* or something?" I asked.

"Grow up, Julie," she answered. "The blood curse is silent. There are no words that go with it. How can you be so ignorant?"

I knew she was trying to get even with me because Willi had taken my side instead of hers over the school play, but I forgave her. I was so grateful to her for helping me get rid of Bette, she could have asked me to give up both my short acquaintance with Willi and the play, and I would have done it.

I went over to the dresser, where I found a note from my father to Bette. It said: *I have been thinking about you all during rehearsal. I want to reblock the entire play with you at centre stage, always, for ever. Come and have dinner with me tonight.*

I dipped my finger into the blood and smeared the edge of the note with it. The sharp paper cut my finger, and I imagined that Papa and Bette had drunk red wine at dinner that night. I began to work earnestly then, in silence. I smeared the blood on one of the dried yellow flowers, the hem of the curtains, a corner of the Chinese rug and the most beautiful of the scarves that hung over the barre.

When I finished, I looked up and saw Ursula watching me. She was grinning and her bright red lips made her mouth look very large. I pulled her over to a space where the mirrored wall was not covered with pictures. We looked at each other's reflections. Then I kissed the mirror and left a print of my red lips on it. Ursula did the same. Next I kissed the print of Ursula's lips and she kissed mine. Finally we kissed each other's real lips. After the cool hardness of the mirror, Ursula's warmth and softness surprised me. I wanted more of her, so I put my arms around her waist, but she pushed me away. She examined the lip prints for a minute and said, "We'll leave them there. It will start Bette thinking about red, which is the right colour, and that will make it easier for the blood curse to work on her."

"Are you sure it'll get rid of the baby?"

"It'll get rid of them both."

After Ursula left, I went into the upstairs bathroom and stood for a long while before the mirror. The lipstick had smeared and faded but my lips still looked fuller and tantalizingly adult. I drew a bath, shed my school clothes and put up my hair. The steam began to fog the mirror and, as I watched my reflection blur, I pretended that my hips had widened and my breasts had grown full; if I squinted, I could imagine the misted shape of my older self looking back at me. Then I stepped into the tub and, squatting down in the water, which was almost too hot, I began to lather myself with a bar of fragrant soap that Bette had left in the soap dish. When I had finished, I smeared a little fresh blood from my vagina on the underside of the soap, where she wouldn't see it.

March 12, 1942

We went to the baths today: Danya, the children and I. They have been closed since December, and have only just reopened. Danya had traded two of her fine lacquered boxes for a small bar of soap. Although she has such difficulty walking, it was she who persuaded the rest of us to go.

"I won't so much mind dying, if only I can be clean again," she said, in a matter-of-fact voice that I did not attempt to contradict. Tanyusha and I had to support her for the last few hundred metres, but once we had gone inside and began to warm up in the steamy air, she revived.

As I pulled off layer after layer of filthy clothing, I felt that I was peeling off my own skin, and I expected to expose raw tissue and bone. I had not seen the children naked for weeks, and Danya not for many months, since the last time she and I had gone to the baths together, in early October. It is not just that our bodies are thin, they are ancient, yet they also appear curiously undeveloped. If we survive, Danya and I will have to grow hips and breasts again. Though Andrusha has been away for so long, I have not wanted to make love for months. I yearn only for the warmth of his body, nothing more.

The children's skin was dry and scaly. Nikolenka had dark marks around his waist from his trousers. Tanya's knees were swollen. Xyusha's body had a parchment-coloured cast. But the warm water was such a comfort for us all, and so was the soap. We passed it among us, lathering ourselves all over. I washed and rinsed my hair, two, three, four times, until my fingers slipped through it easily.

Danya began to sing Massenet's "Pleurez mes yeux". Her voice was so hoarse she hardly got the words out. No one would have believed that, only a few months ago, she had sung Tatiana at the Maly Theatre. The words brought back memories of concerts we had done together, and we found ourselves gossiping about colleagues, many of them dead, just as if the war had never started. The children caught our mood and they threw

the remains of the soap back and forth between them until it
melted away completely. Really we should have saved that scrap
of soap — when I think of those lacquer boxes — but we were in
no mood to be prudent.

My hands no longer felt stiff. They ached a little in the
warmth: a pleasant ache that had more yearning in it than dis-
comfort. I found myself hoping once again: to play; to accom-
pany Danya; to give a recital; to record the Fifth Piano Con-
certo by Prokofiev. But then I looked at Danya closely, not only
at the shapelessness of her body, but at her face, and the dark-
coloured down that has grown on her upper lip and her cheeks
over the last few months. I stopped hoping and began gossiping
once again about the days before the war. We lingered in the
warmth for as long as we could, until the director came in and
warned us that the baths were closing. We got dressed in the
few clean clothes we had, and then put our dirty clothes on top,
layer after layer, until we were ready to go out again into the
frozen air.

March 16, 1942
Danya died yesterday. I was not with her. This morning,
when I was standing in line for our bread rations, I met the
bassoonist who plays in the Kirov orchestra. He lives in the
same building as Dunya, and he told me the news. I wish I
could grieve for her, but instead I keep remembering the strange
hectic light in the streets that evening in September when she
and I watched from her apartment as the Badayev warehouses
burned.

The following Friday, when I came home from Ursula's,
there was a light on in my father's bedroom. As I walked
down the hallway towards it I heard whispering and, arriving at the door, I peered around it. The light came from
Papa's bedside lamp, and in front of it I saw the silhouette of his chair and him sitting in it. At least I thought it
was he, but something was wrong: he looked too large,
hunched, misshapen and threatening. The silhouette
shifted, heaved and moaned. I thought, *He's ill. He's in*

77

pain. I started to go to him but he split in two — became man and woman, Papa and Bette, his hand stroking her thigh, she moaning, he whispering, "Christ Jesus, my love, I can't wait."

"Julie," Bette said, her voice sharp with surprise. She stood up and smoothed a loose-fitting dress over her hips. "Home for the weekend," she explained.

My father watched her with lovesick eyes as she went over to the bedside table. I hated it that she had so much power over him. She picked up her purse and took out a small package. Handing it to me, she said, "I found this in a little store on Fisgard in Chinatown and thought you might like it." I took the package and mumbled an ungracious *Thank you*, remembering that I had not yet got the present my mother had promised to send me when she phoned on Boxing Day. Inside was a ring. It had delicate silver flowers with red centres on a turquoise background.

"It's cloisonné," Bette said.

I caught myself smiling and felt sure she had seen. If only it doesn't fit, I thought to myself, because I loved it already but I didn't want it to be a better gift than the expensive present I knew my mother would eventually send. When I slipped it on my finger, however, it fit perfectly.

I took the ring up to my room. Later, when I came back down for dinner, the door to my father's room was shut. Inside I could hear their voices.

"Oh, the lipstick was Julie. Who else could it be?"

"But where would she get it from?"

"Niki, darling, she's a teenager, after all."

"Well, I don't like it. She's too young. But that's not the point. She should never have been in your room. She's not going—"

"No, Niki, I think it would be better if we didn't even mention it. I want to become friends with her."

"What a lucky girl she is, to have you wanting to be her friend."

In school the following Monday, I worked hard on the play all through guidance class and study period. I got three pages done and, because I looked as if I were working on my school assignments, the teachers left me alone.

After school, when I came out of the gate past the chestnut trees, a car horn honked. I looked around and saw Mrs. von der Linde's Karamann Ghia and, behind the wheel, Willi. He beckoned to me, so I opened the passenger door and looked in.

"Come for a ride?" Willi asked.

"Where?"

"Out beyond the university. I've got something for you."

I hesitated and Willi said, "You're not scared, are you?"

"Of course not," I answered, though my voice wavered a little as I spoke.

I got in, and as Willi started the engine I asked, "Aren't we going to wait for Ursula?" But he pulled out into traffic and headed west.

On Marine Drive, beyond the university, Willi parked the car on a gravel shoulder above a bank that sloped sharply down to a stony beach. I thought we would get out of the car and make our way down the steep and narrow trail to the water, but he just sat. Eventually he pulled something out of his jacket pocket and held it up for me to see. It was a joint. I stayed cool.

"Aren't you going to light it?" I asked.

Miraculously I didn't choke or cough, and after I'd taken four or five tokes the Karamann Ghia's upholstery smelled so strong and rich I could almost taste it. I ran my hand along the piping around the edge of my seat in an attempt to contain the smell and make it mine. I was very thirsty. My throat was beginning to close up a little.

I glanced over at Willi, who was tracing the figures on the speedometer with his little finger. He glanced back at me, raised his hand, which trembled a little, and held it up to the windshield. The watery, sunset-tinged light coloured the nicotine stains and I thought how old his hands looked. His knuckles were already wrinkled, and there were thin dry lines down the sides of his index finger. I lifted my hand to the windshield and touched the nicotine stains with my fingertip. I thought, *These are the hands of someone who knows about the danger just below the surface.*

We sat looking through the window, side by side in the bucket seats, for what felt like a very long time, and during those moments I was without memory. When my memory came back, I discovered that I needed to speak, and I willed my inarticulate lips and tongue to move.

"I promised...," I began, and had to start over again because I had already forgotten what I was trying to say. "I promised to meet Papa...downtown after school."

"But you're with me instead."

"No. I have to meet Papa."

"Forget it."

"Please...take me."

"Okay, okay. Where?"

"He's rehearsing . . . on Thurlow . . . yes, Thurlow Street."

It was dusk as we drove down the long hill to Fourth Avenue. The sky had clouded over and it was raining heavily. The reflections on the wet pavement confused me so that I could make no sense of the road: a green neon sign disappeared under our wheels; the white lines marking off the lanes vanished into a multicoloured slick of water. I tried to huddle into the familiarity of my school uniform, but it had become a derangement of textures: scratchy, silky, stiff, smooth.

Willi punched the car radio on and fiddled with the dial. He stopped at the sound of a solo cello piece and turned the dial back and forth carefully until the station was as clear as he could get it.

"Are you a musician?" I asked.

"I play cello a little. Used to."

"So why did you quit?" I asked.

"Only idiots like my parents think music's going to save the world," Willi said, "but my father thinks I quit because of my bad blood. I'm not his kid, you know. My mother was pregnant when he married her, but not by him. Whenever I quit something or get expelled, they say it's the bad blood I got from my real father."

The car slowed down. We were on the approaches to the Burrard Street bridge and a brightness lit up the air on the far side.

"Holy shit," Willi murmured, "something's on fire."

He stopped the car, then opened the door and got out.

"A burning truck."

The distant brightness lit up his face as he rushed towards it, his arms and legs lithe, greedy for destruction. All around, people got out of their stalled cars, brought out umbrellas, put on raincoats and gloves. Sirens screamed. Some people ran to the crest of the bridge to get a better view. Others hung back for a moment until a crowd gathered; then, feeling safer, they ran forward to catch up to the excitement. I stayed where I was. My grandmother's diary had shown me enough suffering, and I had no desire to gawk if I couldn't help. Also, I remembered my father describing how the bystanders stared at him when he was brought out of the bush after his plane crash. They couldn't get enough of his smashed body — not the rescue team or the medics, just those who had gathered out of curiosity and a fascination with catastrophe.

The fire grew brighter. An ambulance picked its slow way among the stopped cars, looking oddly inept, its sirens sounding hysterical, as if screaming was the only thing it could do effectively. I felt trapped inside the impassive metal body of the Karamann Ghia. And in my mind there was an ever-growing urgency to get to my father, to keep my promise to meet him after rehearsal, as if his life or mine depended on it.

The distant brightness began to dim and the onlookers returned to their cars, stamping their feet, rubbing their arms, their breath clouding the night air. All around me people started up their motors; then, when they couldn't move forward, they started honking, until the few straggling witnesses came back. Willi was the last.

He got in, smelling of car exhaust and wet wool, his hair slick against his forehead. I thought, *It's the stink of someone who knows how to bring hidden disasters to the surface.* It was almost as if he had caused the accident.

"Holy fuck," he said, "that guy was burned black as a roast pig."

"Is he alive?"

"For the moment."

Slowly we started moving forward, until I could see the wreck of the truck lying upside-down in the middle of the bridge. The cab was crushed and the metal was blackened and blistered. As we circled around it I felt suffused with a pleasure that was inexplicable until I understood that it wasn't pleasure but relief, because neither I nor anyone I loved was the victim.

March 27, 1942

There was a loud knock on the door this morning. When I opened it a young Komsomol girl stood on the threshold with letters in her hand.

"Kabalevskaya, V. M.?" she asked.

"Yes," I said, and she handed me a large bundle of letters, the first I had received in months. I told her thank you, and was about to close the door when the rest of the letters she was carrying dropped from her hands and she fell forward into my arms. Tanyusha helped me carry her over to the table, where we sat her down, and when she had recovered a little I poured her a glass of tea.

"Are you ill?" I asked, when she finished it.

She shook her head.

"What is it then?"

She began to cry. I held her hand as Tanya sat down

opposite her, on the other side of the table, and started to sort through the letters.

At last the girl, staring down at the table, said to me, "All of them are dead. My friend Luba, her mama and papa and uncle and babushka. I was delivering letters over on Nekrasov Street and I was excited about seeing my friend Luba again. The door was open, so I knocked and went in. Luba's mama and babushka were in the living-room. They were both sitting on the couch and they were dead. Then I went into the bedroom. I heard a rat. Luba was there, and the rat.... She was dead, and the rat...."

I put my arm around the girl. She was only a year or two older than Tanya. I said to her, "You must not talk any more. You have had a bad shock."

Tanya had stopped sorting through the letters as the girl was speaking.

"Luba?" she asked. "Luba Sokolova?"

The girl nodded. Tanya and I looked at each other. Luba had been a student at the conservatory. Her mother was a tall, elegant woman who wore expensive furs because her husband, who had survived the purges of 1937, was one of the high party officials. Luba, who was a little older than Tanya, played violin. She was talented, and I knew that Tanya admired her. Though I kept my arm around the Komsomol girl, all my concern shifted to my Tanyusha. Her hands lay still on the pile of letters she had been sorting.

"I wanted to play like Luba," she said. She lifted her hands from the table and dropped them limply into her lap.

When the Komsomol girl left I began to sort through the letters myself, while Tanya stayed seated in silence. Most of the letters were from my dear Andrusha, though one was from his commanding officer. It said he had been wounded and was missing, but it had been written last year, in November, and the most recent of the letters from Andrusha was dated February 12 of this year.

Xyusha and Nikolenka arrived home with a bundle of firewood for which I had traded my pearl earrings. Nikolenka's legs are no longer swollen, and he is able to run errands again.

After we had eaten a meal of kasha and tea, I began to read the letters out loud, from the earliest to the most recent. It must have taken me at least an hour and a half, but not even Nikolenka was restless.

My poor Andrusha is fighting under conditions that are as bad as those here in Leningrad. After he was wounded some peasants found him and took care of him. When he recovered, he joined a regiment of partisans who carry out operations against the Fascists behind enemy lines.

Sometimes with exuberance, sometimes with anger, sometimes with exhaustion, Andrusha wrote about his life as a partisan. He works near the Polish border, though the partisans change their bases regularly, travelling through miles of marshy forest to establish new camps. He wrote of derailing trains, blowing up bridges, slashing telephone and telegraph lines. He said that food and supplies were scarce. Often he had used homemade vodka to disinfect his wounds.

For a weapon, instead of one of our own Mosins, he uses a rifle he captured from the Germans during a raid. He also has a German machine-gun, and always sleeps with both it and the rifle by his side.

"My teeth are falling out," he wrote in one letter. "We eat mushrooms and rowanberries and potatoes taken from the storage bins of burned-out villages. Sometimes we dine on the flesh of horses killed in the fighting, but we never get enough green vegetables, and so many of us have scurvy."

He talked of how the Germans retaliated against the partisans, or any civilian suspected of being sympathetic to them.

"One day, when I went into a certain village to barter for milk, I found all the villagers gathered in the square. A gallows had been built in the centre of it. Twenty or more German soldiers stood around the perimeter as three prisoners, an old man, a younger man in his forties and a middle-aged woman, were brought bound to the gallows. One of the Germans walked towards them. He was smoking a cigarette. He pushed the two men to the ground and began speaking German to the woman. She did not understand what he was saying, so he spoke louder, and when she still did not answer him correctly he began

slapping her. She sank to her knees and, trying to shield her face with her arms, cried out, 'Mercy, Herr. Mercy, Soldat.'

"He stopped slapping her then and motioned for her to stand up. He turned from her, began to walk away, turned back to her suddenly, held her head against his chest as if he were trying to comfort her, then jabbed his burning cigarette end into her eye.

"As she cried out a young man rushed towards her from the crowd of villagers, but he was immediately felled by a machine-gun. The three prisoners then had signs placed around their necks which said, in both Russian and German, I gave food and shelter to enemies of the German fatherland. I slipped around the side of a storehouse before the three prisoners were hanged, because I knew I could expect no help from the villagers on that day."

When I had finished reading the letters we all sat in silence until Xyusha asked, "When is Papa coming home?" Then Nikolenka said, "Read the part about blowing up the bridge again." Tanyusha said nothing, but sat still with her limp hands in her lap.

March 28, 1942

I could not sleep last night because of the artillery fire and Andrusha's letters. All through the winter I have lived without hope, expecting that either he or I would die before we saw each other again. But now I know he was still alive as recently as a month ago, so I have begun to hope again, and the world feels much more dangerous. Even the artillery fire frightens me, though we hear it almost every night.

I got out of bed and went to the window, where, through the blackout curtains, I saw that the moon was shining brightly. It bleached the old winter snow of all its stains so that it looked new again, like the first snow of autumn. For a moment I was bathed in a happiness as bright as the moon. Then suddenly I became frightened again, because the clear night made the city such an easy target for bombing or shelling. I thought of the Sokolovs, all of them lying dead in their apartment, and knew, as I had known on New Year's Eve, that at least one of us would die. Danya was already gone. But who else, I wondered. And straight away I understood it would be Tanyusha.

SIX

When Willi dropped me off at the Fourth Wall Theatre offices, I closed the door on his thin-lipped smile with relief, glad to escape his cynicism and his fascination with disaster despite the tenderness I was beginning to feel for him. Though I had not been to Fourth Wall for more than two years, it looked exactly as I remembered it. On the right of the vestibule a nubbly glass door led to the administration office. Directly in front of me was an elevator, old and unreliable, used only by my father and to move costumes and props. On my left was the dimly lit and footworn staircase that most people preferred to the elevator — the actors especially, who were proud of their fit bodies and often ran up two stairs at a time. A clumsily lettered sign read:

Rehearsal Hall — Second Floor
Costumes, Props — Third Floor

Climbing slowly, I listened through the silence for rehearsal sounds, at first worrying that my father might have left without me, but when I reached the second floor I heard voices and, opening the door into the main hall, I saw two actors rehearsing a scene within a playing space marked with masking tape. In the middle of the room sat my father and the stage manager, watching the actors and making notes. Around the periphery stood four other people, among them Pip Salisbury, the costume designer, who was taking the in-seam leg measurement of a blonde-haired actor. It was all so familiar: the only spoken words

86

coming from a different time, translated from another language; the room alive with many-minded focus on the singular task of producing a play. For me it was like entering a sanctuary, or rediscovering home.

On the wall opposite, a large, round clock said 5:37. It was earlier than I'd thought. As the minute-hand clicked over to 5:38, the scene on the makeshift stage ended. The actors relaxed out of their characters' stances. My father sat without speaking, his muteness slowly gathering everyone's attention. One of the actors started pulling at her hair. The other coughed. I glanced down at the rough fir floor, dark from years of waxing and stripping and rewaxing. My father pushed down on the arms of his chair, lifted himself and settled back again. He picked up a pen and at last began to speak: "Technically I can't complain — the pacing is good, the intensity is right — but what I am missing is history. I do not yet sense all those years of rancour and mistrust...that must be palpable too, you know...it is ancient, that rancour...."

As my father went on talking, relief sluiced through the rehearsal hall. But long silences were typical of him. In an interview once, an actor who had just finished working with Papa for the first time insisted that he used silence to wield power. But she was wrong. It was my father's fragility that created the silences. Those who had worked often with him understood this, as I did now that I had read Babushka's diary of the Siege. It was as if he were freezing to death and he had only one match left to light a fire. His silence was a prayer that the fire would catch, and fear that it might not. Each play was his last chance, and the designers, actors and crew, who sensed that he was giving the production all that was left of his frail energy, usually gave much more of themselves than they did to other plays rehearsed by more robust directors.

"Psst," I heard from somewhere on my left. When I turned around, Pip was standing at the door with his tape measure in his hand. He beckoned, and I followed him out of the rehearsal hall and up the dim stairwell to the costume department.

As he opened the door into the shop he asked, "Why is it that the measurements actors send me ahead of time bear not the slightest relationship to their bodies when they get here? I can understand an actor losing or gaining ten pounds, but how on earth can their legs shrink?"

The shop was brilliant with light. On a large table in the centre of the room lay a piece of pale green cloth, partially cut out, and behind, a rack of costumes in various stages of readiness. I went over to the rack and began to finger the materials, all so much richer-looking and heavier than street clothes, as if the stage were more durable and far more real than everyday life.

"Careful, there are pins," Pip said.

Each of the costumes was labelled with the name of a character from *Blood Wedding*: Leonardo, Bridegroom, L's Mother, Woodcutter/Moon, Beggar-Woman/Death. Above the rack on a corkboard were pinned Pip's original designs. Even if the costumes hadn't been labelled I'd have been able to match them up with the drawings, the costumes looking substantial though unfinished, the drawings unrealized but complete.

To my right the uncurtained window looked out onto the dripping neoned streets, where cars swished over the reflective pavement and people ran from the shelter of one shop awning to the next. I stood with my hands on the sill, warming my thighs through the wool of my tunic against the scalding radiator pipes. Behind me I heard the sound of Pip's scissors amplified by the wooden table as he cut through the cloth that lay on top of it.

"It's good to see you again, lovey," he said, "and your dad. We're all so glad to have him back."

"Yes," I answered. And that was all I managed to say before my throat closed up. For an instant I thought it was the lingering effect of the dope. But then came the tears, part despair from being exiled for the past two years from the Fourth Wall offices where I'd spent so many childhood hours, and part relief at feeling welcome again. A moment later Pip was standing behind me, rubbing my shoulder and pushing a hanky into my hand. He didn't make me explain my tears or try to comfort me with words, but when I had dried my eyes he went over to the wall where he kept his hundred spools of coloured thread on nail after nail. He lifted off a bright yellow spool, took an old-fashioned latchkey from behind it and handed it to me. It was the key to the costume closet.

The costume closet wasn't a closet at all, but a large room where all the costumes were hung, women's to the right of the door, men's to the left, according to period or, if they weren't European or North American, according to country of origin.

All through my childhood, whenever I'd gone up to visit Pip, he'd given me the key. It was his to offer, not mine to ask for, and I'd always accepted it, as I did now, because the costume closet was a place where I could dream.

I put the key into the lock and turned it. The door opened into dimness and the smell of sweat and cleaning fluid. The air was warmer than in the shop. Closing the door, I took a few steps down the dark, narrow corridor between the costumes. I searched the air for the string that hung down from the light, but when I found it I stood for a moment in the centre of the darkness and listened to the blades of Pip's scissors beyond the door. I could hear the faint in-out of my own breath as I stood amid century after century of costumes, half wishing, half fearing, that they would take up the rhythm of my breathing and come to life in the dark.

I pulled the string and the bright bulb clicked on. The costumes were draped with dust-covers which I pulled off, one by one, as I went down the row, running my hands over the material of sleeves and bodices. I sniffed at the armpits for the smell of each character, pushed my way between the hangers, lifted up skirts, draped myself in capes, reached into the pockets of smoking jackets and greatcoats. Oh, this was heaven.

At last I chose a colonel's uniform from the nineteenth century. It was Vershinin's costume from an old production of *Three Sisters*. It was too large for me, but not by much. The man who had played Vershinin was smallish, about Papa's size. Standing in front of the mirror at the end of the corridor, I saw that the dark cloth suited me and, although the arms were too long, the coat had a slender cut so that it didn't overwhelm me.

The headgear was stored along the wall, on shelves that reached from floor to ceiling. There were crowns of gold, of laurels; a crown of thorns; wigs, wimples, helmets, headdresses and an entire shelf of military caps. I tried on several of the caps but they all came down over my ears. Finally, at the back of the shelf, I found a small one labelled *bellboy*. There was a band of red and gold around it and, when I pushed my hair under it, it was a perfect fit.

When I went back to the mirror I discovered that I looked like Nick, but I told myself I was a soldier from many eras, dressed to go to many wars. I heard the staccato of drums, the rhythm of marching feet, the call to duty, honour, glory. Standing with the Tsar's troops as the holy procession passed by — the priests in their vestments, the deacons, the choristers — I listened to the endless chanting, smelled the incense, knelt down before the icon of the Holy Mother. With God I prepared to march against Napoleon.

Or, like Dedushka, I fought against the Fascists. I holed up in swamps, foraged for mushrooms and rowanberries, tore meat from the carcasses of slaughtered horses. I raided German convoys and mined railway tracks, or set fire to the woods where German tanks were hiding.

But even as I played these games, I knew I'd outgrown them. Babushka's diaries had taught me that war, especially for women, was quite different: heroism had much more to do with enduring hopelessness than with singular acts of bravery. As I looked in the mirror at my face, hot-cheeked with fantasy, handsome but implausible in pseudo-uniform, I began to think about my play, in which the only battlefield was a small Leningrad apartment where minds as well as bodies struggled against starvation, where battledress was everyday clothes and weapons were whatever might be bartered for food or fuel.

I turned around and stared at the rows of costumes, and found myself taking off the bellboy cap and undoing the buttons on the Vershinin jacket. I put the cap back on the shelf exactly where I'd found it, and hung up the jacket again, brushing some lint off the sleeve and pulling the dust-cover over it, because I knew that the costumes were no longer for my dreaming. Somewhere in that room, if I looked carefully, I was sure I'd find something for my play too.

I discovered it at last, in a cardboard box on one of the shelves that ran the length of the far wall. It was a fringed woollen shawl painted with red and blue flowers, warm enough to be useful and beautiful enough to trade for bread or firewood. I came out of the costume closet with it draped around my shoulders.

"My God," Pip said, "I haven't seen that for years." He took the shawl from me, put it around his shoulders and stood in front of the mirror.

"Those cerise flowers are a problem," he said. "They clash with my hair." He patted the few red strands left on his almost bald head. "But wouldn't it just look terrific on Simon?" Simon was Pip's lover, slender and boyish, a dancer who'd lived with him for about five years.

"Pip," I said, "can I borrow it? I really need it."

"What on earth for?" he demanded. I had never before asked for anything from his costume closet.

I looked down and began fingering the heavy green material on his cutting table.

"I'm writing a play," I said. "It's for school, and my friend Ursula and I are going to put it on just before Easter. Oh, please, Pip, I really need it."

"Yulochka," I heard my father call from downstairs,

"time to go."

Pip took off the shawl, folded it up carefully, put it in a plastic bag and handed it to me, saying, "The rules are that you return anything you borrow in as good condition as when you took it away."

"For sure," I said.

I gave him a quick kiss on the cheek and ran downstairs to meet my father.

"The Survivor," Ursula declaimed in a metallic voice. "Leningrad, 1942. Scene One." She looked up at me and said, "This *must* be a play about the Siege."

I said nothing, but looked back down at my handwritten copy of the scene. We were having our first reading of it in Ursula's basement. I'd decided to see how she reacted to the play before I brought out the shawl, but I had it with me, packed neatly away in my school satchel, like a secret cache of food: there if I needed it, but to be used only in an emergency.

She continued. "Characters: Luba Sokolova, a talented musician. Tanya, her friend."

"You play Luba," I explained.

"Luba," she spat, as if the word tasted bad. "Russian names are so ugly. Why couldn't you give me a beautiful name like Rosamunde or Sabine?"

I knew this was all talk. She still hadn't forgiven me for insisting on the Leningrad play instead of hers. But I couldn't help wondering if she thought the Russian version of my name, Yuliya, was ugly too.

She began looking through the script. "Most of the lines are for me," she said. There was still mockery in her voice but it was lighter, and it sounded as if she was using it to hide her pleasure. She started reading the lines.

"A fir branch, a bowl of cabbage soup and a glass of potato wine. That's no way to bring in the new year."

"At least we are both still alive," I said.

Ursula laughed, but I didn't even look up. She continued reading. Sometimes she made remarks like "Gross" or "Are you kidding?" I didn't let them distract me. Her remarks became rarer, and by the end of the third page she was speaking only the lines. Her usually cool voice became warmer and more intense. It was a strong voice, more suited to acting than mine, which was quiet and often cracked if I tried to shout. Before long she was standing, and she began to speak the lines with her entire body — not thrashing about like an amateur, but with an understated grace that left me feeling awkward by comparison.

We read through to the end of the scene, where Luba caught Tanya stealing her only piece of bread but, instead of throwing her out, urged her to eat all of it. As I turned away from her and mimed gobbling it up, she poured the last of the imaginary potato wine into my glass. "Go on, drink," she told me. "Happy New Year."

Our rehearsals were mostly like that. At each one I'd have to win Ursula over to the play. To each I brought my satchel with the shawl, in case I needed to barter it for her commitment. Gradually it became a kind of talisman: as long as I had it with me, the rehearsals would go well.

Though Ursula left all the writing of the play to me and, like a prima donna, always needed to be cajoled into rehearsing, once she got started she worked hard. The more hours we spent on the play, the more she chose to spend her free time with me, which was usually Saturday afternoon, because she practised piano two hours a day and had to go to a music lesson every Saturday morning. When I remember those afternoons, I see the two of us walking through the streets of a downtown shimmering in late winter sun, our laughter fogging the cold air, though I know perfectly well there were many more cloudy, drizzling days than sunny ones. We window-shopped endlessly, and the stores we went into were mostly expensive, the displays tasteful, with no price-tags to mar the window-dresser's artistry. Invariably a clerk would come up to us and ask in a patronizing voice, "May I help you *girls*?" Ursula always answered them, in a tone that was marginally disdainful but never quite insulting, "Thank you, if we decide we'd like to try anything on we'll let you know." After that we were left alone. But I felt uncomfortable, and more than once she said to me, "Don't skulk. I hate the way you sneak around doorways as if you didn't belong. We've got as much right to be in here as anyone else."

I invited her to the opening night of *Blood Wedding*, and after looking through the clothes in my closet Ursula decided that I needed a new outfit for the occasion. I didn't have any money except the ten dollars Dedushka had given me at Christmas. I told her I was broke, but she simply said, "Ask your father." And when I explained that he never had any extra cash, she said, "Well then, ask your mother. Mutti never refuses me anything."

I dreaded phoning my mother. Not that she wouldn't say yes, especially since she hadn't sent me my Christmas present yet, but I knew her well enough to predict that she'd forget to mail the money, and I'd have to phone her again to remind her and probably get her answering service or James on the line.

"Look," Ursula said, "either you get the money from somewhere or we'll have to steal everything."

"You're bluffing."

"Am I?"

I knew Ursula was bold enough to steal if she decided to, and clever enough to get away with it, but the very idea made me sweat and in the end, after days of hesitation, I put a call through to my mother late one night.

It was seven a.m. in London and a sleepy James answered the phone.

"Is Mama there?"

"Who?"

"Julia Holmes, my mother."

"Ah, Julie, hello. It's damnably early for a phone call."

"Well, it's really late here."

There was some muttering in the background, the

sound of what must have been sheets against the mouthpiece, then my mother's half-conscious voice.

"Darling? Anything wrong?"

"I just wanted to make sure I'd get you in."

"You did that."

I was an honest kid but clumsy, and I asked for money before I thought to employ any of the pleasantries, the protestations of affection, the flattery with which supplicants manipulate their benefactors. And when my mother asked what I needed it for, instead of explaining, I blurted out that I was tired of looking like a geek, and she owed me something because she still hadn't sent me my Christmas present. My rudeness surprised even me, but my mother said, "Oh, my darling, I'm so sorry." Then she fell silent. There was a long pause during which I heard her quiet breathing at the other end of the line. At last she asked, "How much do you want?"

I'd been so concerned about whether she'd say yes that I hadn't thought how much I should ask for, so I said the first number that came into my head. "A hundred dollars."

"A hundred?"

The question in her voice intimidated me, but the emotional energy it had cost me to pick up the phone made me stubborn, and I outwaited her silence. Eventually she said, "A hundred dollars seems reasonable. I'll send you a postal order today."

Of course, she didn't send it that day, and I had to phone her back to remind her. But eventually my hundred dollars arrived.

On the Saturday Ursula took me to buy my new outfit, we met early in the afternoon at her house. She prepared me for the shopping expedition by making up my eyes and mouth, and arranging my hair on top of my head. She wound one of her own scarves casually around my neck, but sighed when she looked at my shoes, which had T-straps and fastened with buckles.

"Anyone would think you were eight years old,"

she said. She was wearing open-toed shoes with platform soles.

She decided we would go to Kerrisdale instead of downtown, and there she took over the sidewalks the way a character in a movie does — the camera focused on her, while everyone else is just an extra. I walked one step behind her, suffused with the brightness of her aura, trailing light. Never had shop windows been so full of possibilities. We entered and left each store like an elemental force. In one of them Ursula found me a long cream-coloured skirt and a silk blouse patterned with cerise and purple flowers, in another cerise pantyhose, and — in a shoe store no larger than the von der Lindes' front porch — my first pair of platform shoes. By the time we'd finished, she looked haggard and drained of all her brightness. I suggested we go to a coffee shop for a snack, and on the way I pointed to a pair of velvet hot pants in one of the windows and said jokingly, "Maybe we should take everything back and get those instead." I'd expected a smile, but she snapped at me, "Don't be so stupid, your legs are too short."

Abruptly she turned into a doorway I didn't recognize and began to finger through the racks of clothes.

I couldn't imagine what else she thought we needed to buy.

"What're you looking for?" I asked.

"Since you're not a virgin," she said, "I thought we should look here just in case."

When she lifted a shapeless blue denim tent off one of the racks, I realized she'd taken me into a maternity store. "I'm sure you'd look *great* in this," she said. There was no mirth in her voice.

A salesclerk confronted us. "May I help you?" It was more a challenge than a question. I shook my head and started towards the door, but Ursula answered with a question of her own.

"Do you know what *Schlumpe* means?" When the clerk didn't respond, Ursula said, "It means "slut". It's what my little friend is."

"Let's go, Ursula, please," I pleaded, my hand already pulling at the door, but she had become someone quite different from the patient mentor who had spent all afternoon watching me try on clothes, urging me towards the sophisticated choices that would transform me into a young woman. She was out for blood and couldn't be stopped.

"Schlumpe. That's what she is. She's done it with her cousin and she wants to do it with my brother too. A little Slavic Schlumpe." Ursula laughed at the comic assonance of those two words placed so awkwardly together. I withered.

At that moment a woman came out from the back of the shop. She was thin and elegant and, like us, she had her hair piled up on top of her head.

"Get out of my store," she said quietly, with a slight accent that might have been German.

Ursula laughed.

"Get out of my store," she repeated. "You don't belong here."

There was a long pause during which she and Ursula stared at each other. Finally Ursula said to me, "Let's go." She sauntered bravely but I crept out the door.

"Ursula, why...?" I asked, not yet able to find words to describe what she'd just done to me.

"It's a warning," she said.

There my courage failed, and we continued in silence to the coffee shop.

We ordered mushroom burgers and chocolate shakes. In the background "Age of Aquarius" was playing.

"What schmaltz," Ursula said.

I sat fingering the cutlery, head down, bewildered that an afternoon begun so luminously had turned so vicious. There was a fury in me that I held back, knowing I couldn't express it without tears and determined not to give Ursula the satisfaction of seeing me cry. In the end all I could find to say — such a flimsy retort — was "I think "Age of Aquarius" is a *great* song."

To my surprise Ursula said, "You're probably right."

She was trying to woo me back. After a moment's silence she said, "My feet are killing me. I guess there's a place in the world for buckles and T-straps after all."

Just then the burgers and shakes arrived, and while we chewed and sucked on our straws my anger slowly leached away.

With food in my stomach, tears no longer threatened. I felt bolder and able to confront her on safer territory: Bette, whose belly was growing larger every day.

"So how come the blood curse hasn't worked?" I asked casually, as if I didn't care.

"What makes you think it hasn't?" Ursula demanded.

"Bette's still holed up in Mama's room, *and* she's started to show."

Ursula took a long pull on her straw, then said, "Of course, she might not lose the baby at all. It could turn out to be a monster instead."

"A monster?"

"Yeah, you know, it might turn out to have one eye in the middle of its forehead."

I nodded, trying to picture this miniature Cyclops. Would it have one eyebrow, or two, or none?

"Or it might have no brain," Ursula continued.

"Or flippers like those thalidomide kids?" I asked, feeling my way into the malice of Ursula's new game.

She nodded. "Or a gigantic head but just a tiny little body."

"Or both legs joined at the ankles, but only one foot."

"Or three feet, but only one leg."

Ursula suddenly wrapped her arm around her head. "Or with one arm fused to its skull," she said, rolling her eyes.

I began to giggle. "Or with its elbow fused to its foot." I brought my foot up onto the booth's padded seat and pushed my elbow hard into my shoe.

"Or it's pee-er where its poo-er should be." Ursula grimaced.

"Or its cock where its nose should be," I said, pretending I was jacking off my nose.

Ursula pointed at me and laughed and laughed, holding her stomach. "That's disgusting," she said.

"It's sick."

"Gross."

"Insane."

Gasping, she rolled back and forth against the back of the booth. And I laughed too, so hard that tears slipped down my cheeks.

July 25, 1942

This morning after I picked up our bread rations I walked along Liteiny towards Nevsky Prospekt. There had been a rumour that all the German prisoners of war were going to be paraded through the centre of Leningrad because it was Navy Day. I wanted to see the faces of our enemies, and yet the thought of them marching down the Nevsky, even as prisoners, disgusted me. It was a warm day and the summer weather made me feel, for a few moments, more at ease than I have for over a year. But then I remembered that there had been sightings of German troop movements and warnings of a new offensive against the city.

I thought how empty the streets looked now that the crowds of corpses had been cleared away and so many people had been evacuated. On one of the street corners, I found a group of ten or fifteen people. As I walked towards it, the group parted a little and I saw a set of scales standing on the pavement. The man who owned them had no lack of customers. They all wanted to know how much weight they had lost over the winter. I joined the group and saw that the man was charging a ruble for each weighing. A ruble is far too high a price for a few seconds on a set of scales, but no one argued with him or offered him less.

He had no hands. I thought that perhaps they had been blown off in a bomb blast, because his stumps were covered with burn scars. Even so, he moved the weights so quickly and accurately that it was hard to believe he had no fingers.

When I stepped on the scale he smiled at me. His teeth were badly pitted. One was chipped and another was missing. Yet it was a kind smile, and I almost forgot to take note of my weight before I stepped off. What I saw shocked me: thirty-seven kilos. The last time I weighed myself, which was probably in September, I was over fifty-eight.

I continued on my way down Liteiny to the Nevsky, and when I got there I found a crowd, mostly women, lining both sides of the street. It was not nearly as large as the usual crowd one might have seen any afternoon before the war when all the streetcars were running, but it was large enough to make me understand that we had survived a year of war and were still a city.

I watched two women and a little girl walk towards me across the Nevsky. One of the women limped slightly and supported herself with a stick, while the other gripped a string bag in one hand and the little girl in the other hand with the same firmness. The string bag contained two or three wrapped parcels that looked like food. Though the day was warm, both women wore coats and berets. They had heavy shoes and ankle socks on their feet, but their starved, pale legs were exposed to the warm air and the sunshine and the glances of the crowd. For that reason, or so I thought, they walked with their eyes downcast. Only the child, wearing a dress and a bow in her hair, walked with her head up and skipped every few steps, her knees rising rhythmically and looking grotesquely large in comparison to her emaciated calves.

Most of the rubble had been cleared away from the street, and in the gaps where buildings had been destroyed by shells, false fronts rose up, all of them carefully painted to look like the exteriors of the buildings they replaced. If I glanced up the Nevsky or down it, if I didn't examine the false fronts too closely, I could almost believe that the city had never known war. We might all have gathered there to watch a May Day parade.

Beside me I heard a voice say, "They are going to reopen Philharmonic Hall soon. Have you heard?"

"Yes. Certainly," said another. "They flew in the score of

the new symphony by Shostakovich in June, you know, and the orchestra has already been rehearsing for several weeks. Ah, what a concert that will be."

My throat went tight and my chin began to tremble. So there will be music again, *I said to myself, and tried not to think too much about Danya, or Luba Sokolova, or my Tanyusha, who lies in bed most of the day and never takes her violin out of its case any more.*

A murmur began in the crowd, and around me voices asked, "What is that? The prisoners? Can you see them yet?"

Down at the far end of the Nevsky the crowd looked thicker. Then, slowly, an uneven line of plodding figures separated themselves from the onlookers. A voice rose in the crowd. "Fascists. Scum," it said, and beneath it I heard incomprehensible growls and mutters, while other, louder voices cried out, "Give them to us. Give them to us." My pulse raced and I thought to myself, I am going to see my enemies. *As the prisoners came closer my hands began to sweat. I strained to see their faces. I wanted a confrontation, I wanted violence, but their plodding, stumbling walk aroused my pity before I could make out their features.*

When at last I saw the prisoners — unshaven, dirty, their jackets torn, eyes averted — I wanted to turn my glance away from them too, but I could not. Around me, the words "Give them to us" were repeated over and over until they became a chant. I heard moaning near me, and when I looked I saw that it came from the mouth of the woman I had watched earlier as, supported by a stick, she crossed the street. The little girl in the dress and bow bent down and picked a stone from the gutter. As the chant "Give them to us. Give them to us" crescendoed, she lifted her arm and threw the stone at the prisoners. It hit one of them, a bareheaded, grimy, lean-faced boy, on the cheek. He looked up, turned to us, and his lips parted in a grimace. Suddenly he began laughing. The prisoner behind him gave him a poke. Another turned round and thumped his shoulder, but he did not stop. The undercurrent of voices in the crowd became angry. That anger reawakened my own, and buoyed it up. Soon I was chanting too. "Give them to us. Give them to us." I felt

101

myself being carried towards the column of enemy soldiers. I caught sight of a piece of broken plaster lying in the road. I stooped, picked it up, threw it, saw it hit a chest that was protected only by a torn shirt, watched the figure hunch, stumble, straighten — and at last I saw the face. It was blue-eyed and arrogant: just the way an enemy face should look.

I felt a pressure on my chest. I looked down and saw a uniformed arm pushing me back. One of ours, I thought. A Red Army soldier. "Quietly. Quietly," he said, as he pushed the crowd back like a benevolent shepherd. His face came very close to mine, so that I could see drops of sweat trickling down from his hair. His jaw was square with determination but his eyes looked violent, and I knew he was speaking the words "Quietly, quietly" to calm the hatred within himself as much as to control the crowd. I looked past his shoulder at the line of trudging prisoners: at their filth and their dejection. One of them scratched and scratched at his belly. I realized that they must all be half mad with lice. I at least had been able to keep myself clean.

SEVEN

On the opening night of *Blood Wedding* Papa, Bette and I arrived at the Regent Theatre a good half-hour before the curtain, so he would have enough time to go backstage and wish all the actors and crew a good show. I didn't go with him because Ursula and I had decided to meet in the foyer at a quarter to eight. She was taking a piano master class that didn't end until seven-thirty.

I went immediately to the women's washroom and stood gazing at myself in the mirror. With the ten dollars Dedushka had given me at Christmas I'd bought make-up: powder, lipstick, eyeliner and eyeshadow. For days I'd practised: eyeshadow first, putting the right amount on each lid, not too dark, not too light, smoothing it out with my finger; then with the eyeliner drawing a thin green outline around my lashes once, twice, starting all over again because one eye looked larger than the other, keeping the line smooth, as tricky as using a paintbrush; next the lipstick, which I put not only on my lips but on my cheeks as well, rubbing it in until I glowed; and finally powder. This evening I'd got it just right. I was beautiful and, more important, I was still myself — not the false adult Ursula had made of me, lips too bright, hair piled high. I stood steady in my platform shoes. The blouse was perfect and so was the skirt. A slit in it revealed my cerise calf. The only thing I was unsure of was the shawl Pip had given me for the play. I hadn't been able to resist it, so soft to the touch: the flowers almost matched my blouse, and the background was only a shade darker than my skirt.

"*Velikolepna,*" my father had said as he watched me come down the staircase at home, my left hand lightly holding the bannister rail for safety rather than balance. "Stunning."

I opened the washroom door and went out into the foyer. A large corkboard displayed glossies of the cast, with their bios. The photo of my father was recent, shot professionally and designed to give the effect of Romantic intensity — his strong cheekbones highlighted, the grey in his hair made to look distinguished — while the handles of his chair were carefully concealed behind his shoulders. The bio spoke of a welcome return to Fourth Wall after two years' absence; no mention of the weeks he'd spent in hospital, his resignation as artistic director or the difficult way back, via a mediocre production of *Medea* and more illness, to this particular opening night. Yet while the photograph and the bio didn't tell all the truth, it was a relief for me to know that sometimes it was possible, even appropriate, to leave history behind and arrive newly and, as the bio asserted, *in triumph*.

I turned away from the glossies and discovered that the foyer had filled while I'd been looking at them. Pip, dressed in a burgundy velours shirt and wine-and-beige-striped silk pants, stood amid a group of women with Simon, light-boned and blond, at his elbow, lifting his arms in exclamation, looking as if he might fly up to the mezzanine. I began to move towards them through a crush of people already swallowing champagne from long-stemmed glasses made of plastic. I felt serene and unassailable in my new costume, as if, like Papa, I too had just returned in triumph to Fourth Wall. Pip saw me, frowned as if he didn't quite recognize me, smiled when he realized he did, caught sight of the shawl around my shoulders, frowned again and turned back to the women. Immediately I knew that I had done something wrong. He'd lent me the shawl on the understanding that I was going to use it for my play; to wear it off-stage was like an actor wearing stage make-up to a post-performance party; it was unprofessional; worse, it was a betrayal of Pip's generosity and trust. And so he snubbed me.

I felt a hand on my arm. It was Bradley. "Yule," he said, "what a lovely young woman you are." Not "Hello, chicken," which was what he'd called me all the years he and my father had run Fourth Wall together. He began asking me the questions that adults always ask children: about school, friends, activities; but they were sincere, he wanted to get reacquainted after the hiatus during which his life and my father's had diverged so drastically. The reunion was swift and easy. After only a few minutes I found myself telling him about my play, and how it was based on my grandmother's Siege diaries, and I thought how strange it was that my father and I had never talked about the Siege, or even Babushka. I wondered why it was so much easier to tell Bradley, whom I'd hardly seen in the past two years, than Papa. And then it occurred to me that, from very early on, I'd been muzzled by a profound and inarticulate sense of duty to protect Papa from even the smallest hurts (the assumption was that he'd already suffered far too much); and I asked myself why I should have to play guardian, when after all he was the adult and supposed to protect *me*.

As I was telling Bradley the plot of my play, his gaze suddenly shifted from my face to somewhere beyond my shoulder, and I knew he'd stopped listening. I turned around and saw why. Slowly down the stairs from the mezzanine came a black-caped figure, tall, with some of her blonde hair piled up on her head while the rest curled down in ringlets in front of her ears. It was Ursula, of course, and what had caught Bradley's attention was that beneath her cape she was wearing the black velvet hot pants she and I had seen in a Kerrisdale shop window.

Her long legs were stockinged in the sheerest black hose, and she was wearing a blue-grey silk blouse that was the very colour of her eyes. She advanced towards us. I could see that Bradley was enchanted. He gave a slight bow, a smile quivering at the edges of his formality.

"This is my friend Ursula," I mumbled.

"Delighted," Bradley said.

When Ursula looked me up and down, I dropped the shawl from around my shoulders as if that would make it invisible. She said nothing, but I felt her disapproval. Then the warning bell rang.

Bradley said, "I'd better go see if your dad needs any help," and left us by the corridor that led backstage.

Ursula strode towards the auditorium and the crowd stared after her. Wearing hot pants to opening night was both daring and not quite respectable.

As we settled into our seats she asked, "Where did you get that shawl? It's totally wrong with what I chose for you. Did Bette give it to you?" There was disdain in her voice, but by the way she fingered the material I knew she found the shawl beautiful, and probably far too good for the likes of me.

"I got it from Fourth Wall's costume department," I told her. "It's for our play."

"Oh?" Ursula said.

I paused for a moment for what I considered to be dramatic effect, then added, "You're going to wear it."

Ursula nodded as if she had known all along that the shawl was destined for her. She sat with her cape draped over the back of her seat and the arm between us. Its lining was an icy blue that contrasted perfectly with the blue grey of her blouse. A faint sheen of flesh showed through her black hose, and her thighs, which spread only a little against the seat, looked both elegant and athletic. I was tempted to reach out and run my hands over her just for the sensation of all her textures, from her elaborately fine hair, down over the filmy silk of her blouse, the nap of her velvet hot pants, the smooth, cool satin of her cape's lining and especially her stockinged legs.

As the lights dimmed briefly to warn the audience that the curtain would go up in another few minutes, my father appeared, with Bette walking beside him and Bradley pushing his chair up the aisle, as he had always done from the time they'd mounted their first production together, Jean Genet's *The Maids*, eleven years earlier. Bette sat down beside Ursula and Papa transferred into the aisle seat beside Bette; Bradley took his chair away and, just as the lights dimmed a second time, slipped into the row in front of us and gave my father a thumbs-up sign.

When the curtain went up, a surprised but approving *ahh* went through the audience, not just because of the intense yellow light that heated up the scene, but also because the stage was covered in sand, and as the actor playing the bridegroom entered from upstage left it rasped under his feet.

"Weird," Ursula whispered to me.

I looked over to where Papa sat at the end of the row and saw that he had taken out a notepad and his special pen with a light on it. He'd discovered the pen during one of his stays in hospital, when he'd watched the night nurse writing a note on his chart with such a pen so that, without carrying a flashlight, she could see what she was writing. He'd carried one in his pocket ever since, and now, as he made his first note, the light jiggled and leapt just beyond the outline of Bette's spreading belly.

For the second scene the lighting became rose and copper, still hot but more benevolent, as the mother-in-law began to sing a lullaby to the child while the mother sat nearby mending stockings. The melody keened through the audience while the words told the legend of a great horse who came wounded and dying to a stream but would not drink. The song was both terrifying and a talisman against terror. I glanced towards the aisle and once again saw my father's pen flickering just beyond Bette's belly, it too warding off danger with its leaping, jiggling dance — a formidable enemy for the blood with which Ursula and I had cursed Bette and the foetus growing inside her. For the first time, as I watched that light dancing its fairy jig, I connected the foetus with my father, and understood that, by cursing it, I had also cursed him.

At intermission the audience came up to my father in ones and twos to welcome him back to Fourth Wall and congratulate him on the staging of *Blood Wedding*. It had always been easy to tell if a show was going to be a success by how many people stopped on their way up the aisle to speak to him. If a play wasn't going well they hurried past with averted eyes, or in implausibly intense conversations with their companions. And all the time, because Bradley had parked his chair in the check room, Papa was trapped in his seat. I often thought that, whether or not the play was a success, those intermissions must have been among the worst moments he ever spent as a director.

When Ursula and I headed up the aisle to get coffee, we met Pip on his way down. I was no longer wearing the shawl, and apparently he'd forgotten about it, because as he jogged past us he called out, "Hello, lovey. Can't talk now. Word is that Leonardo's darts are too tight, so I've been summoned." He fluttered his hand at us in greeting and farewell. Meanwhile on stage two crew members dressed in their blacks raked the sand smooth, as if they were trying to tidy up the passions of the lead characters before the play turned into a tragedy.

When we got back to our seats, Ursula turned to Bette and asked her, "Have you ever worked on sand?"

Bette said, "No," and they continued talking, too quietly for me to hear, until the house lights went down.

Later, up in the mezzanine at the reception that followed the play, I asked Ursula, "Why are you being so nice to Bette? Don't you want the blood curse to work?"

She answered, "I'm not being nice to her, I'm using her. You want me to act Luba just as well as I possibly can, don't you?"

"Yeah, sure, I suppose...but...."

"Don't you understand? I've got her to give me all kinds of tips about acting. Maybe I'll have her come to one of our rehearsals."

"Don't you dare," I said. I didn't want Bette and her fat belly anywhere near my play.

Across the mezzanine Pip and Simon stood close together, sculpting the small space between them into a discreet tenderness. I knew that after the reception there would be another party for just the cast and crew, and there they would be able to abandon discretion and touch each other as they needed, dancing together perhaps, Simon resting his head against Pip's burgundy velours shirt like an infant lying on a velvet pillow.

Near the staircase, Bradley and Bette were toasting my father with champagne served in crystal glasses instead of the plastic ones from the downstairs bar. I pulled Ursula away from an admirer, a short, loquacious woman I'd seen around the theatre many times but whose name I didn't know, and took her over to Papa.

"That sand was pretty strange," Ursula said to him. "It made me want to take a shower, but that scene with the moon and the beggar-woman who turned out to be death — that was just great."

My father thanked her and turned to me, hungry for praise, or perhaps only reassurance. I wanted to say something lavish or daring, as if I were the one wearing hot pants, but instead I could only echo Ursula.

"It was great," I said, and as I spoke I felt tears in my eyes because everything was the same as it had been in the past — the theatre; opening-night nerves and exhilaration; the reception with champagne — yet somehow it was all infinitely more fragile. My father said to me, "You are so grown up." There was tenderness in his voice, but also reproach, as if my grown-upness was pulling him towards something faster than he wanted to be pulled. I remembered how, at the end of the first scene in Act Three, the beggar-woman had hobbled on with her back to the audience. When she reached centre stage, in one swift predatory movement she lifted her arms so that her shawl flew out like the great dark wings of a dreadful bird. Then the lights faded to black in absolute silence.

Notes for *The Survivor*. Scene Two.

Luba arrives weak, cold and frightened at Tanya's apartment. Tanya calms her down, gives her something warm to drink. Luba tells how she lost her sled because of a man who offered her black-market meat (like Babushka and Lev Antonich). While Luba tells the story, Tanya takes down Luba's hair and combs it. (Ursula will love this, the whole school will get to see how beautiful it is. I'll get to touch it. I wish my hair was like hers.) Tanya promises Luba that she'll find her another sled.

At our next rehearsal, Ursula drawled her words so that she sounded the way Papa once had when he was in hospital for an operation on his spine and the doctor gave him morphine to ease the pain. I thought she was making fun of me or the script so at first I ignored her, but when she suddenly started to recite the lines very quickly, so the words exploded like the artillery fire in Babushka's diary, I said, "Are you going to work like a serious actor or what?"

Ursula dropped her script on the table, walked over to me slowly and folded her arms over her chest.

"Don't you know what I'm doing? It's something Bette taught me. She said you can learn a lot about a character by alternately reading the lines slowly with the emphasis on the vowels and fast with the emphasis on the consonants. That's how you learn about a character's energy level."

She stared down at me and I thought to myself, *If I don't come up with something good, she's going to take over the play.* I looked up into her eyes and said quietly, "That's just an exercise. It's the sort of thing you try when you're working on the script by yourself, which *you* never do. If you were a professional actor you'd already be *off book.*" I used "off book" purposely, to prove I knew far more about theatre than she did. Her steady gaze only tottered for a moment before she answered, "*You* haven't even finished writing the play. You're just a typical lazy Slav."

I tried to laugh away Ursula's words, which I knew originated not in her mind but in her parents' minds, perhaps, or their parents' — words out of history that sent a shiver of rage up my spine. I thought, *She's not my best friend at all. She's the enemy.*

Just then Willi walked in and sat down on a chair at the opposite end of the room.

"I've come to watch," he said, as he took out a cigarette and lit it around his words. "Mutti says I ought to attend plays and concerts instead of driving about in her car all day, so here I am." He drew in the smoke, held it for a minute and then exhaled. "By the way," he said to Ursula, "Mutti wants you upstairs."

"What for?" she demanded. "Doesn't she know we're rehearsing?"

"She says you didn't wash the dishes properly."

Ursula looked at Willi, then at me. She suspected something and didn't want to leave. I looked at Willi to see if he was playing a trick, but his thin lips were set naturally and his eyes told me nothing.

Ursula threw the script down and left the room. Her feet pounded the stairs as she went up. Willi laughed. "That'll keep her busy for a while," he said. "Come on. Let's go."

"Where?"

He took a joint from his jeans pocket and held it up with his fingertips for me to see. I followed him to the basement door and out into the garden, though it felt like a betrayal, not so much of Ursula as of the play. It was a cold night and I was wearing a thin sweater. He led me in among the shrubs at the side of the house, where we were sheltered a little from the wind. I looked up at the sky, where a crescent moon lay on its back, lazy and cold-looking. Beside me I heard the strike of a match. I turned to see Willi bring the flame to his mouth, where he was holding the joint between two fingers. He sucked at it, the tip caught fire, then he inhaled with three sharp hisses. A few moments later smoke meandered upwards to a lit window six feet above us. I began to shiver. He put his arm around me and passed me the joint.

"You didn't invite me to the opening night of *Blood Wedding*," he said. "I think you like Ursula more than you like me."

"She's my best friend," I answered, trying to ignore what I'd thought about her just a few minutes earlier.

"And what am I?"

I looked up at his strong cheekbones. He had a half-starved look about him, just like the captured German soldiers in Babushka's diary. I almost said to him, *I think you might be the enemy too.* But he put his hands on my shoulders and kissed my lips. His breath smelled of cigarettes. I kissed him back, put my arms around him, rubbed my hands up and down his back and over his shoulder-blades. Immediately I felt warmer.

"So you like me a little," he said, and a strange, almost flabby look, which I understood as gratitude, came over his face.

I wondered if the soldier in Babushka's diary might have looked like that if, instead of throwing the piece of broken plaster at him, she had offered him a crust of bread.

Willi sucked on the joint again. Slowly he brought

his face close to mine and touched my lips very gently with his, again and again, until my own lips parted and he blew the smoke into my mouth. I choked and started to cough.

"Shh," he whispered, pulling my head to his chest to muffle the sound. "Papa's upstairs and he has very good ears." Then he started to laugh silently, his chest shaking beneath my cheek.

I heard Ursula's voice calling me and felt myself stiffen in Willi's arms.

"She's really got you scared, hasn't she?" he whispered.

"We're supposed to be rehearsing," I answered.

As I pulled away from him, the basement door opened and Ursula walked into the square of light cast by the upstairs window.

"Julie," she called again, and walked across the lawn into the darkness.

I crept past the shrubs and back through the basement door. Willi didn't try to stop me. When I got inside I made for the washroom, and ran the tap until the water was as cold as the air outside. Bending over the sink, I washed out my mouth to rid it of the taste of smoke; then I stood before the mirror, combing my hair and waiting for the excitement to fade from my eyes and cheeks. Beyond the bathroom door I heard Willi saying, "How should I know? I went outside for a smoke." I flushed the toilet so that Ursula would think I had good reason to be in the bathroom; then I went out to meet her.

"You weren't in there a few minutes ago," she said, speaking in a tone that demanded an explanation, but I didn't answer her, and we walked in silence back to the rec room.

Even though the opening night of *Blood Wedding* was over, Ursula and I still kept going downtown on Saturday afternoons. But without any shopping to do we dawdled around the stores, our hands moving listlessly through racks of clothing, all energy gone from our fingertips, which were used to exploring the texture, colour, drape and possibilities of this or that blouse, dress, scarf, coat, trousers, skirt. Both of us were bored. I began to dream about Willi. I played and replayed the night he'd interrupted our rehearsal: the lazy moon, his arms around me in the cold night, the light from the window above us, the psychic shift in the world after a few tokes. These dreams devalued Ursula, making her an obstacle, interesting chiefly for the fact that she was Willi's half-sister. I searched her face and her demeanour for resemblances. She and Willi had the same forehead. They shared a gesture of the hand, abrupt and dismissive — a rapid flick of the wrist away from the body, the fingers stretching almost to rigidity before they relaxed back into grace — and I found myself ready to provoke Ursula's annoyance just so I could watch her use it. Almost. What kept me secretive and circumspect was the warning she'd given me in the maternity shop, but I found myself more and more inclined to disregard it.

Of course there was still the play. I'd finished Scene Two, and one afternoon when we'd scheduled a rehearsal for four o'clock I suggested that, instead of going downtown, we might stay home and start working earlier. But Ursula's refusal was fierce.

"I want some fun," she said. "I'm so bored with all that Russian suffering. We suffered during the war too, you know. I'd rather go slumming around department stores than start rehearsing any sooner than I absolutely have to."

And that's what we did: Woodward's, The Bay, until we got to the cosmetics counter in Eaton's and she announced that she had to go to the washroom. I didn't go with her, but stayed to sample the lipstick testers on the counter beside me.

Mechanically I marked the white skin on my wrist with all the colours of lipstick, from orange through red and fuchsia to purple. There was no sense of discovery about it. I was putting in time.

"I'd get that one if I were you," a voice said, as a nicotine-stained finger touched the slash of fuchsia on my wrist.

It was Willi.

"What are you doing here?" I asked.

"I've been following you."

"Ursula's gone to the can," I said.

"I know," he answered. "Let's get out of here."

"But she...."

"You'll have a lot more fun with me than with her," he said.

I hesitated. *Slavic Schlumpe...just a warning*, Ursula had said. Twice now I'd followed Willi when he asked me to. He was becoming a habit. I knew that when Ursula gave warnings they were meant to be heeded, but I couldn't resist: it was as if this were a natural consequence. Enlisting his help to persuade Ursula to do my play had led, by way of an after-school drive and a cold moonlight toke-up, to this moment, and so I went with him, all the while knowing that there would be still more consequences, and that they all had been set in motion by histories we were helpless to ignore.

Willi led me down and down concrete steps to the lowest level of the parking lot, where his mother's Karamann Ghia was parked.

"Where are we going?" I asked.

"Up and out and into the light," he said. He turned on the ignition and the engine roared off the concrete walls. Level by level we spiralled up through the parked cars, and true to his word he drove out into the light, which did not shimmer or flash against the chrome of headlight casings or hood ornaments, but descended in a grey drizzle from beyond the tops of office towers whose windows reflected only other office towers.

We drove over the Burrard Street bridge, where a few weeks earlier we had been stopped in the dark by the burning wreck. I wondered what had become of the driver: if he was still a prisoner of pain in a charred body, or if, like us, he'd risen up and out and into the light, neither shimmering nor flashing nor drizzle-grey, but merely blank.

There were trees and the light was greener on the Kitsilano side of the bridge. Willi drove among leafless chestnuts along streets with evergreen names — Arbutus, Hemlock, Larch — until we reached Trafalgar, named for a battle a century and a half earlier and a continent and ocean away. He pulled up in front of a dark green, dark-windowed clapboard house that looked unwelcoming in spite of a straight path that led to an open front door.

"Who lives here?" I asked.

"It's not who lives here, it's what we can get here," Willi answered, holding his thumb and forefinger together in what I might have mistaken for an okay sign or the eyehole in half of an exotic mask, but when he brought them to his lips I knew he was making as if to smoke a joint.

"They're drug pushers?" I cried.

"Shh," he said, throwing his arm around me and laughing. "We don't want the neighbours to know, they're only supposed to *guess*."

Inside, the rooms were as dark as the windows had hinted. The smell of dog hung around the dim and tattered couch and overstuffed chairs, and there was also the stronger odour of rotting dog food.

"Hello," Willi called out, his voice faint, travelling only as far as the short distance we could see. From one of the back rooms came the sound of electronic music with a heavy rock beat.

"Anybody home?" Willi called again, his voice more self-assured this time.

"Yeah, whadda you want?" A bearded face appeared in a doorway. "Oh, it's you." The face belonged to a thin, ropy man in his mid-twenties who was dressed in a collarless Indian cotton shirt and jeans. "Come on in," he said; then, as if seeing me for the first time, he added gruffly, "Not her."

So Willi left me alone in the front room. If I hadn't needed to pee I'd have stayed where I was, but my full bladder sent me searching for a bathroom. When I started down the hallway a large shape emerged out of the murk at the far end. It was a woolly mongrel, part English sheep dog, old and fat, and as it came closer my nostrils caught the stink of shit and another unhealthy smell that I couldn't identify. How different from Callack, who smelled of the fields and woods of Lisii Nos; even when she found something stomach-turning to roll in, she always came back to the house full of doggy pride as if to say, *Smell how clever I am; I know you don't like it, but you'll just have to accept it because it's me.* But this old mongrel passed by me, a stranger, without even stopping to sniff, and went on into the front room, where I heard it groan as it settled itself heavily on the floor.

I reached the doorway of the room the music was coming from and couldn't resist looking in. No daylight illuminated it, only a small bedside lamp with a red scarf draped over the shade.

"Come in," a throaty woman's voice said. "Welcome to my night."

I hesitated, almost ducked out, then changed my mind.

A woman of about thirty, but with a ruined face that made her look more like fifty, sat cross-legged in one corner of the room. She was wearing what looked like a bedsheet wrapped around her torso. A leather thong fastened around her neck kept the cloth in place over her large breasts. Though the room was chilly, her shoulders were bare, and her feet were bare too. Her one concession to the cold was that she wore a pair of long johns beneath the sheet.

All four walls were painted black, and on them were the heavens: the solar system along one wall, the northern sky on another and the southern sky on a third. The windows were covered over with tarpaper to which were tacked luminous cutouts of the sun in various stages of eclipse, and one very large and lurid globe.

"That's the sun in its death throes," the woman explained. "And that is the dog-star, Sirius," she added, pointing to a bright star near the edge of the northern sky. "Sirius the *dog* passed you in the hallway."

She looked at me as if what she had said was full of significance. The electronic music narrowed into a high-pitched waspish noise that flew through my cranium, back and forth between the speakers. It was the sound of spiteful galaxies beaming maledictions at the earth, and all earth's creatures were its victims: the dog-star cursing the dog, killing the sun, shrivelling friendship.

The electronic noise dwindled into the helpless sound of the tape as it spun off its reel, like a fish flopping in the bottom of a boat. Then there was a silence that lasted and lasted — not like my father's taut silence, full of desperate creation, but flaccid, with an unhealthy smell like the dog's. When I looked back at the woman her eyes were long-standing blank, as if she'd forgotten all about me hours ago.

I left her just as I had found her, sitting cross-legged in her artificial night, and continued to the end of the hall, where through a half-open doorway I saw a dingy toilet and smelled something foul enough to make me gag. I had to pee so badly that I went in anyway. As I squatted over the toilet bowl I saw, in the opposite corner under the sink, a pool of vomit and another of soupy shit. I tried closing my eyes to keep from retching, but it didn't help, and as soon as I'd finished peeing I ran back up the hallway, through the front door, and burst into the fresh air.

Willi was waiting for me on the curb with a small parcel in his hand. Neither of us was inclined to loiter. We got into the car and drove off.

118

August 7, 1942

Today I took Xyusha and Nikolenka for a walk. In the Summer Garden people were harvesting cabbages: row after row where there used to be lawns. If the Siege is not lifted, we will at least have cabbages for the winter.

We walked along the Moika to where it meets the Griboyedov Canal, which we then followed down to Nevsky Prospekt. It was a fine day, and I noticed how ruddy Nikolenka's skin has become. He and Xyusha both are beginning to look healthy again, though they are still very thin.

On the buildings there were signs posted: In case of shelling this side of the street is most dangerous. *We heard artillery fire in the distance. We hear it almost every day.*

A man with a hand-held line was fishing in the canal, and for a moment we stopped to watch.

"Good day," he said to us. He had a bald spot on the crown of his head that was fierce red and peeling, though he did not appear to be bothered about it, and had no hat to protect himself from the sun. Beside him stood a cane basket that must have been thirty years old. The children were fascinated and went to inspect it, but when he opened it up for them there was nothing inside.

"Do you really expect to catch fish here?" I asked.

"Oh yes," he said and, turning to Xyusha, added, "Maybe even a sturgeon." It took her only a moment to see that he was joking, though Nikolenka repeated to himself, "A sturgeon. A sturgeon," as though he could almost taste it.

I gazed down at the water, where the façades of the buildings opposite us were reflected. It was calm, so that the image was perfect, and the very stillness of it reminded me of a photograph from before the Revolution.

We said goodbye to the fisherman and began to retrace our steps, towards the Church of the Blood. One of its domes was hit by a shell, but it has since been repaired with plywood and, though I looked carefully, I could not tell from where I stood which dome was damaged.

Suddenly there was a shrieking sound and a crash that deafened me. I tried to gather Xyusha and Nikolenka to me, but a shock wave knocked me to the ground. As I fell, I thought I saw the fisherman get to his feet, but he kept rising into the air and, limbs splayed awkwardly, he floated for a moment like a bird held aloft by wind currents before falling into the heaving canal waters, which only a few minutes earlier had been so calm.

I think I must have lost consciousness. When I came to myself, the shock waves had subsided and my ears were ringing so that I could not hear anything. There was a moment of calm or numbness, I am not sure which, and then I remembered the children. I felt a warm body at my side, looked, saw Xyusha and, a few feet beyond her, Nikolenka, face down on the pavement.

"I am all right," I heard him say through the ringing sound. Beside me Xyusha whimpered.

"Are you hurt?" I asked her.

"My leg."

I sat up and examined her. She had a cut down her right shin, but nothing looked broken. Nikolenka crawled over to us. He was bleeding from the mouth.

The ringing in my ears still had not gone away, and I thought that perhaps it never would. I might be going deaf, and I wondered what would happen to me if I could not hear the notes on the piano as I played them. But through the ringing came cries of My God; Help me; My arm; Mercy, oh, mercy. *I wanted to run away from those cries, with the children, but I knew I had to stay and help.*

I stood up and told the children to go to the Church of the Blood and wait for me at the entrance.

"The worst is over," I said. "Do not be afraid."

Nikolenka looked up at me and replied, "I am not afraid." And I saw that what he said was true: neither was he trying to be brave, nor was he in shock. Xyusha took him by the hand, and I watched them stumble down along the canal towards the church before I started walking back to the place where the shell had exploded.

A woman stood up, began to brush herself off, stopped and sank back to the ground. I went over to her and found her unconscious. At first she didn't appear injured, but when I lifted her head my hand suddenly felt warm and wet and, pulling her face towards me, I discovered a heavily flowing wound on the side of her head, just above her ear.

There was the sound of running footsteps, and a motor. A grey-haired woman carrying a canvas bag crouched down beside me.

"Can you help her?" I asked.

"I will try," she answered. Then she looked at me and asked, "Are you injured?"

"No," I said. "I do not know. I cannot hear properly." I began to get up, because I could still hear cries and groans through the ringing in my ears. I caught a glimpse of a foot in a laced-up boot ten metres away from me. I sat back down. It occurred to me that there was something wrong with that foot, but it took me several seconds to understand that it had been blown off someone's leg. All around me I heard shouts and soothing murmurs as the cries and moans began to subside. Two men passed me carrying a stretcher. The injured were bandaged, lifted, carried away. The ringing in my ears distanced me from the scene as I watched it. It was clear that the injured had no need of me, and I turned towards the canal. The water was still again, and it reflected the façades of the buildings on the opposite bank, but in the middle of that reflection the fisherman's body floated, his legs tangled in his line.

EIGHT

Willi drove the car along Broadway, past Alma, to where it merged with Eighth Avenue, and up to a playing-field that overlooked Jericho School. He parked and, taking a packet of cigarette papers out of the glove compartment, opened the brown parcel of dope and rolled a joint with his yellowed and agile fingers. I looked out past the school, its walls as white as deafness, to English Bay, where two freighters were anchored, and beyond to the mountainous North Shore. The afternoon had begun to brighten, and the long light of the sun marked out the contours of the slopes and the upstanding trees, snow-covered near the summit and lower down a hue that had something of the sea in it, more glaucous than evergreen, while the late blue shadow in the valleys was so dark it was almost black.

Willi lit the joint and passed it to me. I sucked on it, my mind anticipating the easy high before it suffused my body.

"Give it to me quick," he said suddenly, and for a moment I wondered at his greed before he hissed, "Cops."

A police cruiser was coming up Eighth Avenue, and as it crested the hill an officer wearing a peaked cap peered at us through the passenger window. I lowered my eyes and listened. The car slowed down, stopped for a long moment, then continued. When I looked up again it was turning left three blocks away.

"The pigs think only hippies in vans toke up," Willi said, "so I wear short hair and drive Mutti's car, so respectable because it's expensive. Anyway the hips are dying out because they're just a bunch of brain-fried sheep."

We sat passing the joint back and forth while a cruise ship steamed out past Brockton Point and the late sunlight gilded the large windows of what must have been its forward lounge. I felt settled and leisurely, as if we were two middle-aged people sitting on its deck somewhere in the Caribbean, sipping at our evening drinks while we passed nuts back and forth instead of the joint. I'd have been content to stay there the rest of the afternoon.

"Ever seen *Last Tango in Paris*?" Willi asked, and in that question I sensed a purpose and immediately felt wary.

"I'm not old enough," I said. "Neither are you."

He rolled his eyes. "What a prude. If you obey all the rules you'll never get anywhere. I've already seen it twice, and I can get you in too, even though you're only fourteen, if you stop behaving like a silly schoolgirl."

I looked at my watch. It was a quarter to four. If Willi drove me straight home I'd just make it on time to my rehearsal with Ursula. But what excuse could I make up for abandoning her in Eaton's? I knew I shouldn't worry about that when the really important thing was the play, but Willi had already turned on the ignition. The dope had left me inarticulate, as had the dread of confronting Ursula. And beyond that, and more significant, was a growing conviction that whatever Willi did was inevitable, as if he knew exactly where he was going and how to get there; his avidity was stronger than my own inchoate aspirations. As we turned onto Discovery I felt that being dragged away from the serene view of English Bay with its ambience of physical comfort and peace of mind was like being a child abducted from her parent. Willi drove as far as Tenth Avenue and

123

parked in front of the University Cinema.

"Wait here," he said.

He got out, went straight up to the open door and talked to the ticket-taker, who disappeared for a moment and came back with a woman who walked with Willi outside the theatre past posters advertising *Cabaret* with Liza Minelli and *Man of La Mancha*. They stood together, she with her back to the wall, he facing her, hemming her in on one side with his hand pressed against the white tile façade. From where I sat it looked as if he might be kissing her, their faces were so close. At last he nodded, released her and they parted, she heading back into the theatre, he whistling towards the car.

"All set," he said as he got in. He drove onto a side street and parked.

As he led me up an alley to the back of the theatre, he put his arm around my waist, then stopped and kissed me full on the lips, his tongue exploring my mouth, his saliva familiar with the taste of dope. My own tongue was so sensitized I felt minutely each ridge of his hard palate. A car honked at us, and honked again. Only when a voice said, "Hey, you kids get off the road," did Willi and I, laughing, pull each other out of the way. For several minutes we stood outside one of the rear exits, until with a quiet thump it opened a crack. Willi opened it farther, just a body's width, then pushed me in in front of him and right away pulled the door shut again. We stood behind a velours curtain, his arms around my waist and his cheek against my hair, as we waited for the lights to dim, and I began to enjoy myself; I had stepped past the threshold of my compunctions and was safely inside an adventure.

As soon as the lights went down, before the audience had quite got used to the darkness, we sneaked out into the aisle and settled in seats near the front. When the curtain rose a cold draft blew over us, then there was saxophone music, and as the titles appeared on the screen beside Francis Bacon paintings the film slowly enclosed us.

I watched the film by touch. Instead of looking at luminous images projected onto a screen, I felt them through my vision: the vibration of a train roaring along an elevated rail; Marlon Brando's despair when he blocked his ears and screamed. It was as if I were groping at Maria Schneider's fur-trimmed coat, her hat, high boots, the very short yellow dress with the wide belt loosely slung over her fashionable hips. This was envy, and also arousal to what was beautiful and sophisticated and not within my fourteen-year-old range. I was particularly envious because at first glance Schneider reminded me of Ursula — not her colouring or her face, but her long legs and a sense of style that was European.

When Brando and Schneider, still wearing their clothes, began to fuck so abruptly, with much lust and very little passion, I remembered Christmas, when Nick and I had made love. Up until that moment the memory of it had warmed me with a sense of belonging, and it had made me feel more grownup than my classmates who did not yet make love with their boyfriends. But now my explorations with Nick seemed awkward and juvenile and not daring enough. I was aware of Willi sitting beside me, and I sensed how he divided his attention between me and the images on the screen. I wondered if he would put his hand on my leg, and when he didn't I tried putting my hand on his. He pushed it away. I guessed that he didn't want to dismiss me so much as divert my attention back to the film. But then I forgot about him altogether, because what came next was entirely familiar.

It took place in the hotel where Brando had lived with his wife, who had committed suicide. Brando's mother-in-law was searching through her daughter's room for a clue, an explanation of why she had killed herself. I remembered how doggedly I had searched through my mother's room the morning after she left. I was convinced I'd find a note written especially for me, which would explain clearly why my mother had gone, justify it and so make her abandoning me forgivable.

But there were other scenes that shocked me because I'd never imagined such things might happen. For example, Brando ordered Schneider to bring him a package of butter, then forced her onto her stomach and pushed his cock up her bum. It was only much later that I learned the word for what had happened was *buggery*. Beside me I sensed Willi's strong attention, no longer divided but focused entirely on me. I sat very still, trying not to let my naivety show. I wanted to be alone in a private screening-room where I could play and replay those images, not so much to understand them as to make them mine. This was what I'd been doing with my grandmother's diary: reading and rereading each entry until it became part of me. I didn't want to study it or analyse it or judge it or explain it, I merely wanted to transform what was outside into something inside.

When the film was over and the lights went up, Willi and I followed the paying audience out the same door we'd come in so surreptitiously. It was dark. I felt divided. I wanted to go home and sit alone in my upstairs room to think over all I'd seen that afternoon. I also wanted to stay with Willi, but in darkness, as we'd sat in the cinema, perhaps touching but without any words at all.

"I've got a place where we can be alone together," Willi said. His voice pleaded. It was an admission that he needed me and so I agreed to go with him. While we were driving down Tenth Avenue, I remembered a scene when Brando and Schneider were sitting together naked on the mattress that was the only furniture in the entire room. Instead of telling each other their names, they spoke their being in animal sounds, Schneider chattering like a monkey or some bright-plumed jungle bird while Brando grunted at her. I wished that I didn't know Willi's name and that he wasn't Ursula's brother. How much easier it would be if I were able to say to her breezily, "But Ursula, it was quite fantastic, a complete stranger came up to me while I was standing there waiting for you at the cosmetics counter and swept me right off my feet. I had to go with him. There was no other choice." I might have squeaked by with that; but to abandon her and go off with her brother.... I knew she wouldn't forgive me.

I hadn't been paying attention to where Willi was driving, so when he stopped the car, told me to get out and led me down a residential street planted, as many were in Kitsilano, with chestnut trees, I wasn't immediately sure why the solid lamplit steps halfway down the block looked familiar.

"But that's your place," I said a moment later, and began to pull away from him. "We can't go there. If Ursula—"

"She'll never know," he said. "Why do you think I parked so far away?" He put his hand on my shoulder and steered me past the steps to a gravel path that ran alongside the house under well-lit windows to the basement door. Once inside, he didn't switch on the light but, taking hold of my hand, and without once banging into a wall or doorway, led me into a darkness so labyrinthine I felt as if we were threading our way towards some secret hideaway far beyond the concrete foundations of the von der Lindes' house. At last I heard an ill-fitting door shudder as he pushed it open. The air was warmer inside and there was a smell of oil.

"Just a moment," he said. He let go of my hand and moved off silently, so that I couldn't even keep track of him by the sound of his footsteps. A moment later a light went on, and beyond the jog of a metal duct I saw him standing with an electric lantern in his hand. The light cast dark shadows onto his face, so that where his eyes were I could see only blackness. Beside me stood a furnace, monolithic in the small room, and behind it just enough space for the mattress that lay on the floor.

"Not bad, huh?" Willi said. "Warm, comfortable." He sat down on the mattress to indicate where, in that

127

cramped little room, the comfort was. "And the best thing about it is that nobody will ever guess we're down here." He sounded younger than the hard-smoking seventeen-year-old I'd first met; more like a nine-year-old trying to win me over so I'd join his game.

"It's kind of stuffy," I answered, but I made my way round the heating duct to be with him in the light.

He undid my coat and pulled it off my shoulders and, because I was warm and wanted to be rid of it, I kept my arms slack and let it drop to the floor. As I unzipped Willi's jacket, we knelt down together on the mattress. I expected him to be urgent and demanding, to want inside me right away, but what he wanted more was comfort, and he spent a long time arranging our coats, some old pillows and an afghan into a nest for us to lie in.

"You hungry? Thirsty?" he asked.

"Both," I answered. I hadn't had anything to eat or drink since one o'clock, when Ursula and I had stopped at a Chinese restaurant for lunch.

"Back in a minute," he said, tossed a joint and matches at me and left the furnace room, taking the lantern with him. He must have left the door open because its light swayed up and down the wall for a moment after he was gone, and cold air began niggling at my shoulders. I pulled the afghan over me like a shawl, lit the joint, and as I started sucking at it the furnace lumbered to work. I expected to feel warmer, but most of its energy went into heating other rooms, though its good-natured roar, which rattled the duct above my head, made that small, utilitarian room more friendly.

Not long afterwards light once again swayed up and down the wall towards me, and Willi appeared around the furnace carrying a feast.

"Mutti keeps an extra fridge down here," he explained as he set down a tray of dark bread, cheese, sausage, butter, a pot of water, instant coffee, cream and two large pottery mugs. "Very handy at a moment like this."

"But she must know when that much food's missing."

"Oh, we help ourselves to whatever we want."

He looked so easily domestic as he put the tray down, plugged in an immersion heater and set the pot of water to boil that I wondered if he had entertained other girls in his hideaway.

It was the best meal I had ever eaten. We lay in our nest of coats, propped up against the pillows, buttering bread, cutting slices of cheese and sausage, sipping at coffee. Hunger and dope made it all taste miraculous. And Willi was right: the furnace room was warm and comfortable, though we left the door open a crack so the air didn't get too oppressive.

"When I was a kid," he said, "my father used to make me sit and listen to symphonies by Mahler and Bruckner, and God, I hated them. It was like being in a straitjacket. I thought I'd go nuts. I thought I *was* nuts. I had to sit still in the living-room for an hour, two hours. Those guys were both so long-winded. I've never heard anything so fucking boring in my life."

"Did Ursula have to sit there with you?" I wondered. Ursula loved Mahler. She'd even sung me bits of *Songs of a Wayfarer* and *The Song of the Earth*.

"Ursula? She was just a baby. And anyway, my father would never make her do anything she didn't want to." He gave me a reproachful look, as if bringing up Ursula when he was talking about himself was an insult.

"But afterwards," he continued, "Mutti would feed me cheese just like this, and sausage and rye bread, and tell me how good I was to sit so still for so long and listen so well. Sometimes, Mutti would get out her cello."

"I thought your mother was a singer," I said.

Willi paused for a moment as if caught out. "She used to play cello too," he said.

He turned over, facing away from me. I put my arm around his waist so I wouldn't lose contact with him.

When he started speaking again his voice had a different quality, more remote but also more intense.

"She'd sit with the cello in front of her, I'd stand between her legs holding the bow, and with her own hand over mine she'd guide the bow over the strings. The sound was so deep and real, nothing like the cacophony of those Mahler symphonies: pure and singular and not a punishment; just Mutti and me; my father could go to hell."

He said the last words in a gasp, and the anger in them caught at somewhere inside me, just beyond memory: my prehistory, I thought. As I lay beside him I let his emotion wash away the debris around some precious fossil, a moment forgotten aeons before — not lost, but preserved like a fly in amber. I could almost see it, touch it; and then Willi said, "I have to fuck you. You're going to let me, aren't you?"

I was astounded that he had any doubts. From the moment he had seduced me away from Ursula in Eaton's it had been what I expected, and though his timing was off because he'd interrupted me when I was about to make a rediscovery, I still whispered to him, "I have to fuck you too."

They were the wrong words, and together with Willi's bad timing they stopped us hard up against an obstacle of incompatibility that we had to find our way around. So I helped him gather up the remains of our feast, and as I did we touched each other's hands, by accident at first and then more purposefully, until our separate skins were once again sympathetic.

We lay down together in our nest and took off our pants. As Willi pulled the afghan up over us, he kissed me on the lips and I felt a tension in him that I tried to ease by stroking his chest. He allowed it, but when I moved my hand down over his thighs he jerked away from me and I was reminded of the spasms my father sometimes got in his legs. Willi rubbed his hands over my belly, then reached inside my underpants and found my vagina, though I wasn't sure I wanted his nicotine-stained fingers there. I reached for his penis. This time he didn't jerk away, but when I found it, it was soft.

Suddenly I heard footsteps above us. "Who's that?" I whispered.

"It's probably just my father. That's the living-room up there."

I could also hear the sound of water running through pipes.

"Are you sure it's safe here?" I asked.

He took his hands out of my underpants and held his penis. Slowly at first, he began moving his hand back and forth.

"Tell me you like my cock," he said.

"Oh, yes, I do," I answered.

"Tell me how big you think it is," he said.

I thought it was probably not as large as Nick's penis, but I knew I had better not say so.

"It's...it's huge," I managed to stammer.

"How huge?" He was now moving his hand back and forth furiously and was getting red in the face.

"Twelve inches," I said.

"Twelve inches?" he replied, and the question mark in his voice sounded both threatening and comical.

"Oh, fifteen inches, at least...twenty inches."

"*Scheisse*," he said loudly and harshly.

"Shh," I whispered, "your father might hear."

"Fuck him," he said. "Fuck you, too." Then he pulled me roughly onto my stomach.

"It's going to be just like *Last Tango in Paris*, isn't it?" I asked.

"Yeah," he said, "even the butter."

I grew very still and alert. I thought to myself that I could, if I wanted, refuse to play Willi's game. But partly I was curious to live what I had so recently seen, partly I was mesmerized by the strength of his determination, partly I believed that, if I let him do whatever he wanted instead of imposing things on him as his father had, the

131

pain that his rebelliousness and love of destruction hardly masked would abate. He might end up writing a play like Ursula and me, or taking cello lessons again and becoming a musician. That was how people saved themselves. That was how my father had, so of course I believed it was possible for Willi — inevitable, if I could love him enough.

But as he slathered the butter around my bum and pushed it with his finger up into me, I discovered something quite different from what I believed about myself: I was incapable of making a choice; it was laughable to think I could impose anything on Willi; I was afraid of him, and so I submitted. My stillness was a paralysis of will, as real as my father's physical paralysis, and my alertness as futile as that of the citizens of Leningrad when German troops crossed the border and invaded the western forests of Russia.

And so I endured Willi as he pushed his now erect penis hard up inside me and tore the delicate tissue in a mock deflowering. He thrust hard against the back of my womb, and I retched from the pain of it but couldn't speak.

"What I told you before," he said, gasping, thrusting faster and faster as he spoke, "about Mutti and me and the cello was bullshit, complete bullshit, and only fit to stick up your...," he cried out, "*ass*," and he shuddered and shuddered and grew still.

I went black and then, hearing a rushing sound in my ears, came to. I've been in an accident, I thought, and something's fallen on top of me and I can't move. But then I became aware that the thing on top of me was warm and breathing, was Willi. He was the accident, and I'd allowed myself to be his victim. I pushed at him and, curiously tractable now, he rolled over, his penis sliding out of me like shit.

"Where you going?" he murmured.

"Out of here," I said.

"Jesus Christ," he said, "you were perfectly willing

before, and now you're mad at me."

I groped for my clothes, found my pants, my jacket, my socks, my boots, and put them on. I tried to find the electric lantern too, but Willi clamped a strong hand around my arm.

"Don't go," he said, "it's so good here, just the two of us." His voice was warm and like a giant sponge, ready to sop up the small puddle of injury I'd become.

I pulled away from him, stood up, stumbled from the mattress onto the concrete floor and groped around the furnace for the door.

"You'll never find your way out of here in the dark," he said. "Why don't you take the lantern?" But instead of offering it to me, he was taunting me with it.

I kept on going, through that labyrinth of concrete walls and hollow doors that sounded like poorly made drums when I banged into them in my blindness. At last I came through an opening into a paler darkness and, after feeling my way around a wood-panelled corner, discovered a high window with a latch which, when I opened it, gave onto the gravel path that ran along the side of the house. By the light that seeped down from the upper-storey window, I scrambled onto the ledge and escaped into a night that was lit with streetlamps and the newly risen moon.

I walked through the neighbourhood streets, only half knowing where home was, circling, yearning to go there but unsure of my bearings. What I needed was to be allowed to go up to my room, no questions asked about why I had missed dinner or the rehearsal with Ursula, who had probably phoned to ask where I'd got to. I was too distracted to make up lies and too humiliated to be able to tell the truth. The damp air was cold enough that I had to keep moving, and my brisk pace used up just enough energy to keep the recurring scenes from that day, which patterned and repatterned themselves on my retina like the translucent bits of glass in a kaleidoscope, from becoming unbearable. But eventually

133

my stride slowed, and when I looked up and saw the street names Thirteenth Avenue and Trutch I walked the two blocks down to Eleventh, where home was, three houses in from the corner.

Bradley Hamilton's much-loved and fastidiously maintained old Packard was parked outside. The front rooms — Papa's bedroom and the living-room — were both dark, and I thought to myself, *Good, they're all in the kitchen, I'll slip upstairs before anyone notices me.* But as I walked up the ramp to the front porch, the door opened and Bradley stood on the threshold, his back to the dim hallway.

"Thank God you've turned up," he said.

"Oh, I'm okay," I answered. "I just had dinner at a friend's."

I had hardly spoken before I understood it wasn't me he was worried about, and immediately I thought something had happened to Papa. But Bradley confounded me again.

"Your father has taken Bette to the hospital," he said. "She started bleeding...."

For a moment I couldn't grasp what he was talking about, and imagined she'd cut herself badly, with a kitchen knife perhaps.

Bradley went on.

"He phoned a few minutes ago. They're going to keep Bette in hospital. He said it doesn't look too good for the baby."

"She's going to lose it?" I asked, finally understanding.

"Could be."

A day earlier the news would have made me feel triumphant and powerful: proof that I could mould the world to my own needs, with a little help from Ursula and the blood curse; but now I felt injured and mocked by the news, and once again I could hear Willi taunting me: *You were perfectly willing before*, he said.

August 9, 1942

*I took Tanya to hear Dmitri Shostakovich's new sym-
phony this evening. I had to barter my winter hat and three
cucumbers to get a ticket for her, because everyone in Leningrad wanted to hear it. I remember how, in September last
year, Shostakovich spoke over the radio. In spite of the war he
was working steadily on his new composition, and had just
completed the second movement. He said that if he finished
the third and fourth parts, he would call it his Seventh Symphony. But what I remember most about the broadcast is how
he called upon all his fellow musicians to continue working
for music in spite of the bombs and the shells and the nearness
of enemy troops.*

*Tanya did not want to go with me; nothing interests her
any more. But I kept thinking that, if she heard live orchestral
music again, she would somehow be shaken out of her apathy.
I put on my best dress and got out Tanya's best dress too: a
pale blue silk with lace set in the yoke. She stared down at it
and asked, "Is that mine?"*

*I was shocked. She had got it only last summer and had
been so proud of it. "My first really grownup dress," she had
said to me. But today she looked at it as though it puzzled her,
and as though she found it offensive. I left her to take Xyusha
and Nikolenka to stay with our neighbour while we went to
the concert, but when I got back she still had not dressed.*

*"My Tanyusha, my sunshine," I said. "What is the
matter? Why will you not put your dress on?"*

*She said, "Mama, I do not know how to wear a dress
like that." I held her in my arms for a moment. Then slowly
and gently, as though I did not want to frighten a small, wild,
nervous creature, I unbuttoned her blouse. She allowed me to
do it, but she did not help me. I wondered to myself if she could
not. Finally I got her ready for the concert. I gave her my amber beads and even put some lipstick on her mouth. She looked
beautiful, or should have, except that she was not really wearing the dress. It was on her body, that was all. And she walked
stiffly in it, as though the light, delicate material encumbered
her.*

135

When we arrived, the Philharmonic Hall was crowded. It seemed to me that the whole of Leningrad was there: artists, writers, dancers, musicians, military and political leaders. It was such a fashionable crowd, at least by Siege standards. We were all wearing the best we had been able to save from the winter. As Tanya and I passed a woman wearing a ruby brooch with her emerald-coloured dress, I heard her say that she had bartered her best pair of boots for it, because during the winter she had traded her own jewellery for bread.

We sat in good seats in the orchestra. The evening sunlight poured through the windows, most of which had been repaired after the shelling, and glowed in the amber around Tanya's neck. The chandeliers were lit, too. I thought how glorious it was, after a winter of cold and darkness and starvation, to have survived and witnessed the return of light.

But it was not until Karl Eliasberg stepped onto the podium that I really believed the concert was going to take place. The first few bars astounded me. It was so long since I had heard a full orchestra, and the energetic, self-assured, even happy phrases of the first movement reminded me how powerful live music is, because each note filled the hall in a way no radio broadcast can fill a room; and I thought about the circumstances under which the symphony had been written: first under enemy attack; then under siege; then in exile after Shostakovich was evacuated to Moscow.

During the performance there was artillery fire, but the guns hardly interrupted it; the symphony played over the noise and at last vanquished it. Not only was there music again; the triumph was that guns could not silence Shostakovich or the players and could not deafen the ears of the audience. I looked across at Tanyusha to see if she felt what I did, but her hands lay listlessly in her lap as they have ever since she learned of Luba Sokolova's death, and if there was any expression on her face it was one of boredom. Suddenly I felt very angry. I could hardly believe Tatiana was my daughter. If she could remain unmoved by such an experience — the light, the music, the silent audience, the defeated noises of war — then she could not be a Leningrader, or a Russian. It was as if, in her *beautiful pale blue dress, she had betrayed me. I watched as her hand rose slowly to her neck, hesitated and fell back into her lap while she let out a deep, shuddering sigh. I was no longer angry. I was afraid.*

NINE

That night I couldn't sleep, and not only because of the wind that made the clouds churn at the boundary between foul and fair weather. I kept seeing the look my father had when he came back from the hospital, of someone hard up against the edge of suffering — different from how he looked when he was in physical pain. Then the anguish came and went with the twinges in his back, but now it was unremitting.

He asked me, "What if I lose her too?"

And I understood that his misery came not just from his fear that Bette and the baby might die, but from the memory of all the other losses in his life: his childhood because of the war, his ability to walk, his marriage, his health, his job.

I felt guilty for wanting to get rid of the baby, but much more for my father's sake than for Bette's or the baby's. What I felt about the blood curse was more complex. The fact that Bette had gone to hospital bleeding and about to miscarry should have strengthened my belief in it, but I felt responsible for the pain I'd brought my father and Bette: I had excluded myself from the happiness they'd asked me to share and, by wishing Bette harm without considering my father, had brought harm upon them both.

And about the previous day's events I felt only shame. Like a coward I'd sneaked off with Willi without a word to Ursula, and in the end I'd been humiliated.

Willi had hurt me physically, but worse, he'd manipulated me into accepting that hurt by telling me about his mother and the cello and, when he'd got what he wanted, by insisting it was all a lie. But his story was precious to me because it had revealed the edge of a memory of my own, which I now began to uncover.

That night had been turbulent too, but with the moon high, full and restless, wandering in and out among the clouds. My mother was in her pale room, lying on the narrow bed. A basin of water and Epsom salts, once hot, now growing cold, in which she'd been soaking her sore dancer's feet, was sitting on the floor beside it. I'd tiptoed in because I wanted her to sign a slip that gave me permission to go on a nature trip to Manning Park with my school. Usually I got my father to do such things because he was more willing, and took some pleasure in hearing about my school outings and projects; but he was already asleep, and I had to get the slip signed by the next morning or miss out on the trip.

Her eyes were closed, and when I spoke to her in scarcely more than a whisper, asking, "Mama, are you awake?", she groaned, looked at me and answered, "I've got such a headache; I ache all over. Go and get me some Aspirin, will you?"

I hesitated for a moment, wondering if I should ask her to sign the permission slip before I went for the Aspirin. It was almost impossible to get my mother to do what I wanted. She usually sidetracked me so that I'd find myself running errands for her or watching her as she worked out a new dance sequence; and then she'd decide she was late for some appointment or rehearsal and I'd be dismissed before she had to listen to me, never mind respond.

As usual, I did what she asked: went into the bathroom, got her a glass of water and two Aspirins. But as the water was running into the glass I remembered that, whenever my father had a headache, he liked to have a cold damp cloth on his forehead, so I rinsed my facecloth in the basin, wrung it out and took it to my mother as well.

"You took long enough," she said, reaching out for the glass. "God, how I hate that wind." While she was still drinking I folded the damp facecloth and placed it across her forehead.

"What...?" she began, the alarm in her voice almost palpable; then she relaxed into the comfort of it. "Thank you," she said, "my darling."

I pulled the permission slip out of my pocket. My mother's eyes were closed again.

"Mama, I need you to sign this."

She half opened her eyes and glanced at the paper.

"Yes, of course," she said. "Just give me a minute." She touched her hand to my facecloth. "Ooh, that feels good. Come and lie down beside me." She moved over on the narrow bed.

I hardly believed what I'd heard. She rarely offered me more than a kiss, and that only when she was headed off somewhere and could easily escape any threat of intimacy.

Cautiously, as if she were made of glass, I lay down on the bed. My muscles grew tense with the effort of keeping near the edge so that a small space remained between us, and I found myself holding my breath. But she put her arm around me and pulled me closer. Several times she began to speak, but changed her mind. At last she said, "Can you keep a secret?"

"Yes."

"From Bradley, from your Aunt Xenia, from your father, from everyone?"

"Yes."

"You're the only person in the world I'm telling this to, so you must promise not to say anything at all."

"I promise," I whispered, feeling honoured that she thought me worthy to confide in, but alarmed by the knowledge that the secret was so important to her that she wanted no one else in the world to hear of it.

"I'm going to have a baby," she gasped. I lifted myself on my elbow to examine her, thinking she must be in pain, but as I watched, the corners of her mouth turned up into the slightest smile, and her skin, which always appeared taut over her prominent cheekbones, relaxed so that her face became suddenly rounder and kinder. She turned to me.

"Would you like a baby? A little sister? A little brother?"

"Oh, yes," I said, and thought how that meant I'd never feel lonely again.

"Which do you fancy? A boy or a girl?"

"A boy," I answered. Spending summers at Lisii Nos with Nick had made me yearn for a brother.

"Yes," she said, "I think I'd like a son." Then suddenly her voice was sharp. "You understand that your father mustn't know, not just yet. I want to make sure everything's all right before I tell him."

I was used to having to protect my father, and I hardly bothered to imagine what those vague words might mean. A week earlier he'd had a mild bout of flu, and I assumed my mother wanted to make sure he had completely recovered before she gave him the pleasant shock of announcing her pregnancy.

She and I lay on her bed for an hour or more talking about what our lives would be like once we had the new baby, and I think that then, and for the next few weeks, my mother really believed the proliferating cells in her womb were a magic great enough to right all that was wrong in her relationship with my father. At last she dismissed me, saying that it was after nine and I should already be asleep, although I usually didn't get to bed much before ten. After I left her I realized I must have dropped the permission slip somewhere in her room. I thought I'd get her to sign it early in the morning before I left for school, but when I woke up she was already gone, and though I searched her room I never found it.

During the weeks that followed my mother's confession there was a bond between us that I'd never known before and haven't known since. As usual she was too busy to spend much time with me, but I suspect that in our private moments, before we went to sleep at night or during the timelessness between one diurnal event and the next we shared the same dream — to be a real family: mummy and daddy and daughter and son, spending our evenings and weekends together, working on family projects like the building of a sundeck, perhaps, or eating popcorn in front of a blissful fire, or camping beside a wilderness lake, singing songs while my father strummed a guitar, never mind that he didn't own a guitar or that the wilderness was hardly accessible to a man in a wheelchair. If my mother's dreams were different in content, I suspect they were just as unrealistic. She wanted what I did: for the crippling in us all to be healed.

That Friday afternoon when most of the rest of my class left on the nature trip to Manning Park, I came home from school early. As I opened the front door, my mother was just coming out of my father's room. She was wearing a heavy dressing-gown that belonged to him and her hair was uncharacteristically dishevelled. When she saw me, a strange progression of emotions crossed her face: guilt, embarrassment, betrayal, futility; and there was no pleasure. Whatever I did or didn't know about sex at that age, I could see by her wanton hair and my father's dressing-gown so intimately wrapped around her body that she craved pleasure, had expected it and been disappointed.

"It's all right. It's going to be all right," she muttered, as much to reassure herself as to communicate anything to me. "I think maybe I'll make a cup of tea," she added, her Englishness asserting itself in a time of disaster. As she disappeared into the kitchen, I ran upstairs to my own room and pretended the pain I'd seen in her face was less real than the fantasies I'd concocted about the little brother she would never give me.

As the memory slipped away, I got up from the bed and stared out my window. In the darkness the grass, the trees, the hedge had become indistinguishable, lacking density, their presence made real only by the wind that vaguely shaped their movement, but at the end of the yard the telephone pole and the swaying wires, dangerous with electricity, stood out sharp against the light-washed clouds.

Amid everything that had happened that day, probably nothing made me sadder than the sudden realization, while I was watching *Last Tango in Paris,* that the love Nick and I had shared at Christmas had become a devalued and childish thing. By following Willi through his labyrinth to the mattress behind the furnace I'd arrived in a darker world, where motivations were never clear and cruelty was inescapable. He had hurt me and hurt me again. It was no accident. In all the years we had played together, Nick and I had never willingly inflicted pain on each other. Looking back, I realize that I didn't know what innocence was before I met Willi, who taught me what innocence was not. The lovemaking with Nick certainly had been innocent, an adolescent game to replace the childhood games we'd abandoned. Now I knew that if I ever went to him again, I would be wary, afraid of being hurt and capable of hurting. I wanted to protect Nick and the innocence we had shared. At the same time I no longer respected him because he had not yet discovered cruelty.

I decided to write him a letter. After many starts and stops and scratchings out I ended up telling him I'd found a new boyfriend, and he wasn't to expect me to go to bed with him over the spring break, which, as usual, I was going to spend at Lisii Nos. I added that I hoped we would always be friends.

Of course, the letter was a lie — Willi was not my boyfriend — but at least I hadn't declared that I loved him. I suppose I claimed Willi partly to rescue my pride, and partly because I knew another boyfriend was something Nick would understand and accept. If I confessed my hurt, he would simply put his arms around me and kiss me until our separate and personal needs compelled us to make love: his to reclaim me, mine to repair the illusion that sex was an expression of tenderness and regard.

When I'd copied out the final draft of the letter, the wind had died and the clock beside my bed showed twenty-seven minutes after three in the morning. I went to bed and quickly fell into a blank sleep. When I woke up, beams of weak spring sunshine lit up my room. There was even a little warmth in them, and I experienced a moment of wellbeing before memory chafed at the wounds from the day before. It was after eleven, and when I got up and made my sluggish way downstairs, the letter to Nicholas in my hand, I discovered I was alone in the house. Within a few moments I'd convinced myself of catastrophe: Bette had died; my father was alone at the hospital in despair and near death himself. But on the kitchen table I found a note from him that was telegraphically brief but reassuring: *Gone to hospital; Bette improved; Bradley bringing dinner.*

After I'd mailed the letter and made myself a cup of coffee and a slice of toast I went back upstairs. The dilute sunshine lit up the untidiness in my room: the clothes thrown over the chair and tumbled onto the floor, the unmade bed, the layer of dust on the desk. For a sullen moment I flopped down on the bed; then, discovering a need for order as compelling as hunger or thirst, I opened the window to let in the fresh Sunday air, made the bed, put away my clothes, dusted and vacuumed, all the while wondering how to approach Ursula. I hadn't seen her or talked with her since I'd left her in Eaton's, and consequently my head was full of melodrama I'd picked up from movies and TV: she would put a contract out on me (*Julia Kabalevsky sleeps with the fishes*), or poison me with arsenic, or inject air into my veins. I hardly dared think of the more realistic probability that she'd refuse to work with me on the play.

Rescued from chaos, my room became a haven. The sunlight enriched the dark finish on my old desk and made the pad of ruled foolscap look so pristine, so attractive, that I sat down in front of it and took out a pen. That small, unpremeditated act decided me: I was going to finish the play, then seek out Ursula and offer it to her as an apology with the hope that it would lure her back to rehearsals.

"Only let it be good enough," I whispered as I sat pen in hand, hesitant to commit the first word. It was a long time before I jotted down my ideas.

Notes for *The Survivor*, Scene Three, Luba's apartment.

Luba is lying in her coat on the bed, which is piled high with blankets and shawls to keep her warm. The room is lit by a single candle. There is a knock at the door. Tanya enters. She has come to atone for New Year's Eve, when she gobbled down Luba's only piece of bread. *I have a new sled for you*, she says. Tanya has brought it to replace the one Luba lost, but Luba is dying so Tanya can never really atone for her moment of greed. She asks Luba's forgiveness, but Luba doesn't know what she's talking about. Only her own death has significance, and it is very near. Tanya stays with Luba until she dies early the next morning. Unlike Luba, she has not yet understood that her greed doesn't matter. She thinks it is her fault that Luba has died. *If I had not stolen her bread or drunk her wine...*, she tells the audience. *If...if....*

I spent all afternoon writing dialogue from those notes, breaking only long enough to make myself some tea and a cheese sandwich. A little after five I put my pen down. The play was finished and, though I was tired and the muscles in my shoulders ached a little, I felt at ease. The sun was low in the sky and the ill-kept laurel hedge that separated our yard from our western neighbour's cast its long shadow across the grass and partway up the fence on the opposite side. From the front of the house I heard the sound of an engine. I went into Bette's room to find out who it was and saw my father getting out of the car into his chair. I ran downstairs to open the front door for him, and as he wheeled himself up the ramp I saw that his face was serene.

"She's going to be all right," he said, "and the baby...as long as she's very careful and rests, the baby's going to be all right too." He spoke hesitantly, as if the words were not really his and he distrusted them. I wondered if he'd so surely expected a loss that he was now reluctant — almost sad — to let it go, because loss was certain, while hope was capricious and full of peril.

Bradley arrived soon after, and Papa and I gave ourselves up to his pampering. We were both exhausted, Papa from his vigil at Bette's bedside, I from the accident of Willi and the long afternoon with my play. I was light-headed, too, as if I hadn't yet come down from Saturday's dope-induced high. The food Bradley made, an ordinary lasagne, was delicious, almost as good as the meal of bread, cheese and sausage I'd eaten with Willi, and I thought how odd it was that when my head was in chaos I could so much enjoy the very basic pleasure of eating.

That evening I felt especially close to Papa — partly, I think, because Bette wasn't there, but also because the antagonism I'd once felt towards her had set up a barrier between Papa and me that I hadn't noticed until it was gone. And our states of mind were similar: we shared a curious slackness, a passivity that I think Bradley mistook for relief.

I wasn't a stranger to this disquietingly flaccid mood. The summer I turned nine, Uncle Alek, who was still on good terms with my father, drove us — Papa, Mama and me — out to a cabin owned by some friends of his on a lake. We arrived in time for lunch, then spent the afternoon on the float. I don't remember exactly how my father got down there, I only recall him lying on an air mattress at the very edge of the float, his hand trailing in the water. The property was situated in a part of the lake that was no more than a quarter of a mile wide, and Uncle Alek decided to swim across to a dock almost directly opposite. He asked Mama to go with him, but she said the reflection of the sun on the water was too hard on her eyes and she was going up to the cabin to lie down in the shade. I'd been chasing a water strider in the shallows, but as soon as Uncle Alek and my mother left I climbed up onto the dock, dove in, climbed up, dove in again, over and over. Diving was a skill I'd learned only a month before, from Nick, when I was staying at Lisii Nos, and I wanted Papa to see me and applaud me, but I'd been afraid my mother might criticize and Uncle Alek mock me. Papa clapped and shouted, "*Molodets,* good girl," and I preened with a pleasure that came partly from knowing he was himself incapable of diving.

But once when I surfaced I looked up and he wasn't there; only the air mattress lay along the edge of the float. I thought he'd fallen in and was drowning in the depths of the lake. There was no one to help. I dove under and couldn't see him, but when I came up for air a voice called out, "My sunshine." I swung round and saw Papa swimming towards me from ten yards away in a strong overarm stroke. For a moment I thought a miracle had happened, but when he drew up beside me I saw that his legs hung inert in the water, and only his arms propelled him.

"Why don't you and I swim across the lake too?" he asked, pointing to the dock on the far side, which Uncle Alek had just reached.

"I couldn't swim that far," I said as I watched Uncle Alek climb up the ladder to the deck and stand looking

147

across at us, or more likely for my mother, in among the trees.

"I couldn't swim that far either," Papa said, laughing.

Papa and I stayed in the shallows with the water striders. We swam close, matching each other stroke for stroke. I looked across the lake and saw Uncle Alek dive in again and start butterflying his way back. Papa and I luxuriated in the warm water, our feet inadvertently touching bottom from time to time, stirring up silt that muddied the normally clear surface.

"My arms are getting tired," I confessed at last.

"Hold onto me then," he said.

I grabbed his shoulders and my weight pulled him under. When he broke the surface again he was laughing.

"Around my waist, not around my neck, you donkey. Do you want to drown us both? Now, you kick and I'll pull.... That's it," he said when I'd got it right.

Along the shoreline we swam, like the upper and lower parts of the same creature, or like water striders making love. At last he grew tired too; we separated and swam back to the float. Awkwardly he pulled himself out of his freedom into the unsupporting air and lay beached across the air mattress. Just then Uncle Alek arrived back at the float, and as he climbed the long flight of stairs to the house to get changed, Papa sighed and closed his eyes. I was overcome by a sense of inertia. At first I thought I was simply tired, but that didn't explain why I felt so depressed.

Half an hour later Uncle Alek and my mother came back down to the float. Drearily I watched as Alek crouched over my father, offering him a glass of vodka, which he put beside the air mattress. Papa pushed it away and it fell over. "You know I shouldn't drink," he said, as vodka spilled over the smooth wooden planks and trickled down between them into the water. My mother laughed. Not at my father. She was staring with delight at Uncle Alek's muscular thigh as he rubbed suntan oil into his skin.

Bradley left early, around nine o'clock, saying that Papa should try to get a good night's sleep.

As I started up the stairs to my room Papa asked, "My sunshine, what's going on?"

The question confounded me. I hadn't expected him, with all his worry over Bette, to have enough energy left to consider me.

"What do you mean?" I asked, stalling for time to think how to answer him.

"Ursula phoned yesterday in the middle of everything. Her voice was shaking. She said you'd gone off with Willi. But I had to cut her short. And now today you look so fragile."

"I'm just tired," I said quickly.

"And Willi?"

"Nothing happened," I said, but my voice sounded too cool.

"If he did anything...," he said, ready to call up paternal fury.

"No," I answered, because there was nothing he could do to ease the shame I felt for allowing Willi to humiliate me. "I'm okay, Papa, really," I added, and ran upstairs before he could ask any more questions.

I went into Bette's room and dialled the von der Lindes' number, terrified that Willi might pick up the phone. After the third ring Ursula answered.

"I've finished the play," I said.

There was a very long silence. At last Ursula replied in a neutral voice, "So you'd better bring it over tomorrow night. Eight o'clock." Then she hung up.

The next night, in silence, I handed the script over to Ursula. When she finished reading it she looked up and said, "My God, you Russians are so gloomy. If I'd been running the war I wouldn't have bothered to invade

Russia. Who'd want to conquer such a dreary, boring country anyway?"

It was the old, familiar, critical Ursula, in her perverse way inviting me back inside her friendship. It would have been so easy to laugh off her words and pretend they hadn't hurt me. But I didn't. Neither did I have the courage to tell her to stop. I undid my satchel and handed her the shawl.

"Let's do a read-through," I said.

Ursula settled down into the lines faster than I did. In spite of myself I dreaded and hoped that Willi would arrive. Three or four times I thought I heard footsteps on the stairs; but little by little the play world became real, and I forgot him. Instead I held Luba in my arms, and as I helped her through her dying the lines took on all the tenderness Ursula and I felt for each other, and for a few moments brought us closer than we'd ever been before. I touched her hair and her shoulder, felt my cheek close to hers. *I am not afraid*, Luba whispered, and Ursula rested her head against my shoulder. Her hands slipped down over my chest. I kissed her on the temple. When Luba died I pulled the flowered shawl up over Ursula's expressionless face, which the harsh fluorescent light in the rec room had turned cadaverously pale. I watched as the fine wool trembled slightly from Ursula's warm breath, though Luba lay still and cold beneath it. When the scene ended Ursula sat up, the shawl still covering her face. Slowly it slid down from her forehead past her cheeks and mouth. She took hold of my hand. "What if," she asked, "when Luba says, *I am not afraid*, you kiss her on the mouth instead of on the temple?"

"We could try it," I answered, but as soon as I spoke Ursula shook her head.

"No, it was a dumb idea. Let's start the scene again."

For the next two weeks we endured a climate of extremes. At school our encounters were frigid, the few sentences we spoke to each other punctuated by the cold, blank silences of unuttered emotions that centred around Willi. But downstairs in the von der Lindes' rec room we worked steadily, carefully, with increasing concentration and commitment, to prepare the play for its first public run-through, which was to be for our drama class. Gradually the moments of touching between Luba and Tanya became routine. There was nothing of Ursula or me inside the scene except our actor selves, who were trying to find the best way to make the lines work.

Willi had not interrupted our rehearsals once during those two weeks, but suddenly, the night before the run-through, he appeared in the doorway with someone I immediately recognized as the woman from the green clapboard house, who dwelt in the black room full of stars. She was still wrapped in her bedsheet, over which she wore a bulky man's pullover with holes at the elbows.

Slowly Willi took out a cigarette and lit it. The woman didn't acknowledge me. Perhaps she'd forgotten we'd ever met.

"We thought you might want an audience," he said.

"Tomorrow's our dress rehearsal," I replied.

"All the more reason for us to stay and see if it's any good."

Ursula didn't say anything. Her face had the blankness of a mask. She was trying very hard for invulnerability.

"Let's do the last part of the second scene," I said, "from *I felt a hand on my shoulder.*"

We'd become so used to the particular kind of concentration scene work demands that soon I and, I think, Ursula were aware of Willi and the starwoman's presence only as something peripheral and unimportant. For the moment my play had become a shield against the personal anguish Willi so easily aroused. At one point I sensed vaguely that he was kissing the starwoman; then, more keenly, I felt them leave. But as soon as we'd finished, their absence throbbed through me: an insult, a rejection, a condemnation. I guessed that Willi had taken the starwoman through his labyrinth to the mattress behind the furnace. And when I looked at Ursula, her mask dissolved for a moment, and I was sure she knew about the mattress — and I suspected that her parents did too, but that they conspired among themselves to deny it.

After lunch the next day our drama class gathered in the auditorium to run through all the plays for the first time. Ursula and I were on third, and as we sat in the darkness, watching the first two plays, my heart started to pound. I hardly saw what was happening on stage. Tanya's lines kept going through my head, and occasionally Luba's, but whenever I tried to remember what came before or after any particular line I went blank and grew still more nervous, until my hands sweated and trembled in my lap.

When our turn came, we were so busy arranging the stage and checking the props that the tension eased a little; but in that moment of quiet, as we waited for the stage curtains to be pulled back, my mouth went dry and I wanted to both pee and throw up at the same time.

The curtain parted; then the light came up and glared down on us. I was aware of the audience sitting beyond the edge of the stage. They were an expectant, judging blackness, but their faces were indistinguishable. Ursula said the first lines. My memory answered her, while the rest of me searched for something familiar in the stage glare and the blackness to unite me with the freezing apartment in Leningrad where Luba and Tanya tried to celebrate a starving New Year's Eve by candlelight. Then even my memory left me, and I sat under those bright lights not knowing whether Ursula should be speaking or I, or which scene we were performing. *Am I going to faint*, I wondered, *or die?* But Luba was saying, *The Spassky chimes will be playing the Internationale,* and Tanya's voice, my voice, responded, *We must listen to the radio then.*

After that, not only the lines came easily, but the stage movements too. I held the scene and the auditorium in balance. While I knew I was playing before an audience of my own classmates, I was also a starving Leningrader. If anyone had asked me, I could have described the siege world that existed outside Luba's apartment: the corpse in the stairwell beyond her door; a frozen, silent streetcar in the road below; bursts of artillery fire; a knife glimmering in candlelight as it was raised above its victim in some cannibal's lair in the Haymarket. And across the table from me sat Ursula-Luba, both performing and under siege at the same time. She caught me stealing her only piece of bread, which I had cut from a loaf Bradley had baked and brought over to the house the day before. *If you are that hungry, then you were right to eat it,* she said, Luba-magnanimous and Ursula-arrogant.

The scene ended to the sound of applause and the jerky sway of the closing curtain. Ursula stood up from the table with a smooth, self-confident movement. Her cheeks were flushed. I thought that I had never seen her so excited. She put her hand on my arm, but her touch was light and controlled.

"So far, so good," she said, putting the same emphasis on each word; but at the end she added, "huh?", a short, light exclamation that flew up towards the stage lights and released all the expectation and excitement she was otherwise so careful to contain. I wanted to hug her, but during the weeks of rehearsals we had learned to work with a professional discipline I didn't want to betray now that we were enjoying our first success.

Next came the scene at Tanya's apartment, where Luba arrived for comfort and help after she had lost the sled. As Tanya I lit a fire in my tiny, makeshift stove and sat Luba beside it. I heated up some ersatz coffee for her while she talked about the man who had accosted her and offered to sell her meat patties. I listened to her description of the Neva River at twilight, the icy steps that led up to street level, the squeak of the sled runners, a corpse fallen beside a lamppost; and though I was only half aware of what was happening to me, I started to lose my balance. The stage and the audience began to disappear, and the Leningrad apartment became real.

As I took down Luba's hair to comb it, I began to feel cold and weak and hungry. I sat as close to the little stove as I could and enviously watched Luba sipping at the hot coffee. For a moment I wondered why I was spending energy combing her hair; and in the next moment I understood, as I never would have if I had kept the audience and the play in balance, that I was searching for lice. The Siege, the real Siege, had begun to seep through the spaces between the words. I ran the comb carefully through the roots of her hair near her scalp, and after I found each louse and caught it, I squashed it between my thumb and forefinger. I half heard a noise from somewhere beyond the little room where Luba and I were sitting. It sounded as irrelevant as the buzzing of a fly. Luba faltered as she spoke.

What happened after the man showed you where you would have to go to buy the meat patties? I said, to encourage her, because I wanted to hear the rest of her story.

She looked at me hesitantly. I heard the noise again, and this time I recognized it as laughter. Suddenly Luba stood up, except that she wasn't Luba at all, but Ursula.

"What's going on?" she said.

I'm just searching for lice, I answered, still as Tanya, though I was beginning to lose my balance again, and when there was more laughter — loud, derisive, unsympathetic — I fell out of the play world we had created and watched the curtain sway as someone mercifully shut it.

I thought, *They don't understand about lice, not even Ursula. That's how it would be. That's how it really is.* I looked at Ursula's face. Her cheeks were still flushed, but her eyes were hostile. There was a tightness in her neck muscles. Her lips were moving. She was saying words, but I couldn't yet listen to them, because I was fascinated by the miasma rising up between us, the unacknowledged conflict that was in our blood, a legacy from our parents: it was our destiny to play it out as they had a generation earlier, but in our own way.

I felt a pain in my arm and looked down at Ursula's hand as it squeezed me just above the elbow. My white shirtsleeve bunched around her fingers, which looked pale and bloodless. I knew immediately that if I hadn't lost my balance I wouldn't have seen her hair as anything but long and curly and shiny with cleanliness. She thought I'd been trying to make fun of her. I started to tell her I hadn't been, but then I saw her lips move again and I heard her say, "Willi."

"He would never have brought that slut to the house if it hadn't been for you," she said.

The curtains parted and our drama teacher stood in front of us. "I thought this play had another scene in it," she said.

Neither of us could speak.

"I don't know what's going on between you two, but either get on with the show, or get off the stage and give the others a chance. You're wasting everybody's time."

Coming from performing families, both Ursula and I knew she was right: this wasn't the time, not quite yet. For a moment we stared at each other, gauging, challenging, coming at last to an unspoken agreement. Ursula made a show of arranging Pip's shawl around her shoulders.

"Let's take it from the line where Luba says, 'I hadn't seen Alexander Andreyich since the beginning of the war.'"

Ursula nodded. Then she said, in a neutral voice that she had to work at to control, "Only don't touch my hair. Don't come anywhere near me."

She sat down and began to warm her hands over

the make-believe stove.

It was a good play, I thought, and I suppose I expected admiration from my classmates and teachers. I wanted them to come up to me and tell me how it had frightened them, or made them cry, or at least say that they didn't know people in Leningrad had suffered that much. And I expected surprise: we didn't know you could act; we didn't know you could write a play; we didn't know you could make all that history so real. But those few raw moments they'd witnessed between Ursula and me confused them, and made them shy. I suppose they wondered if they should be taking sides, and which side was the right one. Though I sensed that they were more curious about me than they ever had been before, there was something clandestine and prurient in the attention they paid me. That afternoon as I was leaving school a group of girls standing in the hallway started giggling as I walked past them, and immediately I assumed their laughter was directed against me.

Outside I walked behind the tennis courts, down the alley of hawthorn that led to the school's rear gate. Ursula was waiting for me beside one of the older and larger trees, which in a month would be heavy with fragrant blossoms but was now bare, its armour of spines visible among the branches. As soon as I saw her I began to apologize.

"I wasn't trying to make fun of you, please understand," I pleaded. "I love your hair. I would never do anything...I just got lost in the story and I forgot we were acting."

Ursula said nothing, but stood with her arms folded, staring me into silence. And the miasma started rising again.

"You know," she said, "that day in the maternity store when I called you a Schlumpe, a Slavic slut, I thought I was joking, but that's exactly what you are. Look what you did to Willi. You seduced him with your

156

silly lie about smoking dope, then you went off with him and left me all alone in Eaton's and he's never been the same since." She coughed to cover up the emotion that cracked her voice as she spoke.

"What did you do to him?" she demanded. "He would never have brought that woman to the house if it hadn't been for you."

This was the second time she'd spoken about the starwoman, and I remembered how, the night before, her mask of imperturbability had disintegrated for a moment; but the lapse had been so brief that I'd had only a glimpse of the emotion beneath. It was not mere distaste, or even disgust, but undisguised horror — and not because the woman was ruined, but because for the first time she'd understood her brother was ruined too, and that the starwoman was his perfect companion.

"What did you do to him?" she demanded again.

"What did *I* do to *him?*" I said. "You think it's my fault he's such a mess? Why don't you ask him what he did to me? You think I'm the first person he ever fed and fucked on that grubby mattress of his in behind the furnace?"

"Shut up," she cried. "Stop telling those Slavic whore lies."

"You're the one who's lying," I said, "but only to yourself. Willi's a jerk, an asshole; you just don't want to admit it."

Ursula came at me then, screeching like a cat as she pushed me back against branches of the spiny hawthorn. I received the scratches with deep relief, because the frozen silence between us had at last been transformed into pain and blood. When I pushed her to free myself from the spines, she tripped over a root and fell. In a moment I was on top of her. Her hair was spread out, shining and vividly human against the dark subtlety of the earth, and amid the decaying leaves I imagined I could smell the burgeoning shoots and tightly wrapped buds of early spring. She struggled beneath me and I tried to pin her arms down, but she was stronger and heavier than I, and in a moment we had rolled over in the dirt and she was on top. She sat across my pelvis and held me down by the forearms with her strong pianist's hands. As she brought her lovely Teutonic face close to mine, her hair fell across my forehead, and for the first time I noticed a scar at the edge of her eyelid. In a low, intense voice, her lips almost touching my cheek, she said, "During the war we thought the Slavs were subhuman."

Her words invaded me. *Subhuman.* For a moment I believed she had unearthed in me the very deepest truth. *So that's what I am,* I thought. It explained so neatly why my mother had left my father and me. I stared up through the hawthorn branches into the clear sky. Since that day I've never been able to look at that particular blue without anguish. Ursula's face was still very close to mine, and her weight on my pelvis both oppressed me and set up a physical yearning in my groin.

No, I thought. *This isn't real, it's only what Ursula wants me to think. A tactic.* This was, after all, a war.

"No," I said to her out loud, and that one word unbound my speech. "You're a Fascist, is what you are. Do you know what you did to the gypsies and the Jews and the Slavs during the war?"

"Don't blame me for what happened," she said. "I wasn't even born. And what makes you think you Russians are such saints? Just ask my mother what a Russian soldier did to her in East Berlin in 1955. Yes, that's right, the year Willi was born. The reason he's such a mess is because he's half Slav."

"You're lying," I said.

"No I'm not, you Russian whore."

And as I had found my voice a moment before, I now discovered my strength. I struggled free of her and stood up. Then, just as she got to her feet, I ran at her and pushed her off balance.

"Don't lie to me," I growled.

She stumbled and I pushed her again, this time with all my fury. As she fell backwards her face went comic with surprise; then she hit the ground.

"Oh God," she cried.

The thick sound of pain was in her voice. Her right forearm looked as if it had suddenly grown a strange excrescence.

"Look what you've done, you've broken it."

August 27, 1942

As Xyusha and Nikolenka grow fatter and healthier, my Tanyusha continues to lose weight. Her face is sallow, and her skin so dry that it flakes off her legs. Yesterday she had another bout of dysentery. I took her to see the doctor, who gave her some powder and ordered her to rest in bed. This morning she was no better. She said she felt nauseated, though she had not vomited, and she is irritable this evening. When I gave her some cabbage soup at dinner-time, she said that it was too thin, and not good enough to feed even to the Germans. I then gave her some bread and a little of our precious butter to eat with it, but she complained that it tasted worse than the small chunks of cellulose and sawdust we ate last winter. She did not sound like my Tanyusha at all. Her voice was harsh when she spoke. Still, I prefer this irritability to her usual listless state. I do not want to say that it gives me hope, but a person must have energy to be irritable, and it has been so long since my Tanyusha has had any energy at all.

September 21, 1942

For the past few weeks we have heard artillery fire in the distance as our troops attempt to force the Germans back across the Neva. They have tried once already and failed, but there are rumours that they will make another attempt soon.

Meanwhile I teach my three students at the conservatory. After the deaths and evacuations, three is what I have left. We work very hard, all of us, harder than before the Siege, even though we have not yet fully regained our strength. We lost so much time during the winter, when it was too cold and dark and we were too weak to work at all. Next week there will be a recital and all three are ready to perform in it. I am so proud of them. If Tanya is well enough, I want her to attend.

October 9, 1942
My Tanyusha is very ill. She stays in bed all the time, while her bouts of dysentery make her weaker and weaker. She has odd fancies. Two days ago she kept asking for caviar and refused all other food, saying that only a lovely little spoonful of black caviar would make her feel better. I spoke to some of my colleagues at the conservatory and eventually found a man who sold me fifty grams for fifty rubles. How my mouth watered as I spread it on a piece of black bread for Tanya; but when I gave it to her she took a bite and spat it out into her hand. She said it tasted bad and made her feel sick. In the end, Xyusha, Nikolenka and I shared it while Tanya sipped at a glass of tea.

October 10, 1942
Tanya is dead. This morning very early I woke up and heard her calling, "Mama, Mamochka." When I went to her I found that she had soiled her bed. As I cleaned her up, she smiled to herself. I asked her, "Are you happy this morning, my Tanyusha?" She did not answer. Sometimes her lips moved, and when they did I stopped what I was doing and listened, in case she had anything to say to me. Three or four times she said, "Mamochka."

When I had finished cleaning her up and had put fresh linen on her bed, I made her some tea, which she drank only when I held the glass to her lips. At last she said to me, "Everything is kind this morning. You are kind this morning. My bed is kind and so are the walls and the pictures on the walls, and the curtains, and the grey sky." She was looking out the window as she spoke.

I sat quietly beside her. Neither Xyusha nor Nikolenka had awakened yet, and the room was peaceful with their slow, even breathing. I thought how similar Tanya's mood was to the quiet, tender mood I had experienced at dusk last winter when I started to pull Nikolenka's sled with its load of water homeward. I had counted the corpses along Nevsky Prospekt and knew that, if I wished to, I could sink down beside them in the snow. Then I met Lev Antonich. I have since heard that he was shot, but for what crime I do not know. As I sat with Tanya I realized all of a sudden that if it had not been for Lev Antonich, who roused me from my torpor, I might have died that day; and in the same moment I understood that my Tanyusha was dying and there was nothing I could do. I would not even be able to keep her alive long enough for her father — oh, my beloved Andrei — to return from the Front to say good-bye to her.

I sat for a long time and watched the surly grey clouds through the window. I have been busy this autumn and have seen the days pass only out of the corner of my eye: sometimes clear; sometimes dark and squally. I held Tanya's hand, and thought how Leningrad will probably spend another winter under siege. I do not think that our troops are strong enough or that we have enough tanks or weapons to break through the German lines. Yet, even as I sat there with my daughter, who I knew was dying, I felt strangely happy, almost light-headed. Perhaps it was because I knew I had really lost her months earlier, when Luba Sokolova died; or perhaps it was because there was no artillery fire.

At last Xyusha and Nikolenka woke up. They too appeared calm and quietly happy. We ate breakfast with Tanya in the bedroom (she only sipped at some tea), and I think all of us understood that the meal was special, although I do not think either Xyusha or Nikolenka knew it was the last time all four of us would eat together. Afterwards Xyusha and Nikolenka went outside, and again I sat with Tanya, who soon fell asleep. An hour later she groaned once or twice and suddenly awakened.

"Do you want something, my sunshine?" I asked, but she did not appear to know who I was. She closed her eyes again and opened them almost immediately.

"The sun is keeping me awake," she said irritably, and

asked, though I do not believe the question was directed at me, "Can't something be done about it?"

I closed the curtains, even though the grey day was becoming darker and it looked as if there might be a storm. Immediately she went back to sleep for the rest of the morning. In the middle of the afternoon I took some tea in to her, but I could not wake her although she was still breathing. Her arms lay alongside her body, and her palms were turned up. Her eyelids flickered, opened and half closed again, so that she appeared to be staring at me drowsily.

"I have brought you some tea," I said, because I thought that, if her eyes were partly open, she might be able to understand me, but she did not answer. She was completely still, and for a long time I could not tell if she was breathing. Beyond the curtains the day had become brighter again. I put my hand on her forearm and found it cool, and then I realized that it was not merely cool, it was growing cold.

I closed her eyelids and sat beside her body while I waited for Xyusha and Nikolenka to return. At last I heard the door bang.

"I'm so hungry," I heard Xyusha say. A moment later Nikolenka was standing at the bedroom door.

"Look what I found," he said, and held out an old samovar spigot for me to see.

TEN

It was drizzling on Good Friday when Papa and I drove out to Lisii Nos. I was going into exile, a kindly exile — I hoped, surrounded by the people who loved me. Ever since the day of the dress rehearsal I'd been in a mental fever, reliving the fight with Ursula: my elation when I finally found voice enough to call her a Fascist and strength enough to struggle free of her and push her and push her again until she fell, her face stupid with surprise; the sight of her arm, so awkward and ugly, and a small internal voice crying, *I won, I won;* a crowd of blazers and tunics gathering around Ursula and me, and among them a suit of heather tweed, the headmistress asking, "Did you do this? , my choked "Yes but...," and the sensation of something inside me diving — leaping up, out, then curving gracefully into a final sickening plummet as the headmistress's voice said, "Go to my office and wait."

Papa was silent as he steered the car past road signs that promised Hope was only seventy-five miles away, then sixty, then thirty-seven. *It's much farther away than that*, I thought, remembering the interview to which the headmistress had summoned me.

"Can you explain to me why two of our best students were fighting like hooligans?" "It was the play, I guess." "You guess? You don't know why you were fighting?" Oh yes, I do know, you silly old bitch, but I could never even begin to explain to you about Willi and the

163

war and being Russian instead of German, and how much I love Ursula and hate her because she called me a Slavic slut and subhuman, and how it turned out Willi, that asshole, that jerk, is half Slav like me, half slave to Ursula, so beautiful, so superior, and I hope she'll never be able to play the piano again, but her arm, oh, her poor arm, and to think that I've ruined her perfection, what I loved about her most, but you'd never be able to understand because you don't know anything about the Siege and how my grandmother and my father and aunt survived on a few hundred grams of bread a day, how Tanya died from malnutrition and hopelessness, how twenty million others suffered and perished, a million and a half in Leningrad alone.

I stood silent and stared at a letter opener on her broad oak desk as she forbade me to see or talk to Ursula for the rest of the term. Of course that meant the play was cancelled. Oh, the play. No, don't take the play away from me too. "And if I ever hear a whisper of a complaint about you, you'll be expelled." Just like Willi. I'm no better than Willi. "I thought you were a most remarkable young woman, and now I discover that you're a vicious little barbarian." Barbarian. Slavic slut. "I am most disappointed. You may go now."

When Ursula came back to school two days later she was summoned into the headmistress's office too. But later I heard that she had only been reprimanded, not threatened with expulsion, probably because she was the one wearing the cast. The unfairness of it, together with my grief over losing the play and the shock of having broken Ursula's arm, made me raw with conflicting emotions, but I had no close friends apart from Ursula, no one to confide in, and so, with all my energies turned inward, my confusion quickly abscessed into shame.

It's easy to turn someone who already feels ashamed into a pariah, and my classmates did so, while Ursula suffering in her cast became the romantic heroine that her golden hair already suggested. But I discovered that being a pariah was a belonging of sorts. Before Ursula had arrived at our school my classmates had not paid me much attention. Now they actively shunned me, creating and re-creating my isolation from classroom to gymnasium to playing-field. They had to work at it hour by hour, and though I was lonely I sometimes found myself energized by a perverse pride for claiming so much of their interest — until my shame, like a low-grade fever, once again left me enervated and depressed.

When I returned the shawl to Pip, he stood with his hands on his hips and asked bitchily, "So why didn't you invite Simon and me to your première?"

"It was cancelled," I answered, and stared straight at him, daring him to ask another question. A look of bewilderment came over his soft features. And then I realized there was something that had changed in me. Only a month or two earlier I'd have cast my eyes down at the checked cloth laid out on his cutting table — the deference of a supplicant — begging him not to probe any further.

Out of his own discomfort instead of mine, he turned away from me and walked over to the corkboard above the costume rack. With his graceful fingers he pulled the tacks out of a drawing and handed it to me to examine. "Macheath's costume," he said. It was a watercolour drawing of an evil-browed man in a rakish suit designed with tightfitting pants and a sharp-angled notch in the wide lapels. He placed his long hand on the bold black-and-white material on the cutting table.

"Like it?"

"Yeah. It's great," I said, and handed him back the drawing, dismissing not the design, but my old tendency to be overawed and far too humble before other people's cleverness. I handed him a plastic bag that contained the shawl.

He took it out with the delicacy that informed all his gestures. His examination was meticulous. He was making no allowances for the fact that I was little Julia and the daughter of the director who approved or rejected his designs. I loved his professionalism and suddenly found myself wanting to confide in him: to explain all about the play and why it had been cancelled, and maybe talk to him about Ursula. He would understand my loving her more intensely than I had loved any boy. But the memory of my very unprofessional act of wearing a theatre costume to an opening-night reception made me feel shy and unworthy.

He folded the shawl, put it back in the plastic bag and placed it on a small table beside the door to the costume closet. "It looks fine," he said. "You've obviously taken good care of it." And he smiled at me, but only with his lips. Then he went over to the cutting table and picked up his scissors.

"I've got work to do," he said. "You'd better be on your way."

I was already at the door when he asked, "Was it a good play?"

After a hesitation during which I relived the moment when the stage curtains swung jerkily shut on Ursula's hostile face and the audience's jeering laughter, I answered in a very quiet voice, "Yes, I think so."

"I'm sure it was," he said, his tone matching mine.

I opened the door and was half-way down the stairs before I realized that he hadn't offered me the key to the costume closet.

We drove past an access road along which stood a grocery store, a drugstore and a building supply, with its large sign on which a little carpenter was climbing a ladder to nail a red letter B to the white background. It wasn't the building supply where Nick worked, but for me that sign had always marked the border between Vancouver and Lisii Nos. I tried to conjure up the square green-roofed farmhouse, the paddock, the woodpile, the outbuildings, including the shed where Dedushka kept his

traps. Usually, by the time we passed the building supply, Lisii Nos was more real than Vancouver. But today I
was uneasy, and that unease kept it at a distance. In my
suitcase lay the translation of Babushka's diary, which I
intended to return to the trunk in the attic, but because I
couldn't leave behind my shame the attic remained only
a word, not the slope-roofed sanctum with its one
lightbulb where Nick and I had made our first love. And
then there was the letter I'd sent to him. I had put the
actual words I'd used out of my mind, hoping, I suppose, to strip them of power. I thought that if I didn't
acknowledge them, Nick wouldn't either, and between
us things would remain as they had always been.

A few miles down the highway, just before the
turnoff to Lisii Nos, my father slowed the car and pulled
over onto the shoulder. For a moment I felt panic. I
thought that he was going to tell me I'd been banished
even from Lisii Nos, that he'd make me get out and find
my own way up the windingly treacherous Hope-
Princeton highway into the vast exile of sea-to-sea
Canada, unknown to me except for its airports: Gander,
Dorval, Pearson, Winnipeg and Vancouver, all part of
my childhood's follow-the-dots route homeward. But
when I looked at him, I saw that the reason the car had
come to a stop had nothing to do with me. Papa's head
was bent forward, not quite touching the top of the steer-
ing wheel.

"What's the matter?" I asked, and was surprised
to hear more anger, which is so often the obverse of relief, than concern in my voice.

He didn't say anything at first; then he slowly drew
himself up. "I was just waiting for a bad moment to pass,"
he replied, in an offhanded tone that rang false because
of the oracular silence surrounding the words.

I didn't know if he was talking about physical or
psychic pain. I hadn't paid much attention to him during the drive, but if I'd been asked to explain his silence
I'd have said he was still angry about my fight with

Ursula. It wouldn't have occurred to me that he was pre-occupied with his own troubles, whether it was concern over Bette, who wasn't fully recovered from her haemorrhage, or his own health. And I thought how small my world had become over the past weeks, contracted to the breadth of my own unhappiness.

Less than a quarter of an hour later we turned into the drive at Lisii Nos. Aunt Xenia came out of the house, and as soon as I saw her standing so solid in her bulky dark green wool sweater, I thought, *Now everything will be all right.*

"Niki, you look awful," were the first words she said. I touched the cable pattern on her sweater's sleeve. "Yulochka," she mumbled, and only the edge of her smile touched me; her attention was for Papa. As soon as she got him inside the house, she sent him to bed. She went to the kitchen to make tea for us, and I followed her into the aroma of onions and cabbage and beets from a pot of borscht that was simmering on the stove. She took down the glasses and their enamelled holders from the cupboard, setting two on a tray and the third, for me, on the deal table beside the window.

"Your Uncle Michael's taken Kate to Rosedale and Nick's gone to Hope for the day, so, my pigeon, you'll have to amuse yourself this afternoon," she said as she poured the tea and, carrying the tray, started out the door to my father's room. "There's cake in the fridge if you want it."

Instead I took a bowl of cooked potatoes out of the fridge and sat down at the table. The windowpanes were clouded with steam from the borscht, so I couldn't see outside, and as I ran my fingertips over the grain of the deal tabletop I felt close to the comfort I'd been seeking ever since Papa and I had passed the building supply. I added sugar to my tea, and lemon, and as I stirred them together with a spoon that clinked sweetly against the glass, I gazed at the enamel clover that circled the metal holders like a motif from one of Bilibin's fairy-tale illustrations, remembering each curve of petal and stem and leaf from all the other times I had sat drinking tea here, and how one of the holders, though not this one, had a chip out of the white enamel so the grey metal underneath was exposed. I poured salt on one of the potatoes and took a bite. It tasted cold and grainy on my tongue and, as I chewed, the butter that Aunt Xenia always slathered over hot potatoes as soon as she cooked them melted in my mouth. I looked across at the chair opposite and for the smallest fraction of a second thought I saw someone sitting there. It wasn't an apparition but the ghost of a memory, long forgotten and therefore haunting: my babushka, old though she was only in her early sixties, stooped, skin appallingly wrinkled from suffering and cigarettes, eyes regarding me not so much coldly as with indifference, but, like me, biting into a potato, experiencing the same tastes and textures, chewing, swallowing, no longer starving as she had been during the war but starved all the same — of her health, her country and her music, because too many Westerners played it with sentimentality instead of the sentiment that she herself too often forgot, replacing it with a cold technical brilliance that her dying fingers were losing day by day. I didn't want to think about this babushka, who was very different from the resourceful young woman in the war diary, so with the sleeve of my sweater I rubbed a hole in the condensation obscuring the view from the window. As I finished off my potato and drank down the tea, I gazed out at the silvered wooden outbuildings, whose walls looked darker than usual, and morose, in the wet.

I saw that the drizzle had almost stopped, so I went outside. I thought I might go down to the stable and curry the donkeys' coarse, straw-fragrant coats, the repetitive gesture soothing me as I became familiar again with the shapes and smells and sounds of Lisii Nos. But as I neared the toolshed I heard a clinking noise, and I smelled smoke. Knowing it must be Dedushka, I felt a twinge of fear, though I managed to block out the memory that caused it by trying to imitate the song of a nearby towhee. *Wheer?*, I called, as the hint of a tickling sensation crawled unpleasantly along my ribs. The noise stopped. I went past the shed quickly, gazing towards the blistered paint of the stable door, but I couldn't help looking back because the silence was more compelling than the noise, and when I did, Dedushka was peering at me from around the shed's near corner. He beckoned and, as I walked towards him — the obedient granddaughter, feeling so much younger than I had in the car — he disappeared. A moment later the clinking started up again.

I found him sitting on a stump near a fire over which a cauldron hung from a metal frame. In it water boiled and small chunks of bark floated, turning the water dark. Close by was a row of traps resting open on the ground on sheets of newspaper. Dedushka did not look at me but, staring at the water in the cauldron, tapped his cheek to show he wanted to be kissed. I bent over and touched my lips lightly to his skin, which was prickly with stubble. The smell of wood smoke was in his hair and in his heavy dark jacket.

"What are you doing?" I asked, not out of any real curiosity, but to appease a murmur of violence that I sensed deep beneath his sweaty plaid shirt, disguised under an old man's slackening skin. And I thought how much my instincts had grown up since my last visit.

"What I am doing," he said, "I will show you."

He picked up a sturdy stick from the ground and stirred the bark-filled water in the cauldron.

"Yes," he said. "It is dark enough."

He put down the stick and, one by one, lifted the traps and dropped them in the water. As each one clanked against the cauldron wall he gave a grunt of satisfaction. Finally, when all the traps were immersed in the boiling water, he picked up the stick again and used it to push the metal supporting frame away from the fire.

"I will leave them like that over two nights," he

said. "Then the day after tomorrow, I will dip them in hot wax. This keeps the traps from rusting. And afterwards they will not smell of steel or of humans. Especially they must not smell of humans."

Nearby I heard barking. I thought it must be Callack, who had not been at the house to greet Papa and me when we first arrived. Eager to see her and to get away from Dedushka's traps and the unease he aroused in me, I started off in the direction of the barking, which sounded as if it was coming from behind the shed. Dedushka followed and, taking me by the elbow, said, "I have something to show you."

As we turned the corner he stopped and, with a dramatic sweep of his hand, showed me a lean-to he'd built against the back wall. The barking came from inside it. I wondered why on earth he had Callack penned up like that, but then I smelled a wild, high stink that certainly couldn't be her, and when I peered through the metre-high section of chicken wire tacked across the opening I didn't see a dog at all, but a small red fox whose tail was so thin that no one would have described it as a brush. The straw on the floor was filthy. In one corner stood a rusty dish full of water, littered with bits of straw and twigs and a few tufts of the fox's fur. It looked as if it hadn't been changed for several days. The fox stopped barking and stared at us with bright and belligerent eyes. Dedushka picked up a stick and ran it across the chicken wire. With every muscle quivering, the fox drew his mouth back over his sharp dog teeth into a snarl, then lunged at us. But he fell sprawling across the filthy straw. As he scrambled back onto his feet, he looked astonished. And then I saw that one of his hind legs was only a stump, like the little rabbit's whose corpse I had found beneath the cabin floorboards. Dedushka chuckled and ran the stick across the chicken wire again. The fox once more snarled, lunged, fell, picked himself up and looked astonished, as though he would never learn that his hind leg was now a useless thing that would always fail his

171

instincts. When I turned to look at Dedushka there was no cruelty in his face, no hardness at all; I'd seen my father look at Bette with an expression that wasn't so very different.

In the distance I heard an engine, then the weighty give of tires rolling over gravel as a car made its way down the drive. I was sure it must be Nick, and when I looked up at Dedushka my face must have revealed all my anxiety and hope, because he stared at me for a moment, his jaw firming up again and his eyes going hard, before he shouted, "Off with you. Go and see your cousin. What do you want with an old man anyway?"

I ran around the corner of the shed just as a large American four-door was pulling up beside our car. A man was driving, and on the passenger side sat a girl with light brown hair who was about my age. The door behind her opened, Nicholas got out of the back seat, and as he closed the door the girl rolled down her window. It was Suzy Janssen, who had been at Aunt Xenia and Uncle Michael's Christmas party. Nick bent over and called through the open window, "Thanks, Mr. Janssen." His face was very close to Suzy's. For a moment I thought he was going to kiss her, but instead he put his hand on her arm and said, "See you Wednesday," and immediately I knew I had something to fear from this girl who, I noticed as I watched their heads so close together, had hair exactly the same colour as his.

As Nick straightened up, he caught sight of me.

"Yule," he gasped, then blushed.

"Hello, Nick," I said.

"We've been to Hope," he mumbled.

The car started to pull away. Nick called out to Suzy, "This is my cousin."

Suzy nodded and said, "Oh yeah, right, I remember." With a honeyed smile she rolled up her window, and a moment later the car drove out of sight.

"So how come you chose Suzy?" I asked him after dinner

that evening, my awkwardness as blunt as my words. I had been standing with my hands in the warm dishwater, passing clean plates to Nick for drying. Each minute that went by made it harder to speak. I had wanted to say something clever and stinging and subtle that would take him by surprise, but the way he stood beside me, so stolid and imperturbable, had unnerved me.

"Because she's really quite a nice person," he answered, clearing his throat.

I didn't reply, but left his insipid words hanging between us. Through the window above the sink I watched Uncle Michael in the dusky light throwing a ball to Kate, while Callack danced behind her. When Kate missed, Callack fetched the ball and dropped it at her feet. Uncle Michael said, "Good dog," and Kate picked up the ball. She tried to throw it back to him, but her five-year-old hands tossed it far off the mark. Callack fetched it once again and this time dropped it at Uncle Michael's feet.

"Border collies are the smartest dogs on earth," Nick said. Then he blushed. "I never thought of going out with Suzy until you sent that letter. And I chose her because she's not like you. She doesn't do weird things or talk weird like you do: all that stuff about the guy you were going out with, and how he was teaching you so much about your dark side and—"

"Do you and Suzy fuck?" I interrupted.

"Now that's exactly what I mean," Nick said. "She would never talk that way."

"Or do it."

"No, she wouldn't. I mean, Jees, Yule, you're only fourteen and you've already done it with two guys."

"So you think I'm too young? That didn't stop you from fucking with me at Christmas, when I was even younger."

Nick, whose voice up until then had been pleading for understanding, suddenly became angry.

"Just stop it," he said. "Stop using that language.

When are you going to learn to act like a girl?"

"You mean like Suzy?" I answered, putting as much contempt into her name as I knew how. But I wondered if Nick had resented what for him must have been the ungirlish way I'd demanded satisfaction from our lovemaking, insisting he lie on his back so I could be on top and find the place inside me that swelled and blossomed.

By the time we finished the dishes, Uncle Michael and Kate had come back inside. I walked out into the last light feeling worse (and I think Nick did too) than before we'd spoken; we had failed to explain ourselves to each other, and had found no comfort in the knowledge that we didn't really like each other any more, when only a few months earlier we'd been what we thought was in love.

Early the next morning I took Babushka's diary back up to the attic. As I lifted the lid of the trunk, I looked out the little window above it, with its lace-edged slip-curtain. Through the dirt-streaked pane I caught sight of Nick walking up the driveway towards the road, where he was going to thumb a ride to his job at the building supply. His pace was quick but easy, and as I watched him disappearing around a curve until he was hidden among the trees I yearned for him, and found myself grieving for the touch of his hand on my thigh and the newborn smell of his crotch. But then I remembered Suzy's sweetish smile as she'd rolled up the car window, and suddenly I was mad with fantasies of revenge. I'd find a way to get back at them. I'd lure Nick up into the attic, complain how stuffy it was and get him to open up the window. I'd sneak up behind him, push him out. His sneakers would catch on the edge of the slip-curtain before he tumbled down past the kitchen window and cracked his skull open on the hard-packed gravel driveway. *Or* I'd take Suzy into the stable to show her the donkeys, then I'd knock her down onto the floor and get Chornik to kick her head in with his sharp hoofs. *Or* I'd lead them both up to the cabin, invite them in, ply them with vodka stolen from the cupboard above the fridge in Aunt Xenia's kitchen; then, when they'd fallen into a drunken stupor, I'd lock the door on them and set the cabin on fire. I imagined how their perfectly matching heads of hair would first singe and then flame as they lay slack-mouthed in their drunkenness, drifting towards death. *Or* I could take revenge by killing myself, opening up my veins with the carving knife that hung in its wooden holder near the stove. Then wouldn't Nick be sorry, not to mention the rest of the family, even little Kate? Years from now her memory of me would still haunt her: that loving older cousin who died so tragically because her stupid brother took up with an even stupider neighbour. *Or,* better still, I could turn the whole thing into a spectacular mass murder-suicide. I'd buy a gun like those weirdos in the U.S. did, and before I shot myself I'd pick off all the others: Suzy, Nicholas, Kate, all the adults and the animals — Chornik and White Isobel, Callack, the chick, the fox, oh, the poor fox. Looking out from that high attic window I could see, just beyond the roof of Dedushka's shed, one triangular corner of the lean-to where the little fox was imprisoned, scrawny, filthy, lunging in helpless fury whenever Dedushka teased him with a stick. I wondered how Aunt Xenia and Uncle Michael could let him keep such a pathetic creature penned up like that. No, I wouldn't murder the fox after all. I'd spare him. I'd set him free. I'd sic him on Dedushka and let him gnaw his face off, the way the rats had gnawed at Luba Sokolova's face. Suddenly I remembered that Babushka's diary was in my hand, and my stomach went queasy, as if I'd misjudged the depth of a stair and found myself stepping into the void. I lost interest in my vengeful fantasies, which were so vapid beside the terrors my grandmother had known during the war, and instead I did what I'd come up for — I returned the diary to the trunk.

That afternoon I went with Aunt Xenia to tidy up my babushka's grave. It was a ritual that happened every Easter: first the trip in workclothes to weed and scrape away moss and lichens; then later, sometime between Western and Russian Orthodox Easter, the more formal trip to the graveside with flowers and the vodka my grandfather always took. I had never been a part of this ritual before. To me it was a quaint custom my family had imported from Russia — slightly mysterious and very old-fashioned — and I'd always been content to stay at home with Uncle Michael and my cousins. My father, I suppose, had told Aunt Xenia all about the trouble I was in at school, and she, not only to keep me occupied but also because she knew I had been reading Babushka's diary, had insisted I go with her. I went sullenly because I felt embarrassed: Aunt Xenia looked so foreign with her kerchief tied over her head, so unCanadian. I imagined how Ursula would sniff at the square, peasanty look of her in overalls and rubber boots: Slavic, I thought, sub-human. Even though I hadn't talked to Ursula for weeks, she talked to me all the time, chattering in my brain, judging everything I saw around me, judging me most severely of all. "Schlumpe," she said. "Little whore Slav."

I was astonished when Aunt Xenia led me to a grave in the corner of an Anglican churchyard. "Your babushka wanted to be buried in the country," she said. "During the last year she took to attending the evening services here." Aunt Xenia paused. "Maybe just so she could claim a little plot of earth in the churchyard."

Her grave was different from all the others, surrounded by a wrought-iron railing, and the cross was Eastern Orthodox and had a photograph of her set in the stone. She was not beautiful, except perhaps for her wide cheekbones and her eyes, which looked as if they might be green like Papa's and mine, but larger.

"That's the only picture we had of her from before the war," Aunt Xenia said as she took a piece of cloth, a garden claw, two small brushes, a can of black enamel paint and paint thinner out of the mesh bag she was carrying. She started pulling weeds out of the little plot of ground and I knelt down to help her. As we worked I kept stealing glances at the photograph. The glass that protected Babushka from the weather was grimy, and the dirt obscured one side of her face so that she appeared to be looking at me from out of the shadows. Although her eyes were serene, I felt as if her gaze followed me wherever I went. It reminded me of a painting by Vrubel that Aunt Xenia had shown me in a book of Russian art, which she had seen as a child in Leningrad. It was a fantastical painting of a *bogatyr*, one of Russia's folk heroes, on horseback, and Aunt Xenia told me that as she looked at it, no matter where she moved — to the far left or right of the canvas — the horse's eyes followed her.

After about five minutes Aunt Xenia said to me, "Your papa's very concerned about you, you know."

Immediately I went on alert, greedy to hear anything my father had said about me, but defensive because I dreaded having to explain, even to Aunt Xenia, about the play and Ursula. Then there was the letter I'd sent Nick. Had he shown it to her? Or might she have come across it one day when she went into his room to clean? And in that letter had I ever mentioned Willi's name? Oh, I hoped not. I kept my eyes on the notched leaves of the dandelion I was pulling, though all my attention was for the space Aunt Xenia's next words were about to fill.

"He thinks you must be very unhappy at school, and wonders if you'd like to go somewhere else instead."

My stomach lurched, and for the second time that day I had the feeling that I was stepping into the void. If my father had asked that question in the days before Ursula had arrived at school, I'd have said, "Yes, take me away from all these rich kids whose parents own the world." But never to see Ursula again, even at a distance, even though I was forbidden to talk to her?

"St. Mary's is perfectly okay," I said, wondering if the headmistress had quietly suggested to my father that he bundle me off to a school that could handle misfits like me. Oh, the conversations that must have gone on between the teachers and my father, and my father and the von der Lindes: carefully chosen words woven together into a conspiracy of adult opinion, the net inaudible, visible only as an aura of grey around the few direct and everyday words they dared share with me, so that I sensed myself caught, rather than knew it. And not my entire self, only that momentary self who had pushed Ursula down hard onto the ground and cried, *I won. I won.* And this was the person those grownups thought I was, not for an isolated moment but for eternity, just as they thought Willi eternally smoked and drank and got expelled from boarding schools.

Aunt Xenia accepted my answer with a nod and didn't try to probe any deeper. We set to painting the metal railing around the grave. The silent work, the humble, repetitive pulling of dandelions, couchgrass, clover and wild pea, the sunshine dappling our backs through the new leaves of an overhanging willow, the intermittent trill of a red-winged blackbird, all had their effect, soothing and comforting me like the ballads Aunt Xenia sometimes sang to her own accompaniment on the piano.

As she finished painting a section of railing, she put her brush down on the lid from the paint tin and stretched her arms up towards the willow branches. The movement was graceful, and so unlike the way she had hunched over the base of the metal railing a moment earlier: it was as if some crone out of a fairy-tale had suddenly discovered that she was fully human.

"I translated Mama's diary for *you*," she said quite suddenly, but she spoke as if we'd been carrying on a conversation about it all the time we'd been painting. "And of course for Nicholas and Kate, although I don't think Nick is the slightest bit interested."

Looking for reassurance before she could carry on, she held out her hand, which I took for a moment.

"It was after the plane crash. For weeks no one was sure if your papa would live. And then there was Mama. She'd already had her first bout with cancer. Anyway I was afraid that in a very short time there would be no one left who'd gone through the Siege. And you children don't speak Russian."

There was mild reproach in her voice.

"It occurred to me that after I died you might throw the diary away because you couldn't read it. I couldn't bear the thought that that terrible time might vanish for ever, and you wouldn't know anything about it."

She started rubbing at the flecks of enamel spattered across her handsome, wide forehead.

"It was very hard living through it all over again, trying to find the right English words to replace what was hardly describable even in Russian. But I kept thinking that once I'd finished it I could put it away in the attic and forget about it until you were ready—"

There was a loud crack, like the report of a rifle, though I think it was only a car backfiring. I started, but Aunt Xenia crumpled. She held her head in her hands and her fingers clawed at the red roses that bloomed along the border of her kerchief.

"My God," she said at last, looking up at me, her eyes brimming. "How fragile it is. I thought living in the country would make me forget, and sometimes for days, weeks even, I delude myself into thinking that I've forgotten, that I'm free of it, and then...a loud noise...that's all it takes...and the shells start to explode all over again. And sometimes I think it would be easier to go back to the city, where it's noisy all the time and I couldn't be so easily deluded. But in the city there are other things — the smell of diesel oil, for instance, which is exactly the same as that smell from the Kirov Works — and I remember how it all was before the war and the shelling began, and...oh, forgive me...whenever I come here and see that picture of Mama...."

She picked up a rag, got up slowly, looking like a woman in her sixties or seventies even though she was only forty-three, went over to the photograph and began to rub the grime away. As my babushka's face emerged, Aunt Xenia wept. I wanted to cry with her, partly for the war, mainly for myself, for all the little griefs I had already known. But fear choked my tears off, because I suddenly understood that there would be other losses, most of which I couldn't even imagine yet, and that, added together, the griefs of a lifetime might become as pitiless and unassuageable as anything my relatives had known during the Siege.

Aunt Xenia grew quiet again as she scraped away a small patch of moss near the top of the stone cross. When she spoke, it was in a voice so low I had to strain to hear.

"I sometimes think the country is the worst possible place for your Dedushka to live. He spent most of the war in the western forests, trapping animals and ambushing Germans. And now he has that shed of his, with all those dreadful—"

"And what about that poor little fox?" I blurted.

Aunt Xenia's head snapped up.

"Do you think that fox could survive in the wild?" she asked, her voice suddenly gone sharp. "It could not."

"But the pen's filthy, and the water looks as if it hasn't been changed for days, and the fox is so skinny, and he torments it...."

By this time I was in tears — if I was too afraid to cry for myself, I certainly wasn't afraid to cry for the fox — and I expected Aunt Xenia, who had always mothered me far better than my real mother, to take me in her arms, rock me back and forth and tell me the world would turn out all right after all. But she held me by the shoulders instead, and shook me.

"Stop it. Stop it," she said. "I don't want to hear another word about that animal. And you're never to go near that pen again. Do you understand me?"

I looked up at her, and through my tears saw that she saw how bewildered I was. Her face softened and she tried to give me the hug I had expected, but beneath the comfortable pillow of her flesh was something un-yielding and as maimed as the fox she'd forbidden me even to talk about.

ELEVEN

When I got up the next morning — Easter for most of the neighbouring households, but for us just another Sunday — Papa was already dressed and in the kitchen, sitting at the table drinking tea. The phone stood close to his right hand, and by the serenity of his face I knew he'd just been talking to Bette.

"How is she?" I asked, knowing how safe the question was.

He smiled at his own transparency, then answered, "Lucie arrived last night and this morning served her breakfast in bed."

Lucie was Bette's sister and the reason Bette had decided not to come to Lisii Nos over Easter, while her visit meant that Papa could bear to leave Bette on her own for a few days and come to the country for the rest he needed.

"She tells me the baby was very active last night," he said in a muffled voice. He looked away, then back again, pleading for me to understand and approve the depth of his happiness. I glanced at his hand where it lay, fingers curved slightly, as if he had just taken it away from Bette's round belly and could still feel the baby kicking. There was no jealousy left in me; I was ready to believe that if I had been Papa's first miracle, then Bette and the baby were the second, and what I wanted after all was to be included in this happiness that was obviously so much greater than anything he had ever known with my mother or during the few years when I had had him all to myself.

It was the first real contact we'd had since the catastrophe with Willi and Ursula. Certainly he had interviewed me, as the circumstances and probably the headmistress demanded. He had tried to play the stern father, a role he'd never liked, which didn't suit him. He had pronounced his disappointment, and the edicts the headmistress had already imposed on me: that the play was to be cancelled, that I was not to speak to Ursula for the rest of the term and that any more trouble would mean I'd get expelled immediately. No mercy. No appeal. But suddenly he had unmasked himself and his words had sounded very unsure.

"I...understand your play is about the Siege of Leningrad," he'd said, a rawness in his voice belying the formality that he used even thirty years afterwards to distance himself from his memories of the Siege.

"Yes," I'd answered. Our eyes had met and I'd seen in his what he must have seen in mine: shocked disbelief that I had sat up in my room hour after hour working on the play, while he sat downstairs without an inkling that I had read Babushka's diary, let alone that I was writing about the Siege.

"Perhaps sometime you would allow me to read it?" he'd asked, his words carefully constructed into a fortification for the defence of his soul.

"I got...I burned it," I'd lied.

He'd winced, said, "Oh." Then the muscles in his face had gone flaccid with relief.

I hadn't lied only to protect my father from his memories. I was very afraid that what I'd written might be wrong, not factually but in spirit, and that the scenes I'd created might somehow be an affront to him, who after all had lived through the Siege.

Now, as I looked at him sitting so serene, radiant almost, drinking tea at the kitchen table, it crossed my mind that I might give him the play after all. But what if he reacted as Aunt Xenia had to that backfire that sounded like a rifle shot? What if, instead of taking me into his arms, he held me by the shoulders and shook me as she had? I decided I would neither show him the play nor confide in him about the fox.

Because it was Easter Sunday, Nick was sleeping in instead of going off to his job. I wanted to be away from the house before he got up, so for an excuse I took the scrap bucket from under the kitchen sink and told Papa I was going down to feed the donkeys. But as soon as I got out the door I began to wonder if there might not be something in it that I could feed the fox. Not that I knew what foxes ate, but would a starving creature refuse a crust of bread? And I felt defiant. I was convinced that Aunt Xenia was trying to protect herself from the fact of the fox, just as my father protected himself from memories of the Siege. I could have asked Uncle Michael to do something, I suppose, but he had always been curiously oblivious of Dedushka, whose attitudes and actions were so far outside his comprehension that it was easier to live his own busy life and ignore his father-in-law completely. Anyway, in my mind the fox was linked to the war. Aunt Xenia had hinted at it at Babushka's graveside, and I remembered how the old man had once talked about trapping foxes in the forests of German-occupied Russia. Uncle Michael had certainly gone to war, but not the same war, and because I had read Babushka's diary and written the play I somehow felt the fox was my responsibility.

It had rained during the night. As I walked through the long wet grass, by a circuitous route that went down towards the paddock, then out into the fields and back up again through a grove of trees to Dedushka's shed, my socks and the bottoms of my jeans got soaked. I tried to ignore the beginnings of a sore throat. I came out near the cauldron, which still hung from its metal frame, though it was now empty and the traps had disappeared. I made my way around to the lean-to, and as I peered through the mesh the fox stirred in his dingy prison. He looked up out of his sleep, his eyes preconsciously neutral, as yet unaware of hunger or thirst or hopelessness. Then he saw me, became alert rather than alarmed, and for a few brief seconds stared at me as if he were a shy but expectant, even friendly dog. I bent down to pick an apple core out of the scrap bucket; the movement frightened him and he snarled, started barking, lunged and fell sprawling beside his water dish. I threw the apple core over the top of the mesh. He flinched, snarled again, then began sniffing at it, his hunger making him vulnerable for a moment during which my right hand reached for the stick Dedushka had left leaning against the wall. Tempted by my grandfather's example and the impulse to cruelty Willi had taught me about, I very nearly picked the stick up and ran it back and forth across the mesh, just to get another look at the way the creature lunged with such grotesque ferocity. But the moment passed, and instead I noticed how Dedushka had nailed the mesh to a board that was attached to the sides of the lean-to by two large hooks. The fox gulped down the apple core and then started barking at me again, as if to say, *You see, I haven't forgotten that you are the enemy.*

I began to worry that his barks would attract attention. I had not seen Dedushka at all that morning, and assumed he was still asleep; but he was a light sleeper whose hearing was acute, still listening after all those years for signs of the invader: a twig cracking beneath the weight of an army boot, the rustle of branches on a windless morning, the sibilance that might be an insect flying past or a whisper in a foreign tongue. I threw two more apple cores into the pen, then took the rest of the scraps down to the paddock to feed the donkeys. After I dropped the scrap bucket off at the house I made my way to a grove of alder near the shed, where I hid and waited for Dedushka. Soon in the distance I heard his voice singing tunelessly. Pushing my way through some salal towards his song, which I recognized as "Kalinka" by its rock-strong beat, I smelled a wild honeysuckle before I saw it, even though its blossoms had not yet fully opened. Sheltering behind the tangle of its vines, I spied him as he trudged around the curve of the driveway with a sack slung over his shoulder.

I knelt down where the undergrowth was thicker, and where, though I was only a few feet from the driveway, I could be sure Dedushka wouldn't see me. As he passed in front of me — his feet encased in heavy rubber boots, the zipper of the left one undone so that the top flapped with each step — I heard a scratching sound such as a robin makes when it searches for grubs on the woodland floor, and no sooner had I heard it than the sack jerked, the side of it bulged and Dedushka almost lost his grip on it; he would have dropped it if he hadn't grabbed the top with his other hand, his soldierly reflexes still quick, as if at any moment he might have to fight for his life.

I watched until he turned off the driveway; then I crept nearer his shed, trampling mahonia and pushing past huckleberry bushes, moving through the silent spaces between leaves, twigs and roots. And when I came to a parting of fir branches through which I could see the fox's lean-to, I stopped and waited.

Dedushka arrived, dropping his sack on the ground, and once again the creature inside began to struggle so that the whole thing started moving jerkily, as if it were part of some grotesque sack race that had only one contender. Dedushka ignored it, and though I couldn't see because the opening of the lean-to was hidden from me, I heard him run his torture stick back and forth across the mesh. The fox barked madly. By the time Dedushka turned his attention back to the sack it had moved several feet. He pounced on it, chortling and wagging his finger at it to the rhythm of his tuneless, interminable "Kalinka".

Dedushka untied the string around the mouth of the sack and brought out a hen, who in the sudden day-

light gave voice to her indignation with a stream of out-
raged clucking which she interrupted only to peck at his
red ungloved hands. He talked back to her in Russian.
Xoroshenka, he called her, my pretty one. Then, deft and
ruthless, he scooped her up and disappeared around the
corner of the lean-to. Her clucking turned frantic and
terrified. I heard the fox snarl. There was the sound of a
struggle: a thump and then the shiver of the makeshift
wall facing me. Dedushka paced back and forth, visible
for a moment when he reached the edge of the lean-to,
his face radiant, carrying the torture stick in his rough
hand, then vanishing again, calling out, "*Molodets,* well
done," as he cheered on one or the other; I couldn't tell
which. I heard growling, redoubled clucking, more
growling and then silence. Dedushka stumbled back
from the lean-to and sat on the ground, breathing hard,
laughter escaping him in small explosions, tears slipping
down his cheeks as he dabbed at his eyes with a striped
handkerchief. He stayed seated until whatever madness
in him was spent, then got up slowly and trudged towards the house.

At last I was no longer an observer, or even a witness. I stepped out into the clearing and made my way
to the front of the lean-to. The fox, gorging himself on
the carcass of the hen he'd just killed, ignored me until
he'd had his fill, then raised his head and turned to me.
His snout was covered in blood, his fur ornamented with
feathers as if he were some high priest taking part in a
blood ritual. There was nothing pitiable about him now
as he stumbled towards me, a crippled god instead of
the starving creature he had been before Dedushka
brought the sacrificial hen. The struggle had transformed
him, restored his dignity and his cunning. Befeathered,
he stared at me and, with the authority of a descended
angel, demanded his freedom. Obediently I undid the
stiff hooks that fastened the mesh gate to the lean-to,
pulled it open and stood to one side as he slowly limped
back out into the world, abandoning the chicken carcass,

which lay half-eaten on the filthy straw floor.

I was left to endure the consequences — harsh ones, I was sure, because I remembered Nick telling me about the thrashing he'd got when Dedushka suspected him of tampering with his traps. An unpleasant tickling sensation crawled over my ribs for the second time since I'd come back to Lisii Nos, but now I remembered its genesis: the time at Christmas when, like a wild animal, Dedushka had chased me through the upstairs hallway into Kate's bedroom and cornered me with his merciless tickling — like his torture stick, enough to induce madness if Callack and then Nick hadn't driven him off.

I heard snapping twigs and what I thought was the sound of footsteps in the alder grove on the other side of the clearing. Pumped up with an excitement that bordered on terror, I fled along the driveway and across the road, up into the remoter woods. There the ground was still damp from the night's rain, but as I slowed down to a nervous walk the sun came out, and the heat in the rays that seeped down through the trees made steam rise up from the spongy mosses so that, briefly, the woods became a northern jungle. The sunlight cheered me, but within a few minutes the wind came up and blew in dark clouds that began spilling rain. Very quickly I was soaked through but, instead of seeking shelter under some broad-branched cedar, I felt desperate for height and a vantage point from which to keep an eye out for Dedushka, so I made my swift way to the base of the outcrop and began a scrabbling climb up its granite slope.

When I got to the top and looked down on Lisii Nos, Dedushka was nowhere to be seen. The rain had eased, but the farm was still overhung by heavy clouds that scarcely muted the vibrancy of the spring colours. The slopes of the hill were tender green with new foliage. In the orchard the apple trees were haloed with blossoms, and as I gazed at them I thought I could smell their scent wafting up to me, though it must have been some other spring flower hidden in the nearby woods because the orchard was too far away.

But as my eye swept the outbuildings, the driveway and the path down to the paddock where the donkeys stood side by side, patient with each other and the unsettled weather, I felt the past rise up through that familiar landscape: what had been hidden and subterranean was coming to light; Dedushka was not the only reason I didn't feel safe. The rain began again. I was shivering and my throat was worse, but I didn't dare go back down through the woods to the house for a warm bath and dry clothes and glasses of hot tea because I'd defied Aunt Xenia as well as Dedushka, and I knew I couldn't ask her to protect me from whatever revenge he chose to take.

I climbed down from the outcrop and went to the cabin, where there was shelter at least and, if I was lucky, some matches to start a fire. It was very neat inside, neater than I had left it at the end of the Christmas holidays: beside the stove was a pile of carefully stacked dry wood, a bundle of kindling tied with a cord, folded newspapers and, sitting beside them in a jar, the matches I'd hoped for. And someone had swept the floor. I wanted to think Nick had done it, and I said to myself, *It's his way of letting me know he still loves me.* But then I thought maybe he'd done it for Suzy, intended to bring her there, perhaps already had. Or was it Dedushka, whom Nick had seen spying on us at the window during the Christmas holidays? He might have decided to claim the cabin for himself, and claim me with it. But it was useless to guess, especially when I was so wet and cold; better to light a fire in the stove, which I did, and then huddle beside it. By that time it was late in the morning. I hadn't had any breakfast and I was so hungry that, if anyone had offered me a chicken, I think I might have tried to kill it. But it was as if whoever had tidied up the cabin had also anticipated my needs, because I found a tin of beans and a can of peaches in the cupboard. I devoured them in spite of my sore throat, then settled back beside the stove, still shivering though the heat was becoming oppressive.

In the warm room, with a full stomach, I soon fell asleep. When I woke up I was dizzy with weakness, my throat was so sore that I tried to keep from swallowing, all my muscles were aching and I couldn't stop my teeth from chattering. I put more wood on the stove; then, pulling the mattress off the bed, I brought it closer to the fire, where I crumpled down onto it. No sooner had I lain down than I heard a noise outside the cabin, as if someone had just climbed up onto the stoop. My mind struggled against the fever to stay rational. Was it Dedushka? Nick? Could it be Suzy? There was a grating noise as the door handle turned. Had I shot the bolt when I came in? Yes. The handle returned and then turned again, but the door didn't budge. If I stay still and crouching maybe he won't see me. Invisible. Is that what a rabbit believes when it's cornered? Oh God, no, not a rabbit. Under the floorboards. The stench. White teeth luminescent in the dim light. Maggots. Little fox. Little me. No. Don't think about that. Remember there's someone outside trying to get in. Watch the door. Yes, I see the handle and it's still. But someone's out there and I've left the shutters open. Visitor? Visitant? Spies on us through the window. Naked, touching fingertip to mouth. Nick and me, sweating. Our chests making sucking sounds as we stick together and come apart. Nick and Suzy? Me on the outside looking in? No. Don't think about that. Watch the door. Watch the unshuttered window. Who is watching me? Invisible eyes. Mine. Burning. But I'm so cold.

And my feverish muscles ached from crouching rabbit-still on the mattress. I stood up, my calves stiff. So dizzy. Stumbled to the window. And as I closed the shutters — the old wood smooth as skin to my touch — I looked out at the stoop and saw no one.

When I turned around the past had entered the room. It became clear to me that the reason I was shivering had less to do with the fever than with the fact that it was winter; and I was sitting in an apartment without electricity. Even inside the temperature was below freezing, and all I had was a *burzhuika* (that was what my grandmother had called it in her diary — a *little bourgeois*, or makeshift stove) to keep me warm. But a miracle had happened. Like the answer to a prayer, a whole pile of wood, instead of just a few twigs and shavings, had appeared beside the stove. I added a log to the fire, which to my surprise was already burning fiercely. *If I add enough*, I thought to myself, *the stove will become red-hot. Yes, that's what I want: to make it glow.*

I crammed as much as I could inside, and the stove roared louder and louder until the metal began to vibrate. There was a cymbal crash and I saw that the stovepipe had broken away from the wall, and flames were licking upwards, blistering the layers of paint on the wall. This too I had read about in my grandmother's diary: how one of the *burzhuikas* had set the neighbouring apartment building on fire. I struggled up from the mattress. My sickness vanished into fear. As the flames spread, the wall began to smoke and the air, which had been stifling anyway, started to choke me.

And now the flames were licking at the ceiling. I knew I had to get out because my lungs had started to burn. I ran to the door and turned the handle; it squeaked; I pulled; nothing. You've forgotten the bolt. Oh yes. My God, it's hot. Never mind. Pull it anyway. With a thump the door flew open and the flames rushed across the ceiling to catch me. I nearly let them, but the murderous winter cold had turned into mild spring air that filled my lungs: inspiration to live.

And now, instead of stumbling through history, I was running towards the rain-darkened woods. I caught a glimpse of the branches of an alder waving gently in the flowing air, and as I rushed towards it I felt that I was flowing too. I was not skin or blood or bone but a current, for ever moving towards or away from, and nothing could catch me. Then suddenly there was a pain so sharp it went right through me, and in an instant it turned me back into flesh. I fell through the air, through branches and undergrowth, to the ground. The pain was in my right foot and it was so fierce that it choked me as the smoke had. Just like flames it spread up my leg. Behind me I heard a crackling sound which grew more and more intense as each moment passed. I pulled myself up on one elbow and looked back over my shoulder. The whole cabin was on fire, and the heat from the flames made my cheeks burn though I was thirty or forty feet away. Suddenly a figure approached me: a dark silhouette against the leaping fiery background. I said to myself, *Is this Death?* And that thought made me calm. I lay back on the ground, closed my eyes and, a moment later, heard a voice call, "Yuliya."

"Yes," I answered, "I am ready."

TWELVE

All around me I heard incantations: some high-pitched and malevolent, others sweet, firm, round and full, like ripe fruit that I wanted to bite into so I could taste the juicy flesh against my tongue. I was lying on my back, inside a smoky discomfort that was hot in the centre and cold around the edges. The contrast was torment, and I shivered: my body's attempt to outwit its own confusion. And there was also real pain, tidal, that swelled and ebbed. At first I had trouble locating it. I thought its source must be those incantations that were high-pitched and malevolent, but they were outside and the pain was inside, somewhere low in my body. It took me a moment to remember that a body was not just a racket of sensations, but also had a form. Slowly I rediscovered my own bipartite shape: ears, eyes, arms, legs, my right leg, my right foot...where the agony was.

"Yulochka," a voice said, rising from the incantations that were round and sweet. I opened my eyes and found myself in semi-darkness, gazing at an illuminated Christ nailed to a cross.

"Yulochka," the voice said again, close to my ear, as I kept watching the crucified Jesus, whose suffering dribbled slowly down over his ribs from the wound in his side. But at the same time as he hung there transfixed and dying, I saw him arrested in the garden, put on trial and scourged. He bore the cross towards Golgotha. His body was taken down from the cross, wrapped and entombed. And these scenes too were illuminated, though they appeared to be happening very far away in the distance, beyond the crucifixion.

It's the icon, I said to myself, *and the reason it looks illuminated is because there's a light on in the hall.* I was in Aunt Xenia and Uncle Michael's bedroom, and when I turned my eyes away from the icon I saw that Papa was sitting beside the bed. Aunt Xenia was there too, and so was Dedushka. They were speaking in sweet dark voices, and from outside — far beyond the drawn curtains, which kept the room in twilight — I could hear the high-pitched whine of a saw.

My father reached out, whispered, "Yulochka," and stroked my hair with his hand. The smell of smoke was very strong — it came from my hair — but I ignored it, closed my eyes and lay for several moments within a sensation of well-being that briefly overwhelmed the pain. When I opened my eyes again, I looked over at him. His face was very pale, and the corner of his mouth convulsed downwards three or four times. A small shock went through me because I saw that, for the first time in months, all his attention was focused on me. I felt triumphant, and suddenly responsible, because he too was suffering and I was the cause.

"It doesn't hurt that much," I said with martyrish self-pity.

He tried for a smile.

Aunt Xenia said, "We're going to take you to the hospital."

"What's wrong with me?"

"A trap. It was a trap," Dedushka said, interrupting Aunt Xenia just as she was about to speak. "Who set that trap?" he demanded, and added, "*Durak*," as though he was accusing himself — "Fool." Oh yes, I thought, I have been caught in the trap I set at Christmas for Dedushka. But if I had trapped myself, I had caught him too. He kept on saying, "*Durak*," and looked sideways, first at my father, then at Aunt Xenia, afraid of reprisals, revenge.

I began to shiver again: heat and cold taking me over, distorting the wheelrims of Papa's chair, distancing Aunt Xenia's face, rippling the wound in Jesus' side so that it appeared to pulse like heart muscle exposed by a surgeon's knife. When I closed my eyes I began to fall, and on the way down I grabbed at anything I could to save myself: body parts, geometric shapes, strands of hair and rope and light — the mental chaos of a body in distress.

Yet among these hallucinations were moments of physical lucidity. Words clear and dense with actuality:

Uncle Michael. "She's too heavy for you, Andrei."

Dedushka. "Did I not carry her all the way down from the cabin?"

My grandfather's arms lifting me. The wild smell of him: part smoke, part animal.

A glimpse of long-dead Tanya smiling at me from inside her frame on the dressing-table.

The sound of my own whimpering.

My father. "Be careful with her."

As I was lowered into the car, the sensation of a hand on my chest, on my breast. Dedushka's hand.

Then a sharp sudden pain (as I pulled away from him) that exploded through my leg. A rushing sound. Dizziness. Blackness.

It was almost midnight when I came back to Lisii Nos, my foot bandaged, the pain identified as torn ligaments. Crutches came with me, and medicine for the flu I'd caught in the springtime damp. I was put back into Aunt Xenia and Uncle Michael's room, because the bed was larger and the mattress more comfortable than my own, and perhaps so the crucified Jesus could watch over me. The painkillers sent me right off to sleep and I dozed through most of the next day too. Usually when I surfaced for a few moments I found my father sitting beside me. Sometimes he was reading a book. Sometimes he was looking out the window. Often I found him watching me.

"What are you looking for?" I asked him once, when his gaze felt particularly probing.

"I only wanted to be sure you were not in pain," he answered. "It was such a lucky thing that you didn't break your foot in that trap. And thank God your Dedushka just happened to be up in the woods."

Dedushka? Was he the black figure that had come towards me, silhouetted against the flames? Did he call my name? Was it to him I'd answered, "Yes, I am ready?" And was it really he who had carried me all the way down to the house when I was unconscious?

The lingering smell of smoke in my hair made it all the more believable, and remembering how, as he lowered me into the car, I'd felt his hand on my breast, I burst out, "I wish he *hadn't* carried me down here. I wish you'd tell him to leave me alone."

"What do you mean?" my father said sternly. "He saved your life."

I kept silent because it was clear Papa didn't want me to answer, and wouldn't have believed me if I did.

In the distance I heard the saw whining again, just as I had the day before. The sound made me more uncomfortable than did the pain in my foot.

"They are building a new chicken coop," my father said, pointing out the window towards the neighbouring farm. "They've been losing chickens to the coons and foxes."

To Dedushka, I thought.

Papa closed his eyes for a moment against some pain of his own. He had lived inside pain for years, was used to it, maybe even understood it. My injured foot connected me to him. I wanted that connection, but I was wary. As I glanced up at the icon of Christ eternally suffering on his cross, I asked myself, *What if I got trapped inside pain like Papa or Jesus, and had to endure it for ever?* I remembered the day Ursula and I had the fight: how she pushed me hard against the hawthorn and the long spines pierced me, scratched, drew blood. I welcomed that pain. It was as if the thorns had lanced an abscess and some ancient festering poison oozed away. I wondered if my father welcomed the pain that afflicted him. Maybe it kept away memories that hurt even more: of the Siege, perhaps, or his marriage to my mother. And was he really trapped? Was Christ? Or had he simply made a choice?

In mid-afternoon I was awakened out of my feverish dozing by voices in the hallway.

"Meddler. Thief," I heard Dedushka say. There was a scuffling sound. I was shivering and I pulled up the blankets close around me, lifting them carefully so they wouldn't rub against my foot.

"I didn't steal any of your rusty old traps," Nick said. "And I didn't let the fox out. What do I care about a stupid little fox? Leave me alone."

"Liar."

There was more scuffling farther down the hall; then I heard Aunt Xenia's voice, stern, in the distance: "Enough, Papa. That's enough."

"I didn't do it," Nick insisted.

"*Durak.*" Dedushka shouted. And this time it sounded as if he was cursing himself instead of Nick. I found a certain perverse pleasure in knowing I could stop his torment at any moment just by admitting I had set the trap myself. Was that how Dedushka had felt when he ran the torture stick back and forth across the mesh of the little fox's pen, savouring the fact that he could put a stop to the creature's suffering simply by laying down the stick?

After that the voices became fainter so that I couldn't make out the words, and at last there was silence. But when I fell asleep again the echoes of their conflict disturbed my dreams. The fox stumbled through the woods, and I limped after him, pursued by an indefinite fear, trying to avoid the traps that infested the pathways like vermin. And as we fled past long-needled branches that scratched my cheeks, I discovered, nailed to the stringy bark of the cedar trees, all kinds of woodland animals: raccoons, rabbits, deer, coyotes — most of them dead, a few still alive, whimpering the end of their world.

In the heart of the woods I found my father's wheelchair. It lay on its side with mahonia growing up through the spokes of its wheels, their sharp holly-shaped leaves lit by a few rays of wan sunlight that somehow had managed to penetrate the evergreen. He was standing nearby, in front of what, when I looked up through the frondy branches, must have been the tallest cedar in the woods. I felt a pang at seeing him so independent. But then I realized I'd been mistaken. He wasn't standing at all. Like the raccoons, the rabbits, the deer and the coyotes, he was nailed, crucified on the great trunk, and his suffering oozed out of him through a wound in the middle of his back.

I woke up in what was only partly a nightmare sweat. My fever had broken, and I lay in the drenched sheets as if I were floating in a cool pond on a summer's day. Aunt Xenia and Uncle Michael came in and changed the bedding; then, dreamless, I slept the rest of the afternoon away.

At dinner-time Aunt Xenia brought me a bowl of thick soup and black bread with unsalted butter. With the first mouthful I discovered that I was hungry. I gulped down the soup, asked for more, finished that too and at last sat back against the pillows, a glass of tea in my hand, feeling both satisfied and restless. My back ached from lying in bed all day. I wanted something to do, somewhere to go. When I pulled myself over to the edge of the bed, the friction of the bedclothes against my bandages sent unbearably hot flames of pain through my foot, and I fell back, content suddenly just to lie there, belly full, without ambition.

Later Nick arrived. He sidled up to the bed with his hands behind his back, stood grinning for a moment and handed me a jar filled with pussy willows.

198

As I touched one of the furry buds he asked, "You okay?"

I nodded.

"I went up to the cabin," he said. "Holy shit. There's hardly anything left. You're lucky to be alive. How did you ever manage to set the whole place on fire?"

"I was cold," I said, "and I added too much wood to the stove," Just as in the play, I'd let the past overwhelm the present. Ursula hadn't listened when I'd attempted to explain it to her, so with Nick I didn't even try. And anyway the troubled look on his face made it clear that he was the one who needed to be understood.

"Dedushka thought I set that trap, you know. But I didn't," he said.

I looked away.

"You believe me, Yule, don't you?" he pleaded.

I knew I should tell him that I had set the trap myself, but I felt too ashamed, especially when I remembered the sound of his scuffle with Dedushka earlier that day.

"Of course I believe you," I said, and realized it wasn't just shame that stopped me from telling him. I was enjoying my role as the entirely innocent victim of someone's carelessness or malice.

There was a long silence between us. I glanced over at the dresser. Tanya's smile remained steady but her pale eyes looked disapproving. It was as if she knew that my secret pleasure was also revenge against Nick for choosing Suzy over me. I stared down at the bedclothes so Nick couldn't guess at my thoughts. After a minute or two I felt a small softness on my cheek. I looked up. He had taken a pussy-willow branch from the jar and was stroking my face with it.

The next morning my father left. He had a meeting with Bradley that afternoon, and he was going to start rehearsing a new show the following day. He went away looking rested, in spite of the worry I'd caused him and the pain that had revealed itself only in those moments over the past few days when his cheek had twitched or he'd closed his eyes in mid-sentence. The connection our mutual pain had forged was quickly ruptured as I listened to the noise of his car engine slowly diminishing up the drive. I knew his mind was back on his work and on Bette. For him the crisis was over, and so was my brief tenure at the centre of his attention.

Shortly after he left, Aunt Xenia bustled in with some yoghurt and bread and jam.

"When you've finished eating," she said, "I'd like you to get up and try those crutches. I'm making *kulich* and *paskha* and I need your help in the kitchen."

Kulich and *paskha* were traditional Easter cakes. Aunt Xenia always made them a little early, then froze the *kulich* and left the *paskha* to drain in the fridge for several days before she brought them into Vancouver for Russian Easter, when we attended the all-night service at the Orthodox church. Every year, except for one when I was visiting my mother in England, I had helped Aunt Xenia make the cakes. I had always been so proud when they were finished: the *kulich* cylindrical and encircled by coloured eggs; the *paskha* a pyramid with the Cyrillic letters XB written upon it, which stood for *Khristos Voskrese*, "Christ is risen." The cakes made me feel that I belonged in a way I was never quite able to at school: because we had less money than my classmates' families, because my mother lived in a different country, because my father was a stage director instead of a businessman and because I was a hybrid, neither English nor Russian. In a more cosmopolitan city, or at a different school, or at the same school just a few years later, all that wouldn't have mattered, but there and then it made me a little peculiar, so it was always a relief to have that peculiarity celebrated among the cooking smells in Aunt Xenia's kitchen.

But on that day I didn't want to make *kulich* or *paskha*.

"My foot hurts," I told Aunt Xenia, "and my head

200

aches, and I didn't sleep well, and I had awful dreams."

"Dear little pigeon," she said, kissing me on my forehead, "you'll feel better once you're up." And she left me to my breakfast.

Twenty minutes later she came back and handed me the crutches, which I used awkwardly at first, complaining that they didn't work properly and demanding that I be allowed to go back to bed. Aunt Xenia said only, "One, two. Crutches, swing. Yes, that's it," and before long she had shepherded me into the kitchen, where Kate was fumbling to tie the strings of an apron behind her back.

Aunt Xenia sat me down at the deal table.

"Kate will be your helper," she said. "You sit where you are, and she'll bring you whatever you need."

Kate nodded and presented me first with a large bowl, then flour, milk, eggs, butter, raisins and almonds. I mixed them together, rarely needing to ask Aunt Xenia about the order or quantities. As I beat the dough with a wooden spoon, it was almost as if Babushka sat across the table from me, chewing on her cold potato, smiling between bites, encouraging me in the old ways that would keep her memory alive. My headache went away, and I forgot about my foot, or put up with it, at least. I discovered that I enjoyed having things brought to me, and Kate enjoyed bringing them because she was still young enough that she thought being a servant was fun. But even as I filled the cylindrical moulds with partially risen dough, I felt the history about to intrude upon the traditions of Aunt Xenia's homey kitchen, within which I had always felt safe. The small war I'd been waging, not exactly against the past but certainly inside it, wasn't yet over, and this cozy afternoon of cake-making was merely a respite between skirmishes.

"Here," Aunt Xenia said, "taste this." She had just finished mixing curds and butter and raisins into a paste for the *paskha*, and she gave Kate and me each a spoonful. As the rich flavour, both cheesy and sweet, filled my mouth, I said to myself, *Khristos Voskrese*, but the picture I had in my mind was of my father nailed upright to the trunk of the giant cedar.

That day I was considered well enough to move back into my own room, and I was glad to do it, if only to get away from the crucified Jesus. The days that followed were serene. My crutches confined me to even surfaces, which meant that I had to stay inside the house or on the terrace; but the weather was wet and, though the woods had always had a certain charm in the rain, the terrace was depressing, so I kept to the kitchen and the living-room, where every morning Aunt Xenia set a fire in the woodstove.

I saw very little of Nick, who, because it was Easter holidays, always left early to go to his job at the building supply. Kate sometimes got me to read her stories or play hospital with her (she was fascinated by my bandages, and kept begging for my crutches so she could be the hero/patient while I played the sidekick/nurse). Aunt Xenia had me help her with inside chores, but during the dry hours between rainstorms she was busy outside with Uncle Michael, battling disease in the orchard or splitting rounds of wood that had seasoned over the winter in one of the sheds. Consequently I was often left alone and, though I sometimes became bored and depressed, the slow drab days suited me, and I drowsed or read or daydreamed through my hours of solitude, placid if not happy, and feeling safer within the confines of my injury than if I'd been free to roam the woods and meadows. The reason for this was that Dedushka never came into the house any more except at mealtimes, and left right after, preferring to spend all the rainy hours in his shed, and the dry ones tending his traps.

But if my waking moments were peaceful, my sleep was full of nightmares. The crucifixions persisted, became more gruesome. Willi began to appear, sometimes nailing a screaming animal to a tree, sometimes crucified himself, his face contorted with pain. Ursula was there too, though she held herself aloof, neither crucifying nor crucified, sometimes wearing a sardonic smile, her arm always in its cast though it didn't slow her down: she played piano exquisitely and performed marvellous acrobatic feats that would have enchanted me if they had not seemed to mock all the other pathetic, tormented inhabitants of my dream world.

More and more the little fox appeared, often crucified, always imprisoned behind a curtain of wire mesh Three nights in a row I unfastened the mesh and pulled out the nails to free him, only to find him a moment later confined again and tortured. Eventually these images began to worry at my waking hours too. The house was no longer the sanctuary it had been. I grew restless, though I was tired out by my nightmares, and I found myself crutching from window to window, staring out, on the alert for some sign of the crippled fox. At last, though the knowledge filled me with dread, I came to understand that the nightmares wouldn't stop until I went outside myself and discovered what had become of him.

I opened the front door into a light drizzle. My left crutch slipped on the wet wooden step so that I nearly fell before I'd even reached the driveway. After that I made my way gingerly across the gravel. The rutted surface unnerved me at first, but inside the house I'd become adept with my crutches, and I soon learned to test the ground the moment before I put my full weight on them, so that I reached the pen behind Dedushka's shed only a little more slowly than if I'd walked there.

The mesh gate slumped uselessly at the front of the pen and there was no sign of the fox or the chicken carcass he'd half eaten. Not that I'd expected to find him there; it was really only a place to start looking for him. I thought I'd make my way from there to the alder grove, the direction in which I'd last seen him heading, but before I got more than a few yards a voice asked, "How is the foot?" It was Dedushka, of course. I turned around to find him grinning his way towards me. In his right hand he carried a tool that consisted of a blade roughly fashioned from metal with a wooden handle.

"Better," I answered. "It doesn't hurt quite so much. And I was getting bored—"

"You were looking for the fox," he said, snuffing whatever excuse I'd been trying to make up. He turned back to the shed and beckoned for me to follow him, which I did, at a slower pace than my crutches called for.

Because I'd confined myself to the bottom floor of the house ever since my injury, I wasn't much good at negotiating steps, and when we reached the front of the shed I had trouble climbing even the two shallow ones that led up to the door.

"I will help," Dedushka said. He held the handle of the metal tool in his teeth, and with his hands around my waist lifted me like a dancer, so that with the effort of a small hop, using my crutches hardly at all, I suddenly found myself inside. It was like flying, and I supposed that must be how my mother felt when her partners lifted her during a *pas de deux*. No wonder she had chosen the rigours of dance instead of work less demanding but more earthbound.

The calendar girls from 1947 were still smiling down from the wall over Dedushka's worktable. But there was something wrong about Miss April, all abloom in pink and white and tender green, her expression so pertly alluring. She had a dark, evil-looking scar just below her navel, which when I got closer turned out to be a jagged cut in the shiny paper. I was sure it hadn't been there at Christmas.

The air in the shed had a strong chemical smell, which only partly masked the odour of decay. Directly in front of me six traps were laid out in a neat line on top of the worktable. My grandfather slouched down to the end by the window and began scraping at something with the primitive-looking blade he was carrying. As he bent over, he blocked out most of the light, but I could see well enough to tell that the thing he was scraping at looked like a pelt. I edged closer, even though the smell made me queasy. Then I saw the stump of a hind leg. Dedushka turned to me, grinning, and held up the skin of my fox. Its tail and head were still attached, though the eyes were gouged out, and as Dedushka stood there he began to laugh like a little boy who's managed to pull off a joke. "You should have left him in his pen," he said, wagging his finger at me. "He was much safer there. Impossible to leave injured creatures to wander about all alone in the woods." He shook his head. "*Nelzya*. Impossible."

His laughter subsided, and he put the skin back down on the worktable with a slight expulsion of air which he must have intended to be a regretful sigh. I turned towards the door, but as I did, he grabbed one of my crutches away from me and then steadied me, his hand at my elbow.

"I don't like the smell in here," I told him. "I'm going to be sick."

He put his arm around my waist, solicitous now, and steered me towards a bench under the window, as far as possible from the door.

"Please, I feel sick," I said. "I want to go outside."

But he pushed me down on the bench.

"I have been waiting for you," he said in a quiet, confidential tone. He sat down beside me and, though I resisted for a moment, took my other crutch away from me and leaned both of them up against the wall on his far side, where I couldn't reach them.

"You are...," he started, then cleared his throat and continued. "I have things for you...I want to show you...I want to tell you so you will understand...."

He stood up and took a tin down from the shelf above his worktable. When he sat down again he lifted the lid to reveal perhaps eight or nine small reddish balls.

"Candy," he said. "Good." He saw that I was

suspicious and so held the tin up under my nose. "You take a sniff." His hands stank of chemicals and decay, but the balls themselves smelled sweet and sunny. He popped one of the little confections in his mouth, sucked on it for a moment, then nodded for me to do the same. It was as if I were some alien being and he were looking for a way to establish contact.

"Candy," he said again and kept on nodding encouragement. I reached into the tin and took out one of the little balls. It was sticky to the touch. Slowly I brought it to my mouth, wondering all the time why I felt compelled to obey him, and licked at it with my tongue. The flavour was pleasant enough, sweet and berrylike, so I put the whole thing in my mouth.

"Good?" he asked and, answering himself, said, "Yes, very good." He stared at me until I nodded, solely to deflect his gaze, though I had to admit the candy was delicious. "Now," he said, "I will tell you why it is so good." Although we were sitting on a simple, hard bench, he somehow managed to settle himself into it. He put his arm around my shoulder and squeezed it, observing a moment of silence before he spoke.

"Do you know how I get this candy?" He waited while I shook my head, as if my response was an essential part of some private ritual of his, then he continued. "First I search through the woods for wild strawberries. You have seen them growing?" Again I shook my head. "No, I did not think you had." He waited for me to say more, and to relieve the pressure I felt from his silence I added, "Well, maybe just once when I was with Nick...." He grunted — with satisfaction, I thought — and immediately I wished I hadn't spoken Nick's name, especially when I had no real memory of eating wild strawberries with him, though we had often picked blackberries together. Then he went on. "I pound the flesh into a pulp, then I make this candy. You agree it is delicious?" I nodded. "And do you know where I have learned how to make it?" I shook my head. "Behind enemy lines, in

Belorussia, for something to do in between raids...that was the worst: the time in between." He shifted on the bench, cleared his throat and nodded his own affirmation, for a moment not needing mine. "It is also the worst now: the time in between." He stared at me for a moment. "You do not know what I am talking about." I shook my head. "You cannot know." Again I sensed that he thought of me as an alien; part of him wanted to drive me away, but the stronger part was desperate to communicate. Slowly he got up from the bench, then crouched beside the worktable. From under it he pulled out a dusty cardboard box which he immediately opened. As he rummaged about inside, I heard the *tock* of wood against wood and thought to myself, *At least it's not another trap.* By this time the candy in my mouth had dissolved to a thin oval which I crushed against my teeth to suck out the last sweetness, while the odour of decaying flesh from the fox pelt eddied through me, churning my stomach towards sickness.

Moments later Dedushka stood up again with a muttered *K chortu* and held out a statuette carved in wood. It looked like some kind of weasel.

"Polecat," he said. He pushed the carving at me, and I took it and examined it during another of his needy silences. Its body was sinuous with energy, and highly realistic in its detail, as if the artist had tried to carve each hair instead of merely giving the impression of fur.

"It is good?"

"Beautiful," I said, without hesitation.

"You can have it."

"Oh, no."

"You do not want it?"

The truth was that, although I appreciated the artistry of the little carving, I hated the way Dedushka pressed his offerings on me so that I felt compelled to accept them whether I wanted them or not.

He closed my hands over the statuette and pushed it towards me. Staring down at the exquisite wildness in that miniature face, I tried to find words that would make his gift feel less like an importunate demand. Eventually I uttered a cowardly and half-hearted "Thank you."

"I carved that," he replied, his voice brightening with small-boy pride.

"You?" I tried not to let my astonishment show too much.

"I was good carver," he said, leaving out the article, sounding suddenly more Russian.

I nodded, freely this time, without feeling driven to it by his need.

"I did that when I first came to the forest at the beginning of the war. Polecats, you know, their fur is no good for trapping." He shifted on the bench and cleared his throat. "It was the last carving I did." He cleared his throat again. "But I kept it...right through the war." A moment of silence. "Later on I tried to carve other things. Other animals. I had lived for three years in forest, and in that time martens, polecats, deer, pigeons, had become creatures to stalk — only that: their flesh was for eating, their skins for clothing or shelter. Do you understand? I could not see them any other way." A pause. "But you cannot understand." His voice sounded at once contemptuous and despairing.

"I sort of understand," I murmured. "I think I do." I had sensed something similar in Willi, and in my father too. It was as if an essential part of them had been injured beyond healing. For my father, of course, this was literally true. But for Willi and Dedushka it felt no less real. And the consequences were not just their obvious, palpable suffering, but a capacity to make others suffer. In my father it manifested itself as neglect, both of himself and of those he claimed to love; in Willi and Dedushka, as small and not so small verbal and physical cruelties.

"The best times," my grandfather continued, "were when we stalked wild things: plants, animals, Germans." He chuckled. "Germans running wild with terror through our forests. No, they did not like it in there. Suddenly they find themselves surrounded by a ring of flaming trees. No thunderstorms, no lightning. How could the forest catch on fire? Spontaneous combustion?" Dedushka shook his head and chuckled some more. "We stalkers, we just wanted to cook our supper; it was simple to cook Germans at same time." He gave a belly laugh.

"Do I shock you? You are so young. You have not yet suffered. You are still innocent," he said, and looked at me as if he did not quite believe the words he had just spoken. I remembered how it had been at Christmas, when he had stalked me in the upstairs hallway and the next day I had stalked him in the woods, wanting nothing more than a quick revenge; and now I understood that that had been only one play in a game that Dedushka, by showing me the imprisoned fox, had enticed me to resume as soon as I'd come back to Lisii Nos. For the moment he had chosen words to stalk me with — only words — but I sensed that, minute by minute, those words were turning the game into a battle.

The carving of the polecat had grown warm in my hands, and it complicated my exchange with Dedushka. Its finely worked paws scrabbled for my attention: admit that your grandfather is, or at least was, an artist, they insisted, with not merely an artist's skills but an artist's perceptions; admit that he is more fully human than you thought he was; admit that he has a claim on your sympathies. I did admit, and was thereby disarmed, as he had no doubt intended when he pushed the carving towards me.

He took another candy for himself and pressed one on me. As I sucked it, I tried to imagine Dedushka at some temporary camp in the birch forest, mashing strawberries into a pulp which he then cooked over a fire — with sugar stolen from where? The provisions of some murdered German soldier?

"Yes," he said, rolling the candy over his tongue,

"in between was the worst, when there was little to do and nowhere to go but still I had to stay on alert. Impossible to get proper rest. Three years I had without proper rest. And in between was when wounds hurt the most, and when, if I was already sick, I felt even sicker. I missed your grandmother, and your papa, and your aunt. I tried to carve, you know." His voice quavered. "Again and again I tried, but I could not work when all the time I had to listen for the enemy."

The polecat's coarse fur had come alive in my hand. Its wild, sharp-featured muzzle spoke: *I am the soul of your grandfather; have pity on me. I am his failed aspirations; love me. I am his loneliness; embrace me. I am his hope revived; grant me sanctuary.*

"After the war there was no more stalking. All time was time in between. Your babushka...the way she looked at me...as if I was enemy. And I kept thinking: *What have I turned into?* And I kept listening for that false tone in her voice that meant she did not recognize me any more. Others did not recognize me either. Why? I could not see what had changed when I looked in mirrors. My face was thinner. It was older. I knew something was missing, but I could not remember how I looked before the war, when I was able to carve with steady hand and impeccable eye. Impeccable: eye without sin. Had the war made me sinner? Was it sin to fight for my country, my wife, my children? To kill an enemy who would otherwise kill me? Now the war was over, was I good for nothing but stalking? All right, then, that is what I would become — a stalker.

"I left behind the memory of my old life, my family life that had once been whole. Now it was in pieces because one of my children, my Tanya, my little girl, my innocent child was gone. I came to Canada, and your babushka, though she would have nothing to do with me, came too, and brought Nikolenka and Xyusha. I found civilized work teaching Lermontov and Pushkin. In Canada it is easy to pretend you are civilized when so many are not. Like all exiles I taught out of yearning for what I no longer had. My colleagues, my students, thought I had merely lost a country; they did not know I had once been able to carve. They did not know that in the guise of a teacher I stalked them. Oh, I was careful. They hardly knew when I made a kill. But kill I did: their vitality, their curiosity, their innocence. Not everyone's. Only those who were most vulnerable. That was my real work.

"Your babushka, as I said, would have nothing to do with me. Of course she was quite willing to take my salary to support the children. So I stalked her too, and eventually I caught her. And the result was Aleksandr. A stalker's son. Far more ruthless than I will ever be. As your father found out. And your mother. Your fine, elegant, remote, calculating mother."

I had got used to having to think about Aleksandr, my Uncle Alek, only once a year, at Christmas, when I stood on guard against him for my father's sake. Otherwise I tried to drive away all memories of him. And as for my mother, I was indignant that Dedushka had found such apt adjectives to describe her, especially in a language that was not quite his own. They were adjectives that I would have liked to use, and somehow I felt that only I had a right to use them, because, unlike my grandfather, I knew they were both true and not true: she was more vulnerable than he made her sound, and Uncle Alek more at fault.

"In between are the worst times," Dedushka was saying. He was trying for my interest again. It was as if he'd realized that he'd made a mistake talking about my mother and Uncle Alek, that unintentionally he'd deflected my attention away from himself, and he wanted it back. He opened up his tin and again offered me a candy. Only this time those little red balls looked to me like bait: the plastic roe sometimes used to lure salmon. I pushed the tin aside. My hands had gone sweaty around the polecat's wooden sinuosity.

"I am all right," Dedushka went on, "when I am setting traps. I am all right when I check my lines. But there aren't so many creatures in the woods any more. And they are cunning."

He nodded at me as if I were one of his creatures — the most cunning of all. Then he brought his lips close to my ear and whispered, "Nicholas."

I felt heat rise up my neck and into my cheeks. It was as if the very mention of my cousin's name insinuated everything that was to come. But a moment later he'd veered back towards self-pity.

"When Vera was dying," he said, "I saw how much I'd lost and how long ago I had lost it." He stared at the floor. "She did not want me there. In the hospital. At her bedside." A shudder went through him as he gave a sigh — very real this time. "She was in pain. She was coughing her lungs to shreds, but she did not want me." His voice suddenly went cold. "She lifted her hand. She pushed me away. She turned to the wall. A blank, green, institutional wall. That was what she preferred." He turned to me. "Why?" he asked.

I shook my head and smiled vaguely at him. It occurred to me that Papa must have taken me with him to see Babushka in her hospital bed, and I remembered or perhaps fantasized her lying in the institutionally green room, but not with her face turned to the wall. The head of the bed was raised so that she was almost in a sitting position, and she was smoking — assiduously, without pleasure, sucking on an unfiltered cigarette, as if it were the bottled oxygen that sustained her later in her illness.

Dedushka began to cry, muttering "Verochka, Verochka," over and over again, as he had at the Christmas party in Aunt Xenia's kitchen when he'd got himself drunk. I laid the polecat down on the bench beside me and, remembering how I'd mourned unremittingly for months after my mother left, I put my arms around him in his crumbling leather jacket to try to give him comfort. With his head against my chest he shuddered

212

and blubbered and sighed.

"Yulochka," he pleaded, clasping me by the shoulders, "you will be good to me?"

I was trapped, and like all trapped creatures I tried to pull free, but Dedushka only held me tighter.

"You were good to Nicholas," he said. "You must also be good to me. I saved your life, didn't I?"

There was a slight relief in knowing for certain that he had spied on Nick and me when we'd made love in the cabin at Christmas, that what had sometimes felt like mad fear was in fact quite sane, a response to real danger; but it further cheapened the intimacy Nick and I had once shared. Willi had already devalued it to the level of naivety; Dedushka turned it into a peepshow.

"I gave you money, didn't I?"

So the ten dollars he'd given me at Christmas was a whore's wages. *Schlumpe, slut, little Slavic whore.* And what about all the other times he'd given me money? Did he do it intentionally, thinking that one day, when I was old enough, he'd ask for repayment?

He began to unzip my jacket. I went very quiet, convinced that struggling would only touch off the warrior violence in him. If, on the other hand, I could keep him pleading, I'd still have some control.

And those were the last rational thoughts I had. From that moment on I was no more than a body scheming to live, waging its own small defensive war by instinct rather than strategy. As Dedushka caressed my breast, my hand reached up and touched his hand, neither pushing it away nor caressing it, to confuse him with a sense of maybe. I was aware of the sharpness of things: the metal scraping tool he'd used on my fox's pelt, the teeth of the largest of the leghold traps, the edge of the tin box in which he kept his candy. I was aware of my body's weakness: queasy stomach and aching foot; and its strength: the adrenaline clarity of vision, hearing and sensation that I have known only rarely — at the centre of danger; that instant and almost mystical perfectibility

213

of the senses.

Dedushka crooned to me. *"Daleko...daleko,"* his thin voice quavered, and I swear that, for the first and only time, he sang on key. He undid my shirt and the button at my pant-waist, and still my body stayed neutral to his touch. But then suddenly he was all urgency, though he went on pleading, "Be good to me. You must be good to me as you were to Nicholas. I saved your life. I gave you money." He pressed me against the wall, his shoulder hard into my chest, stifling my breath as he undid his belt buckle and his fly; and in the compressed space between us I smelled his underwear, a whiff of urine. My hip began to hurt, too, and I wondered why, until I remembered that I'd laid the polecat down beside me on the bench and it was now digging into my pelvis.

"You must be good to me," Dedushka kept repeating. By now he'd taken out his penis and was rubbing it against the crotch of my jeans. My body ached as I tried to hold onto my neutrality, as if, instead of doing me harm, it still protected me. My vision blurred and fastened on an inner image: the Jesus icon of eternal suffering, the terrible passivity of his face, or my father's face, or my face as it must have been when Willi buggered me, or as it was now, waiting for Dedushka.

And my body said no, began to struggle, adrenalin once again restoring clarity and the instinct to survive, which is the larger part of will. I fought my way towards the nearest sharpness, the tin candy box, but when my hand was only an inch or two from it Dedushka, whether by accident or on purpose, hit my bandaged foot, and pain blacked out the shed and sent wind rushing past my ears. I grappled my way back to consciousness, literally, because the first thing I saw was Dedushka's arm lifted to fend me off. The sharp tin box was within my reach. I grabbed it and, in a single blow that had in it more strength than I knew I possessed, carved a deep wound into Dedushka's cheek. He yowled like a crazed cat and pulled away, blood flowing down the front of his jacket onto me, into my mouth. The foreign salt taste turned my stomach. I gagged and retched and threw up all over the bench where a moment before Dedushka had had me pinned down, the vomit splashing his pant-leg, repulsing him more effectively than had the sharp edge of tin.

"*Bozhe moi*, my God," he said (he had stanched the blood from his wound with the heel of his hand), "are you mad? Get out of here."

Without even bothering to wipe my mouth or do up my clothes, I grabbed for my crutches and hobbled out into the fine April rain. Fear made me so agile that I scarcely noticed how I got down the steps to the driveway, but I had not gone more than a few paces when Dedushka was suddenly beside me, his feet dancing, with a bloody kerchief pressed hard against his cheek.

"You will not say anything?" he half pleaded, half commanded. "This will be our secret...how I got this wound...."

He danced in front of me, blocking my way so I'd be forced to answer him, but just at that moment the back door to the house opened and Aunt Xenia came out carrying the scrap bucket. She looked at us, face friendly during the second before she truly saw us, and I was less aware of the change in her expression than the change in me as I plummeted from my adrenaline high down into shame. I pulled my jacket closed over my unbuttoned and vomit-spattered blouse, manoeuvring frantically to keep my balance on the crutches. Sensing the change in me, Dedushka wheeled around and, seeing Aunt Xenia, froze. Cautiously she put the scrap bucket down, as if it were filled to the brim with some volatile liquid that might set the incendiary moment on fire. She came towards us slowly with a grave, authoritative step. She didn't demand explanations, but appraised us with a stare that was both ardent and detached, as though some part of her believed that what had happened between Dedushka and me had been inevitable, and her only concern was how to respond.

She stepped towards Dedushka and grimaced as she pulled his bloody handkerchief away from his cheek, before she turned to me and said, "Go into the house and get cleaned up." Meekly I hobbled towards the back door and went in while she followed, bringing Dedushka along by the elbow. Kate was in the kitchen, and in the split second before I looked away I saw how she came alert.

"Go down to the orchard and get your father," Aunt Xenia said to her. "Tell him your grandfather's hurt himself and needs to go to the hospital."

I heard Dedushka grunt in protest before I headed down the hall to the bathroom.

I was already in the tub when Aunt Xenia arrived. Immediately she took away my dirty clothes. When she came back and knelt down beside me, I saw that her pants were spattered with Dedushka's blood. Without a word she shampooed my hair and soaped me all over, gently sponging my right leg above the bandage, treating me like an infant, as if she could somehow take me back in time and undo what had happened. Later, after she'd settled Kate in front of the TV to watch "The Waltons", she took me into the kitchen, where she sat me down at the deal table with a glass of tea.

"Tell me," she said, and when I looked out the window for some sign of Uncle Michael's truck she added, "Don't worry. They won't be back for ages."

I didn't want to talk. The hot bath and Aunt Xenia's attentions had unknotted both my muscles and the high, tight fear that had given me the physical strength and the will to stop Dedushka. I only wanted to rest; and I also knew that, if I spoke, I'd have to reveal too much that was secret: large and small disobediences, the long vicious game with Dedushka and, worst of all, the physical passion in my relationship with Nick, which was supposed to be no more than a teenage crush. On the other hand I knew that I'd better speak before Dedushka had the chance, because he would uncover anything against me that might help him in his own defence.

When at last I did speak, it was in a detached, tight-jawed monotone. Only the words were confessional; the emotions I kept locked up. Aunt Xenia didn't say a word, but her expressive eyes, the way her lips parted and then compressed, revealed shock, anger and what I dreaded most, disgust. I finished my tea and the narrative at the same moment and, putting down the glass, begged to be allowed to go to my room.

The sound of electronic happiness issued from the den as I passed by on my way down the hall: "Good-night, Mama; good-night, Papa; good-night, John Boy."

When I reached my bedroom I shut the door and locked it.

I lay down on the bed, huddling under the comforter, and closed my eyes, but as soon as I did so my imagination was filled with that moment in the shed when Dedushka had clasped me by the shoulders and I'd known I was trapped. I began to shiver, and all the emotion I had so carefully suppressed in front of Aunt Xenia suddenly tumbled me into self-defensive chaos. I played the scene in the shed over and over, changing the words I'd spoken, fighting Dedushka even before he pushed me down on the bench: biting, kicking, clawing, pounding him, intent on destroying him so I wouldn't have to reveal my secret self, twisting in a fury that was more self-hatred than catharsis. There was a knock on the door. My whole body went stiff. "Who is it?" I asked, knowing that I had no strength left to fend off anyone or anything.

"Yule, it's me," Nick said.

I got up, faltered towards the door, then unlocked it.

"Oh, thank God, thank God," I heard myself saying in a high-pitched, trembling voice that quickly turned into sobs while Nick put his arms around me. The sweet cloying smell of Suzy permeated his hair, and I remembered how, as he leaned against Mr. Janssen's car, he had said to her, "See you Wednesday." *So today must be Wednesday*, I thought, and found some comfort in being able to name the day of the week because it made life ordinary again. For a brief moment I hung onto my old jealousy over Suzy, then let it go because it no longer had any meaning: what really mattered was that, by confessing to Aunt Xenia, I'd lost my right to secrecy. I couldn't risk hiding anything from Nick when I'd already revealed so much to her.

"Forgive me," I said as soon as I got my tears under doubtful control, "I was the one who set that trap."

"Huh?"

I nodded and started sobbing again. When at last I'd blotted my eyes dry, Nick said to me, "Why did you have to go and tell Mum everything?"

"Because if I hadn't, Dedushka would have. You know, you were right about him spying on us up at the cabin."

"Well, we're in deep shit," he said. He left a moment of silence — on purpose, I thought, for dramatic effect — before he continued. "And I suppose it was you let the fox out."

I nodded.

"And as if that wasn't enough, you had to go and get Dedushka all heated up."

"I didn't get him heated up. He attacked me."

"Oh yeah, sure, they all say that," he said, trying for a joke.

The space between us turned hostile.

"Sorry," he said. "It's just that, Jesus, Yule, you always take things too far."

I stared at him.

"Yule, I said I was sorry."

In the semi-darkness of my room we sat for a long time, unwilling to part when there was bad blood between us, and as the moments passed his loyalty and good intentions began to feel as solid as his stocky, muscular presence. It was as if, just by being there, he calmed me down so I could think clearly.

"What I want," I finally said, "is to go up to the cabin."

I felt him retreating, baffled by what must have sounded like another of my crazy whims, so I took hold of his hand to make him stay. "I haven't been up there since the fire," I told him. "I need to see it for myself, do you understand?"

"But Yule," he murmured, "you can't go up there. Not when you're on crutches. The trail's too rough."

I felt myself turning stubborn. Making the trek up through the woods suddenly became a compulsion, just like freeing the fox. I didn't try to justify it or explain it.

"I'm going tomorrow," I told him, "and I want you to take me."

The following morning I awakened to the sound of loud braying, and a moment later Nicholas came in.

"Chornik," he said. "You can ride Chornik up to the cabin."

When I got to the back door Chornik was standing in the driveway, bridled, with a blanket strapped around him. With Nick's help (first he held one of my crutches, then he gave me a leg up) I was able to mount. Aunt Xenia, her eyes puffy from lack of sleep, handed me a parcel. "Your breakfast," she said, in a sorrowful voice that sounded resigned at the worst, approving at the very best. It was obvious that we weren't *in deep shit*, as Nicholas had supposed, and I imagined that for him our love had already become a myth that was more about his own manliness than about me. Perhaps he already told it at the lumberyard, seasoned with allusions to his and my sexual appetite. For certain he would tell it years from now to his current lover, or more likely his wife: an expurgated version, the words chaste but suggestive, as if, like a troubadour, he was improvising a song of romantic love.

We set off. I sat astride Chornik, on the blanket, while Nick led him by the bridle and carried my crutches in his free hand. After the closeness of the house and the chemical-masked smell of decay in Dedushka's shed, the air smelled very sweet. As Chornik walked up the driveway and onto the trail that led to the cabin, the archaic rhythm of his gait freed me from my own tense locus in time. The sun had begun to warm the woods and release the spring fragrances of cedar and fir. A woodpecker hammered against a tree trunk. Because our pace was so slow, much slower than if Nick and I had walked up the path alone, I found myself looking at each tree as we passed by: the texture and patterns of the bark; the colours in the trunks and branches; the shape of the leaves or needles. I noticed every rustle in the undergrowth; watched each bird as it flew from branch to branch; spotted the slime trails of slugs that had crossed the path in the cool, damp night. In front of me Nick occasionally shifted my crutches and carried them on his shoulder for a while, until his arm got tired and he dropped them once again to his side.

I was so absorbed in each detail along the path that the blackened trunks and singed branches of the trees at the edge of the clearing took me by surprise. Beyond them, among ashes and half-burned timbers, stood a stove: my *burzhuika*, which I had stuffed with miraculous wood. The cabin's frame had collapsed but I could tell where the door had been, because for some reason the fire had left the stoop only a little charred.

Nick helped me down from Chornik's back and handed me my crutches. Slowly we walked right around the ruins, among which I recognized the collapsed metal frame of the bed and a cup whose handle had been missing even before the fire. My nostrils were filled with the smell of dew-dampened ash, like a doused camp-fire or the smell in my hair when I had lain in Uncle Michael and Aunt Xenia's bed half-delirious beneath Christ crucified; and I realized that not once in the plodding journey up through the woods had I thought about the nightmare crucifixions that had invaded my sleep. Beyond the ruins and the charred trees at the clearing's edge, the woods extended as green as they had always been, with the same dense undergrowth, and the same rustlings and bird calls. Nick and I found a large, dry rock and sat down to eat our breakfast. As I chewed on a piece of cheese and black bread I looked up through some fire-blackened branches at the sky, which, although it was only April, was already a deep summer blue. Nick followed my gaze and said, "It's a good thing this isn't July, otherwise the whole forest would have gone up in smoke."

The thought of the entire wood in flames made me gag. In my imagination I saw birds and squirrels and field mice fleeing from the fire that had started somewhere deep inside me. I turned away from the sight of the devastation and looked at the new spring growth on the tips of the branches of an old Douglas fir. The green was so tender that I felt it rather than saw it, and the sunlight that seeped down through the trees was even more comforting than it was warm. Chornik came up to me and nudged my arm for his share of the breakfast. I unwrapped an apple, holding it out to him on the flat of my hand, and when he bit into it, his velvety lips stroking my palm, the juice dribbled down and anointed my grateful hand. The violence that shrouded my world was beginning to dissipate.

THIRTEEN

The image of the dead Christ had been carried out of the church. It was almost midnight, and there was a lull as the whole congregation stood waiting for the bells to peal. I was sitting near the wall, where a few chairs had been placed for the old people to use during the long Easter service. In front of me sat a woman with heavy, swollen legs. Varicose veins crawled over her calves, and her ankles swelled above her laced-up shoes. On her head, like so many of the older women, she wore a floral-print kerchief. I felt both privileged and a little guilty about being allowed to sit while almost everyone else stood. My crutches and bandages gave me the right, but the injury to my foot was healing quickly and I could already walk on it a little, though I still needed the crutches for support.

Kate stood beside me, Nick behind, and near my father, on the other side of Uncle Michael and Aunt Xenia, stood Bette. In the ten days I'd been at Lisii Nos, her belly had suddenly grown large. Her face had got rounder and it glowed in the candlelight. I thought how healthy she looked, now fully recovered from the haemorrhage, and how happy — so different from my mother, who had often told me that she had been sick for the entire nine months she carried me.

My father looked depressed and withdrawn. That afternoon, when Aunt Xenia and Uncle Michael had brought me home, he'd taken me into his bedroom and shut the door against their preparations for our Easter feast. For a long time he said nothing at all, but examined me with a scrutiny as intense as that of a doctor palpating a patient for signs of broken bones. When he cleared his throat at last and asked, "Are you sure you're all right?" he sounded almost disappointed that I wasn't more fragile. I think he felt very fragile himself, and needed the comfort of someone as sickened as he had been by Dedushka's attack on me. Now, in the candlelight, his face was an unhealthy yellow, and I knew he should be in bed instead of at the long service, which wouldn't end until dawn.

Dedushka had stayed at Lisii Nos, furious with me, Nick, Aunt Xenia and especially Uncle Michael after a scene that had taken place the day Nick and I went up to see the ruins of the cabin. As we came back down the trail towards the house, Nick again walked in front of Chornik and me, swinging my crutches, no longer just doing me a favour but enjoying himself, his tread exuberant in his runners; and I thought what a relief it must be for him not to wear his heavy steel-toed boots, which the conventions of the lumberyard forced him to put on for manliness as much as safety. Chornik wasn't used to carrying burdens, and when we reached the small rise at the top of the driveway he stopped suddenly and wouldn't budge despite Nick's gentle tongue-clicks of encouragement. As Nick searched in his pocket for a lump of sugar he'd put there for just such an emergency, the sound of angry voices rose through the silence, then faded again when Chornik, his neck craning for his treat, started to plod after him. Nick made a game of it, holding out the lump of sugar just beyond Chornik's reach, walking faster and faster, trotting, running while Chornik pursued him, and I hung on with my arms around Chornik's neck, leaning over the dark cross at his shoulders until his bouncing began to hurt my bandaged foot and I called out for Nick to stop. I heard the angry voices again, this time distinguishable as Dedushka's and Uncle Michael's, and when the house came into view I saw that Uncle Michael had parked his truck in front of Dedushka's shed, and was carrying a cardboard carton out to it. Dedushka circled around the back of the truck to confront him, but the bandage on his cheek made him look like a clown.

"What do you think you are doing, taking away my things? Those are my traps, my pelts. You have no right to touch them."

Beneath his baby-fine hair, Uncle Michael was blushing with anger, as if he were embarrassed at his own fury.

"You should be in jail," he said. "If I'd had my way, you would be."

"Jail? Jail? I was the one who saved this family. If it were not for me, Xenia could never have become your wife. She'd have died years ago in some Siberian prison camp."

Beneath me Chornik stirred nervously, and to calm him I patted his neck with palms that had become grimy with ash from the site of the fire and the natural oils in his coat.

Aunt Xenia paced back and forth along the driveway, hugging herself, lifting her head every few moments, crying, "Aiy, aiy," and then dropping it, eyes staring down at the gravel, in the throes of some private agony that had nothing to do with Uncle Michael and Dedushka.

As Nick helped me dismount, he said, "Ah, Jesus, I hate it when Mum gets Russian." But there was no contempt in his words — rather a tension and fine alertness that made him look older than he really was.

Dedushka suddenly turned from the truck and ran over to Aunt Xenia, who put out her hand, trying to protect the small space around her.

"Tell him," he said, "how I got you all out of Leningrad. To Lisii Nos. Through the marshes to the fishing boat that took us to Porvoo. How I got you from there to

Gotland to Kristiansand to Skegness to London to Montreal. Tell him how I led you past the German sentries, how I snared rabbits for you so you didn't starve. Tell him he should not hate me and my traps."

Aunt Xenia nodded and wept as he spoke.

He placed his rough outdoor hands on either side of her face.

"Pretty. Pretty," he said. "Do you think you would be so pretty if I hadn't got you out? How pretty do you think you'd look after ten years of forced labour? A mouthful of steel teeth, that's how pretty. Do you think your Michael would have looked at you twice if you'd had a mouthful of steel teeth?"

Nick, whose expression had changed from wounded to puzzled to fierce, suddenly ran at Dedushka.

"Don't you speak to her like that." He was the same height as Dedushka, and shouted right into his face as he grabbed his shoulders and shook him.

"You leave my mother alone," he said, "and my cousin, and my little sister and...." Pride wouldn't let him finish, but I knew he was thinking about all the false accusations Dedushka had manufactured over the years to bully and beat him. His hand rounded into a fist.

"Nick. Nick." Uncle Michael said, wedging himself into the space between them. "That's enough." Not angry, but firm. "Take Chornik back down to the paddock."

Nick looked relieved as he took hold of Chornik's bridle and led him away. I went over to the truck to find out what Uncle Michael was going to cart off, but as I came closer the stink got so high I had to hold my nose and breathe through my fingers.

In the box were packed all the contents of Dedushka's shed: traps, snares, sharpening tools, tanning tools, even the calendar girls smiling up at me from their cardboard carton, voluptuous paper bodies wrinkled and ripped. The stink came from the carton beside them, full of badly tanned pelts — my fox's on top, but I could also see a raccoon tail and the sleek brown fur of what must have been a weasel. The polecat was there too, dropped tail-first into the corner of the box, its exquisite wild face staring up at me. It was mine. Dedushka had given it to me, and I knew I must rescue it, not just because it belonged to me but because he had once been capable of carving it. I reached down into the stink and dead fur, my hand disturbing flies, touching coarse and then fine soft hair as I pulled the carving out. Uncle Michael came back to the truck and started the engine while Dedushka yelled at him that he was a thief.

"Well then, you'd better call in the police," Uncle Michael told him, "and we'll see which one of us ends up in jail."

For the first time Dedushka seemed to take the threat seriously. He stepped back, lips suddenly pale, eyes stricken: an expression that reminded me of my father. And the bandage on his cheek made him look so vulnerable that for a moment I thought I'd done wrong in wounding him.

"*Znaiyu*," he said, looking down at his once gifted hands, "I know I am not as I should be." He turned towards his shed and with a broad, dramatic gesture cried out, "But this is all I have...all in the world...and you have taken it away from me."

Ignoring him, Uncle Michael pumped the gas and released the handbrake. For a moment Dedushka held his pose, but when the truck accelerated up the driveway he ran after it, fists punching the air, until it disappeared around a curve and he came to a moment's stop, panting, then veered off into the woods, followed by Callack, whose high-pitched bark declared her glee.

When I turned around, Aunt Xenia was sitting on the back steps, hugging herself, rocking back and forth. Kate stood behind her, hesitant, in the open kitchen doorway. I made my way towards them awkwardly because I was trying to hold onto the crutches and the polecat at the same time. "It's okay," I told Kate, who was teary-eyed with bewilderment. "Can you hold onto this?" I asked her, handing her the polecat, both to distract her and to make it easier to sit myself down beside Aunt Xenia. As Kate took the carving from me her lips trembled. "Your mummy's going to be all right," I said. But as soon as I touched Aunt Xenia she started to sob. I put my crutches down to take her in my arms, but instead she took me, so that she became the comforter and I the comforted. She stroked my hair and my cheek, whispering, "Precious, my darling." And though I had always kept her at a distance, for the sole reason that she was not my mother, I found myself giving in at last to her generous tears, which were as much for me as for herself, and I started to cry the tears I should have shed the day before, when I'd confessed the events to her, but not the emotions. It was at that moment that I stopped needing my own mother quite so much, and discovered that, after all, there was nothing about myself that I wanted to keep secret from Aunt Xenia.

Suddenly the bells began to peal. The doors to the sanctuary opened and the priests, accompanied by the chanting of the choir, came out carrying candles. I had got used to the sobriety of our late-night vigil, and I wasn't at all prepared for the abrupt shift in mood as the priests passed by in their brocaded robes: a hot excitement that affected everyone, even my father, who usually endured events without expecting anything from them. I imagined that any one of us with no more than a glance might have set the iconostasis on fire. And it was the surge of real, naked flame as the candle-bearing congregation started to follow the priests to the door — like the flames in the cabin, leaping from the stove across the ceiling — that made me frantic. In the cacophony of bells I got to my feet, nearly upsetting my own candle, handing one of my crutches to Nick because I couldn't manage both them and the candle too. I stumbled through the crowd, not caring whom I pushed aside, in a panic to get out before the whole church flared up. I felt a hand on my arm, and for a second my terror shifted from fear of fire to fear of violation, until I realized that it was Nick who was touching me, and that he was only trying to calm me down.

At last I broke through to the cold outside. The sound of the bells became clearer and reverberated less in the open night, beneath the safely cold glimmer of stars. There was a smell of damp earth and a fresh, sweet scent from the flowering trees along the boulevard, and in the steady light of the streetlamp I decided that from that moment on I would see things only as they really were, with clear vision, unadorned by fancy; but as I glanced up, the blossoms in the trees looked much whiter than they did in the day and I had to remind myself that it was the peculiar spectrum of artificial light, not immanence, that made them glow.

As we began our procession around the church I looked up at its bulb-shaped dome and, with my newly controlled vision, examined the metal Orthodox cross mounted on it, noting how clean-lined and elegant it looked because no Christ was nailed to it. The paved pathway around the church turned to gravel, which hurt my injured foot if I put any weight on it, and made it more difficult for me to balance on my crutch. I was careful to hold my candle upright, so that the wax dripped evenly down the sides and congealed into tiny globules before it reached my fingers. Nick walked beside me, and I noticed that he was using my crutch to support an imagined limp.

"I have come to find the Christ. Do you think He can cure me?" he asked, limping more dramatically.

I recognized an invitation to the kind of game we had played throughout our childhood summers, and for the briefest moment I was tempted to accept, but I squelched the impulse.

"Don't be so childish," I told him, and focused my attention on the walkway's monotonous grey pebbles, which threatened to heave and flow beneath the unsteady flame of my candle.

Nick sounded hurt but not put off. "*You* may not believe, but *I* do," he said. "Yes, I can feel it. Tonight I will be cured."

Ignoring him, I stared ahead to where my father was struggling over the gravel in his chair. Bette, because she was holding both his and her own candle, couldn't give him any help, but when she turned towards him her look was admiring — he might have been an Olympic weightlifter straining against hundreds of kilos. I saw her lips move and his respond, though I couldn't hear what they said, and his skin had a translucent quality, though my scrupulously objective vision denied it: sweat and candlelight, it insisted; the rest is just your imagination.

The procession stopped, and ahead of me I could see that the priests had made a complete circle and were standing once more at the entrance to the church.

The doors opened. A deep voice chanted, "*Khristos voskrese iz mertvykh; cmertiyu cmert poprav.* Christ is risen from the dead; by His death He has conquered death."

"What did I tell you?" Nick whispered; then, raising his voice, he added, "I'm going to get cured. Just see if I don't." A middle-aged woman tapped him on the shoulder from behind and said, "For shame. Show some respect."

His face turned sober, but he continued to limp and leaned even more heavily on the crutch.

Inside, the church blazed with candlelight — only candlelight, there was no conflagration — which glanced off the metal icon covers and the priests' vestments. Easter matins began, and soon the choir started singing the ecstatic stammering chant *Paskha velikaya. Paskha* was the Russian word for Easter, as well as for the delicious cheesy pyramid I'd helped Aunt Xenia make, and the chant's rhythms were like those of a folk-dance, with strong downbeats and skipping, staccato upbeats. Nick thrust my crutch back at me and did a discreet little dance beneath the church's high dome.

"I'm cured, I'm cured," he whispered to me excitedly, and I knew it wasn't a joke because I couldn't stop myself from getting out of my chair, rising, discovering my fancy resurrected, become caprice, caper, firelit dance to Russian Orthodox liturgy, the voices of my ancestors in old Slavonic curing me of my limitations, my pain of both body and mind, in one sweet physical moment: when I put my full weight on my foot and it no longer hurt.

"*Khristos voskres*. Christ is risen," I said to Nick. It was the traditional Easter greeting, and he answered with the traditional response, "*Voistinu voskres*. He is risen indeed." Then, staring at me with wide-open, credulous eyes, he began dancing again. Behind us I heard a tchtch of disapproval and some muttering, but no one else appeared to care that he was dancing in the middle of Easter matins, and I wondered if others among the worshippers had felt what we had, had been cured of their afflictions, like us, and had wanted to dance their own particular joy.

I looked over at my father, but his expression was grim. As I watched, a violent spasm ran through his leg and lifted his foot for an instant from the footrest.

The church had grown warm with all the people and the heat from the flickering candles. The air was heavy with incense, unlike the air outside, where the blossoms and the earth had smelled so fresh, and as I grew drowsy I felt myself swaying on my crutches, blown back and forth by the rhythms of the chanting, which alternately crescendoed and grew faint until the service finally ended at dawn.

Then I found myself caught up in the flow of the crowd as the worshippers moved forward to kiss the cross that the priest held out to us. Against my lips the metal felt clammy from the Easter rejoicing.

"*Khristos voskres*."

"Voistinu voskres."

I repeated the greeting or its response over and over as I kissed Nick, Kate, Aunt Xenia and Uncle Michael, and gave thanks that Dedushka wasn't there. I kissed Bette too, because it was expected, and then my father. As I bent over him I saw that his eyes were glittering and for a moment I thought, *He believes it. He believes that Christ is risen.* But when my lips touched his cheek it was very hot, and the phrase *Voistinu voskres* smelled bad as he said it.

Out on the sidewalk a rapt Kate eyed me while I showed off my small miracle: walking without my crutches, without limping, convincing myself there was no pain. Nicholas cheered me on: "Way to go, Yule. Right on." We were a tiny joyful knot of believers, light-headed from lack of sleep, filled with hope because we were all three of us young, healthy and therefore curable. From the centre of our microcelebration I looked out and saw my father speaking to Aunt Xenia, who suddenly went still and blanched.

"What?" Bette asked, still smiling at something Uncle Michael had said to her when she turned towards them.

"I think someone had better drive me to the hospital," my father said clearly, and his words snuffed out the expectant mother's glow in Bette's face.

"Show me the miracle again," Kate begged, tugging at my arm.

"Shh," Nick warned her.

My mouth went dry with fear, but I was also furious with my father for ruining our Easter celebration.

Giving himself up to illness, Papa slumped in his chair, while Bette assumed a steely efficiency that made her look pounds lighter, as if she'd traded away her motherhood.

"I'll get the car," she said.

Aunt Xenia bent over my father, mumbling comforting endearments to him in Russian ("Nikolenka, *bednyaga,* poor thing, my Nikolenka"), and stroked his hair. For his part Uncle Michael stood by calm and reliable, ready as usual to assist in yet another episode of what appeared to be a permanent state of emergency.

The weeks went by and my father stayed in hospital on dialysis, because the damage done to his kidneys by chronic infections was severe and irreversible. At first it was like any other time he had been ill. He suffered the dialysis just as he had suffered the operations on his spine or the physiotherapy or the doses of antibiotics. But then there began to be signs, though it took me a long time to recognize them. For instance, Bette and Aunt Xenia, instead of calling each other about once a week, as they had when my father first went into hospital, began to talk to each other every day, sometimes twice a day. Then Aunt Xenia brought Dedushka into Vancouver one weekend to visit Papa. He arrived complaining about the noise of the city and almost everything else; but after he had seen Papa he became silent, and when he left the following day he looked shrivelled and exhausted, as if a sleepless night was the least he'd endured. Next, Uncle Alek, who had never visited my father in hospital before, flew in from Edmonton. A few days later, when Bradley was visiting him, Papa announced that he would never direct another play; two days after that I saw Pip Salisbury in tears as he left the hospital.

But there were more obvious signs too. My father had been on dialysis before for acute kidney failure, but this time he needed it every three or four days, and each treatment left him more debilitated than the last. His skin, which had often looked sallow, became permanently yellow. His face was swollen. He was often irritable and kept demanding that something be done, but one day when Bette tried to find out exactly what it was he wanted, he became confused and shut his eyes against all her questions. With me he was overly solicitous: long after my foot had healed he asked me if I was in pain, as though searching for some hereditary defect he might have passed on to me. He kept saying that I probably had my mother's strong constitution — but regretfully, I thought. Not that he wished me harm, but it was as though he was trying to rediscover the connection he and I had shared just after the fire, and every time I visited him I was left with the impression that, rather than terminally ill, he was fatally lonely.

In the midst of all this I went back to school for the summer term. The first week I was still on my crutches — my Easter cure, like an analgesic, had worn off after a few hours — and whether it was because I was visibly injured, or because I'd been forgiven, or because it was a new term with new preoccupations, I was no longer a pariah: one or another of my classmates always offered to carry my books as we moved between classrooms, or found me a chair during assembly.

Ursula, who had spent the Easter vacation in Germany, didn't come back until the second week. I remember the morning she arrived, her arm still in its cast. She stood in the doorway, surveying the classroom, and it occurred to me that she'd stopped there not out of some histrionic impulse to make an entrance, but out of self-doubt: as if she couldn't take her authority for granted, and needed a moment to convince herself she had a right to claim it. I must have been the only one who noticed, because the pre-bell chatter stopped almost immediately, and I thought that the moment of silence was as real a gesture of reverence as the lighting of a candle before an icon. As the chatter began again, Ursula walked among the desks acknowledging each votive greeting with a smile, but when she started down my row there was another silence, and I knew my fate for the summer term was being decided: if Ursula snubbed me, all the friendly gestures would stop and once again I'd be an outcast. But instead Ursula looked at my crutches and bandaged foot, then at her own cast, and burst out with a laugh that was so free-throated and good-humoured that I started laughing myself, and I knew this was another sign that the violence between me and the world had stopped. Not that Ursula and I became friends again, not yet; it wasn't only our bodies that needed healing. I think we were both traumatized by how easily our intimacy had turned into a savagery neither of us understood because it had come partly from outside our experience, by way of our war-shocked parents: a legacy of hatred and deprivation that suddenly manifested itself amid our teen-aged vitality and North American privilege.

Meanwhile Willi disrupted my consciousness like a migraine shimmer at the edge of sight, especially now that I was back in Vancouver and routinely walked the streets of the neighbourhood where the von der Lindes lived. But I didn't actually meet up with him until one magnolia-laden afternoon in late spring.

The traffic was heavy on Tenth Avenue; even so, I heard the Karamann Ghia approach and slow down to the pace I was walking at on my way to buy olives from the Demeter grocery store on Broadway. The excitement I felt the moment before I turned around was part impulse to flight, part titillation: what was that dangerous boy going to demand of me this time?

The door on the passenger side opened and I saw Willi leaning across the seat towards me.

"Hi, Willi. Still driving your mum's car," I said, establishing myself before he had a chance to speak, forestalling words that might give him power over me: *Come for a drive. You'll have a lot more fun with me than with Ursula. I've got a place where we can be alone together.* The odour of cigarette smoke, a sharp relief from the cloying fragrance of magnolia, wafted up from the interior. Willi was thinner than I remembered, his face derelict. He coughed before he asked, "So where are the crutches?" to let me know he'd been keeping tabs on me. I was flattered.

"I'm cured," I answered. "A miracle." And sat in the passenger seat, daring fate, but staying in control by keeping the door open and my right foot on the no-park yellow curb for a quick getaway.

"Wanna go for a drive to the Endowment Lands?"

"No thanks."

"Still a sissy schoolgirl, huh?"

"I don't trust you," I said.

His face reddened; then, sighing, he took out a small flask that looked to be made of silver, an antique.

"Nobody does," he replied. He took a swig, then offered the flask to me. I shook my head. It occurred to me that the flask might be stolen from some genteel shop, in Kerrisdale perhaps, that didn't have security enough to protect itself from the likes of Willi. A truck passed us, the driver leaning on the horn, yelling, "That's no fucking place to stop, shithead." Willi gave him the finger. Then he took another swig from the flask and lit a cigarette with his shaky nicotine-stained hands.

"I'm getting out of this piss place soon," he said, giving voice to a monologue that must already have been going on inside his head. "Going down to L.A., me and some other guys, to start a band. You gotta be where it's happening, not in this dead fucking town." The traffic noise affected his words the way a strobe illuminates an actor's gestures, blocking out some, emphasizing others, changing what is smooth and linear into something jerky and intermittent: *down there...fierce...couldn't survive...Mutti...never thought...life is change or there can't...just fucking dinosaurs.* He went on like that for perhaps fifteen minutes, taking swigs from the flask, fumbling the cap back on, gazing at me with eyes he couldn't focus. And I realized that it wasn't just the traffic noise or the drink that made his words incomprehensible. He was raving.

Fear: *He's nuts — he's got a screw loose. What if, like Dedushka...?* Panic: *Get me out of here.* Anger: *He's trying to force me beyond myself, just as he always does.* Fascination: *I know he's right to rave. The world...parts of it...don't make any sense. Maybe he's going to lead me...and I'll under-*

stand.... Contempt: *You're starting to rave just like him. He's drunk, that's all, just a boring loser drunk.* Compassion: *But he's half Slav like me, and I love...what?...that excess of sensitivity that makes him suffer.* Hopelessness: *He's never going to get out. I'm never going to get out.*

I felt his hand on my forearm. "The Endowment Lands, Julie. You have to come with me," he said, his words suddenly coherent again and his intention clear.

"I don't want to."

"But I need you, Julie. Can't you see that?" His words slurred just a little, as if they were some slight defect he was offering up for me to pity and be swayed by.

"Fucking me isn't going to help," I said, neutral.

His hand tightened around my arm.

"Won't help at all," I insisted, revealing my determination, hiding my fear. Slowly I pulled away from him. His head dropped against the back of the seat.

"I have to go," I said, but I sat with him for a moment of commemorative silence before I got out of the car with one smooth, agile and wary movement.

When I'd bought the olives I went home by a different route, but for days afterwards I worried about him. I imagined that in his drunken state he'd had an accident, or had lost himself in the logic of the numbered avenues or the chestnut-treed sameness of the boulevards. Every morning, as I sat on the bus cradling my slapdash homework, I vowed that I'd ask Ursula how he was, and if he'd got home all right; but at school, where all the talk centred around make-up and boyfriends or — among the athletes — swimming and track and field, my worry had no context, and I knew that even if I dared bring it up, Ursula would misunderstand and perhaps turn rageful, like the goddess everyone at school thought she was.

All this time Bette and I lived alone together. When I got home from school she would put on the kettle and make me a cup of tea, which I immediately took up to my room. But then one day, when we were expecting a phone call from Aunt Xenia, I stayed downstairs with her. That became a habit, and I didn't realize how much I depended on it until the afternoon she was doing a voice-over for a commercial, and wasn't there to make the tea.

But my relationship with her really began to change one evening when I went to her in her room to get permission for a tuberculin test at school. Lying on a couch near the window, her hair falling loose around her shoulders, she was knitting in the late spring twilight. She had not yet turned on the light, but a moment after I arrived a streetlamp came on and shone in strongly through the window, which was open because the May night was so warm, casting the filigree shadow of the rowan tree over the parquet floor. She lay barefoot with one knee raised, which gave her body an elegant line in spite of her bulk, and above her belly her agile fingers were purling a row of stitches (in the artificial light I wasn't sure what colour it was: some pastel shade of yellow, perhaps, or was it green?) into what might have been the back of a baby-sized sweater. It was as if her real purpose were to knit together the foetal strands of DNA, by a patient and expert magic, into a human soul.

She signed the permission slip right away, and I turned to leave, but she called me back.

"Do you want to feel him kick?" she asked. She had spoken the word *him* with imperturbable confidence, even though it was before the days of amniocentesis and there was no technology to confirm what her body already knew. I held out my hand and she placed it gently on her abdomen. Through the thin cotton of her smock, her belly button obtruded. Something jolted my palm, and as soon as I realized that what I'd felt was the kick of a minuscule foot, the foetus became a child for me. I thought of the blood I'd smeared so discreetly all over Bette's room. The baby had survived a haemorrhage, but what if, as Ursula had suggested, the blood curse transformed it into a monster? My archaic self believed this could happen, and I suddenly grew frantic at the thought that Bette might unknowingly knit my malediction into the child's proliferating cells.

Though I didn't speak about it, I knew my father was dying, and the foetus, now that I'd acknowledged it, became an essential link with him. For that reason more than any other, I began to cast about for some way to undo the blood curse. Later that night, in my own room, I rediscovered the cloisonné ring Bette had bought for me in Victoria. Unthinking, I slipped it over the index finger of my left hand, and when I looked down at that miniature wire and enamel rosary I felt honour-bound to protect Bette, the foetus, my father and me: the remnants of family.

The following day was a Saturday, and while Bette was out shopping I wore the cloisonné ring into her room. For a long moment I stood at the window and stared at the fading blossoms on the rowan tree, which were small and delicate, and clustered like the berries that would soon appear and ripen to a bold, bright red during the fall. I thought of calling on the Christian god for protection, but in my imagination all I could see was the suffering, dying man on the cross, and I thought that with all that pain he had enough on his mind, and could hardly be expected to take seriously a heathen spell worked by two teen-aged amateur witches.

I began twisting the ring around my finger and, as I did, words came to me which I spoke haltingly at first and then repeated over and over until they became a chant: *Protect Bette, protect the baby, protect me and bring Papa relief from his pain.* Dimly I was aware that, although I stood in the room that had once been my mother's, I had left her out of the chant: I knew she no longer belonged in that house, though for so long I'd clung to the delusion that she'd one day return. Over and over again as I twisted the ring I spoke my spell to protect and comfort, and it was as if my words knotted the dappled afternoon into a luminous, four-cornered net of benediction that fell gently over the room: the couch and bed where Bette lay at night, the chest of drawers, the closet, the dressing-table with its chair and mirror, where every morning she powdered, pencilled, lipsticked and brushed her reflection into being, and every night creamed and wiped it away.

While I was chanting I felt that I could go on for ever, but as soon as I stopped I discovered that I was so thoroughly tired I couldn't keep my eyes open. So I dropped down on the couch and slept.

I awakened to a fragrance. For moments I lay with my eyes closed, unwilling to diffuse the sweetness with vision. A smooth, cool material touched my cheek, and I guessed that it must be the source of the fragrance. Soon I heard a voice, only a little louder than a whisper, but clear and rich.

"Julie, are you okay?"

There was a pause while I kept inhaling the sweet smell.

"What are you doing in here, anyway?"

I opened my eyes because the voice, Bette's voice, was demanding an explanation. I saw that she had covered me with a pale dressing-gown made of a slippery material like silk. As I stretched, she sat down beside me, her dress pulling tight over her belly. Briefly I tried to manufacture some excuse for being there, but soon gave up and instead held out my index finger, now burning from the continual spell-twisting of the ring, as if I were offering up a wound that she was supposed to kiss and make better. She took my hand in hers and for the second time placed it on her belly, where the baby was kicking healthy and hard.

I thought to myself, *When he's born, I'll no longer be alone.*

That evening she invited me into the upstairs bathroom while she was taking a bath. I went in reluctant at first to see her full-blown naked body, and standing above her, with all my clothes on, I began to sweat claustrophobically in the steamy air. Her belly was huge and streaked with lines; her nipples brown and swollen. When she asked me, I scrubbed her back for her, but again I felt reluctant...to actually touch such unabashed fecundity.

"Inside," she said, "I feel so immense and sated, there's scarcely anything I need." With her left foot she reached towards the tap and with fabulous agility turned the hot water on. Laughing, she said, "A few months ago I couldn't have done that. I'm magic." She turned the water off again, and lay back resting her hands on her belly. "I only wish your father could share this with me." She sighed. And suddenly I realized she'd asked me into the bathroom in my father's stead. For a long thoughtful moment she stared at me in my jeans, my shirt, my sweater, my socks and shoes.

"Aren't you hot?"

"I'm dying," I said, laughing and at ease, now I knew that she needed me.

"Well, for God's sake take off your clothes."

I did, shyly at first but gratefully, and with each piece I shed I felt my inhibitions melt away, until at last I stood beside her equal in nakedness, she the mother, I the maid, as if we'd both just been created out of archetypal steam.

"There's not much room," she laughed, holding her gibbous breasts as if she were about to offer me milk, "but come on in if you want."

I sat down on the edge of the tub and dangled my feet in the hot water. One by one she took my legs and soaped them; then she picked up her razor from the rim of the bathtub and, with sure delicate strokes, began shaving them from ankle to knee, her touch so gentle that the blade merely stroked my calves. Later, when we were out of the tub and dried, she massaged lotion into my shaved skin and, with my foot resting on what was left of her lap, painted my toenails red.

"Growing up isn't so bad," she said.

I thrived in the new intimacy she offered me, because she wasn't just being dutiful; she needed me to help her through the slow disentanglement from my father. Together we went to visit him, endured his complaints and anger, his periods of withdrawal, and tried to comfort him, more often with touch than with words. And we talked about it afterwards: not just my father, but the hospital's long corridors down which Bette waddled maternally, the disinfectant smell of illness, the nursing staff, some of whom were saccharine, others rough and ready, still others ostentatiously efficient, all working out strategies for survival in the ghetto of the dying.

Then, one Sunday morning just as Bette and I were finishing a late breakfast of too many pancakes, the doorbell rang. Uncle Alek had phoned to say he might fly out for a visit with my father, so we weren't really surprised, and, because I was in the middle of making a second pot of coffee, Bette went to answer. I heard voices in the front hall. A moment later Bette pushed open the kitchen door. A frown lined her usually serene forehead.

"Julie," she said, "it's your mother."

FOURTEEN

When I went out into the hallway, I discovered two people: my mother and James. He was wearing a jacket of nondescript brown tweed, and though he was much taller than she was, he stood behind her, stooped and somehow lesser. Like a visitation she came towards me in her black dress. At her neck was a string of crystals, iridescent in the strong June light that flowed through the glass panel at the side of the front door. But I noticed that on her finger she wore a humble garnet ring. My father had given it to her in the early days of their marriage, and I wondered if she was wearing it out of sentimentality or to make some kind of emotional claim on him or me or both of us. Her hair was swept up and bound back in a chignon as severe and uncompromising as the professional demands she made on herself and her colleagues.

"My dearest darling, how are you?" she asked, as I sidestepped a hug because I wanted to punish her for assuming she could barge into my life and Bette's without warning. She touched a cold hand to my cheek, and when, relenting a little, I put my own hand over hers — unable to believe that on such a warm day anyone's flesh could be so icy — she explained that the rented car she had been driving was air-conditioned. Then she pushed James forward. He walked with a slight limp and looked ineffectual behind his greying, gingery beard, but his pianist hands were long-fingered and supple as a conjuror's. I thought of him performing feats of presti-digitation on her cold skin as they lay together in some hermetic and temperature-controlled hotel room. For his part, James was clearly embarrassed by his role as my mother's protector/pet, and a sharp look in her direc-tion told me that the absurdity of it made him angry. I was angry too, because my mother's sudden arrival had disturbed the small peace I'd begun to make with the world.

Looking beyond me, my mother said, "I'd like you to meet my friend and colleague James Walther." She was speaking to Bette, who had followed me into the hallway, though I hadn't noticed her because all my at-tention was on my mother. Just by putting in an appear-ance, she had already diverted the flow of my affection away from Bette and back towards herself.

All four of us stood uncertainly while hostility flashed in the air between us, consuming oxygen, I im-agined, because I found it difficult to breathe. It was ob-vious that my mother disliked Bette, and she tried to encase her in a disdainful stare, but Bette's very stillness, that round, stolid self-assurance, was equal to my moth-er's contempt. For all her iciness, I could see something had shocked Mama, and suddenly I felt sure that she hadn't known Bette was pregnant.

"We'd like to take you out to lunch," my mother said, turning her attention back to me — reluctantly, I thought, as if Bette's swollen belly was a fascination she didn't want to give up. Briefly I worried about the baby, thinking that my mother in her crone-black dress might curse him as I once had, but much more powerfully, be-cause she had the knack of accomplishing whatever she set out to do. But within a few moments she'd bundled me out the door and into the rented car, whose air con-ditioning brought out goose bumps all over my bare arms.

We sat down for lunch at a sidewalk table at a res-taurant on Fourth Avenue. The traffic flowing past was heavy and made conversation even more difficult than our incompatibility. James hid his simmering anger behind politeness, I tore at the edges of my paper serviette, my mother tried to control the conversation with expansive chatter about herself and vague questions to me about school. When she brought up the play I'd written, instead of trying to explain why it had been cancelled, I turned on them both.

"Why are you asking me all these stupid questions? What are you doing here? What do you want?"

James turned away in disgust from my outburst, but my mother answered quietly during a break in the traffic, "Your Aunt Xenia rang me."

Those words made the air go still, and I wished I hadn't interrupted my mother. To have explained to her all about the fight between Ursula and me would have made me feel ashamed, but it would also have meant that for a moment or two longer I could have pretended Mama's visit was nothing out of the ordinary.

James called the waiter and asked for the bill while I brushed away the lint from my mutilated serviette.

"I feel something of a gooseberry," he said, "so I'll drive you to the hospital, but then, if you don't mind, I'll leave you to yourselves."

I sneezed as I got out of the air-conditioned car into the sunlight, and sneezed again as my mother and I stepped through the automatic doors — she looked back for a moment to watch James drive away — and into the broad hospital corridor that led past Admissions and down towards the gift shop and X-ray. Bette and I had walked this corridor many times, together and separately, but my mother transformed it with her long lithe strides into a conduit for her own resolve. Nurses stared at her as they passed, then looked away shyly. It was as if they sensed in her a force greater than her mere physical presence, and I began to wonder if she was being propelled by something outside her, or if she was herself a conduit:

the flesh-and-blood channel for some titanic will. In the institutional light her necklace and her make-up had lost their iridescence. If she was possessed by a superhuman will, it was a grim one that sucked all energy away from external show and redirected it inward to feed its own purpose. We reached the elevator and the door opened to reveal half a dozen people: staff, visitors, a patient in an ankle-length blue terrycloth robe. There was a general murmur of conversation, but in the few moments it took for their eyes to glance up and notice my mother all speech was stifled. Four people came out of the elevator, my mother and I got in and we travelled up to the fifth floor in a silence so complete that it was as if we'd all suddenly lost the ability to make words.

Through the doorway to my father's room, I saw Bradley standing at the foot of the bed. When he noticed my mother he moved around to the side, closer to my father, as if he was trying to protect him. Then abruptly his body relaxed and, looking back at my mother, I saw that she had faltered. Or was it that just by entering the room she had already delivered into it what she must, what I had sensed when she arrived at our front door and then again at lunch in those simple words *Your Aunt Xenia rang me*: the certainty and imminence of my father's death?

I went to my father as Bradley moved away from him towards my mother, whose hand he took in his, formally but with compassion too, and as if he was really pleased to see her.

"It's been so long, my dear."

"Too long."

Papa was having a bad day. His face was yellow and badly swollen into a mask that had no human affect, but looked more like an overripe fruit that had already begun to spoil. I kissed his puffy cheek and, as I did, caught a whiff of putrefaction on his breath. Then I glanced back at my mother, who looked lost now that she was only herself. Realizing that she needed a guide,

I kissed Papa's cheek once again, then moved away. As soon as she understood what was expected of her — the kiss was part of the ritual of the daily visits, and if she wanted to participate she must do the same — she strode to Papa's bedside, bent over him, kissed him and asked briskly, "Well, then, how are you?"

"As you see," he replied. He didn't look either pleased or upset by her arrival, but then it was hard to tell with his face swollen like that.

The light coming through the window restored the radiance to my mother's necklace, brightened her voice, speeded up her words as if they ran off solar cells.

"We had a terribly good flight over."

"Over?" Papa asked. He sounded genuinely confused.

"The Atlantic Ocean. Greenland. The Pole. From England, you know, where I've lived most of my life except for those nine glorious years in Canada." Her words still so very bright, bantering, almost flirtatious. "We got in last night." A slight emphasis on *we*. And I realized she was trying to provoke him, make him jealous. "*We're* staying at the Hotel Vancouver. I didn't get much sleep, so I'm feeling a bit logy. But of course it's your health *we're* concerned about."

At last my father caught on. "We?"

"We. James. Do you remember? He wanted to come and see you, but I thought better not. Was I right?"

"Right," my father repeated. I had the impression he said it because it caused him the least effort. He didn't have to think anything up, only speak the last word my mother had said as a statement rather than a question. I don't think he cared or even thought about James, although a year earlier the very idea of my mother sharing her life with someone else would have mired him in a week-long depression. I would have liked to believe it was a sign of how much he'd healed since meeting Bette, but I knew it was really the measure of how much he had already detached himself from life.

"Yule," Bradley said, "let's leave them to themselves. There's nothing you or I can do." He put his hand on my shoulder, and I allowed him to edge me towards the door. I think I knew that only if my mother was left alone with Papa would she become real.

A half-hour later, when Bradley and I were walking back down the corridor towards my father's room, his door opened and my mother came out holding her hand to her mouth. She hesitated for a moment, then turned away from us and ran down towards the far end of the hall. A man came after her carrying a plant. My father? Impossible. It was Uncle Alek. He saw us and lifted his hand in an automatic greeting. Looking down the hallway, from which my mother had already disappeared, he said, more to himself than to us, "I don't know what got into her. She started talking about some guy named James, then bolted like a frightened pony."

But I was more concerned about Papa, so while Bradley went off down the hall after my mother, I went back into his room. He was lying on his side, his swollen face distorted by the pressure of the pillow against his cheek. The bedclothes were tangled up in his feet. I straightened the blankets, put a pillow between his ankles to protect the skin and checked that the tube running down to his bag had no kinks in it. I became aware that someone was watching me. Turning around I saw Uncle Alek — the stalker's son, as I now thought of him ever since my run-in with Dedushka. He was smiling a smile that had the need for superiority in it.

"Maybe some day you'll want to train to be a nurse," he said. I felt him trying to control me, make me into someone lesser.

"Or a doctor," I replied, to re-establish myself.

"Aleksandr. How are you?" my father asked. His words sounded laboured, formal, ceremonious.

But Uncle Alek answered with a laugh, "Oh, just as nasty as ever." As he put the plant down on the bedside table and brought a chair up to the bed he added,

"But not as nasty as you think." Between them there was immediate intimacy, a triumph of blood over events which made me feel excluded because I refused to forget, and would have left the room anyway, even without the glance of dismissal Uncle Alek cast back towards me over his shoulder.

I went down the corridor to where Bradley was standing outside the women's washroom. From inside came a howl — fox-like, I thought, remembering Dedushka's starving prisoner. I wondered what that sound had to do with Mama and looked at Bradley for an explanation, but he'd pushed his hands deep into his pockets and kept shifting his weight from one foot to the other. I looked at the skirted stick-person on the door, then back at Bradley, and realized that it warded him off like a charm or a No Trespassing sign.

"She's *your* mother," he said.

I pushed open the door. No one was in sight; only the greenish glare from the fluorescent tubes and a steady clicking sound. There was another howl that was a mere echo of the first, then I noticed my mother's strong ankles and her feet in their slender shoes behind one of the cubicle doors. Click. Click. Click.

"Mama, what are you doing?" I asked. The clicking continued for a moment. Then stopped. Slowly the cubicle door opened and she came out. The tip of her straight, severe nose was red, her eyes bloodshot. With her arms outstretched she walked up to me, pulled me to her chest and held me there. I stood rigid inside her arms.

"It's all too much," she said. "The flight. Meeting Bette. Your father. Alek. Christ, I'm exhausted."

I almost said, *You might as well have stayed at home. You're not doing us any good.* But I felt her feeding off me and there was pleasure in it, as if she were suckling at my breast, so I stayed still inside her arms until she was done.

She went over to a tap that had an attachment for

drinking, turned it on and began to gulp at the curving column of water. Her right hand rested on the countertop. As she drank, she clicked and clicked the garnet ring against its surface.

Then she straightened up as if she'd been some withered plant — "Flying makes you so dehydrated," she explained — and examined her reflection in the mirror: those taut cords in her neck; the prominent collarbones; the lines carved downward from her nose and around her mouth. Her hair, which had come loose from its controlled upsweep, fell thick and curly but fine-stranded around her face. It was like my hair, though I had forgotten, because I had so rarely seen it down and loose since she and Papa had separated. There was nothing else about her that was like me: we had different noses, eyes, cheekbones, mouths, chins. But my eyes were continually drawn back to those loose, dark, unruly strands: the sign that she was my mother; the explanation for why my whole body said yes to her body even though it was beginning to grow scrawny around her cold centre.

She saw me looking at her reflection, and in the mirror I watched her hand move towards me: an elegant hand, though the veins stood out along its back. There had been no real intimacy between us since those few weeks when I alone knew she was pregnant and dreamed of a baby brother, while she dreamed that a second child, even by another man, would transform us into a real family. After that, there'd been all those years when she concentrated so on her work that I always felt in the way. But now she'd decided that she needed me again, or at least needed something from me, and as her hand reached out for mine I went stiff with the fear of once more being used or betrayed.

"I...," she began in a constricted voice, "wanted your father—"

I interrupted her. "Papa doesn't care any more; he doesn't love you."

My mother's jaw fell, not in surprise but in recognition that what I'd said was the truth. Then her whole body rose, looking so light that I didn't know if she floated or stood. It was grief that lifted her, and with the grief came tears. She wept and wept, her face raised to the harsh light, her arms floating away from the sides of her body dancing its grief, while her hair unfurled over her shoulders. I knew some part of her was performing, but her grief was genuine and she couldn't help her body being a dancer's, a choreographer's, after all those years of training and hard work. Inside me I felt a light pulse, perhaps just the beat of my own heart, but the point was that I hadn't noticed it before, wouldn't have now if I hadn't been with her. It was like an undeveloped sense or a gift long neglected, something of my mother I had rejected along with her theatricality and self-absorption. And — perhaps because she was soon to be my only surviving parent, or perhaps because for the first time in years I had seen her in disarray and vulnerable — I admitted to myself that I loved her, even if Papa no longer did, if only for the vague sense of possibility I got from her simply being there.

I heard gentle knocking on the door and Bradley's voice calling very quietly, "Yule."

I went out to him in the corridor.

"You've been in there so long," he said. I just wanted to know...."

"Mama's okay," I told him. "Everything's quiet in there now."

We both listened for a moment to make sure.

Then Bradley asked me, "Are you all right?"

"Course," I said, but found myself unable to look straight at him without blinking something back.

"You can go home now," I told him.

He hesitated for a moment.

"If you're sure...," he said. He turned and walked away, his step reluctant at first, then suddenly brisk, as if he'd remembered some business he had to attend to.

Just as I was about to go back into the washroom, a woman pushed by and went in ahead of me. I followed and found my mother standing in front of the mirror. She had brushed back her hair and was fastening it into its neat, severe upsweep. Carefully she put her face back together with mascara, eyeliner, powder, rouge and lipstick. We didn't speak, both because of the woman who had just come in and because Mama had regained control and I knew she didn't want to lose it again. And for the first time I was able to regard her need for control affectionately, as a foible instead of that enviable but formidable trait that drove her to excellence and gave her such command whenever she performed or choreographed or taught. But I felt no less resentful for all the times it had shut me out. And suddenly I realized that what I'd blinked back, when I was talking to Bradley, was bitterness.

My mother stayed for a week, and though I saw her every day I always came away with the feeling that she'd left something unsaid, until the evening when, without James, we went down to Spanish Banks, carrying a Thermos of coffee and some souvlaki wrapped in aluminum foil. A crescent of old moon hung palely in the sky as the sun eased towards the horizon. I spread out a blanket I'd brought from home and we sat with our backs to a log; my mother kicked off her shoes.

"They're killing me," she said, flexing feet damaged from years *en pointe*, the small toes red and knobby, the big toe of her right foot deformed into a bunion.

I unwrapped my souvlaki and gazed across the wide stretch of beach to where an oystercatcher was probing the rocks with its bright red bill. When I bit into the pita bread the tzatziki dribbled onto my wrist and down my forearm. My mother was looking across to the North Shore mountains.

"It's the best reason I know to come back to Vancouver, that view," she said, then added quickly, "Apart from the chance to see the people I love, of course."

I licked the tzatziki from my arm.

"Hard to maintain one's dignity when one is eating souvlaki from silver paper," she said, laughing and wiping at her chin.

We sat without speaking for several minutes, working at the souvlaki, companionable as we watched the sun set.

At last she said, "I'm thinking about retiring." She wriggled her toes as she spoke.

I must have looked stunned, because she added, "From performing only, my darling."

I knew that was what she meant. But with my father so sick, any change in her identity, and consequently mine, no matter how small, was more than I wanted to think about.

"So what do you say?"

I nodded, wondering if it meant she'd have more time for me.

"Is that all? No 'Congratulations, Mama, for lasting so long'? I mean, my God, most dancers are finished by the end of their thirties."

"There's Margot Fonteyn."

"Oh, well, Margot Fonteyn...."

I looked down at her deformed big toe: "Your feet'll be a lot happier."

She laughed, then sat for a long time contemplating them as if they were a piece of sculpture.

When we'd finished the souvlaki and drunk most of the coffee, we strolled down to the water's edge. The tide was coming in, and we waded through the shallow water that lapped up over the warm sand. Walking behind her, I watched the waves eddy around her feet and caress the prints she left behind, only to obliterate them in receding: briny rhythms in which she was caught up and then released, as if the ocean showed a moment's interest in her before slipping back into indifference. For the second time I became aware of that small pulse inside me, and I began to understand that I noticed it when I was with my mother because she had the same pulse inside her — but while I usually ignored it, she was aware of it all the time, listened to it when she danced or worked as a choreographer. I knew, of course, that I wasn't a dancer, couldn't ever be, but that pulse was a legacy from her to me, and I needed her help to discover how I might use it.

With her toe she began to draw elegant curving lines in the sand; writing in a language I didn't understand. Perhaps it was her own private notation for the choreography of a new dance. Once when I was staying at her flat in London, she was furious with me for writing a phone message on the back of a piece of paper that was scribbled over with what I thought were meaningless doodles.

"They're notes for my new *pas de deux*, for God's sake. Can't you tell notes when you see them?"

I felt stupid and furious at the same time. How was I supposed to know? I saw her for only a few weeks a year, and anyway she tried to keep me out of her professional life, hardly ever letting me watch rehearsals because she said I distracted her, even though I always sat at the back of the hall and never made demands on her when she was working.

But now my mother didn't seem to mind that the water kept washing away her cryptic doodles. She'd stopped looking down at them, although her toe continued to write. Her eyes were closed, her face was raised in the dusky light, which softened all the marks of age in her skin, so that she might have been Prokofiev's young Juliet, whom she'd danced in her twenties and thirties and had only recently given up.

"Niki," she said, as tears slipped from under her closed eyelids.

"I never could stand it when he was ill, and now...Christ, he looks as if they've got him on the rack." Her in-breath shuddered as she stroked the garnet ring with her left hand. She'd worn it every day since she arrived, as if it wedded her to my father's dying.

I refused to feel any sympathy for her. She was the one who'd had the affair with Uncle Alek. She was the one who'd left.

She must have guessed I'd been thinking about him, because she suddenly sniffed away her tears and said, in a voice that was both aggressive and defiant, "Alek came to the hotel."

At the hospital she'd run away from him. And now they were seeing each other again? Even with James hanging around?

"We met in the coffee shop."

I remembered one afternoon when I was about nine — it must have been the second time Papa was in hospital — and I came home from school and found Mama and Uncle Alek sitting across from each other at the kitchen table, drinking coffee. He made me sit down with them and started asking me about school, but I was more interested in showing them how I could snap my fingers; at recess that morning I had been dancing flamenco. Uncle Alek immediately became an expert and insisted that using the fourth finger instead of the third would make a better snap. Mama did a fast-rhythmed solo that sounded almost as good as castanets, then went back to drinking her coffee. Uncle Alek reached across the table and took her hand in his. She frowned at him and pulled away, while he sat there with a smirk on his face, looking from her to me and back again.

"I spent twenty, maybe twenty-five minutes with him," Mama said. Then her face crumpled. "But, dear God, it was twenty-five minutes more than I wanted to spend." Once again she lifted her face to the dusk. "He wanted to talk about the baby. The baby, he called it after all these years. Told me that, ever since, something's been missing from his life. So easy for him to say, as if after five years you can declare yourself cured of loving and grieving."

The air was getting cooler and we left the water for the warmer sand, which stuck to our wet feet and ankles as we made our way back to the blanket. We settled down again, leaning back against the log, which still radiated a little of the departed sun's heat.

"I sat in that damned coffee shop trying not to let anything show, especially not to him. And he enjoyed it. I swear he enjoyed watching me struggle. In public. There was a woman sitting opposite with long nails, honey-haired, in an ankle-length skirt all jade and yellow and golden. And I thought, *I'm not going to cry. Damned if I'm going to give you the satisfaction of seeing me blubber in front of that honey woman.* He was admiring her and she knew it. And there I was, twenty years older than she'll ever be, and on the edge of tears."

My mother held onto my forearm as if she was afraid of toppling over, and the pressure of her fingers made my wrist ache.

"Mama, it hurts."

"Oh God, yes," she said, "because he was so sweet to me when your father was first in hospital, and he talked me through all that emotion. You can't imagine what I was feeling. I mean, your father and I had been married for nine and a half years. And some of it had been fine, and some just bloody awful. I hadn't thought it would matter, all those things he couldn't do, because I could, you see. And he was so talented.... And he worshipped me. But I just couldn't abide all those illnesses and all that pain. They turned him into a part-time director, and you can't be really great if you're only doing something part-time. I should have—"

Her grip on my arm was making it impossible for me to listen any more. "Mama, you're hurting me," I said.

She looked at me, then down at her hand as if she didn't quite recognize it, and, finally understanding what I wanted, let go, leaving white marks where her fingers had been. I felt relief as a deep pleasure, and when I surfaced from it my mother was still talking.

"I thought it wouldn't matter as much because they were brothers. I was convinced, or he convinced me, that it was a reasonable thing to do, understandable, excusable and, above all, within the family. And then as soon as I did it, I was so torn. Well, he was such a good lover, don't you see? I shouldn't be telling you this. You're only thirteen."

"Fourteen." In spite of myself the curious logic of my mother's story had won me over, and my growing fascination overwhelmed whatever loyalty I felt for my father.

"Fourteen? Are you? Oh well then, it's not so bad, really, and I want you to understand how it was for me. You've heard only your father's side, after all, from him or Xenia. And from that perfectly dreadful old man, no doubt. So it's time you heard mine.

"It was so good for a week, maybe two. It was just like the days when your father and I first knew each other — better, really, because your father was more... limited...though I had never minded that; in a way it made it more interesting. I really shouldn't be saying these things to you. But I want you to understand. Alek. Niki. It was almost like making love to the same person. Oh, God...."

She covered her face with her hands.

"Ha...," she said. A small explosion that was meant to pass for a laugh.

"But in the end, of course, Alek turned out quite different, an impostor like those baby cuckoos born into other birds' nests. He began to change as soon as he discovered he'd made me happy, even before I got pregnant. He began to hurt me. Small hurts. Pinches. Bites. The odd slap. He was never out of control. Always knew just how much injury he was inflicting and exactly how I was reacting."

"A stalker," I murmured.

"What did you say?"

"Uncle Alek's a stalker."

My mother looked at me as if for the first time in her life she'd really seen me; then she answered, "Yes, precisely. And those small injuries were to hurt your father as much as me. But he was always so nice to me afterwards, not so I believed he was sorry he'd done it, but so I thought I'd imagined it all. And then the day I told him I was pregnant, he put his hands round my neck and pressed his thumbs into my windpipe. And I thought, *Well, he's only trying to give me a scare and then he'll stop. Any moment now he's going to stop.* And then I saw he wasn't in control any more; his eyes were glazed over; nobody home."

She coughed and touched her hand to her throat.

"And then he came to, just like that," she said, snapping her fingers.

I tried to beat down the first stirrings of compassion. Didn't she deserve what she got? He hadn't killed her, after all. And suppose he had? Wouldn't that have been better than her leaving the way she did? No goodbye. No letter. But that wasn't the point. Like me, she'd sensed the past rising up through her relationship with my father. She hadn't read the Siege diaries, and probably wouldn't have wanted to even if she'd had the opportunity. She found my father's suffering both inexplicable and unbearable because it was so much more than paralysis and physical pain. And that had distorted their life together, made her vulnerable to Uncle Alek, who had himself been deformed by the experiences of his parents and siblings.

My mother continued. "When your father came home from hospital, Alek didn't dare show up at the house any more. Your papa was keeping me safe, and so, of course, I fell in love with him all over again, and I began to think that I could have the baby after all. We could pass it off as his. The same genes. Niki and Alek always looked so much alike. And I wanted us to be a family. Your papa and you and the baby and me. I didn't want to always have to work and work and work to keep myself sane."

She put her arms around me and clung to me, and the warmth was welcome, thinly dressed as we were in the expanding night.

"I went to your father. For a whole week I went to him every afternoon. But he knew. Somehow he guessed. And I couldn't salvage anything. And now that damned Alek tells me that, ever since, he's felt something's been missing from his life. Something. Well, I know bloody well what's been missing from mine: your papa, the baby, you."

Stroking my cheek she whispered, "You, you."

"Mama, don't." I pulled my hand away, embarrassed by how she transformed even affectionate gestures into melodrama.

She turned from me, sulking.

"It's a fucking soap opera," I said. I pulled the edge of the blanket we were sitting on up over my shoulder. "Why didn't you just tell Uncle Alek no?"

"Oh but, my darling, you don't know what an evil man he is. He's not the sort of person you can say no to."

I knew this was only partly true. The violence that had ruined Dedushka had ruined his son Alek. That was its nature — to rise up and engulf the next person and the next, unless it was faced, understood and stopped. I had done it with the help of Aunt Xenia and Uncle Michael and Nick. And I think at last my mother had too, by admitting that she mourned for the baby she'd wanted but hadn't dared have.

I brushed off my feet and put my sandals back on.

"Let's go," I said.

When I'd packed away the Thermos and had begun to gather up the foil from the souvlaki, my mother took hold of my arm so that I couldn't avoid her.

"When this is all over...," she began.

Dead, you mean, when Papa's dead.

"...I'd like you to come and live with me at my flat in London."

258

"Oh, very nice," I answered. "Life with you and James and the ballet."

"James won't be there. Just the two of us."

As soon as she'd spoken, I was afraid she'd change her mind, and then I was afraid she wouldn't.

"You don't have to give me an answer right now," she said. "Just think it over."

FIFTEEN

When my mother left three days later I had not yet given her my answer, and she had not asked for it, but between us there was, if not a bond, then a lessening of alienation. The tension that had always charged the moments we spent together slackened: her voice lost its brittleness, and mine the high anxiety that every meeting with her had excited. It was disorienting at first, a let-down that might have spiralled into depression. I began to experience moments of tedium when we were together; once when she was talking too technically about some aspect of choreography that I didn't understand, she said to me, "My darling, you must find all this very boring," and I said, "Yes, I do," instead of denying it as I would have done before our talk on the beach. Suddenly she seemed ordinary, like the mother of any one of my classmates, and it occurred to me that perhaps I no longer needed to resent her accomplishments. After all those strained and distant years, we both discovered how much we needed contact, so, with a kind of prepubescent excitement, we began to touch each other: hands, shoulders, arms, knees, always on the skittish edge of intimacy.

On the way to the airport my mother had James drive by the house so she could stop and say goodbye. As she got out of the air-conditioned car I saw that she had put on her long, thin, professional look: calf-length travelling skirt split up the side for comfort, narrow jacket fitting snug around her dancer waist, hair swept back and tightly secured.

"I'm not going to cry, my darling," she said, and I couldn't resist the cynical thought that she was less brave than vain, unwilling to compromise her carefully manufactured appearance with tears. She held me in her arms and I was aware how much easier it was for me to relax into her embrace now than a week earlier, when I'd been all rigidity and suspicion; but already I felt a distance growing between us, and it wasn't unwelcome — rather a sense of relief that we didn't yet have to test our new intimacy too severely.

"You *will* think it over," she said, and then added with unnecessary coyness, as if it were only one of three or four things I had to consider, and not the most important, "Coming to live with me in London, that is."

She must have thought I was going to speak, because she touched her finger to my lips and said in quick, panicky syllables, "No, not yet. Think very carefully and then write to me. It's better if you write."

I wondered if she was expecting a yes or a no, and which she dreaded more.

"In the meantime, my dearest darling, I'll love you and leave you," she said, kissing the air beside my cheeks in a gesture that had in it equal amounts of theatricality and caution lest she mar the perfection she'd painted onto her lips. And then she was gone — out the door and into the air-conditioned interior of the car, from which she waved while James gave a peremptory salute as he pulled away from the curb.

Unusually, I didn't brood over this last meeting, but that was because the next three weeks were so unexpected and so singular that, while they lasted, my relationship with my mother didn't even signify.

What happened was that my father suddenly improved and came back home from the hospital. Bette, Aunt Xenia and I took care of him. During that time I kept on going to school, and everyone except Ursula treated me with a mixture of indulgence and diffidence — the teachers especially, as if they were ashamed that there was nothing in the curriculum to prepare me for death. They tried to telegraph their compassion with soft looks, but they spoke not a word about my father. Yet I was obsessed with dying, and any mention of it in our textbooks, whether of a historical figure, or a sun, or an entire species, set me to reading and rereading passages in which death sometimes was cited only in passing, as if the knowledge I needed were hidden in the shapes of the surrounding words. Literally. I began to search the contours of letters, believing that answers might be contained in the fork of a Y or the easy curves of an S, or in the intervening spaces that made each letter discrete and potentially meaningful.

As for Ursula, we had not yet become close friends again, but she treated me with an easy nonchalance — *You seen my ruler? Save me a place in line, okay? There goes the Trojan Horse, looks like she's off to a funeral or something. Don't you think Robert Frost is the absolutely most boring poet in the whole world?* — so that I felt more at ease with her than with all the others who were being so kind and careful.

When I came home in the afternoon, it was to an utterly different existence, a life whose sole purpose was to nurse my father. We cooked meals in order to eat so that we would have the strength to lift him into his chair when he wanted to get up for a few hours. We mowed the lawn and weeded the beds so that the garden would be at its best when he sat looking out at it. We did load after load of washing so that he could have clean sheets every day. We cleaned and dusted and aired out the house only so he would feel more comfortable. And that common goal joined us all in a most extraordinary way.

I became aware of it on the first Saturday my father spent at home. None of us left the house that day. I remember we were all dressed in summery light colours: Bette in green, Aunt Xenia in yellow, I in white. Aunt

Xenia and I bathed my father after Bette had changed his catheter. He smiled as we wiped warm soapy sponges over his skin, and cried out once when Aunt Xenia touched a spot on his paralysed leg that instead of being numb was hypersensitive. Afterwards we dressed him in cream-coloured pyjamas. Then Bette and I changed the bed. The sheets snapped as Bette threw them out towards me over the mattress. Smelling of sunshine and grass cuttings, for a few moments they overcame the faint odour of urine which tainted Papa's bedroom even though we opened the window every day to let the breeze blow through.

Later that afternoon, when we'd done a wash and hung it out on the line to dry, Aunt Xenia brought us all tea in my father's room. Papa lay lucid and serene in his pale pyjamas against the fresh white pillows. We took small sips from our glasses; it was a day for savouring.

Papa said, "I can see a woman eating a sandwich in the treetops." He was staring out the window. As we stared back at him, he began to laugh. "You think it's all those pills they've given me, but take a look for yourselves and you'll see whether or not I'm hallucinating. Come. Come here," he said to me.

I put down my tea, and as I went over to him I felt a gentle tug at my waist, like a current in a slow-moving stream. I crouched down beside him so I could see out the window from his point of view and, sure enough, there across the lane from us sat a woman in the top of a small tree, and as I watched she took a bite out of a sandwich, then lifted up a glass to her lips and drank from it.

"It's true, it's true," I cried, and I felt another tug.

"What?" Aunt Xenia.

"You must be joking." Bette.

They both came over, Aunt Xenia credulous, Bette skeptical. And this time it was as though a rope, like an umbilical cord, vibrated and pulled at my diaphragm, and I had the sense that it was *their* movement that caused it.

"Oh, really," Bette said. "It's just Mrs. Esher eating lunch on her deck."

"But isn't it marvellous," Aunt Xenia said, "the way the windowframe blocks out the house so she looks like some giant eagle sitting there overseeing the world."

Bette settled back down into the one chair in the room that was large enough to contain her and the baby. She sat for a moment with her hands folded benignly over her belly, then she said:

> Mrs. Eagle Esher lunch
> In the top branch of a tree
> Then she fell out and went crunch
> So she didn't have her tea.

My father laughed as if it were the best joke in the world. We all did, and there was a luminous instant when what joined us promised to become visible. And when it passed there was no disappointment, only a deeper sense that the joining was real.

The afternoon changed to evening. My father took morphine. The protracted light reached into his room through the west-facing window and lengthened the spaces between us, so that we had to peer to see one another distinctly.

"It's cool enough to eat now," Bette said. "I'll make a salad." She pushed herself up out of the armchair, and as she walked towards the door I felt our joining stretch and grow thinner, and I wondered if it would break when she left the room, but it was infinitely elastic, and connected us even while she was away in the kitchen.

Outside, two hummingbirds were fighting over the late nectar in a buddleia. The oncoming night had already drained the colour from its blossoms, which now looked merely dark instead of purple. My father's eyes followed the soaring, darting creatures as they defended their claims on the flowers. He said something in Russian that I didn't understand.

"What?" I asked and, when he didn't answer, looked at Aunt Xenia for an explanation.

"The Yak-7," she said. "It was a fighter plane during the war. Your papa thinks the hummingbirds look like Yak-7s."

I smelled salt air on a momentary breeze that came through the window. It was unusual for the sea to penetrate that far into Kitsilano. Aunt Xenia switched on the lamp that was standing beside her chair.

"No," my father said. "Turn it off. Are you mad? Someone might see."

"But Nikolenka," Aunt Xenia answered, "how can it possibly matter if anyone sees? Are you not safe? In your own house, with your family, who love you?" She knew my father was beginning to hallucinate and she was trying to reorient him to the world she and I perceived, but he was moving resolutely towards his own visions.

More Russian.

Then he switched to English.

"...supposed to be deserted. If anyone sees the light, we're lost."

I heard, almost heard, the shriek of nails, and like a double exposure I saw, superimposed on the twilit bedroom, a plank of wood crack and split as it was wrenched away from the doorway it barred: the doorway to a cabin in the woods.

"Lisii Nos," Aunt Xenia said, nodding enthusiastically, as if she understood what was happening.

But it can't be the cabin at Lisii Nos, I thought.

And when, an instant later, the image came clear, I saw that although there were shutters on the windows just like at Lisii Nos, their frames were peaked and carved with a pattern of leaf and vine. I was sure I had never seen — sensed — those windows before; they had risen up from the past just when I imagined I was through with history.

As the image faded, my father began to ramble,

speaking Russian most of the time. I could see by Aunt Xenia's look of bewilderment that he no longer made any more sense to her than to me.

Bette came back from the kitchen with tea and a salad of leftover chicken. She tried to feed some to my father, but he would only sip at the tea, saying that we should remember to pack some to take with us, because it would be cold out in the marsh at dusk.

"Meanwhile we must sleep," he said, and closed his eyes. Within a few moments his breathing had become slow and even, so the rest of us left the room, carrying our half-eaten meal out into the hallway.

That night in my dreams I saw a floor parqueted with rough wood in a herringbone pattern, and double windows, the mullions thick with coat after coat of paint. I didn't recognize the place but I felt it to be more real than dreamed, because it remained in my consciousness, as iconic and luminous as my most significant memories.

The next day I listened hard among my father's words (and Bette's, and Aunt Xenia's) for reverberations from the night before but it wasn't until mid-week that for the second time I smelled salt air through my father's open window. I was now convinced it couldn't be the smell of English Bay. Neither Bette nor Aunt Xenia was in the room at that moment, but at other times I saw them with odd looks on their faces, as if they too were experiencing something on the edge of their perception, not quite present, and for that reason more compelling than the everyday routines we'd settled into since my father had come home.

I began to dream of new details: a basin and a pitcher of water sitting on a chest, the sound of a button dropping and rolling across a floor, the flame of an oil lamp quickly turned down and then out. And there was an outside to that dreamscape, too: the salt smell from waking moments, the wave-like movement of reeds in the wind, a sensation of wading through murky water up to my knees, thighs, hips. And inside and outside, fear — pervasive, so real it became physical, crossing from dream into daylight, so that I'd wake up with pounding heart and sweating hands and be astonished to find myself under the pitched ceiling of my own bedroom.

Then one evening when I was sitting with my father, Aunt Xenia and Bette — the sense of our joining palpable — I heard, as I had in my dreams, the sound of a metal button rolling across a herringbone floor, saw a hand pick the button up and examine it.

"NKGB," my father said, and almost simultaneously Aunt Xenia spoke: "The secret police. My God, it *is* Lisii Nos."

But that was impossible. There was nothing about it that reminded me of the farm: the square green-roofed house, the paddock, the stable; not even Dedushka's shed. Then in a flash I understood. Of course it wasn't the same Lisii Nos I'd known all my childhood, it was the house near the village of Lisii Nos outside Leningrad, and the faintly salt smell was from the Gulf of Finland. I balked at entering this world. Babushka hadn't written about it in her diary and I knew by the feel of it that it was dangerous. But this time I wasn't alone; my father was leading me and Aunt Xenia and Bette were companions. It occurred to me that perhaps all my other experiences of the past had been leading to this one, and that all I had to do was accept it.

"We can't stay here." It was Dedushka's voice and I wasn't afraid of him. I saw a hand reach out to the oil lamp and turn down the flame. "We have to leave now. That button was a message." The flame went out. "They'll be back to look for us."

Then out into the pre-dawn, afraid to stay, afraid to leave, with no lantern to guide us and only first birdsong promising daylight. We moved away from the sea, inland through birch and scrub pine to the bogs — auroral sedges, cattails, sphagnum — the ground quaking beneath our feet. And thunder?

"It's only a heavy truck going by on the road," Aunt Xenia said. She picked up some knitting and settled deeper into her chair.

"Are you all right, Niki?" Bette asked.

"Yes," Papa answered.

"We must stop here." It was Dedushka's voice.

"Just until nightfall." A woman's voice. Neither Bette's nor Aunt Xenia's. My babushka? Trying to reassure herself and the rest of us.

One pair of hands beat down reeds, another pulled blankets from the bundles we carried and laid them on top. When I sat down the sharp tips pricked up through the wool into my thighs and anxiety made my chest go tight. Then Bette reached over and took my hand, pressing it to her belly, and I felt the baby kick and smelled her perfume in the air. But when she moved, when any one of us moved, the ground moved too, and somewhere beneath us water gurgled and oozed through the layers of moss, and it was all too easy to imagine being sucked down into the depths of the bog.

The rising sun was a boon. It brought us warmth and clarity and the belief that somewhere we would find drier, more solid ground. But as the heat evaporated the night's chill, the insects came alive, filling the air with a hum that by noon had escalated to a constant shriek. And they bit. Bites on top of bites, until the only way to escape madness was to cover ourselves from head to foot in the blankets we'd been sitting on, which we first soaked in the water so we could keep ourselves a little cool. Yet even muffled by our blankets the bog was preternaturally alive. Through an opening just large enough for my eyes I watched the bog creatures cross the narrowed circle of my vision. A snail oozed slowly up a reed, and then stopped a few inches from the top, and as I gazed at it I swear I heard the rasp of its tongue filing away at the green blade. As I scratched at the bites on my thighs inside my steamy blanket, a swallow flew through the air above the water, darting, swooping after insects, an ally in the teeming wilderness. And on the far bank, running through the sedges, a mouse suddenly transformed itself into a bird — or so I thought, until I realized that it had really been a sparrow that ran like a mouse down the shore, and then stopped and raised its head, glancing around for predators, before it disappeared into the sound of Aunt Xenia's contralto as she sang the song about a birch tree and the end of love, and all the while her supple fingers purled in the lamplight.

Bette lay back among the reeds and dozed, her hand protective over her belly. We all tried to sleep through the afternoon heat, but a sense of nearby danger kept me alert, and I was not at all surprised when through my peephole I saw a hawk plummet into the reeds a hundred yards away and fly off with a rat screaming in its talons. Then there was gunfire and voices too indistinct to understand. *This is not really me, it's happening to someone else. It's what happened to Papa.* And five or ten suffocating minutes when a hand held me down and my nostrils were filled with the dank, decaying smell of the shuddering layers beneath us, and all around us the scurrying and creeping of the bog went still. But there were no more shots, no human voices, and slowly the bog came back to life.

In the oblique light of evening, we opened up our rations. Slender hands peeled an egg. So deft. My babushka's hands running scales over the keyboard: only a professional musician could play scales that fast. I ate a hunk of cheese and black bread and drank some tea. Then we folded up our blankets and headed off again.

"We must be at the lake by dawn." This spoken in Russian, but understood in English.

Water began to seep into my shoes as we left the tentative security of the quaking ground, carrying our lives on our shoulders: those few things light enough to bring with us and too precious to leave behind. I had Babushka's diary. Aunt Xenia carried the string of amber beads that Tanya had worn to the Shostakovich concert. There was a lacquered box and the icon of Christ crucified that hung in Aunt Xenia and Uncle Michael's bedroom. Bette handed me a letter.

"It came in this morning's mail," she said. "My arms were full of laundry, so I put it in my pocket and then forgot all about it."

It was from my mother. She had known how to reach me even here where I waded ankle-deep in the black water.

My dearest darling,

I have found the most delightful surprise for you, which I am sending as soon as I can get it safely packed. Oh, there now, I've already let slip a clue. Yes, my dear, it's fragile, *and very delicate, and so beautiful. You're not to think I'm trying to tempt you, or God forbid, buy you, though it did cost a pretty penny; but what's life for if not to occasionally lavish expensive presents on loved ones? And I hope you know, my dearest darling, how much I love you.*

I tucked the letter into my bundle along with the other treasures, which I was determined to carry to safety, even though I knew most of them would slip away into the murk or be traded for food.

Soon we were up to our knees in the water, welcome at first because it was cool, but soon too cold in the waning light, and irritating to the skin. My calves felt raw, as if the water rats which occasionally swam past us took the opportunity to gnaw at our legs for the brief moment before fear of the unfamiliar sent them fleeing deeper into the marsh. The reeds grew high all around us and very quickly we lost all sense of perspective, and would have lost our direction too, if it hadn't been for the slow dependable arc of the sun along the horizon.

An owl flew out over the reeds to begin its evening search for rats and the other small creatures who, like us, were foolhardy enough to stray into the evening. The water grew deeper. Ahead I caught sight of something dark and bulky half hidden in the reeds. I found myself drawn to it, even though it frightened me, its hard edges so alien in the creeping wetland. I wanted to name it, transform it into something known that would either put an end to my fear or make it rational. As we got close, the sun, still low on the summer horizon, lit up one edge of the thing and revealed it to be metal and rusting. A moment later the image grew clear: a gun turret, wheels surrounded by caterpillar treads rearing up out of the marsh.

"*Panther,*" my father said, and Aunt Xenia added, "A German tank."

And then something touched my leg, and I looked down and saw what I thought was an old tree branch but at second glance turned out to be a bone — quite long, an arm bone perhaps — picked clean by the bog creatures and now trailing ribbons of weed.

"1941," my father said.

Bette, trudging beside me with her hands protecting her belly, said, "Don't be afraid. They're gone. Years ago."

And so we continued. At last the sun dipped below the horizon. Night fell. A lantern flared.

"But what if they see us?"

"Unlikely now we've come this far."

Then far away the dance of another lantern. On and off, in some kind of code which we answered with our lantern, opening and closing the shutter. Then birdsong and later shadows, and at last, in the first grey light after the short northern dark, a vast stretch of open water and the faint outline of a skiff.

"That's it?"

"Yes, and see the boatman? He'll take us across to the other side."

For over a week this went on, night after night, when

the four of us were gathered together in my father's room.

"Why do we keep letting him do this to us?" Bette asked more than once, when she and Aunt Xenia and I emerged into the hallway, our minds stumbling and exhausted, but relieved to be back in three stable dimensions.

"Because afterwards he always has a quiet night."

"Lucky bastard."

"Don't you?"

"God, no. It takes me hours to go to sleep."

"I can't dream any more."

"Then maybe whenever it starts to happen we should just...leave?"

"Once it starts happening it's too late."

Long pause.

"But we could send him back to the hospital, couldn't we?"

"Let the doctors and nurses deal with it."

"The nurses. It would be the nurses."

"Well, damn it all, at least they can go off shift."

"Not like us."

"No."

We never had any intention of sending my father back to hospital, not until there was no other choice. Bette and I especially wanted to share in this half-hallucination, half-memory, because we had not lived through the actual events. Aunt Xenia, unlike other times when recalling events from the war upset her, appeared to find comfort in talking about that flight from the Soviet Union, as if she was at last able to extricate herself from the trauma of war and transform it into personal history. She explained to me that after the Siege the purges began again, first of the military and the high party officials and, soon after, of the intellectuals and artists. Dedushka and my babushka, who was vulnerable because she was a friend of Vera Ketlinskaya, decided it was better to slip out of the country in the general chaos at the end of the war. Aunt Xenia said they began their journey at the house near Lisii Nos, and she remembers that part of it was on foot through wetlands and part by small boat, before they came out at the coast again and then went by sea to Finland. But whatever the facts, those hours we spent with my father, when we surrendered to the obsessions of his mind, were as important as nursing his physical body. I knew I couldn't have done it if I hadn't read my grandmother's diaries and allowed history to rise up and overwhelm the events of that past winter and spring. I felt like a true participant, equal with Aunt Xenia and Bette. One evening after my father had fallen asleep, when the rest of us were drinking tea in the kitchen, I said, "This is his way of getting ready for death, isn't it?" to which Aunt Xenia immediately replied, "Yes," and Bette added, "Ours too."

The very next evening the sense of our joining ended. The doorbell rang and Bette gestured for Aunt Xenia and me to stay seated. "I need the exercise," she said, then stood, straightened and rubbed her back. Slowly she waddled from the room and, as usual, I felt the gentle pull at my stomach as the joining stretched and stretched after her but didn't break. I heard the front door open, then Bette's voice and a faint suggestion of another voice, but so quiet I couldn't hear who it was. A moment later she came back and said, "It's for you."

There was a flurry in my throat. I hesitated for an instant, on the edge of some inexplicable excitement, then ran out into the hall, where I found Ursula waiting for me. There was a faint shimmer about her, as if she had brought the bright western evening into the house.

"I needed to see you," she said. "It's all right?"

I nodded and led her out through the kitchen to the back porch.

We sat at the top of the steps that ran down into the garden. The sun was already off the lawn, but it still lit up the washing, which billowed from the line in the summer wind. I saw that Ursula's right arm, the broken one, was a little paler than her left, although she appeared to have got back all her muscle-tone. I waited for her to speak. She frowned, then stood up and ran down the stairs, as if what she wanted to say was chasing her.

"It's Willi," she called up to me from the shadowy lawn.

"What about him?"

As suddenly as she'd run down the steps, she ran back up. She crouched on the step below me and, staring hard into my face, said, "He tried to kill himself."

In the first moment of shock I wondered if I'd begun to slip off into another hallucination, this time shared with Ursula, but the grass and the flowerbed and the hedge at the end of the yard all remained imperturbably solid.

"What?"

"You heard me."

Willi tried to kill himself? But when I spoke those words to my inner ear, they didn't sound so surprising.

Oh, Willi, poor Willi. If only I.... But I couldn't think what I might have done to help him.

"We were all going to drive out to Alice Lake this morning," Ursula said, "but when we got up, Willi was gone and so was Mutti's car."

I remembered the burned-out truck Willi and I had seen on the Burrard Street bridge, and Willi's face avid for destruction.

"Was there an accident?"

Ursula ignored me.

"We decided to drive out to the lake anyway," she said. "There's a dirt road that leads down to a tiny beach at the far end of the lake. And that's where we always go. The main beach is impossibly crowded, you know, and who can stand all those people anyway? But when we got there we could hear the sound of a motor running, and we found the Karamann Ghia in the bushes."

She leaned her cheek against the wooden railing and stared out at the billowing sheets and towels.

274

"There was a piece of tubing that ran from the exhaust pipe and curled around and up into the car's back window. It was vibrating. The whole car was vibrating. It was hard to see through the windows because there was smoke inside. But I did notice that the back of the driver's seat was tipped back, and then I saw Willi lying there very still with his eyes wide open."

She paused and began to pick at a blister in the paint on the railing.

"My father made Mutti and me go back to the other car. We held onto each other. We couldn't even speak. Then we heard the sound of glass breaking. And then the engine stopped and my father called for us.

"He had pulled Willi out of the car onto the ground, but Willi just sat there, staring. His eyes were wide open and he was breathing okay, but he couldn't even speak. He looked like...I don't know...he looked so young. Mutti kept asking him what his name was, and he just stared and stared and finally he said his name was Willi. And then my father and Mutti lifted him to his feet, and they sort of dragged him and he sort of walked to the car. All the way into town Mutti kept asking things like what day it was and how old he was and where he lived and what was his birthday, and a couple of times she slapped him, and I think she was really angry."

Ursula stopped talking. Her back was still turned to me. We sat quietly for a long time, and I saw that her shoulders were shaking. I touched her. She shook even more. Then I heard her gasp.

"It's okay. It's okay," I said to her, and began massaging her shoulder-blades. Suddenly she threw back her head and let out a high-pitched sob. I thought it was a sob, but when she turned to me I saw she was laughing.

"Ursula," I said, "what's so funny? Are you nuts?"

"I...I...can't," she gasped, and started laughing again, loudly and madly, until I wondered if I should slap her as Mrs. von der Linde had Willi. But at last she stopped and her breathing calmed, though her face was still red and her cheeks were wet.

"It was that piece of plastic tubing," she said. "The way it curled round and up into the little back window. And there were rags stuffed around it. And the whole car was vibrating...and the tubing was vibrating...." Here she laughed again, laughed and gasped while she held her stomach.

"The car and the tubing were vibrating together, and it looked like the car was jacking off...or Willi was jacking off...or, God, I don't know...."

Ursula's shoulders began shaking again. She giggled and snorted, then sighed.

"It was so weird," she said, "and I just had to tell someone, and I could hardly say anything to Papa or Mutti, now, could I?"

Ursula smiled at me and only the corners of her mouth twitched with laughter. Then her face grew sober once more.

"Is Willi going to be all right?" I asked.

"Well, they're keeping him in hospital right now, and then he's going to stay in a nut house for a while, I guess."

I hated the thought of Willi being locked away, until I remembered how, the last time I'd seen him, he was so off balance I was worried he'd get lost in the few familiar blocks between Carnarvon Street and his own house. A hospital room might be the only place he'd feel safe.

Suddenly Ursula said, "I'm sorry about your father."

I wasn't prepared for her words and I began to cry. She put her arms around me.

"It's so good to see you again," I told her, as I pulled out an old Kleenex and blew my nose.

We sat on the back step until the sun was completely gone from the garden and even the washing was in shadow. I began braiding her hair into one long rope down her back. It felt so thick and silky.

"Your arm," I asked, "is it...?"

"I'm playing better than ever," she said. "I'm so fucking good I'm brilliant."

"I know you are."

"Oh God, Yule," she said, "that's what I love about you. I can be such an asshole, but you still believe in me."

"Will your parents let you come here again?" I asked.

"I'm not even going to tell them," she answered, "and anyway, they're too worried about Willi right now to care what I do."

"So you'll come and visit me sometimes?"

"I guess so. Sure," she said coolly as she pulled her braid out of my hand.

It was after I'd said goodbye to her on the sidewalk in front of the house that I began to understand that the joining with Bette, Aunt Xenia and my father had ruptured; and not just because of the absence of that gentle but compelling tug at my centre. I knew it by the absolute clarity of the twilight air, and the exhilaration I felt at the thought *I am alive.* I stood for a few moments watching Ursula disappear into the dusk, and before I went back inside I had to take a deep breath, as if I were diving down into an atmosphere suddenly become alien. And in fact, when I got to my father's room, I knew there truly had been a transformation: for everyone the joining had ruptured. It wasn't just my imagination or the diversion that Ursula's visit had been.

Aunt Xenia was standing at the window, her pale yellow dress bleached colourless by the streetlamp. Bette was standing over my father.

"What time is it?" my father asked.

"Nine-thirty."

"But I haven't had my breakfast."

None of my father's hallucinations over the past weeks had disturbed me as much as those words did. They lacked the sense of purpose that had convinced us to follow wherever his fantasies led. Now he was utterly bewildered, caught out by a mind that had begun to give up making connections.

"What day is it, Niki?" Bette asked, her voice abrupt with anxiety. I thought of Mrs. von der Linde asking Willi the same question, and slapping him hard across the face.

My father didn't answer. Instead he muttered, "Bradley was here this afternoon."

"No, darling, it was Ursula to see Julie."

"Julie?" He paused. "Ah yes, Yulochka."

My father had forgotten who I was — only for a moment, but he had forgotten. I crept to the foot of the bed and stood watching him.

He closed his eyes. His face was beginning to swell again, and the skin was stretched tight over his cheeks.

"Is there anything you'd like?" Bette asked him.

He didn't answer.

"Niki, do you want something to drink?" she asked louder.

He opened his eyes.

"My God, can't you leave me alone?" he muttered. He turned his head away from her, saw Aunt Xenia at the window and said with arbitrary tenderness, "You must come across to this side of the street. If they start the shelling again you'll be safer over here."

Aunt Xenia ran to the bed and lifted Papa into her arms.

"Nikolenka, Nikolenka," she sobbed.

My father's head lolled on her shoulder.

Bette went around to the other side of the bed, stood behind Aunt Xenia and hesitantly stroked her hair. Aunt Xenia began murmuring to Papa in Russian, calling him endearing names: *solnishka moe, golubchik*. At last she let go of him and he collapsed onto his pillows with a groan. A moment later he said, "If someone doesn't take that samovar from the end of the bed I won't be able to move my legs."

I giggled miserably.

278

Bette said, "I'm going to call an ambulance," and went out of the room.

My father reached for my hand.

"Yulochka," he whispered. And I thought, *Right now, this moment, he knows who I am.*

SIXTEEN

Five days later my father died in hospital, with his arms by his sides and his palms turned up. On the morning of the funeral I received the present my mother had told me she was sending: a small multifaceted egg made of silver crystal that shattered sunlight. I put it in my skirt pocket and all during the service I fingered its surface, the *wrongness* of something that is naturally ovoid and smooth transformed into a polyhedron. The air was laden with incense from a *kadilo* the priest swung too conscientiously over the open coffin. I remember how a fly crawled slowly up the icon of the *Transfiguration* as a bass voice in the choir, so deep it sounded subterranean, pulled at me like a gravitational force. But I could not accept that my father's death, even though it released him from all that suffering, was absolute. I kept looking for some slight movement to reanimate him: a twitch in his cheek or a sudden contraction of his neck muscles; some minute response to the chanting, the incense, the candlelight, the sighs and weeping that filled the church. A response to his family and colleagues who had congregated there to mourn him: Bradley looking both drained and relieved at the same time; Pip not touching but standing close to Simon; Aunt Xenia holding Kate by the hand; Nick and Uncle Michael behind me; Bette, who stood beside me holding her great belly as she wept; Uncle Alek, so much like my father, whose expression changed from willed detachment to professional concern as he reached out to support Dedushka who swayed and stumbled when the priest motioned us forward for the last kiss.

When my turn came I walked alongside the coffin, then bent over my father's hand and kissed it. For a moment I held my lips against his fingers and waited for some movement, a secret communication showing that, although he no longer existed, he still remembered me. His skin was neither hot nor cold. He lay there inert and neutral, suspended between the moment of death and the onset of decay.

Later, at the graveside, I watched his closed coffin sink into the ground. Then, after the priest had sung a final chant, I looked on as Aunt Xenia threw a handful of soil on top of it. The whole family did, Nick and I included, and I couldn't help thinking that it was all make-believe, and soon we'd give it up and go home for dinner.

The next day Bette left to stay with her sister, Lucie, in Kelowna, and I went to Lisii Nos. The weather was still fine, as it had been for weeks, and, as in Camelot, the rain fell only in the middle of the night. I prayed for the rain to wash away the image of my father's death from my mind. I tried to picture soily microbes breaking down his flesh, or maggots like those I'd seen crawling over the dead rabbit under the floorboards in the cabin. But my last memory of him, when I'd kissed his hand and his stillness had felt so isolate, stuck in my mind like a piece of bone in the throat.

And there was no comfort in the company of my cousins or Aunt Xenia. My father had been the locus of suffering in the family, and without him we'd fallen away from each other into our separate griefs. Aunt Xenia's took the form of exhaustion. Most days she went to bed right after lunch and didn't get up again until it was time to make supper. Nick went off every morning to his job at the building supply, and I was too abstracted to keep

Kate good company playing dolls or house or mummies and daddies. So instead I spent all day outside, convinced that my own grief, so desiccated and tearless, was somehow nobler in the fresh air than in a stuffy house.

Often, accompanied only by Callack, I took my lunch up to the outcrop and, while I ate, sat looking down at Lisii Nos: the orchards, the stable, the donkeys in the field, Dedushka's shed, the house and the beginning of the driveway, which soon lost itself in the trees and then reappeared just below the road. Each detail of that landscape tugged at me, made something in me stretch almost to the point of tearing, and my eyes burned while I nibbled at my ragged sandwich but fed most of it to Callack. Even though I hadn't told my mother for certain that I'd go and live with her, I felt my ties with Lisii Nos, like the invisible cords that had joined Bette, Aunt Xenia and me to my father during the final weeks of his life, pull thinner and thinner with each visit. After I'd eaten, I lay back against the granite and, shielding my eyes with my hand, squinted up past the sun at the barbarously blue and cloudless sky. My skin was tanned so that I looked healthy and fit, even though I spent the night hours buried with the memory of my father in his coffin.

One morning early in July the phone rang. Thinking it was probably for Uncle Michael or Aunt Xenia, who were trying to sell off ten acres so they could keep up with their mortgage payments, I answered it with my finger poised to ring the buzzer that sounded in the barn. But it was my mother.

"My dearest darling," she said. And right away my occluded grief opened towards anxiety.

"Hi, Mama."

"It's so good to hear your voice. And oh God, it's good to sit with my feet up for five minutes. You know I have to have physio every day now? And that's just to control the pain. I'll be a cripple by the time I'm fifty. Why I got into this racket I'll never know."

There was a pause, as if she was trying to remember why she'd phoned, and then she said, "Well, my dearest darling, how are you? Tell me everything."

"I'm okay," I said. "I've been spending lots of time outside."

"That's nice." Another pause.

"I loved the egg."

"The egg?"

She forgot what she had given just as easily as she forgot to give.

"The crystal egg. It arrived the day of Papa's funeral," I said, because I hoped we could turn the conversation to him. And perhaps, if she had enough time and she listened as thoughtfully as she did to her own internal pulse when she danced, she'd be able to tell me how to rid my imagination of his intractable corpse.

"Oh, that egg."

"It shatters sunlight."

"Well, it's a prism. You know, when I was very young and still a student, I once got to rehearse in the most exquisite room. It was long and narrow, and had once been the gallery of a fine Georgian house. I can't remember why I was rehearsing there. But that floor. So kind to the feet. The best damned floor I've ever worked on. Warm. The wood was a warm gold. Oak, it must have been. But the rest of the room was so cool. Pale green walls, decorated with scrolls and lyres standing out in white relief. And a bank of mirrors that took up most of the length of the gallery, interrupted only occasionally by columns that rose to within a few feet of the ceiling. And right in the middle of that ceiling — it was just as ornate as the walls: vases and vines and God knows what — there was a crystal chandelier that hung from a brass hook. And the sun came out from behind a cloud and shone through the chandelier's prisms and showered us with rainbows as we worked."

"Good God. Look at the time. I'm supposed to meet the new rehearsal pianist for a drink in fifteen minutes. I really must go. But you will let me know when you're coming? No later than the middle of August, please, my darling, so we can get you settled before I head off to Milan."

"But Mama, I never said I'd come."

"Oh nonsense, you must. You're my daughter, after all."

"But I might want to stay here with Aunt Xenia and Uncle Michael."

"And learn how to be a farmer? Oh, Xenia and Michael are wonderful people, but they've already given you everything they can. What you need now is a real education in a great city like London, otherwise you'll learn to be mediocre. And if you spend much longer in that bucolic paradise out there on the edge of the Western hemisphere, that's just exactly how you'll end up. You see, my dearest darling, I've been thinking very hard about this, and I'm absolutely convinced it's the best thing."

"But it was supposed to be *my* choice."

"Oh, I know, my darling, but you're simply too young to decide what's best. Please understand I love you very much, and remember, I'm the one who's had experience in this funny old world. If you're going to get by, you've got to be prepared."

There was a didactic pause, then she said, "So you'll let me know as soon as you've booked your ticket? Must go. Goodbye, my dearest darling."

I put down the receiver. It was decided. Inevitably. Perhaps it was even what I wanted. And as I looked across the deal table where I had once watched my babushka bite into a cold potato, Lisii Nos seemed very brittle, as if it might crack down the middle and crumble away.

Aunt Xenia came in a few minutes later, the armpits of her shirt wet with sweat, a few strands of hair stuck to her forehead. When I told her about the phone call, she took me into her arms and held me against her hot thick body and began to cry. Not so much at the thought of losing me, I understood that, but because she felt as fragile as I'd imagined Lisii Nos to be.

"Go," she said, as she took a Kleenex out of her pocket and blew her nose. "Give Michael a hand staking the tomatoes, and I'll bring you out some *kvass* as soon as you're done."

That evening when I was having a bath the door suddenly opened.

"Hey," I shouted and recognized my atavistic fear of Dedushka, who had hardly bothered to speak to me since Papa's death.

"Hey," came the reply, a female voice. Ursula stepped into the steam.

"You?" My voice tender and frightened.

"Me." She went over to the mirror, rubbed away the condensation and stared at her face, lifting her hair to examine what must have been a small blemish on her forehead. "Your auntie thinks you've been spending too much time on your own, so she's brought me here to cheer you up." She turned away from the mirror and examined me with the same objectivity she'd applied to herself. I lay very still, like a rabbit freezing when it senses danger, and wished for the water to turn opaque.

"You've got breasts," she commented.

I didn't dare look down, but kept my eyes on her. She was wearing a red blouse and khaki shorts. Slipping off her sandals, she came over to the tub and sat down on the rim. Stretching out one of her long, tanned legs, she touched a toe to the nipple of my left breast. Instantly a shock went through me, as I'm sure she intended, but the next moment I understood that her touch was approval and, beyond that, permission to be the young woman I was becoming.

She smiled at me and then said, "You know I'm going to Vienna for the whole of August, so I have to practise at least two hours a day. I should do more, but

I'm considering this my vacation. It's a good thing your auntie has a piano, otherwise I wouldn't have come."

She left me while I got dry, and I towelled my breasts with special care, gazing at them indistinct in the steamy mirror. When I was dressed, I took Ursula to the living-room so she could try the piano.

She played muscular runs up and down the keyboard.

"Not bad," she said. "Some of those bass notes sound pretty awful."

"It'll just have to do, Ursula," I said, knowing that Aunt Xenia and Uncle Michael couldn't afford to bring in a piano tuner.

"It'll do fine," she laughed. She settled down to a Bach piece. As she played I watched her right arm, now tanned as brown as her left. No sign of the injury. No trace of the fight. God, she could play, her sense of rhythm infallible, each note crisp, each voice distinct. Out of the corner of my eye I caught a movement, and when I turned Aunt Xenia was leaning against the doorframe, frowning slightly, appreciative and envious at the same time. She disappeared before Ursula had finished.

"Nice action," Ursula said, breaking the silence that had followed the last note. "I'll work for a couple of hours every afternoon."

"Aunt Xenia sometimes sleeps in the afternoon," I said, a catch of hesitation in my voice, afraid she might not want it known.

"Oh, but she likes music, doesn't she? The way I play, she'll have nothing but good dreams."

That night, as Ursula snored sweetly in the bed next to mine, I once again went underground to be with my father's corpse. But I felt less haunted by his blank, insensible face because I could hear Ursula so near and remember the brief moment of approval as her toe touched my breast. The next morning I dressed more carefully than usual: instead of a T-shirt, a blouse that was cut low enough to show I had breasts; shorts that fit close around my bum. After breakfast Ursula trailed after me down to the paddock and, while I fed scraps to Chornik and White Isobel, chewed on a stalk of meadow grass and stared off into the distance towards the highway.

Later we drove with Uncle Michael to the building supply. When we arrived I whispered, "This is where Nick works."

"Yeah," she said, raising one eyebrow, "I met him last night when I first arrived."

Nick was in awe of Ursula. He scarcely looked up from the counter as we talked to him, and when she asked if he worked there full time he blushed as he mumbled, "Naw. Only on weekends and during the holidays."

"I'd like to get a job," she said. "All I ever earn is scholarships." She wasn't boasting, her voice sounded regretful, and Nick didn't know how to respond: her kind of excellence was foreign to him, made him uneasy. When a customer came in looking for a socket set and he had to go into the back to search for it, his relief was so obvious that Ursula hardly waited until he was out of hearing before she broke into laughter.

We stood outside while Uncle Michael took the truck to the loading bay to pick up some two-by-sixes. Ursula glanced back through the plate-glass window at Nick who was writing up a bill for a customer.

"So you actually fucked with him?"

"Shh. Not so loud. Yes, you know I did."

"Twice?"

"Ursula, I told you all this way back in January."

"Okay, okay, don't have a bird," she laughed, and after a pause she added, "He's cute, but he's not your type."

"What do you mean?"

"He's too wholesome."

I turned the slight insult back on her. "Unlike Willi?"

A stupid mistake. She looked away and didn't

answer. Why had I squandered his name on a payback? Now I'd have to wait until she was good and ready to tell me if institutionalized psychiatry was helping him.

That afternoon, as soon as we'd finished lunch, Ursula — suddenly eager and completely focused — sat down at Aunt Xenia's piano. I left her alone to practise, partly out of respect for her seriousness, partly out of relief that for two hours I wouldn't be responsible for keeping her entertained. And I felt a bit depressed, too, knowing that for the whole time she worked I would simply disappear from her consciousness. I went out onto the veranda with a magazine, one of Aunt Xenia's, full of photographs of sweaters with instructions for knitting them. Ursula was running one-handed scales that sounded almost too fluid to be merely sound. Then she began to play something heavily percussive, full of dissonant urban energy. It was the sort of piece that gets played for encores, more entertaining than moving, more pyrotechnic than profound. Yet I felt a small delight bleed into my abdomen at those expansive, flashy chords, which burst through the solemnity of Lisii Nos like that one day towards the end of winter when every living thing suddenly shouts, *Here I am. Didn't think I'd make it this year, did you? Almost had you fooled.*

The brash, full-handed chords became a Mozart adagio, then something troubled and rippling that may have been Schumann. After that there was silence, and Ursula came out onto the veranda looking like someone newly bathed. But the next afternoon didn't go as well. She kept playing one of the passages from the Schumann over and over. "Shit," she shouted. "Shit, shit, shit." Her distress drew me in from the veranda. When she saw me standing in the doorway, she said, "It's my right arm. It's no damned good any more." There was a ripping sensation in my chest that my face must have betrayed.

"Don't worry," she said, "I can always become a specialist in concertos for the left hand."

"Jesus, Ursula...."

"Just kidding. It happens to be a very difficult passage. I learned it wrong the first time and now I have to relearn it, and it pisses me off is all."

"Oh Ursula, I couldn't bear it...."

"For God's sake, don't get melodramatic. The arm's perfectly fine, where I'm screwed up is in the head." She waited a beat; her timing was impeccable. "But only over this one passage, I want to make that absolutely clear."

"Bu..ull..shit."

"Fu..uck..you," she retaliated, giggling. "Clear out of here, will you? How am I supposed to get any work done?"

I listened as she practised that passage over and over until she got it right, not only for herself but to reassure me.

By the third afternoon Ursula's playing had drawn Aunt Xenia out onto the veranda. She sat knitting from the magazine I'd taken to read on the first day: a baby's jacket. It was the first inkling I had that Aunt Xenia and Bette still intended to keep in touch; and then I reflected that the baby, when it was born, would be as close a relative to Aunt Xenia as I was.

Because the weather was so fine, Ursula and I spent mornings outside. She was content to follow me around, and even help, while I did a few odd chores like feeding the donkeys or picking strawberries and digging out potatoes in Aunt Xenia's garden. In our free time we walked through the woods on the high side of the road. I avoided the trail to the burned-out cabin, and always made for the outcrop, where we could sit and talk and gaze down at the rolling farmland below us.

One morning I took the crystal egg with me and watched the sun play through the facets, casting rainbows onto the granite where we sat, and onto our clothing and our flesh. The farmhouse and outbuildings looked very far away; my connection to them was now as thin as a ray of winter light, and when I played the prism out towards them all the rainbows were absorbed by the distance.

"I wish I had something like this," Ursula was saying "Not just the place. Knowing me, I'd pretty soon get bored with all this beauty. It's your aunt and uncle and cousins, and just the way you fit here."

"But I don't fit here."

"Of course you do. You only say you don't because you have to leave."

My cord-like connection with Lisii Nos began to vibrate, even though it was now so attenuated, and it made me ache from my centre.

"Something happened to me," Ursula continued, "when I broke my arm. When *you* broke my arm." Pause. "Oh, don't look so abject. Don't give me that *Galgengesicht*. That's what Mutti would say. The point is, you did something to me, and I'm glad of it."

I played the crystal over Ursula's right arm. "What?"

"I guess I've always thought I was somebody."

"Uh-huh."

"I mean, I'm lucky to have my talent, and I know it. But when my arm was broken it was like I suddenly wasn't me any more. All I'd been was my talent, and without it I was nothing."

"That's how you *felt*. It's not how you were...are."

I was thinking how easily the crystal egg might fall from my hand onto the granite and smash.

"But *you* would never feel that way."

"I don't have your talent. I don't have any talent."

"Oh, don't be so fucking modest."

If I smashed the crystal, would it mean I could tell my mother I wasn't going to live with her in London?

"When your father was dying, everyone at school thought you were so damned magnificent. By comparison I was nobody. You know, at recess the little kids would make up games about you. *Let's play Julie at the hospital. Let's play Julie goes to her dad's funeral.*"

"Don't be silly."

"It's true. And I wish you could have seen their version of a Russian funeral. They chanted stuff like *Krushchevmoskowbolshoivolgakievkommunist*. I'm not kidding. They wanted to be like you. They knew you were special."

"I'm not. I don't want to be."

If I smashed the crystal, would the image of my father in his coffin vanish, or would I just descend to him in the night through shattered glass?

"And the point is, I want to be like you too."

"That's ridiculous."

"I'll never be a really good pianist if I don't change. I'm too hard. I don't care about anyone else." Her eyes wavered. "Not enough."

The cord was vibrating so wildly and the ache was so strong that I thought the crystal might simply shatter on its own. I handed it over to Ursula. "Take it for me. I'm scared I'm going to drop it, and then my mother will be really pissed off."

She put it in her pocket and stood up.

"You know, I can describe what it's like to attend opening night at the Berlin Staatsoper, and I can tell you that Otto Klemperer and Dietrich Fischer-Dieskau and Elisabeth Schwarzkopf have all made a fuss over me, but I hardly ever cry or get excited or passionate about anything or anyone."

"I haven't cried once since my father died."

"No?"

I shook my head.

"That's not how the little kids at school played you. They had you weeping gallons. One afternoon the whole damned schoolyard was wailing like the weird sisters."

"Why are you making up these stories?"

"It's the truth. The grade sixes think you're a fucking heroine."

"Well, I'm not."

I then told her about my father's corpse: how I couldn't remember what he looked like when he was alive, and all I could see when I tried to imagine him was his coffin-bound flesh steadfastly resisting decay.

"Must you? That's absolutely disgusting."

"But Ursula, what I'm trying to say is, I don't feel passionate about anything either. I feel just as unreal as you."

She gave me one of her long, frighteningly objective looks. "Yes, I see. I understand that." Then after a long pause she sighed and said, "Well, at least *I'm* beautiful.

"You may be beautiful," I said, "but *I'm* not a virgin."

She started running down the path, throwing the crystal egg up into the air and catching it at the last possible moment.

"Ursula, don't, don't."

She threw it into the air one last time, high up, then stood back with her hands on her hips. I dove, catching it just before it hit the ground. She started to laugh.

"Bitch." I looked down to see blood oozing from my elbow. My knees were stinging. "Look what you made me do. My knees are all skinned."

She was still laughing.

"It hurts, goddamnit."

"Yes, Julie, real flesh, real blood, real pain. Don't tell me you feel unreal."

I got up slowly, pulling a twig away from the cut on my elbow. Ursula brushed at the dirt on my legs.

"Ow. Be careful. It hurts."

"You're sure?"

She wiped the dirt away very gently, tenderly, from the grazes on my knee. Suddenly she put a hand on my arm and shook her head, warning me not to speak. There was a rustling sound off the pathway to our left.

I pulled her close to me and whispered, "It's probably just a towhee, scratching about in the undergrowth." But the noise sounded louder than a towhee, and came from farther off.

I led her off the main path onto a scarcely visible deer trail that meandered through the salal back towards the outcrop. Twenty feet down it we both stopped. Across a clearing we saw a squatting figure, his back to us, wearing a leather jacket.

"Who...?" Ursula asked.

"My grandfather."

He looked as if he was manipulating something on the ground in front of him. My stomach turned queasy.

"What's he doing?"

"Setting a trap."

Dedushka turned partway towards us, as if he'd heard something, the movement of his arms interrupted for no more than a breath.

"But he doesn't have anything in his hands," Ursula whispered.

How could he be setting one of his traps when I had seen Uncle Michael cart off all of them in the back of his pick-up? Yet, as we watched, Dedushka pried open the jaws and set the bait. His gestures were totally accurate, but his hands were empty.

"He's pretending."

"A grown man?"

I found myself wanting to shield Dedushka, of all people, from Ursula's skeptical curiosity, so I pulled her back down the trail, where we could no longer see him and he couldn't hear us.

"He used to run a trapline through the woods, just like when he was fighting with the partisans during the war."

"So how come he's not baiting a real trap?"

"He did something bad and Uncle Michael carted all his traps away."

"You make him sound like a naughty little boy who's been punished."

"Oh, leave it alone, will you, Ursula? He's just trying to survive, is all."

"What are you trying to hide?"

I gave up. It had been me I was wanting to protect all along, and I knew Ursula would keep at me until I confessed.

"He was cruel to the animals. And then one day he attacked me."

"Attacked...? Come on, Julie, tell."

So I told her about the crippled fox, and Dedushka's shed, and what he had tried to do to me there. And as I spoke I cringed inside, waiting for her to make a comment like Nick's: *Jesus, Yule, you always take things too far.* But when I finished, without saying a word she took me by the hand and drew me back to our viewpoint, where we were just in time to see Dedushka hoist an invisible sack to his shoulders and, looking more hunched than I remembered, creep along the path and out of sight. When he had gone, Ursula said in a normal voice, "Now he can only pretend, Julie. Do you understand?"

On our way back down to the house I showed Ursula Dedushka's shed. It was the first time I'd gone near it since the day Uncle Michael had taken the traps. The lean-to where Dedushka had imprisoned the fox had been dismantled, the boards and wire mesh carried away for some more benign use. I climbed the two steps to the door and opened it slowly so my first glimpse of the interior would be partial, but the calendar girls had been taken down, the workbench was bare and I remembered that Uncle Michael had trucked off the pelts and pin-ups along with the traps.

"Not much to see," Ursula said.

On one of the high shelves, though, I found the little tin from which Dedushka had offered me the boiled sweets he'd made from wild strawberries.

I started to gag.

"What's the matter?" Ursula said. "They're just candies. Can I take one?"

"No, Ursula, don't. They're awful."

"Okay, okay." She appraised me. "I think you

should leave."

"No," I said, "there's nothing here now. I want to remember it like this, instead of the other way."

I took a deep breath. There was still a trace of the acid smell, from the chemical Dedushka used to scrape the pelts. Ursula was examining the bench on the far side of the room, where Dedushka had made me sit with him.

"You know," she said, "this would be a good place for a practice room, if you were a violinist or something like that. The acoustics in here are really great. You could build shelving above the workbench for music and books and tapes. The light's not bad either, and you could always cut out a new window at the far end."

"But Ursula, no one in our family plays an instrument except Aunt Xenia, and her piano would never fit in here."

"Well, she could buy an upright."

"She's more likely to have to sell the piano she already has."

"But the point I'm making is, it's a perfect room for some kind of studio. You could compose music or paint pictures or weave tapestries or write books. It doesn't have to stay the way it is."

"Nobody has time for that kind of stuff here."

"Bull. Your auntie sleeps half the day away."

"Just since my father died."

"All the more reason why she should have a space like this. And what about you?"

"I don't have a talent for anything."

"What about the play? I wish I could get into my music the way you got into that whole Leningrad thing. You should try writing something else. Maybe we could work on it together."

"But Ursula, I'm going to England, remember?"

"Yeah." She paused for a moment to think about it; then she said, "It'll be good for you."

That night I couldn't sleep. The moon was approaching

full and shone with the brightness of an interrogation light through the flimsy curtains. The crystal egg lay on the bedside table glowing dully, as if it were made of precious metal instead of glass, and I thought, *Yes, of course, it's silver crystal after all. By day it's crystal, by night it's silver; there is some sort of magic in that.* The grazes on my knees hurt as I shifted in bed. What I had seen and heard during the day had left me feeling dislocated. That I should be considered a heroine in a school where I had never felt at ease, and which I had already left, made me feel both gratified and cheated: in my last few weeks there I'd achieved status as well as acceptance, but I couldn't go back to enjoy it.

Turning over, I bent my arm, and the skin on my elbow stretched so that the healing cut pained. There had been some comfort in seeing Dedushka reduced to a pantomime of setting and baiting his traps. It made me feel safer, as did Ursula's words: *Now he can only pretend, Julie. Do you understand?* But I felt sorry for him too, and for that part of me that had been willing to become a victim, the part that didn't dare believe his shed might one day be transformed into a studio. I tried to imagine it, but without Ursula's clear-sightedness the possibilities all collapsed into the remembered smell of acid and the sound of the sharp-bladed hand tool scraping on skin. It occurred to me that, with so little imagination, I'd never be rid of my father's corpse: his dead but not yet decayed face and his passive hand lying against coffin silk.

Perhaps it was the cold glow of the moonlight, or witnessing the replay of Dedushka's warbound pantomime, that thrust my mind back to my grandmother's siege diary. During the months I had kept it, I had read and reread the pages leading up to and including Tanya's death, but I had merely skimmed the pages that led beyond, to the end of the war and my family's clandestine departure from Leningrad. When dawn came I got up quietly and dressed, leaving Ursula to sleep, though not before she murmured a grumpy "What's going on?", and climbed the stairs to the attic.

It was only four-thirty when the sun came up, shining directly into the one small window that faced slightly north of east. The rays were already warm on my face as I opened the trunk and took out the bundle, paper yellowed and ink turned brown, that contained the diary and Aunt Xenia's translation. After a sleepless night I felt enormously tired, and the early-morning room was so cheerful and welcoming that I couldn't resist curling up to sleep like a cat in the pool of light spilling onto the fir floor. When I awakened the room was already getting stuffy. The light was much stronger, casting the lacy pattern around the edge of the curtain onto the paper bundle and the very pale skin of my inner arm. I got up to open the window, and through the dirty pane I saw Nicholas walking up the driveway with Callack. It was as if, instead of seeing him in actuality, I were seeing him in memory. The morning turned elegiac as I realized that this was probably the last time I would ever stand at the attic window and watch him set off to his job at the building supply. Each of these summer days at Lisii Nos would contain last moments: some I would be aware of, others not. When would I go down to the paddock to feed Chornik and White Isobel for the last time? Or make my way up to the outcrop? Or sit at the deal table in Aunt Xenia's kitchen? If I came back for a visit next summer, I'd be a guest, the farm no longer mine the way it was right now. *It's almost over*, I thought to myself, as if I were saying goodbye to long-term suffering.

I didn't look at the diary until that afternoon as I sat out on the veranda listening to Ursula practise. I turned the pages until the shaky writing that characterized my grandmother's descriptions of the worst days of the siege became steady again. The excerpt was headed *23 aprelya, 1944 g*. I turned to the translation.

April 23, 1944

I am restless this spring. Whenever I have a free moment, I find myself walking through the streets of the city. Early this evening I made my way past the Summer Garden along the Kutuzov Embankment. Across the river the spire of the Peter and Paul Cathedral pierced the low sun, which shone with a weary gold light over the last fragments of ice from the spring break-up on the Neva. How quiet it was without the sound of artillery fire, and how safe.

I continued along the river, down the Palace Embankment and past the Hermitage. The rubble is still being cleared away. Small wonder: they say the Winter Palace was shelled at least thirty times. When I walked up towards the Nevsky past Palace Square, I saw two workers starting to take the scaffolding down from the Alexander Column. Suddenly my mood became so light, so giddy, that I heard myself laughing out loud. I thought that Leningrad really was coming back to life, and began to believe all the rumours I have heard about there being a grand plan for a Leningrad Renaissance: a magnificent square in front of Smolny, a monument to Lenin at the Finland Station, an even vaster Palace Square; and most extraordinary of all, I have heard whisperings that the capital is going to be moved back here from Moscow. Oh yes, people are talking, and there are other, darker rumours too, spoken quietly but with greater conviction: continued purges, but this time carried out in secret; charges of conspiracy and treason; suppression of archival materials, plays, novels, poetry. The old story.

May 3, 1944

Yesterday I took Xyusha and Nikolenka to Solyany Park, where an exhibition on the defence of Leningrad has just been opened in one of the few buildings still left intact. Outside on Market Street stood a collection of German weapons that our troops had captured: cannon, siege guns, Panthers, Tiger tanks. Nikolenka ran up to them, climbed over them, peered into them, all the while doing such accurate imitations of artillery fire and bombs, I was almost afraid the Germans had once again surrounded the city. He became quite wild, as if he were possessed, so that I had to take hold of him and shake him to calm him down. Even so an old babushka scolded him and then me as we went into the building. Xyusha walked far ahead of us and pretended she didn't know who we were.

Inside, the exhibition filled fourteen rooms, and all the rooms were crowded with people. We walked slowly from one exhibit to the next, rarely speaking, and then only in a whisper. For a long time Xyusha stood in front of a model of a bread shop. Through its window we could see a scale with weights on one side and, on the other, 125 grams of bread. There were panoramas depicting each stage of the Siege, maps, diaries, letters, photographs of the Road of Life across Lake Ladoga, the fire that destroyed the Badayev warehouses, the Bronze Horseman sandbagged for protection, air-raid victims on Liteiny Prospekt. Nikolenka looked at them all, solemnly but without lingering, until he came to one that showed a woman pulling a sled on which lay a sheet-wrapped corpse. I became so absorbed by it myself, remembering the dying woman whose sled I had taken, that I did not notice anything wrong until he started trembling beside me.

"Nikolenka," I whispered, "what is the matter?"

He began to whimper, then he cried out, "Take me away. I hate it here. I want you to take me home."

I tried to calm him down. In reality he had seen corpse after corpse on sled after sled. But for some reason he found the photograph more terrible.

"I want you to take me home," he kept saying. So in the end I did, though I would rather have stayed.

On the way back he began to cry, but it was only at home, after I had poured him and Xyusha each a glass of tea, that he spoke.

"It was me on that sled," he said. "I was all wrapped up in those sheets. Why was there a picture of me all wrapped up in those sheets?"

I held him in my arms and tried to tell him that the picture had nothing to do with him, but he would not listen.

Xyusha got up and stomped over to pour herself another glass of tea. "You are so stupid, Kolka," she said. "You cannot even tell the difference between a picture and what is real." But Nikolenka just stared at her, and the look in his eyes was of contempt.

Today I went back to the exhibition. I must have spent three hours there, maybe more, wandering from room to room, wanting to remember, needing to remember: Danya, Lev Antonich, Yelizaveta Andreyevna and her child who died, the woman with the sled, the Komsomol girl from whom we learned about Luba Sokolova's death, the letters from my Andrusha, who is still fighting, but now at the front instead of behind enemy lines. All those memories were still vivid for me, but somehow sealed off from the ordinariness of my daily life, just as the photographs in the exhibition are sealed away behind glass. Some part of that extraordinary time has already become inaccessible, perhaps the better part, and the rest, I'm afraid, will only feed our nightmares, so that instead of fighting Germans we will be fighting the enemy inside us, whom we cannot conquer by weapons or will.

June 24, 1945

Andrei has returned. He was discharged from the army at the end of May and arrived home two weeks ago. When I first set eyes on him — he could tell how shocked I was — I saw only cunning, as if a predator had killed and eaten his humanity. I dare not imagine what happened to him during those months and years in the western forests. His letters revealed almost nothing of what I can read in his eyes. Not merely hardship and deprivation, but some sort of transformation, a metamorphosis. It is only now, after two weeks, that I can think of writing any of this down. I must write in order to sort out my own confusion.

And the children are confused too. In the first moment Xyusha was delighted to see him, and in the next she denied he was her father. Nikolenka will only look at him sideways. And in response Andrei casts his eyes down, in a gesture that is at once guilty, apologetic and sly. But we should not feel

300

guilt, any one of us. We survived the war and now we have to discover how to keep on surviving.

Andrei is uncomfortable in the apartment and spends most of his time away. There is nothing casual about his leaving. He stands at the door, checking each pocket by touch; he never shows us what he has put inside. It is as if he has undergone a secret arming, and his strategy is never to reveal the nature of his weapons; but it is clear he needs to feel battle-ready even though there has not been any fighting near Leningrad for the better part of a year.

July 8, 1945

I persuaded Andrei to come with me to the victory parade today in Palace Square. He himself is not taking part. It is strange that he fought for so long, but never gives the sense of having belonged to a fighting unit, although I have seen his discharge papers. Doubtless this is because he spent so many months caught behind enemy lines, fighting the war of the partisans. He never speaks of that time. Of any time. Except once when he described how he crossed the Dnieper under bombardment. He had to carry his greatcoat and gas mask and helmet. And what else? Flask, mess tin, rifle, ammunition, anti-tank grenade. Imperative to keep all that gear from getting wet. Impossible to do so. For other soldiers, such a crossing would already have been turned into a story full of self-deprecating jokes, told over and over, embellished a little more with each telling. But Andrei has told this story with a coldness that says he will never tell it again. He spoke because I insisted on knowing what he had done to be awarded the citation "Hero of the Soviet Union".

On our way to Palace Square we walked down the Nevsky. Briefly. He scrutinized each person we passed, looking at their hands especially, and he kept glancing behind, to the left, to the right. Then straight ahead, the hands again. After only a few minutes he pulled me onto Mayakovsky Street, which is narrower and less crowded, where he could walk close to the buildings, with the walls behind him, facing out. We circled around to Palace Square by way of the Cathedral of the

Transfiguration, Pestelya Street, across the Fontanka Canal, along the Moika to Khalturina Street. For me all those places are filled with memories that I am beginning to reclaim from before the war; for him they are pathways blazed through hostile forests.

By the time we arrived, the parade was well under way. The square was packed with civilians and column upon column of soldiers, their faces softened by victory — no longer any need to strain towards combat — but dazed by the prospect of peace after so many months battling westward.

"Beware the rejoicing of thousands," Andrei said.

I am no longer able to call him Andrusha, even though some part of me knows he is right. Already there are whisperings against partisans who fought in the environs of Leningrad behind enemy lines. It is by such whisperings that Heroes of the Soviet Union become traitors.

July 14, 1945

Last night I woke up and Andrei was gone from our bed. Usually in the middle of the night, when I find him beside me after so long apart, I lie very still, thinking that I may be able to surprise his true form, this other creature he has become, into revealing itself; so when I knew he was gone I felt at least as relieved as afraid. I waited in the dark and imagined life without him again. Then I fell back to sleep, dreaming that he had returned and that his footfall had the sound of a benediction. When he really came back I do not know, but at dawn he was sitting at the table, his jacket over the lamp, not so much to shield my eyes from the light, I thought, as to create a private world where I could not see what he was doing. Eventually he folded up a piece of paper and put it in his pocket. When he saw that I was looking at him, he said, "Documents." Perhaps a half-hour later, he said, "I need 120 rubles. Can you get it for me?" Today I took all my savings, and begged and borrowed, and came up with over 90 rubles and, without asking why, I gave it to him. Not out of fear. I believe that he has something important to do, and that he is doing it for Xyusha and Nikolenka and me.

July 31, 1945

Such tenderness at the conservatory today. I met with Liudmilla Vassilevna and Georgi Lvovich and we selected the music for our concert in September. The first Beethoven piano trio, the Shostakovich we worked on last year and the fourth Brahms. We spent two hours rehearsing. We squabbled and joked and laughed. Anna Mikhailovna knocked on the door, sure that a party had started, and asked if she might join us for a toast. I embraced her on my way out, and wondered if I would ever see her again. Peculiar. I have not had such thoughts since the deepest days of the Siege. I am not ill. She did not look ill. She is not going away. Why should I think such a thing?

August 3, 1945

Disturbing news today. Vera Sergeevna says that her novel about the Siege is running into trouble at the publisher's. They want rewrites. According to them it is too gloomy, too defeatist. "My editor was not even in Leningrad during the Siege," she said. "How dare he censor my work?" But her indignation was not so vivid as her fear.

August 6, 1945

A bomb has been dropped on Hiroshima, Japan, by the Americans.

August 11, 1945

Today Andrei asked me if I would like to go out to Lisii Nos tomorrow. As he spoke he held matches towards me, and when I reached for them he pulled them back to his chest and said, "Waterproof. I wish I had had these...." Then he laughed. He has spent all evening packing up little bundles. "I can only stay for one day," I told him. "I have to rehearse. I have to see my students." "Still, you must be prepared," he said. And so I began packing too. He is right, I think. These days one dare not leave valuables behind. Apartments are broken into. Anything may be taken. And then, of course, August is a strange month, sometimes summery, sometimes chill. Naturally one has to take warm clothes as well as light ones.

And that was how my grandmother's diary ended; the last words she wrote in the Soviet Union. Though I hardly remembered her, I knew very well she had never been as naive as they made her sound. I don't know if she was deluding herself or if she was censoring herself. Whichever it was, I am sure it must have been a strategy for survival.

Ursula was once again working on the Schumann. The tricky passage she'd had to relearn now flowed smoothly from the phrase that preceded it into the one that followed. I thought about my father, that little boy who could imitate the sound of artillery fire to perfection, who saw a single photograph — a sheet-wrapped corpse on a sled — that must have stayed with him the rest of his life, just as the image of his coffin-bound corpse would always stay with me. Images so similar that I began to think of one as the legacy of the other, both to be cherished rather than got rid of. And as they dissolved into each other, my monolithic imagination began to crumble into disparate memories of my father: at work, at Lisii Nos, with my mother, with Bette; and one from my early childhood, when every night before I went to bed I'd sit on his lap and he'd recite a rhyme my grandmother had taught him:

> *Kotyonok, kotyonok*
> *Nye potsarapai*
> *Ya tolko rebyonok*
> *Nu, zamurlykai*

> *Kitty, oh, kitty,*
> *Don't scratch, now.*
> *I'm only little,*
> *Mrow, mrow.*

And at the end of the rhyme he'd nuzzle up to me and make a purring sound that sent a small ecstasy down my spine. As soon as he stopped I'd beg him to repeat the rhyme, just so I could have the purring again. After four or five repetitions he made me get into bed, and as he pulled the covers up over me, I remember, I felt completely safe.

Safe enough to weep as Ursula began working on the adagio section of her Mozart sonata. *Ya tolko rebyonok.* The liquid sound as he spoke the palatalized "l". Evening stubble on his jaw. The starved-beast-in-winter feel of his thighs. The secure pressure of his hands on my ribs. And the purr of the creature that we became each evening when I sat on his lap. Not just a memory: the soul of what we were to each other.

The yearning of the notes Ursula was playing drew me to my feet. I went into the house and, instead of waiting respectfully at the living-room door, walked right in and stood beside the piano bench. Ursula stopped in the middle of an upward phrase. She turned and looked at me, ready to be annoyed, but when she saw my tears she stopped and gazed. I expected her to put her arms around me. Instead she played a descending passage, highly romantic — it must have been Tchaikovsky — that crashed down into the lower and slightly out-of-tune notes at the bottom of the keyboard: both an acknowledgement of my grief and a pastiche. I sobbed in the silence that followed, dropping to my knees beside her. And when I grew quiet she started playing again, a teasing ragtime rhythm that began in the bass, to which she added a fast, intricate melody line full of jaunty humour. Out in the hallway the phone was ringing. I laughed. I couldn't help it. Tricked by the sudden transformation, I too was transformed and danced syncopated, self-mocking steps somewhere between a Charleston and the jazzy five-six-seven-eight of a Broadway production number. I went on dancing until, out of breath and at the end of the music, I surrendered to teary *in extremis* laughter, and only came back to myself when I turned and saw Aunt Xenia standing in the doorway.

"That was Bette on the phone," she said, eyes brimming, a catch in her voice. "She's given birth to a baby boy, nine pounds seven ounces, and she's naming him Kolya for your father."

"Is he okay?" I asked, even now a little appalled at the memory of the blood curse.

"Perfectly," she answered.

The next day was Ursula's last at Lisii Nos. Together we wandered up through the woods, taking the path that led to the clearing where the cabin had once stood. There, the forest was beginning to claim back the land: salal covered the door stoop and a blackberry vine crawled over a charred beam. Three fir seedlings had pushed their way up through the ash, the blackberry vine was covered with green berries and somewhere deep in the centre, protected by the thorns, a small animal scuffled. I found a stick and began poking around in the ruins.

"What are you looking for?" Ursula asked.

"A souvenir to take with me to England."

But when I disturbed a snake beneath the rusting remains of the stove and it slithered away into the salal, I realized that the site had been taken over by new inhabitants in whose territory I was trespassing. So we moved to the edge and sat down on the log where Nick and I had eaten a picnic breakfast just a week after the fire at Easter. I thought how much more acute my distress had been then, but realized that now my sadness was deeper. To remember back to Easter was like entering my own personal museum, and what remained in the clearing and in my memory were artefacts, more evocative than indispensable.

Ursula said, "I'm going to see Willi tomorrow."

He too an artefact, but in memory only. I knew a real and suffering Willi at that moment inhabited a psychiatric ward.

"What an asshole," she said. "Just imagine anyone trying to kill themselves on a day like that. Perfect.

A morning in late spring when the air positively reeks of new life and hope, and there he is fucking himself to death. That's what he was doing. Fuck you, life. Breathing in those exhaust fumes, all sealed away. Having a hell of a good time."

But to me it sounded as if it was exactly the sort of day to commit suicide. A day for understanding unequivocally how much you are at odds with the world. A day I would choose. If I could be sure of oblivion. What would stop me would be the fear of ending up like my image of my father in his coffin, able to hear the tunnelling of worms but for ever suspended between death and the mercy of decay, with all my pains and yearnings stuck there with me, inside a claustrophobia intensified by the knowledge that I had rejected the world on a day when nuthatches were smearing pitch around the entrances to their nestholes.

"You mean to tell me you've never thought about killing yourself?"

"Of course not."

"Not even after you broke your arm and you didn't know if you'd ever be able to play again?"

She didn't answer immediately, but sat fingering a small indentation in her right arm.

"It was more like I was in prison. The only other times I've felt like that were when Mutti talked about the war: ersatz coffee and bread, the Hammer and Sickle over the Reichstag, death of the Übermensch, Götterdämmerung. She fucking well almost ruined Wagner for me."

After a pause she said, "And when I go and visit Willi, it's the same. Even going up in the elevator there are people talking to themselves, going over all their old hurts; and up in the ward everything is so calm and cool: plants and chairs upholstered in blue, and the only bars are across people's minds, but you know they're there because of the way they walk — shuffling or stiff or vacant — and all those nutsy gestures and tics. There's one woman who keeps making this weird popping sound with her lips. I can't figure out how she does it. And Willi wanders down the corridors. He keeps talking about how you have to learn to love the people who've wounded you, otherwise you'll never be able to probe the mysteries of your wounds. It all sounds like loony talk to me, and yet somehow I think he's better. At least he's happier than he used to be."

There came to me the image of Willi ten years later, standing on a desert mesa preaching to a group of people, women mostly, about the mysteries of wounds, and in his hands holding a machine-gun.

"What's the matter?" Ursula asked.

"Nothing."

"Of course, he may end up being a social worker or a priest."

We looked at each other and started to laugh. I had the uncomfortable feeling that she knew exactly what I had been thinking.

"Are you blushing?" she asked.

But my mind had already veered away to the new baby. Bette was bringing him down to Vancouver at the end of the week, and the next day Aunt Xenia, Kate and I were going in to see them. I wanted to buy him a present. Aunt Xenia had suggested a bonnet and booties to go with the jacket she'd made, but I wanted to get something that would delight him. A mobile, perhaps, to hang above his crib, with iridescent fish, so that whenever he woke up he could watch them navigating the nursery air.